DEAD OF SPRING

Also by Sherry Knowlton

DEAD of SUMMER
DEAD of AUTUMN

DEAD
OF SPRING

SHERRY KNOWLTON

SUNBURY
PRESS

Mechanicsburg, PA USA

Published by Sunbury Press, Inc.
Mechanicsburg, Pennsylvania

www.sunburypress.com

ISBN: 978-1-62006-843-4 (Trade Paperback)
ISBN: 978-1-62006-844-1 (Mobipocket)

Library of Congress Control Number: 2016961287

FIRST SUNBURY PRESS EDITION: April 2017

Product of the United States of America
0 1 1 2 3 5 8 13 21 34 55

Set in Bookman Old Style
Designed by Crystal Devine
Cover by Amber Rendon
Edited by Jennifer Cappello

Continue the Enlightenment!

Earth provides enough to satisfy every man's needs but not every man's greed.
—Mahatma Gandhi

That we may do the thing that is truly wise and just.
—William Penn
(Inscribed in mosaic on the inner rotunda
of the Pennsylvania State Capitol)

For my brother, Rock Rothenberger, who has spent most of his adult life living in and protecting the wild places of our nation.

CHAPTER ONE

ALEXA STOOD ALONE in the looming silence of the deserted rotunda. Above her head, the crimson-paneled dome soared upward more than two hundred feet. Here, in the heart of this dazzling Capitol building, she could almost believe in the grand purpose of government. Alexa tilted her head to gaze up at a panorama of gilded cherubs and luminous mosaics. As she watched, Law, dressed in a red gown, seemed to float from her rondel painting into the dome. Law's face glistened as if bathed in tears. Feeling lightheaded, Alexa blinked to clear her head.

"Get a grip," Alexa muttered aloud AS she sank onto a nearby marble bench to shake off the effects of glitter overload. When the brief dizzy spell passed, she twisted her mouth into a wry smile. Reality check time. How many sex trafficking victims waiting for justice would buy into that whole grand purpose thing? The click of heels echoing down the corridor shook Alexa out of her cynical reverie.

Keisha Washington dashed into the rotunda, her short Afro bouncing with each step. Alexa marveled at the young woman's speed over the century-old, cobbled brick floor. Those heels had to be three inches high. But, Keisha was a rising star, renowned among the Senate staff for her dress-for-success fashion sense.

"Sorry I'm late." Keisha plopped next to Alexa on the concrete bench. "They're going into a late-night session soon, and I had to go over some information with Senator Gabler."

"And I thought lawyers' hours were crazy. I can't believe you have to work all these evenings. Is something big going on tonight?" Alexa asked.

"This will be the umpteenth time the Senate's brought a State Employee Pension bill to the floor. It'll be a miracle if it passes. Pension reform and fracking are the two hot items right now. At

1

this point, they seem closer on fracking. Pensions are going nowhere." Keisha grinned. "I'm so glad we're going to talk about something else. Thanks for meeting tonight."

"No problem. I was in Harrisburg for a deposition. I just got here."

"Let's head up to the office, and we can go over the agenda." Keisha bounced to her feet.

"That's all we have to cover, the agenda for this next commission meeting, right? Can't we just stay here and run through it?" Alexa eyed the empty rotunda. "We won't be disturbing anyone."

Keisha frowned. "I have to keep an eye on the floor discussion. You know, on the closed circuit television. They're breaking out of caucus soon." She glanced down the corridor toward the Senate-side elevators.

Alexa shrugged off her coat. She was losing patience with this whole commission process. "I'm really beat. By the time we walk up to your office, we could have this knocked out. The sooner we're done, the sooner I can hit the road. I need to take care of my dog; he's been alone all day." She stifled a yawn and used a cajoling tone. "You'll only miss a few minutes."

Keisha took another lingering look down the hall before she sighed and joined Alexa on the bench again. "I'm glad I brought the file along. Here's the draft agenda." She shoved a paper at Alexa, a flicker of suppressed anger peeking through her professional façade.

Alexa ignored the attitude and scanned the document. "This looks like a good framework." She shivered and draped her coat over her knees as a blast of cold air swept down the grand central staircase. "Damn, it's chilly in here. How can we avoid the infighting? I don't want to repeat the last meeting."

The young staffer rolled her eyes. "Getting this cast of characters to agree on anything is impossible. Do you have something in mind?"

"Well, one idea—" Alexa broke off when an explosion of angry voices erupted on one of the upper floors.

"I will not be a party to . . ." The rest of the man's raspy protest faded out as several men talked over one another.

Both women looked up, but the mezzanine above blocked their view of the upper floors.

The quarrel flared when one man shouted. "You can't back out now." His heated words reverberated through the dome.

Another man interjected in an icy tone, "He who dances must pay the fiddler." Alexa caught a bit of a drawl in the speaker's voice. A third male murmured something unintelligible in reply as the voices lowered. Although the squabble continued, Alexa could no longer hear what they were saying.

Keisha shifted in her seat. Then she remarked in an apologetic tone, "Typical legislative bickering."

"The governmental process at work." Alexa's reply was sardonic. These guys sounded more like her old boyfriend's rugby team in the scrum than elected officials. She could tell Keisha was embarrassed that Alexa, an outsider, had overheard the senators' rowdy disagreement. But, the staffer was in no way responsible. Alexa glanced down at the agenda in her hand, trying to remember where she had broken off the discussion.

When a sudden silence fell, Alexa and Keisha exchanged an amused look. "Guess you were right about pension reform. Those guys sure aren't on the same page," Alexa observed, raising an eyebrow.

Keisha stifled a laugh. "Glad I'm not responsible for staffing that legislation. Even leadership doesn't agree on whether this current bill is the right way to reform the system. What a nightmare."

Alexa opened her notepad and leafed through a bundle of papers tucked in the inner flap. "Here." She pulled out two pages bound by a red paperclip and handed one of the papers to Keisha. "I typed up some ideas for how to keep us on track . . ."

A subtle shift in light caught Alexa's attention. Her eyes rose from the notebook as she sensed a whisper of motion in the open space above. She gasped as a body sailed through the air, careening toward the grand central staircase. For a moment, time stalled and the body appeared to drift in slow motion as it floated through the bright rotunda. But, as it neared their bench, the body seemed to pick up speed. Alexa watched, frozen in place with hand to her mouth in horror, as it hurtled closer and closer.

Then, with a tremendous crash, the body smashed into one of the tall winged statues that flanked the foot of the stairway, shattering a beaded crystal orb the angel held aloft. A spray of blood and glass beads spiraled in a shiny pink mist from the falling man as he bounced off the statue. Losing forward momentum, the body made an abrupt drop and slammed into the clay cobblestone floor.

Keisha's shrieks muted the leaden thud of body hitting bricks. Recovering from her initial shock, Alexa leapt to her feet, scattering her coat, notebook, and papers to the floor. Slipping on crystal beads and uneven bricks, she rushed toward the motionless form that had landed less than ten feet away.

Alexa knew immediately he was dead. The corpulent, silver-haired man lay face up in a pool of blood. With fatal irony, his flight had brought the man to rest midway between a bat and a dragonfly, two of the famed Moravian mosaics inset into the rotunda floor. His body clung to the tiles like a gray flannel octopus. Its red tentacles appeared to sway as rivulets of blood streamed into channels between the bricks. The back of his crushed head seemed to sink into the cobblestones. Both arms splayed on the floor; one leg twisted at an unnatural angle. Alexa shuddered at the glimpse of bone sticking through his pant leg.

Just as Alexa leaned over the man, two Capitol policemen raced around the corner from their post at the main entrance. One jostled her aside and barked, "Move away. Sit down over there. We've got this."

Alexa reeled back to the bench where Keisha stood, tears streaming down her face. Alexa collapsed onto the seat and tugged the young woman down beside her. "They want us to stay here. Are you OK?" Before Keisha could answer, Alexa's stomach lurched and began to whirl. She leaned forward, elbows on knees, and propped her head in her hands. The vision of the man's crumpled form blurred into the memory of another body. Elizabeth Nelson also had been lying on her back, legs askew, when Alexa had found her lying in the woods.

When her nausea abated, Alexa sat up and turned to Keisha. The staffer sat silent and stone-faced as she watched the whirlwind of activity. A paramedic leaned over the body. A contingent of Capitol Police bustled around, cordoning off the staircase and most of the rotunda with yellow tape. The piercing blare of a siren somewhere outside the Capitol rose and fell in steady waves. Alexa suspected the cops had propped the front doors open. She could feel an icy breeze wrap its tendrils around her ankles. The noise level rose to a frenzy as more policemen thronged the scene. Everyone was shouting to be heard over the din.

Where was the respect for this man whose life had just ebbed away into the historic mosaics? Alexa wanted to scream at everyone to stop talking. Instead, she turned to her still-motionless companion.

"I can't believe this. What a horrible way to die. Keisha, let's try to move away from here." Concerned at the lack of response, Alexa's voice rose. "Keisha? Keisha?"

An officer with an air of authority strode into the midst of the officials surrounding the body, slinging commands. "Put some guys at the front door and the back entrances. Keep the press out. Briggs, CID is on the way. Can you meet them? I have to go upstairs and inform the clerk that the Senate is now out of session. We'll need to organize a detail to interview everyone in the building."

As the officer turned, he noticed Alexa and Keisha sitting on the bench. "Christ almighty. Get these two women out of here. Move them to a secure room. Are they witnesses?"

A burly uniformed policeman approached. "Ladies, please come with me." Solicitous, the policeman asked, "Are you OK?"

When the cop grasped Keisha's elbow to help her up, she jerked her arm away and glared at him before rising. Alexa knelt on the floor to gather up her belongings. The man made no move to assist but allowed Alexa to remove the notebook and papers from the scene.

"Follow me, please." The cop headed toward the House side of the Capitol, Alexa and Keisha trailing behind. Unlocking the door of a big hearing room, he switched on the lights and held the door wide. "I want you to stay in this room. Someone will be coming to question you both in a few minutes. I'm also going out in the hall to radio the paramedics. They should check you both out. Do you need anything?"

"No thanks," Alexa refused as they entered the empty room. Keisha didn't reply. When they were alone, Alexa looked at the distraught young staffer. "My God, what a terrible experience."

"I'll see that body fall through the air every time I close my eyes." Keisha choked back a sob and retreated back into silence.

With little success, Alexa struggled to block the slow-motion video of the moment the man hit the floor from looping through her mind. She sighed in relief when a petite paramedic walked through the door. "Hi. I'm an EMT, Lillian Ortiz. I want to make sure you're both OK. I understand you've just been through a pretty traumatic event." She turned to Keisha and said, "Honey, let's take a look at you first."

Alexa wandered to the far side of the big hearing room and collapsed into a chair along the wall.

How does this keep happening to me? she silently lamented. This is even worse than finding the bodies of Elizabeth Nelson and then Cecily Townes. At least they were already dead. This guy died right in front of me, literally at my feet.

Tears brimmed in her eyes. As Alexa brought her hand to her face to brush them away, she noticed spots on her hand. Blood. The falling man's blood.

Trembling, she grabbed a Kleenex from her purse and rushed to the water cooler. She used the dampened tissue to rub at the spots peppering both hands and the lower sleeves of her gray suit.

With a shudder, she wiped her face with a second tissue. Taking deep breaths to hold back tears, Alexa returned to her chair. When the paramedic approached, Alexa, still fretting, asked, "Is there blood on my face?"

"What?"

"I just cleaned spots of blood from my hands and arms. I can't see if there's any more on my face."

The paramedic leaned close. "No, your face is fine."

Despite her protests, the woman insisted on taking Alexa's blood pressure and pulse. "Elevated, slightly. But, you'll survive." Ortiz nodded toward Keisha. "You know her, right? Does she have someone who can come and pick her up? She's barely said a word. She's pretty broken up."

"Watching someone take a dive into a solid brick floor can do that to you. Do you know the guy's name, the one who fell?"

"Nope. And if I did, I couldn't tell you anyway. That's police business." The paramedic gave Alexa an appraising look. "You seem like a pretty tough cookie, but you might want to call someone too. There can be a delayed reaction to an experience like this. I don't want you to come down with the shakes on the road and wipe out some little old lady driving home from her bridge game."

Alexa managed a wan smile. "You're a pretty tough cookie yourself." She fished her cell phone from her jacket pocket. "I'll call my boyfriend. He's a state cop."

"I'll let the police know they can interview you now." As Ortiz left the room, she patted Keisha on the shoulder. "Hang in there, honey. Your friend is going to call someone to come pick you up as soon as the police finish their questions."

Alexa walked back across the room and sat next to Keisha. "Who can I call to drive you home?"

"I know him." The young woman spoke in a low tone but continued to look at the floor.

Alexa didn't follow at first. Then, she understood. "The man who fell? You know who he is? I mean was."

"Senator Martinelli, Carmine Martinelli. His office is right across the hall from ours. He chairs the Environmental Resources and Energy Committee."

"Did you know him well?" Alexa kept her voice neutral. She didn't want to send Keisha back into another extended silence.

"He was a pretty good guy. I dealt with him quite a bit because my boss is a member of that committee. Senator Martinelli has been in the Senate forever. People always joked he wouldn't quit until they carried him out of here. I guess the prophecy has come true." She dabbed at her eyes and looked back down at the floor.

When her head bobbed up a moment later, Keisha's tone took on a jarring hint of excitement. Her stricken expression hardened into something much more intense. "I just realized. With Senator Martinelli dead, that will leave the chairmanship of Environmental Resources and Energy open. Senator Gabler is next in line, but he'd have to step away from Law and Justice. I bet he'll make that leap in an instant." The flicker of a smile crossed Keisha's face. "I wonder if that would leave an opening for me to become executive director?"

As she listened, appalled, Alexa wondered if the woman realized she spoke aloud. She knew the staffer had reached her current position at a very young age through drive and determination. To witness Keisha calculating how the senator's death could benefit her career, with the body still warm, revealed a ruthless depth to that determination.

Keisha stopped abruptly, then said, "Senator Martinelli had to be in his seventies, but he seemed to be in good health. Why would that old white man jump off a balcony?"

Alexa pictured the shattered body lying on the rotunda floor. "A better question might be: How could a man that old and overweight even get over the railing?"

CHAPTER TWO

SCOUT STOOD JUST inside the cabin door, tail wagging. When Alexa entered, he drew back his lips and bared his teeth in a huge smile. "Buddy, I'm glad to see you too." Alexa scratched the English mastiff's ears then stood aside as John Taylor opened the door wide to let the dog run past them.

John tossed his coat on a chair. "It's cold in here. Let me get some wood in the stove. I guess early March is still more winter than spring."

Emotionally exhausted, Alexa toddled to the big couch and collapsed. "Thanks for coming to my rescue and getting Cannon to drive my car back to Carlisle. If I'd left it on the street overnight, the Harrisburg parking tyrants would probably have towed it."

"He didn't mind. Lucky for us, the Flyers weren't playing tonight."

John walked to the couch and extended his hand. The state trooper towered over Alexa, but his voice was gentle. "Get up and get out of that coat. You'd feel better if you change."

"You're right. I need to shower and wash my hair." Alexa still felt those drops of blood burning like acid into the backs of her hands. Rising to her feet, Alexa nestled into her boyfriend's waiting arms and sighed into his chest.

"I know this has been tough. You didn't say much on the ride home, but I want the whole story." John smoothed Alexa's tumble of curls before he ended the embrace with a kiss to her forehead.

"How about I cook some eggs?"

Alexa grimaced. "I'm not hungry."

"Go upstairs and change. The eggs will be ready when you get back."

Scout greeted Alexa at the foot of the stairs and followed her into the kitchen. She had scrubbed every inch of her body with a loofah and washed her hair before changing into sweats.

John stood at the stove. An egg carton, shells, and an assortment of bowls and utensils sprawled across the adjoining counter. The sharp smell of raw onions permeated the kitchen.

"Do you need me to make toast or anything?" Alexa scooped up the broken eggshells and tipped them into the trash.

"Nope. I've got this operation under control."

"Obviously." She studied John's mess. "Looks like you have absolutely everything you could possibly need to make an omelet." For the first time in hours, Alexa laughed.

"A master chef doesn't skimp on preparation. Just watch those cooking shows, and you'll know I'm right." John divided the fluffy omelet and slid the pieces onto two plates with a flourish.

"Why, this omelet looks like it's been cooked by the Gourmet Chef." Alexa sat at the counter.

"You never get that show right. It's the *Gallic Chef*, not the *Gourmet Chef.*" With a little bow, John placed a basket of toast on the counter. His sandy brown hair fell across his forehead.

"Merci, monsieur." Alexa giggled as John took a stool beside her. Once Alexa nibbled a few bites, her slight nausea disappeared. She dug into the veggie-filled omelet.

After they had both demolished everything on their plates, John turned to Alexa. "What did the Capitol Police ask you?"

"After all that waiting, I expected a whole contingent, but just two guys interviewed me. Officer Sheridan from the Capitol Police. Do you know him? Balding, maybe forty-five. And the other guy said he was with the Dauphin County Criminal Investigation Division. A black guy with salt and pepper hair. Deep voice. Detective Marshall. They said the Capitol Police have jurisdiction over all crimes committed on state property, but CID takes over if it requires forensics and significant investigation."

"I think I met this Marshall on a case last year. I'm not surprised they brought in CID. Did they question you and the other woman together?"

"No, they took Keisha into the far corner of the room and talked to her first. Then I got my turn. But there wasn't really much to tell. We were sitting there on the bench, and this man sailed into the rotunda from one of the higher floors and crashed into the tiles." Alexa shuddered as she recalled the moment of impact. "It was awful."

"So that's it? You didn't see anything more?" John massaged her neck with one hand.

"Not really. A few minutes before it happened, we heard some guys arguing on one of the upper floors. We couldn't see them."

"How many voices?"

"At least three. Maybe four."

"Do you think the dead man was part of that group?"

"I have no idea. It's possible. It's just as possible they were on another floor. They could have been on the mezzanine or up on the fourth floor; there's no real third floor balcony on that side of the rotunda. The argument stopped, and it got quiet before the man fell. So they could have left before it happened."

"I hear this guy was a senator." John stood to clean up the dishes. "No, stay there. I've got this."

"That's what Keisha said. She recognized him. Senator Carmine Martinelli from one of those northwest counties—Warren or maybe McKean." Alexa's voice trailed off for a minute before she resumed speaking. "She called him 'a Senate institution.' I Googled him while we were waiting. His official photo looked a few years old, taken before his hair turned gray and he put on that last twenty pounds." Alexa frowned. "By the time I saw him, gravity had done its worst. But it was the same person as on the Senate website. No doubt Keisha was right."

Scout laid his huge fawn head on Alexa's knee as if he sensed her distress.

John closed the dishwasher and took two cups of tea from the microwave. "Zen tea. Do you want any sugar?"

"No." Alexa managed a wan smile. "Thanks for taking care of me." She couldn't keep from reflecting that John loved to play the knight in shining armor to her damsel in distress. She cringed at the thought of turning into one of those girls who needs a man to rescue her. But, when she looked into John's baby face and guileless brown eyes, she felt like an ungrateful jerk.

"Service is part of my job description." He waved one of the teacups in a flourish, spilling a few drops onto the floor.

"I hardly think holding your girlfriend's hand is what the state police had in mind."

"My boyfriend job description. Come out to the living room."

"Sure, the woodstove should dry this hair." She tugged on her curls, still so damp their usual honey color had darkened to caramel.

"This tea is exactly what I needed." Alexa and John sat side by side on the big leather couch. Scout sprawled on the floor, his back resting on their feet. Alexa barely noticed John's comforting grip on her hand. She couldn't stop thinking about the death in the Capitol rotunda.

"I feel like things are spinning out of control." Her eyes brimmed with tears. "It's happening again. Elizabeth Nelson, Cecily Townes, the Reverend, Quinn Hutton. Now this. I've turned into some sort of death magnet."

"Don't say that, sugarcakes. I know you're trying to deal with a horrible experience. I've only seen one jumper in my years on the job. I'll never forget that feeling of helplessness when she stepped off the building." John scowled. "Or the way her body looked after it hit the ground. But you had nothing to do with this senator's nosedive. And, you aren't responsible for any of those other situations, either. The two women were already dead. You shot Reverend Browne in self-defense. And Quinn Hutton was a stone-cold lunatic killed in a police shoot-out."

"In front of me."

"He planned to kill you and put your head in a box for the gods."

"For a Nat, a Buddhist spirit." Alexa murmured.

"Whatever." John shrugged. "The point is you've had a string of close encounters with death. But, there's no way that you're—what did you call it—a death magnet. Anyway, it looks like the senator was a suicide."

"Suicide?"

"They found a note." John put his teacup on the coffee table. "I used to play softball with one of the Capitol cops working the scene in the rotunda. Terry told me the senator left a note on his computer. The wording sounded sort of weird, something like, *There comes a time when a man has to come to terms with his life. I can't go on any longer.* They're checking to see if he had some type of terminal illness."

"That's a pretty flowery suicide note. But, then, the guy was a politician." Alexa voiced her earlier doubts. "I just don't see how that old man climbed over that railing and jumped into the rotunda."

"I don't know. But, people who want to commit suicide—not the cry-for-help people; the ones who take a long hard look at their lives and decide they prefer death—that group can be remarkably determined once they've made up their minds. So I wouldn't totally reject the possibility that the senator overcame the odds to clamber over the rail to off himself. You didn't hear him scream, right?"

"You're right. Whoa, that would take real determination to jump without a sound." Alexa shuddered.

"No. No. Aaaaayyh!" Yelling, Alexa jerked awake, the terror of the nightmare still fresh in her mind. She'd had this dream before. She was back in Quinn Hutton's crazy temple, still chained to the wall. As always, Quinn explained he planned to kill her and put her skull in a box as an offering. But, this time, her dream changed. Quinn called her name from the rafters of the old barn. When she looked up, Quinn shoved someone off the beam. Alexa screamed as the body plummeted to the floor in front of her, blood oozing into the oriental carpet. As she gazed in horror at the silver-haired old man, his face liquefied, mingling with the puddle of blood. Alexa's eyes followed one of the crimson rivulets from the carpet back up to the body. Her shrieks echoed through the temple when she saw that the face on the broken corpse had become her own.

Eyes open, Alexa recognized her bedroom ceiling. She was awake. Trying to move past the nightmare, she took deep breaths, making each breath last a count longer. She felt John's calming presence on the bed beside her. In the corner, Scout whimpered and kicked his legs, chasing squirrels or bunnies in his slumber. Although her waking cry had seemed loud to Alexa, it hadn't disturbed either John or the dog. Comforted by these mundane connections to the real world, she rolled onto her side and fell into a dreamless sleep.

CHAPTER THREE

THE MATTRESS BOUNCED once, twice, three times until Alexa opened her eyes, squinting at the bright sunshine pouring through the windows. "Scout, give me a break." The mastiff's huge head rested on the bed just inches from her face. When Alexa looked at the dog, he bounced his chin against the mattress again.

"OK, OK." Alexa glanced at the empty space on the other side of her bed. "Didn't John let you out when he went to work?" She swung her feet onto the floor and shuffled to the closet for a robe and slippers while Scout galloped downstairs to the front door.

After she let the dog out for a morning romp, Alexa threw a log in the woodstove and trundled back upstairs to dress. Her cabin sat in the midst of a forest, with acres of woods surrounding it, so she could leave Scout outside alone. As the giant beast moved beyond his puppy years, he stuck close to the house. She knew he'd be sitting on the deck when she arrived downstairs for breakfast.

Alexa ran through her schedule for the day as she showered, then crafted a mental outline of points for the Bowen brief as she dressed. She donned a blue ikat blouse and grabbed the jacket of her pantsuit from its hanger. When Alexa pulled the jacket over her right arm, she stopped short, eyes focused on the lower sleeve. Instead of the black fabric sheathing her arm, Alexa saw yesterday's gray jacket covered in a spray of Senator's Martinelli's blood. Shaking, she sank to the bed, the jacket trailing from her arm.

"You saw a man die yesterday. And it wasn't a pretty death. The senator fell several stories into a solid brick floor. You can't ignore it. It's normal to be upset." Alexa felt better just speaking the words aloud to the empty room. After a few deep, cleansing breaths, she slipped her left arm into the jacket and headed downstairs for breakfast.

Melinda flagged Alexa down the moment she rushed through the doors of the law firm. "You've got a ten o'clock with the Harrisons on their adoption. And you have to be in court at two." Alexa dumped her briefcase on the desk and took off her trench coat. She'd tossed the wool coat she'd worn the night before into the hamper for dry-cleaning.

Her ample assistant scooped the trench coat from the chair and placed it on a hanger by the door. "I'll bring you some tea. How did the deposition go yesterday?"

"Long. I'd say this case is going to trial. But, we're still a few months away from that decision."

"All great achievements take time."

"A Pennsylvania Dutch saying?"

"No, a Facebook post."

By the time Melinda bustled out the door, Alexa's mood had brightened. Her irrepressible coworker had a penchant for timeworn sayings and Pennsylvania Dutch aphorisms that never failed to make Alexa giggle.

When Melinda returned with the tea, she asked Alexa, "Did I mention Graham wants to see you? He's in his office. Now you're a partner, I imagine he'll be consulting you almost every day. Maybe we need to leave an hour free on your schedule every morning."

"Good. I planned to track him down anyway. But, let's see how things go for a few weeks before you change the schedule." Alexa took a quick sip from her teacup before she carried it down the hallway to her brother's office.

A lot of changes had taken place in the law firm over the past few months. After her mother's brush with death last summer, Alexa's parents had decided to spend part of each year in the Italian region of Umbria, a spot they both loved. Her father resigned his position as senior partner in the family firm of Williams, Williams, and O'Donnell. Norris Williams' decision had spurred Pat O'Donnell to take the leap into retirement as well.

Alexa's older brother, Graham, took the helm as senior partner and promoted both Alexa and her sometime nemesis, Brian Stewart, to partner status. They had hired two Dickinson Law School grads to entry-level positions and renamed the firm Williams, Williams, and Stewart.

"Hey, Lexie, come in." Graham rose from behind his big walnut desk and took a seat in one of the big wing chairs by the window.

"I still expect to see Dad here when I walk in." Alexa sank into the opposite facing chair.

"It's going to take awhile until we've settled into our new roles. I'm still struggling with balancing the workload. How much longer are you going to be involved in this trafficking commission?"

"You mean the Commission from Hell?" his sister groaned. "I'm betting it will go another four months before we can reach agreement on what to put into a report. I was naïve to think it would be a quick process. Silas Gabler had to know that when he conned me into this citizen chairmanship. From her staff experience in the legislature, Mom must have known he was feeding me bullshit. But, she probably kept quiet because Dad wanted me to do a favor for his law school buddy, the senator."

Graham gave her a wry smile. "I see you've become cynical after just a few months working with government."

"I've been cynical for a while. This experience just confirms an existing worldview."

"Well, the timing thing. That's not what I wanted to hear. We're losing a hell of a lot of billable hours."

Alexa scowled at her brother. "Look, Graham. You knew all this when you made me partner. I gave up my volunteer hours at the Family Planning Clinic. And, as I recall, you liked the valuable PR my work on the commission would give the firm."

Graham sighed. "You're right. And, you know I support everything you're doing to improve laws against sex trafficking. Those bastards shot Mom and nearly killed her. Not to mention all the lives they ruined. We need to take all the traffickers off the street. But, Brian can't handle any greater workload—and the kids are still getting up to speed."

"Don't let our two new lawyers hear you call them kids. They seem to be doing a pretty good job."

"Agreed, but they're newbies. It's going to take awhile."

"Can we afford to hire someone else; someone who's been practicing for a while and looking for a change?" Alexa glanced at her watch. "I have a client appointment in about ten minutes. Maybe this should be on the partners' agenda for tomorrow." She rose to her feet. "One thing I wanted to tell you," she hesitated. "Did you hear about the senator who died last evening at the Capitol?"

"Yeah. On the news this morning." Graham stood and moved toward his desk, then stopped. "What the hell, Lexie? I recognize that expression. Were you involved in this somehow?"

Alexa nodded. "Keisha Washington and I were sitting in the rotunda when this guy comes crashing into the floor. It was awful."

Graham circled Alexa with his arms and crushed her against his chest. She could feel her curls slip from their clip but pressed her face into her brother's comforting embrace.

"So, another police interview?"

Alexa stepped back. "There wasn't much I could tell them. We heard some guys arguing. Then it got quiet. A few minutes later, this man lands at our feet. John came to Harrisburg and drove me home. Another trooper brought my car back here. I drove the Mini today, so I've got two cars parked in the back lot."

Graham looked at his sister intently. "Are you OK?"

"Physically, yes. But seeing that body hit the floor . . ." Alexa swallowed hard. "I'm freaked out, Graham. Is death following me around? First, I start finding dead bodies. Now living people become corpses right before my eyes."

"I knew it. All those black suits you wear. Just yesterday, I asked Kate if you carry that big purse to hide a scythe," he deadpanned.

"I'm serious, Graham."

"So am I. You've had a weird run, stumbling into these situations. But it's ridiculous to think you're the Grim Reaper or some such shit." Her brother's tone softened. "Do you need counseling? Or maybe you just need to talk to Mom and Dad."

"I don't want to bother them while they're in Umbria working on the new house. I'll talk to them when they get back."

At the knock on the door, Alexa glanced at her watch then fixed her hair. "That's probably Melinda. I've got to go. The Harrisons are here."

"Take care, Lexie. We'll talk more later."

"I've finished researching the case law. It looks pretty good for our argument." Vanessa placed a manila folder at Alexa's elbow on the conference table.

Alexa tossed her unfinished chicken salad sandwich on the plate and wiped her hands on a napkin. Yesterday's nausea had returned, and she could only force down a few bites. "Great. I'll take a look at it after I get back from court. Are there any other angles you think we should take a look at? The Bowens are desperate to win this case."

"We studied a few property dispute cases in my Property Law class. I have some case law that could be helpful. Let me finish the research."

"Good thought. Continue your research this afternoon, and we can talk about some of my ideas tomorrow morning."

As Vanessa gathered her papers and headed toward the door, Alexa studied the recent law school grad. The new associate seemed to enjoy research, and the firm needed that enthusiasm. Having someone to do background work was a real lifesaver.

When Melinda buzzed on the phone, Alexa looked at the time. "No, I still have an hour before I have to leave for the courthouse." She breathed a sigh of relief as she picked up the phone.

"You have a call from Jeannie Demeter. She says she knows you. Do you want to take it?" Melinda used her guard dog voice.

Alexa smiled. "Jeannie? Yes, of course. I roomed with her senior year at Columbia. Undergrad."

"I'll put her through."

Alexa spoke first. "Jeannie, it has been ages since we've talked."

"Far too long. I've thought about getting in touch, but somehow life just gets in the way of good intentions." Alexa recognized her friend's voice although Jeannie seemed a bit subdued.

"Tell me about it. I've lost touch with almost all of my college friends. At least you and I exchange Christmas cards. And I see your posts on Facebook when I have time to go online." Alexa laughed.

"That's why I knew I could reach out to you, Alexa. I need your help. Your legal help."

"What kind of legal help?" Alexa's reaction was wary.

"It's about Tessa. And what the fracking company has done to her." Jeannie's words trailed into sobs.

"Tessa? Has there been an accident?" Alexa tried to remember how old her friend's daughter would be now. Elementary school age?

"No. She's sick, real sick. We should have never gone for the quick money and signed over our land to the drillers. But, Tommy took a big hit when the real estate market went south. And, we weren't farming those fifty acres . . ." Jeannie's voice trailed off.

"Are you trying to terminate your lease?"

Jeannie gave a bitter laugh. "I wish that was all. No, the doctors say Tessa is going to need years of treatment. We've had her to Philadelphia to see the cancer specialists. I want those bastards at Monongas Energy to pay for making her sick and take responsibility for getting her the best medical help." Another sob muffled Jeannie's last words. "She has to get better."

"Jeannie, this sounds like a terrible situation. But, I'm not sure I can give you the legal representation you need. It sounds like you'd do better with a high-powered firm that takes on personal injury or class action cases. Have any of your neighbors been affected?"

"Yes. The entire county has been affected in one way or another by fracking. But it's complicated. A lot of lives have been ruined. People are suffering from all sorts of ailments. Many can't drink their water. Some environmental lawyers have been trying to get us to sign up for a lawsuit, but they have their own agenda." Jeannie's voice dropped to a whisper. "Plus, there are lots of families who are getting rich off the fracking, and they don't care about my sick child. Alexa, I need someone I trust to advise me." Jeannie paused. "I need you."

Alexa looked up from the notes she'd been jotting down and took a deep breath. "OK. I can't guarantee how much help I'll be, but let's talk. Should I drive up to your place?" She looked at her calendar. "I can't do it before Saturday."

"Saturday will be fine. Why don't you plan to stay overnight?"

"Sure. I'll head back home early Sunday morning. Your address is still the same?"

Jeannie's tone became animated. "Yes. We're still at the farm. Thank you so much, Lexie. I can't tell you how much this means to me."

"It's been too long since we've seen each other. And being up there in Tioga County will help me get a better picture of what you're facing. Sorry to cut this short, but I have to be in court soon. I'll see you Saturday, late morning."

"Oh, just one thing more. Don't bring Scout. Too many animals have died up here from drinking contaminated water. It's better to leave him at home."

CHAPTER FOUR

ALEXA CLEARED SECURITY just inside the state Capitol doors and stepped into the rotunda. She couldn't keep from glancing toward the spot on the floor where Senator Martinelli's broken body had lain the last time she'd been in the building. The yellow crime scene tape had disappeared. Nothing marked the site of the recent tragedy. Alexa swallowed a shout of protest when three heedless young boys on a school field trip strode across that patch of cobblestone. The students had no idea they trod where a man had died just days earlier. Alexa steered far left of the central staircase and headed down the hall to the Senate elevators.

When Alexa entered the fourth floor suite of offices, the receptionist looked up. "Go on back to the conference room. Lauren's already there. Keisha will join you soon."

"Thanks."

Lauren Hildebrand, the college intern assigned to support the Commission on Human Trafficking looked up from her iPad as Alexa stepped through the door. A box filled with binders sat on the table in front of her. "Hi. Keisha's running late. She wanted to fill you in on everything that's happening, but she's still in a meeting with Senator Gabler. Maybe we should get started."

Alexa settled into one of the heavy wooden chairs and checked her watch. "The commission meeting begins in less than an hour. Let's walk through the agenda. I'm sure you heard what happened the other day with Senator Martinelli. So, Keisha and I never got a chance to finish discussing the plan for today's meeting."

Lauren leaned forward with an excited look on her face. Her spiky blonde hair rested like a crown on top of the shaved stubble circling the lower half of her head. "You're not going to, like, believe everything that's going on. I know Keisha wanted to be the one to tell you, but the senator's death has triggered a bunch of changes. And it affects the commission."

"Senator Martinelli wasn't involved in our work against human trafficking."

"Right. But Senator Gabler is going to move into Senator Martinelli's role as chairman of Environmental Resources and Energy." Lauren bounced in her seat. "That's, like, a really powerful committee."

Alexa marveled at how astute Keisha had been in predicting this turn of events—the exact scenario she'd outlined the night of Senator Martinelli's death.

Lauren pushed a piece of paper across the table to Alexa as she continued. "Senator Jefferson is going to head up Law and Justice, but she doesn't want to deal with the commission on top of learning a new job. So leadership promised her we'd wrap up the commission work by the end of next month. Senator Gabler will continue as co-chair until we issue the report."

"The end of next month? At this point, the group hasn't even agreed on how to define the problem, let alone issue a report." Alexa's protest sounded half-hearted even to her own ears. The five plus months she'd been involved with this project had been frustrating and exhausting. Pulling the plug on the ordeal had a certain appeal.

"That's the beauty of this whole thing." The intern giggled. "Instead of spending, like, four more months spinning our wheels, we'll just give the group a draft report. We give them one chance to comment, and then finalize the sucker." Lauren flashed a wide grin at Alexa. "Keisha and I went through the minutes from all the meetings and came up with ten, like, broad themes. At today's meeting, we can, you know, update everyone on the new turn of events and discuss these themes. And then after the meeting, we'll turn these ten topics into recommendations and a draft bill."

"I take it this isn't really up for discussion? What does the minority chair, Senator Jacobs, say?" Alexa frowned.

"He's fine with it. His staff agrees producing a quick report is the best way to get a product out of this commission. It's a way to focus all these competing interests."

Alexa picked up the sheet of paper. "Let me take a few minutes to read your ten principles."

"Of course. Do you want coffee?"

"A cup of tea would be great." Alexa turned to read the documents as Lauren slipped out the side door into an anteroom that housed a small kitchen. She had nearly finished reading by the time the intern returned, balancing a brimming Styrofoam cup in each hand. A dangling teabag bounced wildly against one cup as Lauren hiked up a foot and shoved the heavy wooden door behind her.

The petite young woman set the cup in front of Alexa and fished two packets out of the pocket of her suit jacket. "Sugar or Sweet'N Low? Sugar's supposed to be bad for you; but I worry about all those chemicals in artificial sweeteners."

"Neither, thanks." Alexa took a sip of the hot tea. "You did a good job on these themes. I'm fine with using all of these except number nine. I'd like to change the clause—" She broke off as the door to the kitchen area creaked open. Two men had entered through another door and were deep in conversation.

"Look. They have no clue. Don't worry so much. Everything is going according to plan." The man spoke as if trying to calm a toddler.

Alexa glanced toward the door, which stood open at least two feet now. Clearly, these two didn't realize they had an audience.

"Damn, I thought I'd closed that," Lauren muttered under her breath as she jumped up and stepped toward the door.

Just as she put her hand on the knob, the other man replied in a hysterical tone, "Easy for you to say. I'm the one with everything on the line here. You need to make sure—"

"Just a minute," the first speaker barked. His manner turned imperious as he moved close to the door. "This is a private conversation, you dyke bitch. I didn't expect the conference room to be occupied. Are you alone in there?"

Lauren shrank back from the opening and stammered, "I'm sorry. I just wanted to give you some privacy. I'm working on a project."

Alexa rose to intercede. This guy was out of line with both his attitude and language. She moved close enough to just catch a glimpse of snow-white hair and horn-rim glasses before Lauren ducked behind the door and slammed it shut. When they returned to the table, the coed's face had paled.

"What a jerk," Alexa commented. "If he wanted a private conversation, he should have shut the door or gone into an office. He had no right to speak to you like that. You should report him."

Lauren attempted a faint smile. "That guy's a pain in the ass most of the time. He comes from a big family of movers and shakers. Thinks he's hot sh—eesh. I shouldn't be talking to you this way."

Alexa never had a chance to respond. Keisha breezed through the main door and asked with a grin, "Did Lauren fill you in on the plan? I know you've had it up to here with this commission, girl. You should be dancing for joy."

"The idea of fast tracking a report has some appeal," Alexa twisted her mouth into a rueful smile. "My managing partner just complained about the amount of time I've been spending here in Harrisburg. He'll be pleased there's an end in sight."

Lauren piped up. "Alexa wants some changes on number nine. If we can, like, take a look at her notes, I'll make the changes and have copies for the meeting." She looked at her cell phone. "Whoa. We've only got twenty minutes."

As the two staffers huddled over her marked-up copy of the document, Alexa studied Keisha. She could see no trace of the vulnerable young woman who'd fallen apart the night of Senator Martinelli's death. This brash and determined version of Keisha was the familiar one. Of course, Alexa reflected, she hadn't been at her best on Tuesday night either. Having a man crash to his death in front of you could shake even the most self-possessed person.

Keisha looked up from the document. "These changes are fine. Alexa, why don't you and I head down to the meeting room?" She turned to Lauren, "Can you ask Audrey to make these changes and bring us thirty copies?"

"Sure. But do you have just a minute?" Lauren pulled Keisha to the corner and spoke in low, animated tones. Alexa couldn't make out any words but noticed the young woman's look of consternation as she glanced toward the door to the kitchen. Gathering her belongings, Alexa wondered about the identity of the jerk who had blasted Lauren. Apparently, someone important enough to warrant an immediate discussion with her boss.

"My dear," Senator Gabler shook Alexa's hand as she sat next to him at the head of the table. He leaned closer and whispered, "I hope you're on board with winding down this process sooner than anticipated."

"I can live with it." She nodded past him to acknowledge Senator Jacobs and turned to study the group of twenty assembled around the large conference table. A much larger crowd filled the seats in the back of the room. Pennsylvania's Sunshine Law guaranteed that commission meetings were open to the public.

"Well, let's get this show on the road," Gabler muttered as he rose to his feet. "I now call this meeting to order. Thank you all for attending. I want to begin today's session by announcing an unexpected change in direction for the work of this commission."

His voice took on the reverential tone many politicians adopted for public tragedies. "Many of you are aware of the recent death of one of Pennsylvania's most beloved senators, Carmine Martinelli."

As Alexa watched the senator sell this abrupt change to the commission's game plan, she marveled at his skill in working the room. The man was a born salesman. Uncle Silas, as she and Graham had called him, looked a lot like an old-movie version of a politician; from the days when people held their elected leaders in awe. Tall and handsome, Gabler wore expensive suits with a muted pinstripe, expertly tailored to draw attention away from his expanding waistline. Now in his mid-sixties, he had served in the legislature for more than thirty years. When Alexa and Graham were kids, Uncle Silas had always made a point to interact with them during his visits with their father. The charisma she'd warmed to as a child was in full force today.

Two women and one older man dabbed at their eyes as the senator concluded a brief eulogy for Senator Martinelli. Alexa blinked to curb tears of her own as she relived the sickening thud of the legislator's body hitting the Capitol floor.

With his entire audience now in a somber mood, Senator Gabler plunged into the news that the commission's work would end early. Although a buzz arose from the crowd of observers, only one of the commission members objected.

Shoshanna Barr, a sex-trafficking survivor, reached for the nearest microphone the minute the senator finished his remarks. "This work is too important to be cut off because senators are playing musical chairs. We have four more months on the schedule. Alexa and your staff can provide continuity. And this committee thing doesn't affect the minority chair." She looked at Senator Jacobs.

"Shoshanna, we understand your concern," the Democrat replied. "But this group has had months to discuss the issues, and I agree with Senator Gabler. We have had substantive input and developed considerable consensus. In normal circumstances, we would have continued our work for a while longer; but I believe we are in an excellent position to move forward with the development of a report and legislative recommendations."

The outspoken advocate looked around the table for support from her fellow commission members, but Alexa could see no one else dared to object. In fact, one of the women who had been moved to tears during Senator Gabler's speech glared daggers at Shoshanna.

Senator Gabler jumped into the silence. "Let me turn the discussion over to our co-chair, Alexa Williams. Due to the expedited time frame, she and the staff have already put together a set of principles to provide the foundation for the commission's report."

Scout jumped up at the sound of the bell and ran to the door. John had installed a driveway alert system to give Alexa advance warning of cars approaching down the long gravel lane to the cabin. Scout's tail wagged when he recognized the sound of John's car engine.

"Hey, big guy." John walked through the door and rubbed Scout's ears. The dog's entire body wriggled with joy. "Go on, go outside for a run." The trooper let the mastiff outside and dropped his coat on a dining room chair.

"Hi." Alexa smiled but didn't budge from the couch.

John did a mock double take. "Oh, Alexa. You're here too. I didn't see you lying there."

"You don't have to pretend, Taylor. I know you only have eyes for that dog. You fooled me at first, but now I know you're only dating me so you can spend time with Scout." Alexa sat up and held her hands toward the woodstove. "I can't believe it's still so cold. I can't wait for spring."

John sat next to her and drew her into his arms. "I'm with you. I spent most of my day traipsing around outside at a crime scene. A trailer on a hill over toward the North Mountain. Not a tree in sight. The wind was brutal."

Alexa hugged the state trooper. "Was it bad? The case, I mean."

"Yeah, for the victim. A domestic violence thing. The husband got drunk and killed his wife. I have a feeling he tied one on regularly at the end of his night shift. This morning, he stopped at a bar with his buddies."

"Bars are open in the morning?"

"Yes. Remember, it's the end of his workday. So, the guy's already lit when he arrives home. Then he downs another six-pack. The wife asks for money to go grocery shopping. He's pissed because she wants a hundred bucks and he only has fifty left. They get into an argument, and he slams her against the wall. She takes the truck keys and runs out of the house. He picks up the AR-15 he keeps by the door for shooting rounds with his buddies. Said he just wanted to scare her away from his truck because she's not allowed to drive it. But his aim sucked. He meant to fire over her head, but he hit her in the chest."

"How did you find out so much about what happened? "

"Dumb ass told us. The wife's sister showed up to visit and called it in. His blood alcohol level was still off the charts when we got there."

"My God. I don't know how you deal with this, day in and day out."

"Because I need to. Not to sound sappy, but I want to make the world a better place. Of course, fly fishing and a beautiful girlfriend help with the stress levels."

"You're a good man, John," Alexa ruffled his sandy hair before she kissed him.

"Enough about my miserable day. You went to the Capitol this afternoon, right? How did that go?" John flashed her an intense look.

Alexa grimaced. "I have to admit, I gave that spot in the rotunda a wide berth. But I managed. The rest of the day was interesting. With Senator Martinelli's death, there's a big shake up. Senator Gabler is moving to a pretty powerful position in the Environmental Resources and Energy Committee. The new person who would have responsibility for the commission wants it shut down. So, they're skipping ahead to the report phase now."

"Is that good or bad?"

"A little of both." Alexa flashed an impish smile. "Tyrell will probably be pissed when he hears about it. He really wanted the commission to recommend high mandatory sentences for traffickers. But he's an advocate, so he's aiming for the stars. We're looking at eliminating some loopholes in current law, which will make it easier to convict offenders. Another year wouldn't have gotten us any closer to Tyrell's ultimate wish list. But, I have to admit, I'll be glad to see this commission end."

"I know it's been a struggle." John entwined Alexa's hand in his own.

"I'm glad I got involved. Jack Nash and his organization ruined thousands of lives with their trafficking operation. And, that's only the tip of the iceberg. Every state has to do all it can to identify and prosecute traffickers. I'm glad I could play a role in improving things in Pennsylvania, but I'm not sure I'm cut out for the politics."

"You mean the Republicans and Democrats couldn't agree?

"That's to be expected. No, I'm talking about the small-P politics of working with a large group. They all have their own agendas. The whole process has been way more difficult than I imagined."

"I've had some experience with politicians—usually when they want a quick arrest on a high profile murder so their constituents can sleep easy. Not always the most patient or logical people."

At the sound of scratching at the door, Alexa rose from the couch to let Scout inside. "Yeah, I ran into one of them today." She felt anger flare at that morning's incident—the guy who had been too lazy to close the kitchen door to ensure a private conversation. "He jumped all over a college intern for no real reason. Some of these guys get on a real power trip when they're elected. What an arrogant ass."

CHAPTER FIVE

March 28, 1979

It was the first step in a nuclear nightmare, as far as we know at this hour, no worse than that.
                    —*Walter Cronkite,* CBS Evening News

"Babe, did you hear anything at work about this problem at TMI?" Randi nodded toward the radio.

"No. What happened?" Will dropped his shoes and listened to the report in progress on WKBO.

"There has been an incident at the Three Mile Island nuclear power plant during the night. Plant operator Metropolitan Edison says that this issue does not present a problem to the general public."

"You know that in Water Quality we have nothing to do with the nuclear stuff. But I'll talk to the people in Radiation Management today. I'll bet it's just like the news says—there's nothing to worry about." Will Armstrong filled a cup of coffee from the percolator on the stove top and sat down across from his wife at the wobbly kitchen table.

"It's scary." Randi fretted. "What if something terrible happens? Like The China Syndrome. *We're not that far from TMI."*

Will clasped his wife's hand. "If the authorities thought there was a problem, they would tell us."

"Yeah, like they did in The China Syndrome.*"*

"Damn, Randi. That's just a movie. I should have known better than to take you to see it. You're flipping out about everything right now. Last week, it was the polyester in leisure suits. Now you're

getting paranoid about nuclear power plants. TMI had to go through all sorts of hoops to get approval to come on-line. I'm sure it's safe, and they'll fix whatever is going on."

"Can you blame me?" Randi patted her bulging midsection. "This little one is going to arrive in a week or two. I'm a little anxious."

Will rose from his chair and kissed Randi on the top of her head. "I'm more excited than anxious. I can't wait for Walden to arrive."

Randi sighed. "I still haven't agreed on Walden as a name for a boy. Certainly not for a girl, Will."

"We've got time to decide. But I already agreed; no polyester baby clothes. And Walden's a great name. Just remember." He pointed to a Sierra Club poster of huge evergreens on the wall and recited the message. "In wildness is the preservation of the world."

"I know, I know. Henry David Thoreau is your hero, and you want to name our baby after his pond." Randi pushed her bulky body out of the kitchen chair and walked her husband to the door. "You look nice today, babe. Let me straighten your collar." She smoothed Will's wide shirt collar over his sweater vest and kissed him on the cheek.

"Take it easy today. And don't worry." Will pulled on his surplus store army jacket and hurried down the flagstone path to his car, a secondhand Volkswagen Thing. As he exited the lane of their rental farm, Will regretted that the car didn't have a radio. Usually he enjoyed the silence of his brief daily commute, but today, Randi's concerns made him uneasy. He'd like to hear more news about TMI.

Will spied one of his co-workers in the parking lot on City Island. He hurried to join Brad Bittner on the Walnut Street Bridge, calling, "Hey, what's the latest on TMI?"

Brad slowed to let Will catch up. "Met-Ed says they have it under control. I got a call at home to tell me that I might be sent out in the field to take samples later today. My boss is out there at a press conference right now."

"Samples of what?" Will gulped.

"Radiation. The company says they contained everything, but we'll still want to test ourselves. Just a precaution."

"Brad, should I be worried about this? My wife's pregnant."

"We'll know more in a few hours. Based on what I've heard so far, things are fine."

As the two continued to their office in the Fulton Building, Will couldn't shake a niggling sense of disquiet. Although he knew nuclear power was safe, he kept thinking about his dad's advice.

The week before he married Randi, Dad had taken him aside for a talk. "Son, you're taking on a sacred responsibility. You need to put this woman first in your heart and your life. That means making sure she's safe, with a roof over her head, food to eat, and a little money in her pocket. And when you have children, you will have obligations to the entire family."

Will hadn't really paid much attention to his old man at the time. But now the words weighed on his mind.

At noon, Will and two of his work friends went out to The Spot on Second Street for hot dogs. As they waited to order, the radio on the counter blared out the Bee Gees song, "How Deep Is Your Love." The smell of hot grease choked the air.

"I can't stand the Bee Gees, but Randi loves them." Will grimaced as the Gibb brothers launched into a falsetto chorus.

"You had to dig Saturday Night Fever though?" George threw his arms out in a geeky version of John Travolta doing disco.

"Nope, not even Saturday Night Fever. I'm more of a John Denver type of guy."

"Look at you, George," Andy ribbed. "A Travolta fan. I bet you have a disco ball in your living room too."

The music faded to be replaced by a saccharine jingle for a local bank. Then, "And now, the news from Three Mile Island."

"Shh, guys. I want to hear this." Will gestured for his friends to keep quiet.

"We have an update on the situation at Three Mile Island. The Pennsylvania State Police have announced that Metropolitan Edison has called a general emergency for the plant. Although details are few, the problem has been contained in the second unit. Officials are assuring the public that the problem is under control, and personnel continue to work to resolve the issues. State officials are closely monitoring the situation. We understand that Nuclear Regulatory Commission staff are expected to arrive later today."

The three men paid for their hot dogs and made their way to one of the tables in the front of the deli.

"That's a relief to hear that we don't have to worry about a China Syndrome." Andy laughed.

"Yeah. Pretty spooky that the movie comes out, what, two weeks ago? And then we have a scare at TMI. Had me shaking in my shoes." George took a swig of Coca-Cola. "But Jane Fonda was terrific. That woman is a fox. Who cares about that whole Hanoi Jane Vietnam thing?"

Will ignored the Jane Fonda remark. George had a one-track mind when it came to women, even movie stars he'd never meet.

Will confided, "Randi freaked out this morning too. I told her it was just a movie." He noticed Andy's skeptical look. "I know some groups out there are protesting nuclear power plants, but I read a lot about it when Unit One went on-line. I even went to one of those Met-Ed briefings. I believe it's safe."

"You're such a Boy Scout, Will. You'll believe anything the people in charge tell you." Andy scoffed. "Don't you know you can never believe The Man?"

"Calling me a Boy Scout doesn't bother me. I made Eagle Scout. Did my project on raptors at Hawk Mountain. I love hawks and eagles. They're so free."

"Why am I not surprised."George put down his half-eaten Spot Dog and lowered his voice. "But Andy's right. You can't believe everything these people say. I don't know if they're lying about TMI, but the government and corporations lie to us all the time."

Will placed both hands on the metal table and leaned forward. "Look, nuclear power is the future of energy in this country. It doesn't pollute the water and destroy the forests like coal. Look at Centralia. Those coal mines have been burning under the surface since the early sixties."

"You thinking of transferring to the Bureau of Mine Reclamation or something?" George wiped chili sauce and mustard from his mustache before he finished his last bite.

"No way. I love working in Water Quality. It's important work, protecting people and the environment." Will polished off the last of his plain hot dog and looked at his watch. "We better get back to the office. We're late."

Will breezed through the farmhouse door, arms held wide. "Randi, I'm home." Since his wife caught every I Love Lucy rerun she could find on television, Will's Desi Arnaz imitation had become a running joke.

Randi shambled into the kitchen, rubbing her eyes. "I must have fallen asleep. I've been so tired today."

Will dropped his arms before he kissed Randi and stroked the curve of belly straining against her bulky sweater. "How's the little guy?"

"She's kicking like crazy." Randi smiled. "Like she's ready to meet her mom and dad."

"What's for dinner?"

"We could heat up the leftover casserole from the other night. I spent so much time on the phone this afternoon, I didn't have time to cook."

"You sit down and rest." Will gave Randi a gentle nudge toward a chair. "Should I reheat the casserole in the oven?"

"Yeah. That will work better than on the stove."

Will dug a glass storage container out of the refrigerator and dumped its hamburger, macaroni, and cheese concoction into a Corning Ware baking dish. Randi sat in one of the kitchen chairs and watched. "So, who'd you talk to for so long?"

Randi grimaced. "My mom and some of my girlfriends. Mom's freaking out about this whole Three Mile Island thing. She wants us to come home. A lot of people are evacuating the area."

"It seemed like less traffic than usual tonight. People are really evacuating?"

"I talked to Harriet. She and Bob were going to leave town when he got home at three. Then, Sunny called. She and a group of girlfriends drove to Pittsburgh this morning. They're staying with Sunny's family. She said we should leave too—because radiation is even more dangerous for a pregnant woman." Randi's voice caught as she wrung her hands. "I couldn't deal with it anymore so I took a nap." She gave Will a plaintive look. "Are they right? Should we get out of here?"

Will shut the oven door and turned his full attention to his distraught wife.

"I'm really scared, Will." Randi broke into sobs, tears turning her face blotchy. She clasped her hands over her stomach and rocked in her chair. "What if the radiation hurts the baby?"

Will folded her into his arms. "The radio at noon said everything is fine. But let's turn on the television and watch the news. They'll have the latest information. Then, if there's a problem, we'll decide what to do. But, babe, I'm pretty sure all your friends are overreacting. That's what I told Dad when he called me at work."

"So your parents are worried too?"

He led Randi to the big, overstuffed couch in their tiny living room and then switched on the console TV. "Great. We're just in time," he said as the evening news logo flashed on the screen.

The news played part of the press conference that had been held earlier in the day. The mustachioed young lieutenant governor, William Scranton III, stood tall in front of a bank of microphones and said, "We do not expect there to be any kind of necessity for evacuation."

"See, babe? It's exactly what I said." Will seized his wife's hand. "Everything is fine. We can just sit tight. By the time the baby comes, this TMI stuff will be long over."

Randi gave a wan smile. "I'm so relieved. I shouldn't have let Mom and my friends get to me."

"It's natural to be concerned. Especially with the baby only two weeks away."

"You know my due date isn't exact. A lot of first babies come late."

The smell of hamburger and bubbling cheese wafted into the living room. Will laughed as he rose to check on dinner. "Yeah, I know. But I'm going to get the crib ready on Saturday. The Boy Scouts taught me to be prepared."

CHAPTER SIX

ALEXA DOWNSHIFTED THE Land Rover when she saw the sign for Granfeld. An anemic shaft of sunlight that touched the road ahead did little to alleviate the gloom. She cranked up the heat against the morning chill and wondered what she could possibly do for Jeannie and her family. She had no experience in environmental law, but Alexa couldn't ignore her old roommate's heartfelt plea for help.

Although she had been to Granfeld before, those visits had been years ago. Alexa and another friend had spent a weekend at Jeannie's family farm during their college years. And she had come here again for Jeannie's wedding. But she had only sketchy memories of Jeannie's hometown. A little white church surrounded by rolling farm country and fields of black and white jersey cows. In those days, Tioga County had seemed like an idyllic oasis of green in contrast to New York City. She hadn't been back since.

The old Land Rover had been built long before dashboard navigation systems, so Alexa had to rely on her iPhone for directions. The brief hint of sun disappeared when she turned right and plunged into thick ground fog. She slowed, looking for the turn onto Oak Lane, then jammed on the brakes as a towering metal structure loomed ahead in the mist. The menacing gray column, which looked like the love child of Megalon and a Transformer, stood directly in her path. Alexa wrinkled her nose as an acrid smell filled the car.

She glanced into the rearview mirror to check for oncoming cars. Hands clammy, she inched the Land Rover forward. With a sigh of relief, Alexa found that the road angled left to run in front of the hulking tower. She picked up speed, passing the ugly scene. A wide gash of raw earth circled the metal monster, as if it had run amok and trampled the field to mud. A gaggle of trailers that looked like those FEMA mobile homes from Hurricane Katrina dotted the perimeter. A clanking noise rose above the rumble of truck engines. Rows of large tanker trucks lined up at a gate on the far side of the tower. Alexa grimaced.

So, this was fracking.

Continuing on, the road climbed above the mist. A farm perched on the hill above the fracking site. The old limestone farmhouse sat less than a half-mile away from the chaos below.

"How could anyone live with that mess in their backyard?" Alexa exclaimed to the empty car.

As she reached higher ground, visibility improved. Ahead, Alexa could see a sign marked Oak Lane. After a mile or so of driving through thick woods, the tree trunks dark in the humid air, Alexa emerged into farmland. Slowing once or twice to study the numbers on mailboxes, she spotted a white farmhouse with a huge red barn ahead. The buildings sat back from the main road, partially shielded by two old weeping willows, their branches still bare.

"This is it. Nine eighty-seven." Alexa turned right onto the gravel lane. "I know they've got fracking problems, but at least Jeannie doesn't have to live with one of those huge pits in her front yard."

The front of the house faced away from the road. Alexa drove between the willows and followed the driveway to a parking area by the front porch. Just beyond the railroad ties that marked the edge of the parking area, the ground sloped downward then flattened out. Alexa's heart sank when she saw a bewildering network of mechanical equipment and steel pipes dominating the flat below. Several huge metal structures and another small aluminum building sprouting a profusion of pipes stood at one end of the rectangle of packed earth. Below it stood a half-filled earthen pond.

Jeannie came running out of the house as Alexa climbed out of the Rover. "I can't believe you're here. It's wonderful to see you." She pulled Alexa into her arms for a hug.

"It's been too long. Sorry it's taken your daughter's illness to get us together." Alexa sighed.

"Come into the house and we can talk. Did you bring an overnight bag?"

Shouldering the backpack that contained a few toiletries and a change of clothes, Alexa followed Jeannie into the house. The front door spilled into a living room with two leather couches and a big-screen television.

"Would you like a drink? Want to use the facilities?" Jeannie kept walking until they reached a bright, warm kitchen. She gestured to a chair. "Put your backpack there for now. Tessa is napping, so we won't go upstairs until she wakes up."

Alexa headed straight for the fireplace and stood in front of the small fire burning in its wide hearth. "Wow. This is a great room. Could I have a cup of tea? It's at least ten degrees colder up here than at home."

"It's only a few weeks until spring. I have daffodils blooming on the sunny side of the house, but the weather has been brutal this year." Jeannie bustled around the kitchen, drawing water from a big blue plastic jug to make a pot of tea. She wore dark corduroy slacks and a gray cardigan. Alexa noticed a few strands of gray in her friend's black hair. "Tommy had to work today. He should be home by late afternoon."

"Does he still sell real estate?"

"Yes, but the market has been terrible. You probably know most family farming has turned into little more than subsistence living—at least up here in the Northeast. So incomes are low. When a farm folds, few people want to buy it. Unless you can tempt a rich New Yorker looking for a country home. And we're just a little far west for most of the city crowd."

Noticing Jeannie take a tray from the cupboard, Alexa moved to help. She grabbed two cups and a sugar bowl from the counter. Her hostess carried the tray bearing the teapot and a plate of muffins to the table in front of the fire.

"So, times have been hard." Alexa lifted a muffin from the tray.

"That's right." Jeannie looked up from pouring tea. "Tommy's real estate business has been on a downturn for several years. That's why we took the gas deal. Monongas invaded the county. A battalion of salespeople went door to door, buying up leases for gas rights. Lots of people signed right away. They were paying cash up front with the promise of a steady income from the wells on your land.

"Some families held out. They'd heard rumors about problems with fracking. Some just didn't like the idea of drilling equipment on their land. Eventually, even some of the more reluctant landowners caved. Monongas told them they were screwing themselves because the company would pump the gas out of their land anyway through nearby wells." Jeannie twisted her mouth into a sad smile. "Ended up only a few people had enough money or maybe just enough commonsense to send Monongas packing."

"From the equipment out there, I take it you signed a lease?" Alexa took a neutral tone.

"Oh, yes." Jeannie picked up her cup of tea and then put it back down, untouched. "Tommy wanted in the minute Monongas came to Tioga County. I hesitated. The idea of turning part of this beautiful acreage over to drilling—that just didn't sit well with me. The land has been in Tommy's family for years. But we needed the money. Leon Myers rents some of our land for his dairy cattle. And I plant a big garden every year. But Tommy never had any interest in working this land. So most of our acreage just sits idle.

"When Monongas finally knocked on our door, we said yes. Now I can't believe we were so shortsighted. Better to call it what it was—greed, pure and simple. Now our precious angel is paying for her parents' selfish choices."

Alexa flinched at Jeannie's bitter tone. Her sunny, soft-spoken friend had changed. "Don't be so hard on yourself. You didn't know this fracking would turn out to be dangerous, did you? The money must have looked like a lifeline when you were going through hard times."

"But we should have done more research. Listened to guys like Maurice Lewis who talked about the environmental impact and the bad experiences in Dimock and elsewhere."

Alexa took a mental step from her role as friend to lawyer. "Did Monongas disclose any potential problems that could arise from drilling on your land? Did they tell you what the process would be? What chemicals they would use and any dangers from those chemicals? What liability do they assume for problems in the lease?" She'd done just enough reading about fracking on Friday to ask these questions.

"That's why I needed you here, Lexie. To help us figure out our legal options. A major in religion isn't much help in dealing with lawsuits or medical bills. And, to tell you the truth, even my faith has frayed with Tessa's illness. I've found myself wishing I had more options than putting myself in God's hands. Maybe the Hindus have it right. With tons of gods, if Vishnu can't help, you can always try another deity."

"You know I'm the last person to get into a religious discussion, but didn't you always tell me the Hindus worship one god?"

"You haven't changed. I can tell you're trying to distract me, but we're not going to get sidetracked into Hindu theology." Jeannie giggled. "But it's fun you tried. You have no idea how little chance I have to talk about world religions up here. Sunday's church service is my only exposure to theology. And the new minister doesn't seem to have," she paused as if searching for the right word, "an intellectual interest in religious philosophy. He's more doctrinaire in his approach. I miss Reverend Mills."

Alexa scrunched her face. "Reverend Mills. Wasn't he that skinny minister who married you and Tom? I talked to him for a long time at the rehearsal dinner. That guy was a hoot."

"He fostered my interest in religion. You know I considered Divinity School for a while."

"Until you met Tom the summer after junior year."

Jeannie flashed a wistful smile. "That's right. Love and marriage became more important than becoming a minister. That might have been the first step toward losing my moral compass."

Alexa didn't know quite how to respond. Jeannie seemed trapped in a dark place. Although Alexa wasn't an expert, her old friend seemed to exhibit some symptoms of depression. But who wouldn't be depressed with a sick child, a loser husband, and a dangerous industrial operation in your front yard? She broke the lengthening silence. "Tell me more about Tessa."

"Her illness?"

At Alexa's nod, Jeannie took a deep breath and whispered, "It's almost more than a mother can bear. One day your little girl is a healthy, happy six-year-old. The next day she's so sick she can barely lift her head off the pillow." She wiped away a tear and squared her shoulders. "It started about a year after they did the initial drilling."

"Down below, where all those pipes are?" Alexa gestured toward the front of the house.

"Yes. But what you see today is a hundred times better than those first weeks. The place looked like Dante's *Inferno*. They brought in a huge drilling rig and built two open pools, one for freshwater and one to hold the saltwater they brought up from the ground. They tore up the muddy field and sprayed sand everywhere. Big trucks drove in and out constantly. You wouldn't believe the noise. At night, they lit up the area with klieg lights because they drilled twenty-four hours a day."

Alexa grimaced, remembering the ugly tower she'd passed earlier, but didn't interrupt Jeannie's anguished narrative.

"You can't imagine the nightmare until one of these rigs drills right outside your door. I couldn't get Tessa to sleep through the night. She'd wake up at the racket, terrified that monsters were coming for her. Tom spent as much time as possible away from the house." Jeannie shook her head. "The few minutes he stayed at home, we fought about the decision to sign the fracking lease. I blamed Tom, but to tell the truth, I'm just as guilty. I could have said no."

"What you're describing sounds like a terrible situation. Did you know they were going to drill so close to the house?"

"Not really. They leased the entire fifty acres. I guess I expected them to drill somewhere on the outer edge, near the other road. That would have been a mile or so away." She took a sip of tea. "But, once again, Tom and I were fools. The lease said Monongas would survey and drill at the best site. We protested when their tests indicated an optimal site right in front of the house. But the lease we signed included that land. Pennsylvania law says a drilling site can be no closer than five hundred feet from a residence. That's not even the length of two football fields."

"Did Tessa get sick during that initial drilling?"

"Yes and no. We were all cranky because of the noise and lack of sleep. One afternoon, I fell asleep on the couch while she was napping. She woke up and slipped out of the house with the dog. I found them down near the containment area that controls water runoff. She knew she wasn't allowed down there near all those trucks. But Patches ran down, chasing something, and she went to bring him back. The dog died a few weeks later.

"Turned out the saltwater pond had developed a slow leak that seeped into the containment area. The leak riddled the containment run-off water with manganese, arsenic, and radium; all the toxic crap that comes up with salt water from the deep earth and God knows what other chemicals they use for fracking. We hoped Tessa hadn't been contaminated, but, about a year later, she showed the first symptoms." Jeannie plucked a muffin from the tray and shredded the paper liner into slivers as she spoke.

"The day it happened, Tessa swore she didn't go near the containment pond. But she touched the wet dog and kissed him. She carried him back up the hill so he wouldn't get in trouble for running away." Jeannie dropped the mutilated muffin and pressed her index finger to her lip. "I feel so guilty. I should have kept an eye on her. I'll never forget how she wailed when Patches died. And, of course, that's when we knew something terrible had happened. And, for twelve long months, we waited in dread for the other shoe to drop. And then it did. The poison just took longer to affect Tessa."

Alexa's heart ached for her friend, but she pressed ahead. "Did they fix the leak?"

"Yes, when the dog died, we complained. That's when the company discovered the problem. They had lined the saltwater pond with rubber, and something had ripped the rubber at the very bottom of the pond. The Department of Environmental

Programs got involved and cited the company." Jeannie's harsh laugh verged on a snarl. "Soon after, they stopped using the ponds and switched to pumping the salt water into tanker trucks at the site."

"Did they take responsibility for the dog? And for Tessa's illness—" Alexa stopped and looked around at the sound of a child's voice.

"Mama. I'm thirsty."

Jeannie smiled and pointed at the baby monitor on the dry sink. "When Tessa got sick, I pulled this out of storage so I could hear her upstairs. Sometimes she's too weak to walk down the steps on her own. That's why I home school her now." Jeannie filled a plastic cup with water from the blue jug. "She might fall back to sleep. Just sit tight. Have some more tea."

With Jeannie gone, Alexa had a chance to study the big, open room. The old farmhouse had been renovated at some point. This spotless room extended across the entire width of the house, combining kitchen, dining room, and a little sitting area. Warm, wooden antiques, like the dining table and chairs, glowed against cheap fiberboard end tables, a dilapidated coffee table disguised with milk paint, and a slip-covered sofa well past shabby chic. A child-size chair sat against the wall, its fabric patterned with elephants in pink tutus. Medicine bottles filled a clear plastic container on the counter. Jeannie had done her best to brighten the big space with landscape prints and a quilt thrown over the sofa. But, Alexa could see times were hard for her old friend. It looked like any decorating money for the house had gone into that humongous big-screen TV in the living room.

Alexa smiled as she listened to the conversation coming through the baby monitor, Jeannie's soothing words a counterpoint to her daughter's sleepy murmurs. Alexa rose to check out a figurine on the fireplace mantel just as Jeannie breezed back into the room. "Is this the same Ganesh we got in the Village?"

"The very same. That guy has seen me through good times and bad. You know he's associated with obstacles." Jeannie's tone became dry. "He removed a lot of obstacles for me back in my schooldays, but now it feels like he's more interested in throwing them in my way. Tessa should sleep for a while longer. Do you want to take a walk outside?"

Jeannie led Alexa out the back door and around the house where a row of yellow daffodils nestled against the white boards. The happy promise of the daffodils turned to dust when they turned the corner to see the fracking operation at the foot of the hill.

"So, what is this?" Alexa waved toward the rows of steel pipes and metal buildings. The area took up several acres, a harsh scar in the middle of rolling fields tinged with a hint of green.

"The part I told you about earlier, the drilling process. The first one lasted about four months from start to finish. At the end, they pulled out the big drilling equipment, pumped out both the freshwater and saltwater ponds, and filled them in. Then they put in this wellhead to keep the natural gas pumping out of the ground."

"Do they pump it into trucks?"

"No. It flows out through an underground network of pipes. See that station over there?" Jeannie pointed to a collection of pipes at the far corner of the flat area. "That's where the gas lines begin. They go out beneath those fields.

"Of course, there are six wells down there. Four of them working. Monongas came back twice to drill more wells. They didn't do all of them the first time."

"Could they come back again?"

"I guess so—if they decide to drill the last two wells. Compared to the initial drilling, this is bearable." Jeannie waved at the field of metal below. "The noise and dust is gone. You get used to the truck traffic that comes to empty the tanks."

"But it's not exactly idyllic country life anymore, is it?" Alexa bit her lip. "Are you making any money from all of this? That's why you leased the land, right?"

Jeannie frowned. "We got five hundred an acre from the original lease. Most of that went to pay off loans. We've gotten monthly checks since then for royalties—several thousand a month at first, but much, much less now. All in all, not nearly enough to make up for what they did to the land. And how do you put a price on your precious daughter's life? She could die from this cancer." Jeannie put a hand to her forehead and wept.

Alexa wrapped an arm around her friend. "Jeannie, I'm so sorry. Let's go back inside in case Tessa wakes up." Beyond that, she could find no words of comfort.

Tom slammed the front door and boomed, "Where's my little honey bunny?"

Tessa tottered from the kitchen, squealing, "Daddy," and wrapped her thin arms around his leg. Sitting in a living room chair, Alexa winced as the beefy man swung his daughter into the air. Although Tessa giggled in excitement, the child's frail frame looked like it could snap from the motion.

"Be careful, Tom. Just put her down," Jeannie admonished as she ran in from the kitchen.

"We were just having a little fun." Tom returned Tessa to the floor. "Weren't we, honey bunny?"

"Do it again, Daddy." Tessa pleaded but soon lay down on the couch, clutching a blanket to her chest. The child's hair, coal black like her mother's, only accentuated the pallor of her skin.

"Why, if it isn't Alexa Williams. I didn't see you sitting there; you were so quiet. I hear you're a hotshot New York attorney now."

Alexa stood to greet her host, who had turned away to hang up his coat. "Not anymore."

"Huh?" Tom snickered. "Not anymore what?"

"I left New York City a couple of years ago. I still practice law, but with my family firm in Carlisle."

Jeannie interjected. "I told you that already, Tom."

"I thought you were bringing in your old friend who's a big-gun lawyer in one of those fancy New York outfits." Tom's tone veered between scoffing and whiny. "We need some real help in getting money from those bastards who made our little girl sick."

Seeing Jeannie's look of exasperation, Alexa looked at Tom. "I'm here to see if I can offer any advice. My expertise is neither personal injury nor environmental law. But I told Jeannie I would help you find counsel qualified to take on your case—more accurately, Tessa's case."

"Tom, get ready for dinner. I'll feed Tessa now. We can discuss this more while we eat."

As Tom headed up the stairs, Jeannie whispered. "I apologize. Tom talks without thinking half the time. I'm sure he appreciates your help." Her voice rose to its normal level. "Tessa, honey. Time for dinner. "

"I'm too tired, Mommy."

"You have to eat to keep your strength up." Jeannie lifted her daughter off the couch, cradling Tessa in her arms. "Alexa, do you want to come with us?"

Alexa left early Sunday morning, glad to escape the pain and tension in the Demeter household. The morning had dawned clear, so Alexa had an unimpeded view of all the fracking wells and wellheads scattered along her route out of Tioga County. Even on Sunday, she encountered a flow of tractor-trailers, mostly tankers, on the narrow back roads. She breathed a sigh of relief when she hit the four-lane highway.

With the radio tuned to a New Age channel, Alexa soaked in the serene music and reviewed her visit with Jeannie. They had finally discussed the heartbreaking details of Tessa's cancer after dinner. The doctors said this type of brain cancer was very rare, especially in children. The specialists' working theory was that the fracking at the Demeters' had released toxic compounds into the saltwater pool. Tessa was likely contaminated when she and the dog had come into contact with runoff from the leak. The compounds had ravaged the susceptible body of the developing child. Alexa had gasped when Jeannie revealed the doctors' prognosis. The cancer was very aggressive and could be fatal.

Children's Hospital of Philadelphia had already begun chemotherapy on Tessa with more scheduled in two weeks. Jeannie was distraught that Tessa would likely lose her hair on the next round. The bigger problem was Tom's insurance. Although federal law no longer permitted lifetime limits, he had chosen the family plan with the cheapest monthly premiums. They didn't have enough money for the co-pays, let alone the travel and other costs involved in frequent trips to Philly. At least they received free lodging at the Ronald McDonald House. Alexa had suggested applying for Medicaid due to the child's disability but didn't know enough about the rules to be certain Tessa would qualify.

When Alexa's mind drifted to Tom, even the harmonious strains of harp and flute wafting from the Rover's speakers couldn't keep her calm. What a loser. Jeannie had rekindled a romance with her high school sweetheart during the summer before senior year of college. Even the cold hard light of New York City had been unable to shake her infatuation with Tom. So she'd thrown away her plans for Divinity School and returned home to marry after graduation. Alexa had seen through the guy from the moment they met—a salesman whose biggest product was Tom Demeter. It appeared Jeannie had finally recognized some of Tom's bullshit. But she knew her friend. Jeannie would never contemplate divorce.

Alexa turned back to the legal issues. She knew she could track down the right representation for the family. Monongas deserved to pay for the con they'd run on these people who had leased their land for fracking. Most of all, they needed to pay for the medical bills and other harm they'd caused young Tessa. The girl could die.

CHAPTER SEVEN

"FETCH." ALEXA TOSSED a stick and followed Scout into the grove of pines. Her boots crunched through a patch of icy snow still clinging to the shaded edge of the forest. Inside the towering arch of trees, no snow had filtered onto the carpet of pine needles. A calming silence filled the pine cathedral. "Good boy." When the panting mastiff returned the stick, Alexa patted the giant dog on the head and threw it back toward the cabin. She stopped, just inside the pines, and closed her eyes for a moment soaking in the silence.

"Alexa, where are you?" John's voice came from the deck.

"Out here, in the pines." Alexa sighed when the quiet shattered. John ran down the steps and walked in her direction. When Scout spotted John, the dog dropped the stick and ran toward him, tail wagging.

"Hey, Scout." John laughed. As he approached Alexa, he said, "I decided a walk might be nice after all. I spend too much time in front of the TV on Sunday afternoons. With football season over, I'm just watching out of habit. I'm not all that crazy about basketball anyway."

Alexa picked up Scout's stick and moved forward. "Glad you changed your mind. We were going to walk to the far edge of the woods."

"Great. I haven't been out here much. It's sort of eerie, these tall pines blocking out the sun." John shivered.

Alexa gave a thin laugh. "You go into dangerous situations all the time, but you let these trees creep you out? This grove of pines is one of my favorite places. Graham and I played in here all the time when we were kids."

"I guess growing up on a farm, I'm more comfortable with open fields." John darted a nervous look at Alexa. "Speaking of farms, my mom invited us up to State College for Easter. It's two weeks from today. I'd like you to get to know my parents better."

"Do you have that weekend off?" Caught off guard, Alexa stalled.

"Right now, I'm scheduled to work on Friday and Saturday, but I could talk to my boss. I've got a lot of vacation days."

Alexa frowned. "I already told Graham and Kate I'd have dinner with them. I know you'd be welcome too. I didn't know you planned to go home for the weekend."

"But, it never occurred to you—to come home with me?" John's voice was tight.

"Kate's call last week was the first I'd even thought about Easter, to tell you the truth. It's just not something that's high on my radar screen. My parents usually have a big Easter dinner, but Kate stepped in since they're still in Italy." Alexa's tone took on a distinct chill, like when an opponent in court pissed her off.

"Easter's a big deal to my parents."

"Then you should spend the day with them."

"But my mom really wants to get to know you," John cajoled.

"It's not like we've never met. Maybe we can get together when the weather gets warmer."

"You know, when we move in together, we're going to have share holidays between our families; make concessions."

Alexa sighed. "John, I am not ready for that kind of commitment. We've talked about this so many times."

"Right." John muttered. "I should have worn a warmer coat. I'm going back to the house. Maybe finish that trout fly." He turned and shuffled through the pine needles in the direction of the cabin.

"Scout, stay." Alexa held the dog by his collar for a moment and confided, "I just can't deal with John's constant pressure about living with us." Her good mood had evaporated. She kept replaying the conversation as she hiked through the pines. Hell, John spent most of his time at the cabin anyway. Why did he need to move in? She fretted about the situation until, frustrated, she turned back.

When she and Scout reached the cabin, John's car was gone. Walking into the empty house, Alexa switched off the basketball game blaring from the television and collapsed into a chair, angry with John. He kept pushing for more in this relationship than she was ready to give. This crap was getting old.

After a few minutes, Alexa shrugged off her bad mood. She lifted her laptop from the kitchen counter and typed in a search for fracking lawsuits.

"Melinda, I have a project for you." Alexa leaned forward over her desk.

"Okey dokey. How was your weekend, boss?" Melinda raised her pen, ready to take notes on a lavender-hued legal pad. "We went to see that new Pixar movie. My husband wanted to see it more than the kids. I just don't get those computer-animated characters."

"To answer your question, I spent a lot of time driving this weekend," Alexa responded. "I visited my friend, Jeannie Demeter. She and her husband signed a lease with this fracking outfit for extra income. Now they're left with a field of pumping stations in front of their house and a critically ill child. Little Tessa looks so frail. Every time I looked at her, I saw my niece and nephew. I can't imagine Courtney or Jamie being so desperately ill."

"How awful." Melinda wiped a tear from her eye.

"I'd like you to track down an environmental attorney for me. Maybe call the Wildness Cooperative office in Harrisburg first. Find out if they have an expert in fracking or know about any lawsuits. Check with the Sierra Club's state office too. The third option would be the National Resources Defense Council—their headquarters is probably in DC. Then find a time I can meet with one of their people. In person would be better, but phone is an option."

"Doesn't Leonardo DiCaprio work with the NRDC? Maybe you could have him come here to our office?" Melinda suggested with a hopeful expression.

"Yeah, sure. In between movie shoots, right?"

Melinda giggled. "I'll get on this right away."

"Thanks, I'd like to meet with someone this week, if possible. I'm going to ask Vanessa or Ted to do a search for personal injury lawsuits around fracking."

Melinda came through, as always. On Tuesday morning, Alexa headed for Harrisburg, glad to rely on the comforting heft of her Land Rover in the solid stream of truck traffic on I-81. Her vintage Land Rover Defender had been riddled with bullets last summer when she and her mother fled from goons employed by a sex trafficking ring. Alexa had feared her trusty vehicle had driven its last mile. But she'd had it hauled back down to the place outside of Philadelphia that had once refurbished the engine for her. Now the Rover was as good as new, maybe better, with a pristine body. Alexa had never liked the original white color, so she had the vehicle painted a custom blue that reminded her of the sky at dusk. She'd bought a used Mini-Cooper convertible to drive while they repaired the Rover, so Alexa and Scout were now a two-car family.

Alexa found a parking spot in the Walnut Street garage and walked to the restaurant. A tall, tanned woman waved when she entered the room, so Alexa squeezed toward her through the cramped space. When she reached the table, Alexa asked, "Darby Kaplan?"

"Hi. I take it you're Alexa Williams? I recognized you from your LinkedIn photo. Have a seat."

"Thanks for meeting me. Did my assistant tell you what I'd like to discuss?" Alexa pulled out a notepad.

"She did. I take it you've got a client who's being screwed over by the hydraulic fracturing industry?" At Alexa's nod, Darby flashed a sardonic smile. "Welcome to the Marcellus Shale, the State of Independence from adequate taxes and regulation."

Darby's spin on the Commonwealth of Pennsylvania's tourism slogan left little doubt about her position on fracking. Alexa replied, "I've read news reports and some of your Wildness Cooperative articles on fracking. It's something else to see it in operation like I did last weekend. It's destroying the landscape. And my client blames her daughter's cancer on fracking."

"I don't doubt it. I've seen a lot of horror stories come out of the Marcellus Shale. The toxic chemicals. The methane emissions. It's sort of like the Vikings or the Visigoths sailing in to pillage and rape the land and its inhabitants. In this case, the government has helped them dock the boat and then turned a blind eye to the mayhem. So, how can I help?"

As the two women ate their salads, Alexa briefed Darby on Jeannie's situation. The head of the state chapter of the Wildness Cooperative gave the lawyer a mini-course on fracking in the Keystone State.

"When they perfected the hydraulic fracturing techniques, that suddenly made the shale gas in the Marcellus Shale viable. That kicked off a new wave of these companies coming in and buying up leases from farmers and others. Things really got crazy when the state decided against taxing gas production. Most of the states with fracking levy a tax to offset the impact on infrastructure like roads and bridges. We're also finding that the environmental impact may be much larger and much longer lasting than they anticipated. You've probably heard about the almost daily earthquakes in Oklahoma. They've traced them to the injection of fracking wastewater into ground shale. The impacts vary here in Pennsylvania, but there are certain themes that run across counties and locations—water contamination, dying animals. Hell, in Dimock, families could even set the water in their taps on fire because of the high methane levels.

"Most people, like your client, are tempted by the money—which often turns out to be well below what's promised. And very few of them anticipate the havoc it will create on their land, their water, and their health. It's a real shame."

"So Pennsylvania still doesn't tax any of it?" Alexa frowned.

"There's no tax on gas production. A few years back, they finally passed a law that levies an impact fee on every well drilled. They've collected almost a billion dollars from those fees, which mostly go to the municipalities with the biggest infrastructure impacts from fracking. The rest goes to the State. Plus, the State gets money from the leases on state land."

"You mean state parks?"

"Yep. And state forests and game lands. Bambi and the elk and bear have to coexist with drilling platforms and toxic chemicals. Actually, the State has leased out oil and gas rights on state lands for decades. When they opened up bidding on Marcellus Shale leases on state lands, the State did get a lot of new money for improvements in state parks and state forests. But you have to consider the cost-benefit ratio. I don't think drilling and ruining our most pristine public lands is worth any amount of short term money."

"I read something about the new governor putting a ban on drilling in public lands."

"He did issue an executive order. The governor's order leaves in place all the wells that existed before that order. There's a move afoot in the Senate to pass a bill that reinstates shale gas drilling in state parks. If the Senate passes Senate Bill 5100, the House will follow in a heartbeat." Darby sighed. "I hear they might have enough votes to override the governor's veto—especially with Martinelli gone."

At Martinelli's name, Alexa sat bolt upright. "What does he have to do with it? Martinelli's the senator who committed suicide, right?"

"Yeah. As the chair of Environmental Resources and Energy, Martinelli always focused on energy issues. For years, he's been a fracking industry fanboy. A couple of weeks ago, one of his aides told me Martinelli had reversed his position—that he planned to oppose the state parks bill. With his track record, that sudden change of heart sounded pretty farfetched. But, if true, he could have kept the bill locked up in committee forever."

"What about Senator Gabler, the new chair?" Alexa asked.

"When it comes to fracking, he's an unknown quantity. He's shown a tendency to vote in line with his party; and now he's gotten this plum position. My bet is he'll move the fracking bill." Darby curled her lip in a half smile. "Here's hoping I'm wrong."

When the server cleared their empty plates, Alexa reached into her purse for a credit card. "Darby, you've been extremely helpful. I've learned a huge amount about fracking. But I'm looking for a next step to help my client. Do you know of any existing class action suits out there we could explore?"

Darby took a moment to respond. "I would have to ask Aldo Hauck, our expert on all things fracking. He's much closer to the on-the-ground stuff than I am. There might be a citizen's group suit out in Tioga County. I'm not sure it's against Monongas. Let me get back to you."

As the women exited the restaurant, Alexa handed Darby a business card. "Thanks for your time. You can contact me here if you learn about any lawsuits."

On the drive back to the office, Alexa pondered her conversation with Darby. She'd hoped to hear about an existing class action lawsuit Jeannie and Tom could join. Maybe Darby's staff person would come through. But her mind kept wandering to this issue of fracking in the state parks. She couldn't imagine why Silas Gabler would care much about fracking. He represented Franklin County, to the west of her cabin. Not part of the Marcellus Shale boom. Why had he and Keisha been so willing to move onto this new committee when this controversial bill had the potential to ignite a political firestorm?

CHAPTER EIGHT

"I'M SO OUT OF THE LOOP. I haven't talked to any of you this week. I created this huge photo mural for our living room wall. Jim and I have been working on that for days. Move the furniture. Prepare the wall. Move the furniture back. Find out it looks like shit because it blocks the new mural. Rearrange furniture." Melissa's halo of auburn curls shook as she acted out the saga with her hands. An accomplished photographer, Melissa owned a gallery in town.

Haley took a sip of Fiji spring water with lemon. "Oh, I miss the chai," the striking brunette breathed, watching Alexa take a sip of the creamy tea. "I don't know if smelling the aroma makes it better or worse."

"Look, little mama. You've made it this far. Just about three more months to go, right?" Alexa looked at Haley's baby bump. Despite her pregnancy, Haley still managed to look stylish in her Lululemon yoga outfit. She worked in public relations at the local Chamber of Commerce and dressed like a Talbot's catalog model. "Look at you. Melissa, you should do a photo shoot of Haley and call it the Perfect Pregnancy."

"You two can make fun of Haley, but I am in awe. Pregnant, she's nailing all these difficult poses, and I'm still struggling with Tree," Tyrell Jenkins interjected. He had enrolled in their Tuesday night yoga class a few months back and often joined the three childhood friends for their after-class get-together at the Om Café.

"You kept your balance on Tree Pose just fine." Alexa blushed at her unthinking comment. She found Tyrell's presence in yoga distracting at times. The tall, lithe social worker was one of the most physically beautiful men she'd ever seen. With his burnt umber complexion and short, spiraled dreadlocks, he was always surrounded by a group of admiring women. Alexa had long ago decided she wouldn't join that group. But, she cheated sometimes by admiring him during yoga.

Tyrell either didn't pick up on Alexa's admission that she'd been watching him in class or chose to ignore it. "Nice try. My Tree Pose can't hold a candle to your form. I'm just glad you take private lessons with Isabella for all those out-there poses you do."

Melissa laughed. "I'm with you. Most of the class would be up the creek without a paddle if Isabella told us to do Wheel Pose or Scorpion." She looked at Alexa. "We'll leave all the advanced stuff to you."

"Enough banter." Alexa commanded. "I have something serious to discuss about the Human Trafficking Commission." She launched into an update. When she informed the group the commission would end in a month, she could see Tyrell and Melissa frowning. Tyrell worked for an advocacy group: Resolve to Stop Illegal Sex Trafficking, aka RESIST. Melissa volunteered with the organization. Both had pushed Alexa hard to get involved with the commission.

Tyrell fumed. "Why? Why would they stop something so important midstream?"

"It's complicated, but it boils down to a change in committee assignments for a couple of senators. The commission got caught in the middle."

Melissa looked disgusted. "I should have known. Politics trumps compassion and people in need."

"I'm not going to defend any of it. But I couldn't change it if I wanted to." Alexa shrugged. "If it helps, there are extenuating circumstances. This all stems from a senator's death last week."

"Everybody was talking about that at work." Haley shifted in her seat. "Didn't he commit suicide in the Capitol or something? Gruesome."

"He did. Senator Martinelli jumped from one of the upper floors in the Capitol rotunda. He landed right at my feet." Alexa closed her eyes at the memory.

"What?" Haley yelped. Alexa looked up.

"No way." Tyrell looked astonished.

But Melissa sounded like a disappointed schoolteacher. "My God, Alexa. What have you gotten yourself into now?"

"Nothing. Like Haley said, it was suicide. I just happened to be in the wrong place at the wrong time. Believe me, it wasn't pretty."

Haley turned pale and took a quick sip of water. I don't feel very well all of a sudden. I'm going home."

Tyrell stood, "Why don't I drive you? I can walk home from your place. It's only a few blocks."

After Tyrell and Haley rushed out the door, Alexa looked at Melissa. "Let's get out of here. I appreciate Jim dropping you off so you could drive one of my cars home. Do you want to drive the Land Rover or the Mini?"

Following the taillights of the Mini over the narrow country roads to her cabin, Alexa considered Melissa's reaction. She couldn't deny she had a tendency to land in the midst of trouble. And, sometimes, her inability to let things go made it worse. "No," Alexa said aloud, "it's just my healthy curiosity." But, this time, Melissa was wrong. Senator Martinelli's death had nothing to do with Alexa Williams.

Melinda bustled into Alexa's office mid-morning. "We've got schedule problems. The Criminal Investigation Department just called." She glanced at the note in her hand. "A Detective Marshall. He wants you to come to Harrisburg tomorrow for another interview at one o'clock."

Alexa glanced at her packed calendar. "Can't he come here?"

"That was my first question. Says he needs you to walk him through the scene, like in those cop shows."

"Yeah, but that's usually when there's some sort of foul play. This guy committed suicide." Alexa turned back to her schedule and sighed. "At least I don't have any court appearances. Just clear the afternoon. Maybe Vanessa can take my appointment with the Sollenbergers. And we'll have to reschedule the discussion with Jason Durbin. Letting him and his client stew for a couple extra days will give them time to reconsider their claim against the Buchanan estate."

"Don't they know you can't pick a bald chicken?"

Alexa cracked up. "Who would have guessed the Pennsylvania Dutch would have a saying that describes estate law so well? You're right. There's not a whole lot in the Buchanan estate to fight over."

"I'll call that detective about tomorrow." As Melinda turned to leave, the phone rang. She reached over Alexa's desk to pick it up. "Alexa Williams' office. May I help you? Just a moment, I'll see if she's available." Melinda cupped her hand over the receiver and whispered, "Darby Kaplan?"

"I'll take it."

Melinda handed over the phone and left the office, closing the door behind her.

"Hello, Darby." Alexa switched the phone into speaker mode.

"Hi. I haven't been able to track down Aldo Hauck about that lawsuit yet. He's on vacation this week. But I just remembered something this morning. I can't imagine why it didn't hit me yesterday. Your client lives in Tioga County, right?"

"Right." Alexa responded.

"Well, you have to talk to Walt Jordan." The name meant nothing to Alexa, but before she could ask, Darby raced on. "Representative Walt Jordan is leading the charge in the State legislature against fracking. I told you about this new effort to open up drilling in state parks. He's knee-deep in the fight against that bill. Plus, Walt represents Tioga County. So he would know everything that's happening up there." Darby took a breath. "Are you going to be in Harrisburg tomorrow?"

"I have some business in the Capitol tomorrow afternoon."

"I already talked to Walt's assistant, Natalie. She owes me one, so she said she could squeeze you in the schedule tomorrow afternoon at two o'clock?"

"That will work. Thanks, Darby."

"No problem. I'll be in touch."

On the road to Harrisburg the next afternoon, Alexa speculated about why the detective wanted a second interview. And a walk-through. What was that about? Then she switched to the meeting with this legislator. Why had she agreed so quickly to Darby's suggestion? The commission experience had soured Alexa on legislators and the political games they played. She'd found that a good portion of the men and women who represented Pennsylvania's citizenry had only the most rudimentary understanding of human trafficking—and a deep certainty that "it doesn't happen here." To be fair, she'd also encountered flashes of brilliance, in both the rank-and-file and the leadership. But, on something as complicated as hydraulic fracturing? She wasn't holding her breath for this meeting with Walt Jordan.

"Ms. Williams. I understand you're representing one of my constituents in a dispute with Monongas Energy?" Representative Jordan met Alexa at the door of his office with his hand extended.

She shook the proffered hand. "Temporarily. I'm hoping to connect my client with an existing class action lawsuit or another firm that has expertise in damages from natural gas drilling."

"Let's sit." Jordan pointed to a couch and chair in the corner of the room. His committee position must have snagged the legislator this beautiful old office in the main Capitol. The walls were paneled in dark wood, and the sitting area faced a huge fireplace.

But Alexa's impression of the room took a back seat to her reaction to the representative. This man was gorgeous. Tall with broad shoulders, his close-cropped black hair showed a hint of gray at the temples. He wore his charcoal suit with an easy, athletic assurance. Alexa hadn't expected him to be so young. Around forty, she guessed.

She forced her attention to the task at hand. "Thanks for agreeing to meet. Darby Kaplan suggested I speak to you about my client and friend, Jeannie Demeter's, issues. I have her permission to describe her family's experience with Monongas. As I mentioned, I'm looking to find her appropriate representation for potential legal action. With all due respect, I'm not sure there's a political angle here."

Jordan gave a knowing laugh. "Ms. Williams."

"Alexa's fine."

"Alexa, there's always a political angle. And that's especially true with anything that creates as much money as fracking. Would it surprise you to hear that in last year's fiscal code bill, the other side of the aisle tried to sneak in a clause to exempt drillers from damage, personal injury, and environmental lawsuits?"

"Seriously? I know there's a move to expand fracking into state lands. But an exemption from legal action—that's reprehensible." Alexa's shock brought her upright on the couch.

"Are you speaking as a lawyer or a citizen?"

Alexa wasn't sure how to interpret his question. "Both. This sounds like someone is in the industry's pocket."

"Well, you'll be glad to know the provision got dropped when it came to the floor. But I wouldn't be surprised to see it surface again in the budget we're working on now."

"Clearly, a provision like that would disadvantage my client and a lot of others who have been hurt by the fracking industry. I understand you don't support fracking?"

"Hardly." Jordan rose and walked to his desk. "For my constituents, fracking has been," he paused. "Let's call it a mixed blessing. A few have made a tidy sum from leasing their land to Monongas. In Tioga County, the major fracking company is Monongas. They got in first and locked up so many leases that the other companies passed us by. But many of my constituents have battled environmental degradation, water contamination, loss of livestock, or developed health issues. Or all of the above." He returned to his chair carrying a large poster board.

Alexa identified the display. "A map of Tioga County?"

"Yes. The black dots are all sites of wells drilled by Monongas. Most of them are still working. Some are capped. The ones with red squares are the locations where there's been a reported issue."

Alarmed by the amount of red, Alexa took in the profusion of dots that covered a large percentage of the map. She tried to figure out which dot marked Jeannie and Tom's farm, but Alexa didn't know the county geography.

The representative put down the chart. "So you're correct. I don't support the fracking industry. In fact, my focus has been on limiting any further expansion in the state—especially this recent attempt to revive drilling in state parks."

Glancing at her watch, Alexa saw she was running out of time. She'd been allotted a half an hour. "Do you know if there are any legal actions against fracking in your county? My client's main concern is her child. The girl has developed an aggressive brain cancer. The doctor believes it could have been caused by some of the chemicals used in fracking. The family can't handle the cost of co-pays, deductibles, and other supplies. They're driving back and forth to the children's hospital in Philadelphia all the time. And Jeannie had to quit work to care for her daughter. Monongas should be held financially accountable."

"I'm sorry to hear about the child's illness. I wasn't aware of the Demeters' situation." The representative scowled. "Two suggestions. There's a group called Friends of Pine Creek with a major environmental action suit in the works against Monongas. There's a public heath component to that suit. I know they're looking for any negative health impact from fracking in the county. Second idea. One of the big national personal injury law firms represents a few of the families who're dealing with major medical conditions they attribute to fracking. I'll have my assistant track down the name for you."

"I appreciate the help." Alexa handed the legislator her business card. "Here's my contact information." She stood, and Jordan walked her to the door.

He stopped at the threshold. "I've heard about you and some of the bad actors you've exposed. You're chairing this Commission on Human Trafficking. I'm glad you've developed an interest in the fracking problem. Someone with your passion, Ms. Williams, can only help the cause." Jordan opened the door and placed a light hand on Alexa's shoulder to guide her over the doorsill.

"Thanks again," Alexa murmured as she left. The warmth of his hand burned into her shoulder down all three flights of stairs to the main floor.

Detective Marshall stood in the rotunda amid the typical weekday throng of legislators, lobbyists, constituents, and tour groups. His expression gave no indication of how long he'd been waiting. "Thanks for coming, Ms. Williams. I know it's a drive from Carlisle."

"Happy to help. But I'm not sure I have anything new for you. I told you everything I remembered last Tuesday night." Alexa slipped off her coat and slung it over the crook of her arm.

"Let's walk over there to the bench." Marshall led Alexa across the rotunda to the marble bench on the left. "You and Ms. Washington were sitting here, correct?"

"Yes." Alexa felt queasy, sitting on this bench again.

"Which side were you on?"

"The right."

"Let's sit." Marshall gestured to the bench. When they were seated, he turned to Alexa. "Please take me through everything that happened that night again. Who did you see? What did you hear? What happened when Senator Martinelli fell?"

"There was no one around when I got here." Alexa closed her eyes and tried to tune out the noisy throng and the sick feeling in her stomach. She recalled her brief fantasy about the figure of Law floating out of her painting. Shades of Harry Potter. Alexa stifled an inappropriate laugh, remembering they were here to discuss a man's death. She continued in a sober tone. "I sat here alone for a few minutes, and then Keisha Washington arrived."

"From where?"

"She walked down the first floor hall on the Senate side and came directly here." Alexa gestured to the bench. She continued to recount the evening's events with Marshall interrupting every few sentences with a question.

"How many men did you hear arguing above you? Can you describe their voices?" The detective pressed hard when Alexa described the altercation she and Keisha had overheard.

"Three for sure. There could have been a fourth. At the beginning, the voices talked over each other. I got the impression that at least two men were upset with the third guy. He refused to do something the others wanted. They accused him of backing out. I heard three distinct voices. Toward the end, I caught a muffled voice. It could have been one of those three, or it could have been another person."

"A woman?"

"The voices all sounded male to me."

"Did you notice anything distinct about the voices?

Alexa considered the question for a moment. "Maybe. The older guy, the one people were upset with, his voice sounded a little raspy."

"Why do you say he was older?"

"I said that without really thinking. But his voice sounded sort of frail, like my grandfather's before he died."

"Anything else?" Marshall moved on.

"Another guy sounded like an arrogant jerk, talking about paying the piper. But the most distinct thing about his voice was the drawl. He sounded like someone born in the South, who's lived in the North for years. Or the opposite. I have a law school friend from Nebraska. Now that she's lived in Georgia awhile, she speaks with just a hint of a southern accent."

"Would you recognize those two voices again?"

"Maybe." Alexa had cooperated with the police, but she was tiring of this little exercise. She hated reliving that awful night. Why was he questioning her again? "Detective, can I ask why this quarrel is so important? Keisha and I assumed they were fighting about the pension bill. That's what the Senate was debating at the time. Do you think they could have seen Senator Martinelli?"

Marshall ignored her question and pulled his phone from a jacket pocket. He looked around, and Alexa followed his eyes as they swept the rotunda. The crowd had cleared, and they were alone except for two twenty-somethings wearing lobbyist tags, standing on the far side of the stairs. "Listen to this." The cop held the phone near to Alexa's ear and hit a button.

She was surprised to hear some guy giving a political speech. "Pennsylvania faces a bright future thanks to the natural gas industry. Hydraulic fracturing has brought us jobs, increased rural income, and opened up a rich energy source in the Commonwealth. Once again, the Keystone State is proud to reaffirm our significance to the nation. Pennsylvania is the linchpin to the restoration of America's energy independence." Alexa rolled her eyes at the rhetoric but had no doubt as she listened to the raspy voice.

"That's him. That's the older man who had everyone pissed off," Alexa cried. "Who is it?"

Marshall hesitated, and then responded. "Senator Carmine Martinelli."

Alexa raised her eyebrows as she put two and two together. "Who decided to leap over the railing a few minutes after the argument?"

With a serious expression, the policeman put the phone back in his pocket. "We have reason to believe Senator Martinelli's death may not have been a suicide."

CHAPTER NINE

SHOCKED THAT SHE might have witnessed a murder, not a suicide, Alexa huddled on the bench for a few moments after the detective left. She tried to come to grips with this disturbing revelation. Maybe she was a death magnet after all. Finally, searching for a distraction, she decided to check on the progress of the trafficking paper. She hadn't heard from Keisha since the commission meeting.

"Hello, Alexa. Keisha's in a meeting right now, but Lauren's here." Senator Gabler's perky receptionist projected faux cheer.

Lauren met Alexa in the same small conference room they'd used before. The intern tiptoed to the kitchen door and made sure it was latched before she joined Alexa at the conference table.

"Did you ever report that jerk?" Alexa waved toward the door.

"El Jerko Gigundo," Lauren joked. "No. I didn't want to get our office into some big brouhaha with him. Even though the guy gives me the evil eye, like, every time I pass him in the hall, Senator Gabler needs him for a key legislative initiative. It's no big deal. Remember, I'll only be here until the semester ends."

"You're a junior, right?"

"Yes. Next fall I'm back to campus full time. This internship lasts just one semester."

Alexa smiled. "And what has this experience taught you? Are you planning to go into government or politics when you graduate?"

Lauren fiddled with the row of earrings dotting her right ear. "I'm not sure. Maybe I'll go to work for Emily's List or something like that. Or maybe I'll go to grad school and get my master's first. I've got, like, months to figure it out."

"If you ever need a reference, let me know." Alexa grinned. "And if you decide to file a complaint against Mr. Jerko Gigundo, I'm your witness."

"I'm guessing you're here about the report," Lauren sidestepped. "Keisha and I have been working on it. We've got a rough first draft, but it needs some more work before you see it." She looked at the calendar on the wall. "Today's Wednesday. We should be able to get you something by Monday at the latest."

"OK. I'd like to get a first official draft out to the larger group by next Friday. Then, incorporate their comments into a final report."

"Yeah. Keisha's already gotten a few calls from commission members hot to see it."

Alexa stood up. "Can you draft an email with a timetable? I can send it out so everyone knows what to expect."

"Sure. No problemo." The irrepressible intern bounced out of the room, Alexa trailing in her wake.

Alexa never considered going back to the office. Her brain was fried, and she needed fresh air. When she reached the cabin, Alexa changed into jeans and a warm jacket and ran outside. "Scout, let's go for a hike," she called. "Thanks to daylight savings time, we have enough light to walk to Weaver's Pond."

The mastiff charged ahead of Alexa on the trail, then raced back. "Watch it there, buddy," she cautioned as the dog tripped over a log next to the trail. By the time they reached the pond, Scout's tongue was lolling. He collapsed at Alexa's feet when she sat on her favorite log. Together, they contemplated the silent pond, still ringed with a fringe of ice.

Alexa's mind whirled. The police believed Senator Martinelli had been murdered. And, clearly, they suspected one or all of the men who'd been quarreling. Marshall had told Alexa to keep the news quiet, but she wondered if Keisha knew about this new twist in the investigation. Then, her thoughts shifted to Walt Jordan. She had to admit this particular legislator seemed to stand out from the crowd. Perhaps he was a master of charm and deception, but his passion against fracking came across as sincere. There was no doubt about his good looks. And that brief moment of courtesy when his hand rested on her back. Memorable. Alexa shook her head in dismay.

So now I'm letting a pretty face sway me?

She jumped to her feet, rubbing her cold bottom to restore circulation.

"Let's go home, buddy. It's too cold to sit out here." On the walk back, Scout stayed by Alexa's side. Still lost in thought, she patted the mastiff's head every time he bumped against her hand.

Twilight came quickly on the mountain. The light had faded by the time Alexa and Scout arrived at the cabin. "I'm going to the hot tub before dinner," Alexa announced to the dog. She grabbed a beach towel from a hook in the laundry room and stripped out of her clothes. "Come on." Alexa padded across the deck to the new hot tub that sat on the far side of the cabin. Scout settled in on a cushion right next to the steps leading into the tub.

Alexa leaned back in the steaming water and sighed in delight. When she purchased the cabin from her parents this past winter, she had decided to install this hot tub. A contractor had extended the deck across the front of the entire cabin and wrapped it around the bedroom wing of the cabin. The hot tub sat on the elevated deck, screened by the house on one side and open to the forest on the other three. Since the cabin sat in the midst of acres of uninhabited forest, Alexa had few concerns about privacy. She loved to relax and listen to the silence of the forest. Alexa smiled at the sound of geese above her in the darkening sky. The flock was flying high and heading north, a sure sign of spring. Ten more minutes of soaking melted away Alexa's stress. Climbing out of the water, Alexa wrapped a towel around her naked torso and floated into the house.

When the driveway alert rang a half hour later, Scout dashed to the door, tail thumping against a chair. He bounced with delight when John walked through the front door into the open dining room-kitchen.

"Hey. You made good time." Alexa turned back to check the chicken in the oven. "Dinner will be ready in maybe ten minutes."

John dumped his jacket on a chair and grabbed a beer from the fridge. "I had paperwork at the end of my shift, so I came straight from the Carlisle station. Can I help?"

"Nope. Got it under control. What do you want on your salad?" Alexa picked up plates and silverware and headed toward the table

"Ranch." John slowed her progress with a quick kiss. "I'm going upstairs to change."

"What's this flavor?" John pointed to the chicken breast.

"Just rosemary and a dash of olive oil." Alexa plucked a sprig of rosemary from her plate and waved it.

"It's good. How'd your interview go? You talked to Marshall again, right?" John asked between bites of food.

Alexa put down her fork. "It blew me away. He made me go through everything again. This time, he focused on those guys we heard arguing. Then, he had me listen to a short recording. I recognized the voice as one of the men in that quarrel. Turns out it was Senator Martinelli, the dead guy."

"I heard they've moved past suicide to a new theory." John shot her a look as he reached for his beer.

"That's what blew me away. Detective Marshall thinks it was murder. He didn't give me details, of course. I'm supposed to keep it to myself. But, I guess that doesn't apply to you, Trooper Taylor—you already have an inside source." Alexa shook her head.

"That suicide note sounded bogus from the start. The stilted wording. It was on his computer, not handwritten. Odd, especially for a man his age. Terry says they finally figured out that it wasn't a suicide note at all. Those lines about coming to terms with his life and not being able to go on any longer—they were part of a work-related letter that he'd sent earlier that day. It had nothing to do with death. The senator must have had it up on his computer screen, and the killer took advantage of those few sentences. Probably erased the rest of the letter. I doubt he realized that it had already been printed and mailed.

"And the autopsy suggested that the senator may have been knocked unconscious before he was thrown over the rail. Of course, the damage to his head was extensive so the findings weren't conclusive."

Alexa shook her head. "That's right. He didn't cry out as he fell. I don't really know how to process this. Knowing it's murder doesn't change what Keisha and I saw. But it's horrible that someone would throw that man off a balcony. What a way to die." She banged her fork on the plate. "I said right from the beginning it seemed impossible for that old, overweight man to get over the railing."

John had moved into full detective mode. "It's an equally difficult challenge for one person—or even two—to toss a grown man, especially an overweight one, over a three foot railing with enough force to clear the mezzanine. And you never heard a scream or a scuffle?"

"No. The argument stopped. It got quiet. I thought the group had gone back to the Senate floor or something. But then the senator came flying through the air."

"I can see why they're focusing on the guys who were arguing with the victim. It's possible he stayed out there alone and someone else threw him off the balcony. But my money's on one or more of the men involved in the altercation.

"How disappointing." Alexa switched off the television with the remote. "Brian Stewart told me it was a great movie. That I'd love it."

John wrinkled his nose. "Depressing. Not my idea of a happy ending."

"Why are all the recent movies so dark? Seems like they're about zombies, or like this one, set in some bleak dystopian future. It feels like everyone's practicing for the end of the world." Alexa used her foot to scratch Scout, who had stirred at the sound of their voices.

"I love zombie movies." With a ghastly moan, John scrunched his face, pretending to be a zombie.

"Of course you do. You're always talking about that TV series you watch." Alexa slipped from John's zombie grip and stood. "Scout. Time to go out."

When she returned to the living room, John's mood had changed. He kissed Alexa's forehead. "I'll keep you safe from zombies and other dark creatures, sugarcakes." He looked into her eyes. "I'm sorry I made such a big deal about coming home with me at Easter. I know you're close to your family and want to spend the day with them. And I don't see my parents often enough. So I'll just head up there on my own."

Alexa touched John's cheek. "It's no big deal. You just caught me off-guard."

"That's not completely true." His voice remained mild.

"You're right. Sometimes I feel like you're pushing me toward a commitment I'm not ready to make. Visiting your parents. Talking about living together." Alexa sighed. "I've been burned too many times in the past few years. I don't want to rush into anything."

"I know. I know." John grabbed her hands. "Sometimes I just get carried away. Like I did that first time I kissed you."

"The birch beer made you all wild and crazy." Alexa giggled.

"But you like me?" John kissed her cheek.

"Enough." Alexa smiled.

"And you like to spend time with me?" He kissed her other cheek.

"Enough." Alexa's smile broadened.

"And the sex is good?" He kissed her mouth.

"Good enough." Alexa melted into the kiss, then took John's hand and led him upstairs to her bedroom.

Standing beside the bed, John folded Alexa in his arms and pressed his lips into hers. Alexa's body tingled with anticipation as he peeled the turtleneck over her head. He ran his fingers through her messy hair and then gently cupped her head back until her neck lay open to his kisses.

When Alexa unfastened her bra, John trailed a series of kisses down her chest. He rested from his journey when his lips found her erect nipple. A jolt of pleasure ran through Alexa's body as he transferred his attention to her other nipple.

With a sudden urgency, John stepped back. He unbuttoned his shirt and slipped off his jeans and boxers in a single swift motion. Alexa took the opportunity to shed the rest of her clothes before John pushed her back onto the bed. She caught a brief glimpse of his erect manhood before it plunged between her welcoming legs. Soon, Alexa was lost in a sea of warmth and sensation.

Afterward, John leaned over to trace a finger across Alexa's lips. "We are good together."

She snuggled closer, wrapping her body around his nakedness and breathed, "Good enough."

He laughed. "I'm going to stay here tonight, OK?"

"Sure. I need to get to work early tomorrow. Get me up when your alarm rings." Drowsy, Alexa rolled over and pulled up the blanket, then bolted upright. "Scout. He's still outside," she exclaimed. Sliding out of bed, she threw on her robe and ran downstairs.

On the stairs, she slowed to consider her playful words to John. Was their relationship truly good enough? She couldn't help but compare John to Reese Michaels, who had left her for a wildlife research job in Kenya. Although she and Reese had decided to call it quits, he still lingered in her heart. She could never love John the way she had loved Reese.

When Alexa and Scout returned, John was still awake. He turned as she climbed back under the covers and put a hand on her arm. "On this Martinelli case. You need to be very careful until the cops catch his killer. Suicide's one thing, but now we know you witnessed a murder."

CHAPTER TEN

March 29 and March 30, 1979

. . . there is no cause for alarm, nor any reason to disrupt
your daily routine, nor any reason to feel that public health
has been affected by the events on Three Mile Island.
                              —Governor Richard Thornburgh

*Will slammed the switch on the Big Ben alarm clock and
glanced at Randi. Fast asleep, his wife clutched a pillow to her
chest. His heart melted; this woman, who looked like an angel,
would soon be the mother of his child. Will slid out of bed, trying
not to wake her, and padded to the bathroom. When he returned to
the bedroom, Randi opened her eyes.*

*"Good morning, sweetheart." Will walked over and perched on
the bed beside her. "How did you sleep?"*

*"Lousy." Randi groaned and patted her stomach. "This little one
was restless. Her kicks kept waking me up. Then I would waddle
to the bathroom. I don't think I fell asleep until dawn."*

*"Go back to sleep for a few hours. I'll make you breakfast when
you get up." Will kissed her forehead.*

"Yuck. Your hair is wet."

"I just took a shower."

*"You can't stay home to cook me breakfast. Don't you have to
work?" Randi voiced a feeble protest.*

*"I have plenty of sick leave. I'll just call in and tell them I have a
headache or something," Will demurred.*

*"You'd do that for me? You never call in sick, even when you
really don't feel good."*

"Go to sleep." Will smiled. "I'll be downstairs."

Will made coffee and toast then called in to work. Harold, his supervisor, always arrived earlier than the other staff.

"Take some aspirin and rest," Harold directed.

"I will. I'll probably be in the office later." Will felt guilty lying to his boss.

"Only if you're feeling better. Hell, I thought you were going to tell me you left town. This TMI thing has a lot of people scared and fleeing the city. In the past fifteen minutes, I've had four different people call to say they're taking their families out of the area."

Will's throat turned dry. "Did something new happen?"

"No. They're still saying everything is under control out there. But, a lot of people who live near TMI decided not to take any chances. Can't say I blame them. If I looked out my kitchen window at those cooling towers, I might visit my grandma in Scranton for a weekend too." Harold guffawed into the phone.

"I guess so." Will still didn't see why everyone was overreacting to this TMI problem. The plant people said everything was fine. "I should see you later this morning. Thanks." Will untangled the cord and hung the avocado green receiver back on the wall.

He peered out the window. Nothing but fog. At loose ends, he wandered into the living room and switched on the television to Good Morning America with the volume turned low. Lounging on the tattered plaid couch, he watched two men wrestling in a commercial for Irish Spring soap. It felt weird to be home on a weekday morning.

Will sat forward when the show returned with a segment on Three Mile Island. The host introduced Daniel Ford from the Union of Concerned Scientists and Walter Creitz, the President of Met-Ed, the company that owned the Three Mile Island nuclear facility. The men seemed like old adversaries who had argued nuclear power safety many times. The scientist complained about five nuclear power plants that had been shut down for safety problems. He criticized the government's oversight of nuclear power and accused regulators of promoting industry interests over reactor safety. Creitz argued that seventy-two reactors in operation without any injury to the public testified to the safety of nuclear power.

Will listened to the debate, but his main interest was the TMI situation. He nodded with appreciation when Creitz said the plant soon "would be closed down without injury to anyone."

He was still watching the TV show when Randi came downstairs, looking rested. "Don't you look beautiful, little mama?" Will swept her into his arms. "What about eggs and toast for breakfast? Do we have bacon?"

"No bacon." Randi shook her head. "But, I'm dying for a big glass of milk. I'll get that while you make the eggs."

"I already had toast, but I could go for some eggs. They're not expecting me at work until late this morning." Will moved into action in the kitchen.

Over the meal, Will said, "I hope that fretting about this TMI thing wasn't what kept you awake last night. They were just talking about it on TV, and the president of Met-Ed said everything's fine. One of these anti-nuke scientists tried to make a big deal out of what's going on, but he had no proof there's a problem at TMI."

"I did worry about TMI some when I couldn't sleep. But it was more the little one kicking up a storm." Randi smiled and nibbled at a piece of toast. "I'm glad to hear there's nothing to worry about. But I'm sure Mom's going to call again today and try to get us to leave Harrisburg."

"Just tell her everything's fine here. I'm sure they'll have more on the news later if you want to listen to the radio."

When he arrived at work, Will stopped in Harold's tiny office. "Hi. I just wanted you to know I'm here."

"How's the headache?"

"Gone. I feel fine." Will looked over his shoulder toward the half-empty office. "Where is everyone?"

Harold frowned. "Even more people called in and said they were leaving town, at least through the weekend. Governor Thornburgh held a press conference a little while ago. He said there's no cause for alarm; no reason to disrupt your daily routine." The supervisor rapped on the desk as if remembering something. "That's right. This part is important to you. He said public heath hasn't been affected by TMI, and that part also applied to pregnant women. Your wife's expecting soon, isn't she?"

Will smiled. "In a few weeks. She'll be glad to hear that the governor says everything's fine."

Will cursed the fog on his way to work the next morning. The windshield wipers on the Thing were no match for the heavy moisture as he drove along the Susquehanna River. On the walk across the Market Street Bridge from the parking lot, Will's dark hair got so wet that little rivulets of water streamed down his face. He coughed as he breathed in the damp air, tinged with the dank smell of the river below.

"Armstrong," a voice shouted behind him.

Will slowed and turned. "Hey, Brad. I bet you're glad they don't have you out checking radiation today."

"Yes. This weather's miserable. But my boss told me I could be out in the field everyday until this TMI thing is totally put to bed. The Nuclear Regulatory Commission is in charge of the situation with the plant, but the governor wants us to monitor the environment."

"Things are under control, right? That's what both Met-Ed and the governor said yesterday." Will glanced down through the metal grid of the bridge at the river flowing below. For a second, he wobbled, thrown off balance by the rush of the dark water.

Brad leaned closer to Will and spoke in hushed tones. "That's what they're saying. But, back in Nam, we would have called this a real clusterfuck. Met-Ed isn't giving us the full story on the status of the reactor. Prying information out of them is like pulling teeth. The NRC is in charge, but there are some communication gaps between the folks here in the field and the people in Washington. And, on the State side, we're having a hell of a time trying to sift through everything to figure out what's really going on."

"Seriously? Are you saying there's still a problem at the plant?" Will asked in alarm.

"Not necessarily. As of yesterday, things seemed to be under control. But we're not sure we've got all the facts. I'll let you know if I hear anything more."

"Thanks, man. I appreciate it," Will mumbled as Brad dashed through the front doors. Shaken by Brad's words, Will teetered on the edge of panic when he walked into the office and looked at all the unoccupied desks. Andy had accused him of being too trusting of The Man. What if that were true? What if officials were covering up some real problem at TMI?

Will had shrugged off any disquiet and was hard at work at eleven fifteen when the frantic blare of sirens pierced the air. After a moment of disbelief, the few people in the office jumped up in unison and ran to the windows.

"What's going on? Aren't those the air raid sirens?" Harold shouted as he burst from his office.

Out on the street below, people were scattering like ants from a broken mound. Some were running into buildings. Others fled down the sidewalk.

One of the young secretaries wailed, "TMI blew up. Oh my God. We're all going to die." She sank into a chair, sobbing.

"Calm down, everyone. We don't know what's going on. It could be nothing." Harold's shaking voice belied his attempt at comfort.

Will followed Harold back into his office. The supervisor turned on a transistor radio and spun the dial through several channels. All were still playing music.

"Is there someone you can call?" Will prompted.

Just as Harold picked up the phone, the music stopped and a DJ announced, "I have a message for the public. Please stay calm. We understand the recent sirens were activated by mistake. The problem at TMI is still under control. However, a small amount of radiation was released into the atmosphere earlier today. As a precaution, Governor Thornburgh is advising everyone within a ten mile radius of TMI to stay indoors."

Will looked up at the sound of a huge gasp. The entire staff had crowded into the doorway of Harold's office.

Harold looked at the group and tugged at his tie. "Wow. I don't know exactly what to say. We are indoors, of course. And this building is at least twelve or thirteen miles away from TMI. But I'm not going to tell you what to do. If you don't feel safe here, go home. If you need to see to your family, I'm not going to stop you."

Will and the others trailed back out into the open office. A few people grabbed their belongings from their desks and ran out the door. Others stood together talking. Will considered his situation. He wasn't worried about Randi's safety. Their farmhouse sat another ten miles north of the city, too far away for Randi to have heard the sirens. Still, he decided to drive home. She had been so jumpy about this TMI thing. And he was starting to feel pretty uneasy too. He'd feel better if he and Randi were together.

He had just tidied his desk and closed his pencil drawer when Brad burst into the office, panting. His friend from Radiation Management made a beeline to Will's desk. "I'm heading out of here right now, but with your pregnant wife, I wanted you to know."

"Know what?" Will's heart sank at the wild look on Brad's face.

"I just had a call from a guy I served with in Nam. He works at the NRC in Washington. He says this problem at TMI is much worse than they're saying. The plant experienced a huge spike of radiation last night, and they're worried about a hydrogen bubble." Brad gulped. "The whole thing could blow and contaminate everything in the area. Harrisburg could become a wasteland for the rest of our lives." His voice turned bleak. "If we survive it."

Will felt as if the floor had dropped away and left him clinging to a ledge. "What distance? How far will the radiation go if it blows?"

"They're saying forty-five miles. But I'm getting farther away. I'm going home to pick up my family as fast as I can. My wife's on her way to take the kids out of school. Pregnant women and small children are more vulnerable than anyone else. You should get your wife someplace safe. As far away as you can." Brad rested a shaking hand on Will's shoulder.

"Thanks, man. I'm out of here now." Will bolted to his feet, panic surging through his body as Brad sprinted from the room. He rushed into Harold's office and gave him a quick summary of Brad's news. "I'm leaving, Harold. Can you tell the others?"

Will raced to his desk and dialed home. He wanted to alert Randi and tell her to pack an overnight bag. He couldn't get a signal. The phone lines had to be overloaded because of the sirens; everyone was calling to check in with family. By the third try, Will was sweating. He got a dial tone. But the phone rang twenty times; Randi wasn't picking up.

"Shit." Will slammed the phone back on its cradle and bolted for the door. Randi must be taking a nap or visiting their next-door neighbor, Ruth.

Will fretted as he floored the car down Second Street. Traffic clogged the roads as thousands fled the city. With each mile up the road, Will found a new reason to excoriate his earlier complacency. He should have listened to Randi and her mother on Wednesday. The love of his life would bring their first child into the world in a few weeks, and he had failed to protect them.

By the time he reached home, Will's fears had escalated into full-blown panic. He peeled into the farmhouse driveway and jumped out of the car, leaving the door hanging open. Will ran into the house through the unlocked front door, calling, "Randi! Randi!"

Although the radio was playing, the kitchen stood empty. He rushed through the living room and took the stairs, two at a time, to the second floor. But she wasn't in the bedroom either. Thinking his wife must be next door, Will hurried back downstairs. He slowed when he reached the kitchen. Something about the tone of the voice on the radio caught his attention. The newscaster reported in a somber tone with the hint of a quiver. "The governor has just released a new statement regarding Three Mile Island. He is advising those who may be particularly susceptible to the effects of radiation, that is, pregnant women and preschool-age children, to leave the area within a five-mile radius of the Three Mile Island facility until further notice."

Will listened to the announcement with dismay. Their home was located well beyond the five-mile advisory, but this new announcement only confirmed what Brad had told him. Something had gone seriously wrong at TMI. Trembling, Will darted toward the door to look for Randi at Ruth's house next door. He stopped short in horror when a scrawled note on the table caught his eye.

WILL – RANDI WENT INTO LABOR. I'M DRIVING HER TO HARRISBURG HOSPITAL. WE TRIED TO CALL YOU AT THE

OFFICE BUT ALL THE LINES WERE BUSY. I'LL TRY AGAIN AFTER WE GET TO THE HOSPITAL. I'M LEAVING THIS NOTE IN CASE I CAN'T REACH YOU BY PHONE.

RUTH

CHAPTER ELEVEN

"Aren't you going to that memorial service?" Melinda looked up in surprise at Alexa's entrance.

"I am, but it's not until eleven. I wanted to get a few things done before I head for Harrisburg." Alexa sighed. "I'm getting so tired of that stretch of I-81. How do people drive it every day?"

"They have to do it for their jobs," the ever-practical Melinda countered. "Didn't you commute every day in New York?"

"Yes, but I took the subway. So no traffic to contend with. And, if I had to work late, which was most of the time, the firm had a car service to get me home. A perk for female associates."

"Well, I'm sure all these Harrisburg commuters would love to have their own car service too," Melinda sniffed. "You probably had uniformed waitresses to bring you tea at Baylor, Trego, Wilson and Gold, but today, you'll have to settle for me." Her assistant couldn't maintain the disapproving tone and broke into laughter.

"Point taken. But you know I left the firm because I couldn't stand it there. And I can get my own tea."

Melinda leapt to her feet. "No, you get settled. I'll bring you a cup of Constant Comment."

When Alexa sat down, her heart sank to see the headline on the newspaper in the center of the desk—MARTINELLI MURDERED? Even though Detective Marshall had told her the cops were now investigating the case as a murder, seeing it in print made it more real. She remembered John's warning. Yes, she and Keisha could be considered witnesses. But they had witnessed only Martinelli's death, that startling moment when he plummeted into the floor. Neither of them had seen the killer throw the senator off the balcony.

She looked up as Melinda sailed through the door with a brimming teacup. "Interesting news, especially since you're going to his memorial service today."

"Thanks. No doubt people will be buzzing. The church will be packed." Alexa took a sip of tea as Melinda bustled out the door. Then, she dialed the phone.

"Hello."

"Jeannie, this is Alexa." She put the phone on speaker mode.

"Have you found someone who can help us?" Before Alexa could answer, Jeannie spoke again in a muffled voice. "Tessa, honey, eat some Cheerios."

Alexa waited a moment before she responded. "I have two possibilities. Through the Wildness Cooperative and Representative Jordan, I found that a local group, the Friends of Pine Creek, has filed a class action suit. Much of the focus is harm to the environment— watershed and things like that. But they also have a number of named plaintiffs with medical conditions they are alleging were caused by fracking. The second possibility. One of our attorneys, Vanessa Smallwood, has located a personal injury firm that specializes in fracking-related illness. They would represent your family on a contingency basis. You'd have no costs up front, and they'd take a portion of the settlement. That lawsuit would be just about Tessa's illness."

"What do you think we should do?" Jeannie sounded like she was crying.

"That's up to you and Tom. The class action suit has some traction. Plus there's the advantage of other plaintiffs with illnesses that appeared after Monongas started drilling in Tioga County. If you go the personal injury route, the case is all about Tessa, and the attorney will have to build the case entirely on your family's experience with Monongas. I could arrange a meeting with both sets of lawyers so they can explain how it would work and how they'd each approach Tessa's claim."

"Will you go with us? To the meetings?"

"Of course."

"I'm in Philadelphia with Tessa later this week. For more testing." Jeannie sounded distracted.

"How about I try to arrange the meetings for next week then? I'll see if they can come to you—or at least to Wellsboro. I'll be back in touch with some times."

Tessa's plaintive screams of "Mommy, Mommy" all but drowned out Jeannie's reply. "I'll wait to hear from you."

As Alexa hurried down State Street, she wondered why she felt obligated to attend this memorial service for a man she'd never met. Watching Carmine Martinelli bleed to death on the Capitol floor didn't exactly qualify as knowing the senator. Still, when Keisha called to tell her about the service, Alexa felt like she at least owed this small courtesy to the man she'd seen die.

Walking through the doors of St. Patrick's Cathedral, Alexa paused, taking in the size of the crowd. The church was almost full. She headed down the aisle, looking for an empty space in one of the pews. She'd almost reached the altar when a voice on her right called, "Ms. Williams. There's space here." Representative Jordan, looking solemn in dark gray, shifted over and patted the wooden pew next to him.

"Thank you. I didn't expect it to be so crowded. I should have gotten here earlier." Alexa slid into the pew beside the legislator, trying to keep her voice even.

"I didn't realize you knew the senator." Jordan leaned closer to make his voice heard over the hubbub of the crowd. "He wasn't on the Human Trafficking Commission, was he?"

"Um, no. We had just a passing acquaintance." Alexa winced at her word choice. "But Senator Martinelli was a Senate legend. I wanted to pay my respects."

Jordan raised an eyebrow at her response but didn't ask for further explanation. "I knew Carmine very well. He chaired the Environmental Resources and Energy Committee in the Senate. I'm minority chair of the House's counterpart of that committee. We had quite a few knock-down, drag-out fights on energy issues." He smiled. "Like this drilling in State lands issue I told you about. But, I respected the old S.O.B."

"I heard he was pretty pro-industry."

As the rich tones of organ music filled the air, Alexa turned her attention to the front of the church. Still she caught the representative's reply, muttered as if speaking to himself. "But on this one, I had him."

Alexa wanted to ask what Jordan meant, but a priest launched into a singsong prayer. The entire assembly quieted, turning its attention to the front of the cathedral.

The memorial service dragged on forever. Keisha had informed Alexa that Senator Martinelli's funeral and interment would be a family affair in his hometown. But the senator's colleagues in the legislature had wanted to pay their respects with this Harrisburg event. Alexa hadn't anticipated how many politicians would feel the need to speak in person about the deceased. Or how long each of those tributes would last. To keep from nodding off, she studied the rows of people. Almost all were dressed in shades of black and gray like a living chiaroscuro painting.

In the center of the front row, an older, heavyset woman dressed in black dabbed at her eyes. Alexa pegged her as the senator's widow since most of the speakers nodded in her direction at some point during their remarks. Several pairs of black-haired men and women spread out like dark wings on either side of the aging matriarch. Probably the sons, daughters, and their spouses. Alexa's curious gaze came to rest on a teenager, sitting at the end of the aisle in a wheelchair. She noted the boy's pallor. His pale skin seemed to reflect something more than heartbreak at the death of a beloved grandfather. The teen looked ill.

Alexa continued to scan the crowd. She recognized a face here and there, but most of these people were strangers. Several people looked genuinely distraught. An elegant woman with a blonde chignon caught Alexa's eye. She sat ramrod straight as tears flowed down her cheeks onto a purple dress, so plain and dark it looked like old-fashioned mourning clothes.

Fascinated with the woman, Alexa didn't notice that Senator Gabler had taken the microphone immediately after the governor. At the sound of his voice, she turned her attention back to the altar. She soon lost interest; his tribute sounded like more of the same. Looking past Silas, she noticed Detective Marshall sitting with the choir. She stifled a hollow laugh. If Marshall was looking for the killer in this crowd, he had lots of possibilities to choose from. Gabler stepped away from the podium and another politician took his place. And another. The procession of distraught legislators seemed endless. Just when Alexa contemplated making a run for it, the choir broke into "Ave Maria." The priest gave a benediction, and the interminable service finally ended.

As they stood and moved down the crowded aisle, Representative Jordan asked, "Any success in finding a lawyer for your client?"

"Perhaps. I'm arranging meetings with two potential firms next week, up in your district. The Friends of Pine Creek group is one of them." Alexa turned to look up at him and nearly plowed into a man stopped in front of her.

"Next week? We're out of session next week. While you're in Tioga County, why don't I give you a tour of the fracking fields? A little hands-on education to help you better advise your clients."

Startled by the offer, Alexa hesitated.

"I'll have my office coordinate a time. Give me a few hours, and I'll turn you into a full-blown anti-fracking activist by the end of the tour."

Alexa couldn't ignore the dare in Jordan's cocky statement. "You're on." She grinned.

"I'll be in touch," the legislator spoke over his shoulder as a man in a bold pinstripe suit grabbed him by the elbow.

"You came after all." Keisha popped out of a pew to the left. "I saw you before the service, but we were wedged in the middle of the pew."

Lauren followed Keisha out into the main aisle. "Hey, Alexa." The intern lowered her voice. "We were talking the other day about educational experiences. Now that I've got the political memorial service under my belt, I'm ready to roll. I should get, like, an A plus, or at the very least an A, for sitting through this."

Trying hard not to laugh, Keisha turned to her protégé. "Hush. Someone might hear you."

Alexa whispered, "Out of the mouth of babes."

"Now you're calling me a babe." Lauren turned to Keisha with an innocent look on her face. "Boss, is that, like, sexual harassment?"

By the time the three women reached the pavement in front of the cathedral, they were still laughing. Despite a chill in the air, much of the crowd continued to mill around in the bright sunshine. Keisha came to a halt a few yards away from the church entrance. "Did you read the paper today?"

Alexa glanced at Lauren.

"Don't worry. She knows what we saw. I've pledged her to secrecy." Keisha frowned. "But, girlfriend, you know it's going to come out. All those policemen in the rotunda that night. This place leaks like a sieve."

"You know I date a state trooper? He thinks we need to be careful. You and I know we didn't see anything. But, if it gets out that there are witnesses, the bad guys won't know we're clueless."

"Not entirely clueless." Keisha's look held a question.

"Did Marshall ask you about the voices, too? I identified Senator Martinelli from an audiotape. I'd never heard him speak prior to that."

Keisha replied, "That night, I thought Senator Martinelli might be one of the men arguing. He sounded a little frazzled or even desperate during that conversation. So it didn't seem much of a stretch when he decided to end it all a few minutes later. I already told the cops I couldn't identify the other guys."

Lauren had been silent as she listened to Alexa and Keisha talk. With a sudden intake of breath, the intern tensed and stepped behind them. Alexa looked up to see two men walking by. The taller man was striking with a shock of white hair and a tanned face that looked no older than forty. He had that no-neck physique of a one-time football player or weight lifter; the collar of his crisp white shirt pulled taut beneath his expensive tie. The horn-rimmed glasses and tailored suit did little to offset the impression of sheer physical force.

Slight with a wispy gray comb-over, the second man bounced on his toes to keep up with his companion.

"Who are those two?" Alexa asked Keisha. She turned to Lauren. "Isn't that the jerk who chewed you out the other week?"

Lauren nodded.

Keisha sighed. "Jerk is right, but he's not anyone you want to mess with. That's Nason Kurtz, one of the senior partners at Toland." At Alexa's blank look, she explained, "Walker Toland is the most influential lobbyist in Harrisburg. He's been here longer than most legislators, and he has something like twenty associates in his firm."

"Associates? You mean lobbyists?"

"Yeah. But, Nason is Toland's right hand guy. His father and grandfather were both state legislators. But his main claim to fame was as a big football star for Penn State."

Lauren snorted. "I'm not sure he has the brain power to run for public office."

Keisha giggled. "But look at him. He's the Hulk in a tailored suit. Perfect for what he does for Toland." She turned to Alexa. "He's the one they send in when the cause needs a little extra push."

"Sounds a little creepy. I don't remember anyone from Toland approaching us during the Human Trafficking Committee's work." Alexa looked at Lauren with concern. The intern now faced away from them, looking at the street.

Keisha snorted. "Toland is only interested when there's money to be made. Even they might draw the line at representing sex traffickers; more because of bad publicity than any moral reservations."

"Who's his sidekick?" The two men had stopped for an intense discussion with a third man.

Keisha followed her gaze. "The little dipshit is Senator Patterson. I'm surprised you've never run into him before. His office is in our suite."

Lauren finally turned around to join the conversation. "He was the guy with Nason Kurtz that day in the kitchen."

"I had it backwards," Alexa took another look. "I thought Kurtz was the senator."

Lauren interrupted, "Hey, isn't that Walker Toland? The one they're with now."

"Absolutely. They say he's the most powerful man in Harrisburg."

Alexa saw only a tall man, about her parents' age, with thick silver hair. When he moved his hand, gold cufflinks glinted in the sun. Although his tailored suit had money written all over it, he didn't look all that special. "More powerful than the governor?"

Keisha nodded. "More powerful than God. He has enormous influence, and has made so much money lobbying he owns houses in the Caribbean and Aspen. Plus, he has a stable of racehorses. One of his horses won the Preakness last year."

"Is it true his estate has a huge bonsai garden, and he shapes the trees himself?" Lauren asked.

"That's what I hear. Obviously, I've never been there."

Alexa took another skeptical look at this superstar lobbyist and said, "So this guy is the Mr. Miyagi of politics, and this Kurtz character is his Karate Kid? Hard to believe." She drew her attention away from the lobbyists. "I have to get back to the office. You'll let me know when this report is ready?"

"Should be in the next day or two. We'll send it to you for review." Keisha snapped back into professional mode.

Alexa made her way through the clusters of people still hanging around the church. The crowd hadn't thinned much. The news of Senator Martinelli's murder seemed to be the main topic of conversation. At the edge of the sidewalk, a loud voice slowed Alexa to a crawl.

"Did you hear there were witnesses?" An older woman wearing a wide-brimmed hat savored the gossip.

"Witnesses. You mean someone saw the senator being pushed over the railing?" Her mousy companion asked.

A third woman shook her head. "I hear the witnesses were on a lower floor."

The mouse declared, "I hope they catch the monster that killed Senator M. What if he kills other people in the Capitol?"

Alexa sighed. Both John and Keisha were right. The news that someone had witnessed the murder had not only leaked but was spreading like wildfire. She hurried to the Land Rover, hoping the police had at least protected their names.

CHAPTER TWELVE

ISABELLA ENDED TUESDAY'S yoga session with a long period of meditation. Alexa rose from her half-lotus position feeling refreshed and serene. "Namaste." She approached the teacher. "What a wonderful session. I haven't been meditating at home that much these days. I should get back into it."

The tall, slender yogi smiled. "If your heart is telling you to meditate more often, you should listen. Perhaps we need to schedule a few sessions on advanced poses also?"

"Maybe." Alexa hesitated. "My life hasn't gone off the rails like last year, but there are some things going on. Let me see if ramping up my meditation time brings me focus. I'll let you know about the extra sessions."

Haley had missed class because of a social event at the Chamber, but Alexa, Melissa, and Tyrell walked over to the Om Café. When they entered the cozy room, Ariel looked up from the counter. "Two chai teas and a cappuccino, right? No Haley?"

All three nodded to confirm the drink orders, and Melissa responded, "Nope. The Chamber is announcing some big new economic initiative and swore Haley to secrecy. She called it something weird." The redhead frowned. "Embargoed, that's it. The information was embargoed until tonight's event."

"Probably a new warehouse," Alexa grumbled as the three sat at a corner table. Distribution warehouses had descended on the Cumberland Valley like a plague of locusts.

"I know you hate these warehouses, Alexa," Tyrell chided. "But they bring a lot of decent-paying employment to people with marginal skill levels. Some of my kids were able to leave foster care and reunite with their families after their parents got warehouse jobs."

"Not to mention, I can order something from Amazon or that office store, and it shows up that afternoon." Melissa's voice was droll. "Pretty soon, all we'll need to do is think about buying something, and UPS will drop it off at the front door."

"I know there are advantages. I got Scout's last chew toy in one day. But there are so many trucks, and the air quality is getting worse," Alexa countered.

"Speaking of UPS, I got some new display panels for the gallery. I'll use them for my next show."

"That's not until May, right?" Alexa took a sip of the tea Ariel had delivered.

"It will be here before I know it. Can you believe it's officially spring?" Melissa pulled her shawl close. "With this fucking weather, it feels like the first day of winter."

"Girl, I thought you were going to clean up that mouth." Tyrell shook his head in mock disapproval.

"I've made a huge effort, but sometimes you just have to fucking say what you fucking mean."

Alexa tried not to snort a mouthful of chai onto the table. "Tyrell, Melissa's had, let's say, a free-spirited approach to language since the age of . . ." She scrunched her brow in concentration. "Seven. If years of teachers couldn't cure her, you may as well give up now."

Tyrell grinned. "I don't give a rat's ass how you talk, Melissa. So is your landscape show opening in May?"

"No. That's later this summer. The May show features three local artists. Two work in oil. One's a photographer. Put it on your calendars," Melissa ordered.

Alexa checked the calendar on her iPhone. "I might be in Italy visiting my parents."

"Changing the subject." Tyrell glanced up from his phone. "I wanted to ask you about your senator. I hear they're calling it murder now?"

"Yeah." Alexa nodded. "By the way, I'd appreciate it if you didn't tell people I witnessed anything. Which isn't far from the truth. I saw him hurtle through the air and hit the floor. I didn't see anything that happened before that."

Tyrell narrowed his eyes. "Are you worried? From what I heard this morning, the cops are closing in on his killer."

"Really?"

"I went to a big meeting for advocacy organizations this morning in the Burg. Everybody was buzzing about the murder and that the cops think the husband did it."

Melissa asked the question first. "What husband?"

"I guess it was an open secret that Senator Martinelli's been getting it on with some representative." Tyrell took a moment to amp up the suspense. "Her name's Madison Greer. She represents a district near Pittsburgh."

"Didn't you say this guy was some old dude, almost a hundred years old?" Melissa looked at Alexa.

"In his late seventies. I guess he was young at heart." Alexa scrambled to adjust her mental image of Carmine Martinelli.

"Or had an endless supply of little blue pills." Tyrell smirked.

"People say the senator was very charming. Still, I'm wondering what this Representative Greer saw in the old guy?" Alexa reached for her phone to look up Greer.

"Isn't it always about power in these political relationships?" Melissa suggested. "The old quid pro quo."

Alexa showed them the picture of Representative Greer from the Pennsylvania House website. An attractive blond woman in a power suit. "He was very powerful, but jeez." She did the quick math. "This woman is more than twenty years younger than Martinelli."

Melissa sighed. "Maybe it was love."

A vision of Mrs. Martinelli and her brood sitting in the church struck Alexa. "Who knows? I saw his wife at the memorial service yesterday. She looked at least seventy." She paused and turned to Tyrell. "So the police think this is a love triangle? A middle-aged husband dropped an elderly senator off the balcony over an affair."

"He could have just waited a few months and Grandpa would have keeled over," Tyrell drawled. "Now the dude's facing the death penalty. The plus side—if they arrest this husband, you won't have to worry about being a witness. Hell, you might not even have to testify."

On the drive home, Alexa processed this new information— really just gossip at this point. This whole enraged husband theory sounded pretty implausible, but if true, the identities of the men quarreling with the senator wouldn't matter. Alexa imagined a new scenario. The argument ends, and the others leave the senator alone. Then, the cuckolded husband emerges from the shadows to hurl Martinelli into the rotunda. She wanted off the hook as a witness. But Alexa had her doubts about this new version. Of course, the police must have evidence if they were targeting the husband.

As she slowed the Land Rover to turn into her lane, Alexa remembered the weeping woman in deep purple at the memorial service. She'd only seen the woman in profile, but the blonde hair, the age—it could have been Representative Madison Greer. The elegant mourner had seemed very affected by the senator's death. Alexa let out a long breath. Maybe Tyrell's gossip was true.

"Aunt Alexa! She's here. Hey, Scout." Courtney and Jamie tumbled to the door when Alexa and her dog entered the house.

Jamie darted away and came back holding a big chocolate bunny covered in iridescent blue foil. "Look what the Easter Bunny brought me."

"Happy Easter, kiddos." Alexa took off her light coat and carried her basket of apple pies toward the kitchen, following the scent of baking ham. "Guys. Please make sure your candy is up on a table so Scout can't get it. Chocolate can make dogs sick." The two kids and the mastiff raced into the family room.

"Kate, what can I do to help?"

Alexa's petite sister-in-law looked up from stirring a big pan of candied sweet potatoes on the gas range.

"Nothing here. The ham and the baked corn are in the oven. The salad's done and in the fridge. Dinner's probably fifteen minutes away."

"What about the table?"

"That ball's in Graham's court. Maybe you could check? And make sure the kids aren't gorging on candy."

"Sure." Alexa headed first to the dining room, where Graham had completed his mission. Set with the good china, the place settings gleamed in the sunlight filtering through the french doors. She continued down the corridor to the family room, where her brother and his children were glued to a Charlie Brown cartoon. Scout had wedged his huge mass between Courtney and Jamie, who were sitting on big floor pillows.

"Lexie. Happy Easter." Graham rose and kissed his sister on the top of her head. "How's the production line going? I tried to help, but Kate threw me out. You know she's queen of the kitchen."

"Dinner's going to be soon. Do the kids need to wash up first?" Alexa smiled. "I'll help Kate get everything on the table."

"Thanks. I'll handle the kids." Graham drifted back to the couch, and Alexa circled back to the kitchen.

Half an hour later, the family had put a big dent in Kate's feast. The children, eight-year-old Jamie and his seven-year-old sister Courtney, had eaten most of the food on their plates, despite the candy they'd downed earlier in the morning.

"Kate, this is an excellent meal." Alexa took another bite of baked corn.

Her sister-in-law pushed a strand of strawberry blonde hair from her eyes. "I wasn't sure I could pull this off. We're so used to just showing up at your parents' house, and Susan has everything ready. But it turned out to be fun."

"Thanks, sweetheart. You did the Williams family proud, keeping up the tradition." Graham reached for his wife's hand and gave it a squeeze.

"Mommy, may I be excused?" Jamie asked.

"Me too," Courtney squealed, not to be outdone by her brother.

"You may. We'll have some of Aunt Lexie's pie later. After the dishes are done. Finish your Charlie Brown movie."

Courtney and Jamie raced from the room. This time, Scout didn't follow the children. He stuck close to the food.

Graham shook his head. "A lot has happened this year. Mom and Dad bought the house in Umbria. All the changes at the firm with Dad and Pat retiring."

"I miss Mom and Dad, but they'll be back here most winters. I'm anxious to see the villa. It looks pretty great in the photos." Alexa smiled.

"Speaking of changes, did Graham tell you we're looking to buy a beach house in North Carolina? I'd like to spend part of the summers down there with the kids. Since my parents retired and moved south, I don't see as much of them as I'd like." Kate's expression turned wistful.

Her husband jumped in. "We're thinking of this as a two-for; maybe even a three-for. We get to see more of Kate's parents. You know how much we love the beach. And Mom and Dad will be away during the summer anyway. We figure I could do some long weekends and maybe a week here and there. Kate and the kids could spend at least two months during the kids' summer vacation."

"Wow." Alexa pushed aside the selfish thought that the entire family was bailing on her and said, "Go for it. It sounds like a great idea. Are you going to hang on to the cabin at Pine Grove?"

"For now." Kate took a sip of wine. "We still might want to spend weekends there in the fall. We might rent it out while we're at the beach."

"We've selected five beach houses to look at. We're taking a long weekend soon to check them out." Graham assumed his lawyer voice. "We'd like to close a deal next month so we have the place for this coming summer."

"I hope you can find a place you like." Alexa's enthusiasm was sincere. "I can't complain about Mom and Dad deciding to spend summers in Italy. I love that the cabin's mine, now. I've upgraded the lane, the deck, and the house. I'm still considering a garage, but I might wait until the fall to tackle that. I don't want noise and workmen everywhere during the summer. I want to be able to relax on the deck whenever."

"When are you going to visit Mom and Dad?" Graham asked.

"Late May. I'm going to stay two weeks."

"We may fly over in August before the kids go back to school. We need to see how this beach house thing plays out." Graham stood and lifted the platter with the remains of the ham.

"Maybe you can spend a week with us at the beach too," Kate invited as the three adults carried the remnants of the meal to the kitchen. Scout plodded behind, snatching errant crumbs off the floor.

When the dishes were nearly finished, Alexa whispered to Graham and Kate. "Scout and I are going out to hide the eggs."

Kate laughed. "You don't have to whisper. When those two are glued to the TV, they can't hear anything except what they're watching."

Alexa and Scout stashed bright plastic Easter eggs throughout the backyard. Inside the twist-open eggs, Alexa had secreted candies, small change, and miniature images of children's book covers. The actual books rested on the bottom of the pie basket in the kitchen.

A few minutes later, the entire family burst out into the bright, sunny afternoon. Graham, Kate, and Alexa sat in lawn chairs on the patio and watched Courtney and Jamie chase around the yard, trying to find the hidden eggs. Scout ran back and forth between the children.

"How many do you have?" Alexa shouted. "Bring your baskets over and let's check if you found them all."

Each child removed the eggs and placed them on the table. Jamie dumped his nine in a pile. Courtney arranged her eleven in a perfect line.

"Cheater," Jamie yelled. "You have more than me."

"Your sister didn't cheat. She just found more eggs than you did." Graham's tone was stern.

To cut off what she knew would be a lecture, Alexa jumped in. "Plus, you don't know what's in your eggs yet. Some have better prizes than others. Why don't you open them up to see what's inside? I'm going in to get us some apple pie."

By the time they'd opened the eggs, received their books, and eaten a slice of apple pie each, the afternoon sun was setting. Alexa and Scout prepared to leave.

"Happy Easter, Aunt Lexie. Thanks for the Easter egg hunt." Courtney's words were muffled as she raced into the family room.

Jamie stayed and gave Alexa a little hug. "Thanks. You were right, Aunt Lexie. I got better prizes. I got five books, and Courtney only got four."

Alexa laughed. "I hope you and your sister will share the books so you both get to read the stories." She stood and looked at Graham and Kate. "What a great day. Thanks."

CHAPTER THIRTEEN

BY THE TIME THEY arrived home, twilight bathed the forest in shadow. Alexa parked the car, and Scout leapt out. He made a quick trip to the edge of the pines, which towered dark and forbidding in the fading light. Standing on the deck, Alexa felt a frisson of unease as the darkness swallowed the mastiff and he disappeared from sight. She shook off her moment of disquiet, muttering aloud, "Get a grip. You can't let this Martinelli thing take over your life."

"Scout," she called and waited until the huge dog appeared, loping toward the cabin. Inside, the mastiff headed straight toward his pillow in the living room and collapsed with a loud groan. "Kids wear you out, buddy? I'm beat, too. I'm going to run upstairs and change into sweats." Passing through the living room, she noticed the light blinking on the answering machine. When she pressed play, she tensed at the sound of John's voice, expecting him to lay on more guilt for not joining his family this weekend.

"Alexa. I know you're probably at your brother's house, but I wanted to call and say Happy Easter. It's great to be home. I've missed my mom's cooking."

Before the message had finished, Alexa continued toward the stairs. When she reached the top, she paused to hear John's last words. "Give me a call back when you get this."

When she had stepped out of her slacks and shed her top, Alexa swept her hair into a clip and grabbed a large towel.

John can wait, she thought, glad for some solitude after a day with two rambunctious kids. I need a soak in the hot tub.

With the towel flung over her shoulder, Alexa carried her sweats downstairs and tossed them onto the corner wing chair. She stripped off her underwear and wrapped the towel around her torso, glancing toward the dog bed. Scout usually came along on Alexa's trips to the hot tub and snuffled around the woods or stretched out on his deck cushion. But his name died on her lips when she saw the giant mastiff curled up, fast asleep.

"OK. You stay here. I'll feed you when I come back inside." Scout continued to snore through her words, so Alexa picked up a flashlight and walked out the front door. She smiled at the feel of the deck beneath her bare feet and danced a few steps of celebration for the arrival of spring. It was finally warm enough to walk to the hot tub without slippers. She giggled. The joy of living in the middle of the woods, with no neighbors for miles, included soaking naked in the hot tub. So much better than stewing in a soggy bathing suit like they did in the burbs.

She padded down the dark walkway to the far deck. Although ambient light from the big dining room window illuminated the front deck, that light vanished when Alexa rounded the corner. Reaching the hot tub, she switched on the flashlight and laid it on the plastic steps next to the spa. Even with the easy-fold lever, she needed two hands to raise the heavy hot tub cover back against the wall of the house. Dousing the light, Alexa the tossed her towel over a hook and slipped into the steaming water.

"Ahhhhhhh." She leaned back and closed her eyes, feeling the warmth surround her. Truth be told, Graham and Kate's news about the beach house did upset her, just a little. It had only been a few years since Alexa left New York City to return home. She'd been tired of the city and wanted off the fast track at her prestigious law firm. But she had also missed her family and wanted to be near them. Now Mom and Dad were spending spring and summer in Italy. Soon Graham, Kate, and the kids would be away most of the summer too. She and Scout were going to have to do Friday pizza nights on their own.

"Stop whining," she muttered. Alexa knew she was being unreasonable. She also knew if she had a relationship that consumed her heart and soul she wouldn't need her family so much. She'd always want to spend time with them, of course. But, if Reese had stuck around, she'd be wrapped up in their relationship. Wonderful as he was, she didn't envision a lifetime commitment to John. He was handsome, brave, charming, and, above all, nice. But beyond that . . .

Alexa opened her eyes and pushed away any melancholy thoughts. She loved to sit out here at night, luxuriating in the steaming water and watching the stars. With almost no light contamination, night clung to the mountain, dark as velvet. Alexa could see only the narrow swath of open sky that soared over the clearing. The trees blocked a fuller view. But her little slice of the heavens was enough. Gazing at the expanse of stars and planets made Alexa feel small yet connected to a universe so large she couldn't even comprehend its magnitude. She often sat here and pondered the life that existed out there.

She rarely turned on the jets, instead preferring to contemplate the night in silence with only the soothing sounds of the forest to keep her company. The forest harbored many sounds: the sigh of the wind through the trees, the scurrying sounds of small creatures; the hoot of owls at night and birdsong during the day; the chorus of frogs in late spring and the hum of insects in the summer. Alexa relished them all.

A shooting star flashed across the moonless sky. Delighted, Alexa remembered another shooting star she and Reese had watched crease an African night over the Samburu plain. Her nostalgic smile faltered at the sharp crunch of dry leaves on the forest floor.

She peered into the darkness but could see nothing. Charcoal trees against a jet-black hill. The noise had come from high on the mountain that sloped down to the deck. Probably a branch falling to the ground. Hearing nothing more, Alexa resumed her reflection on the universe.

Crunch. Crunch. There it was again. Closer.

Alexa straightened upright, then cocked her head toward the sound. She often heard deer at night, and this sound was similar. Except a lone buck walked with a series of small explosive crunches. And doe and fawns usually traveled in herds, their footsteps crackling the dry leaves in ripples of sound. This animal paused between each footstep.

Crunch. Crunch.

This was no deer. Clearly, a large animal. Alexa ran through the possibilities. A bear? Although early in the season, a bear could have emerged from hibernation. But a bear would pad along, unconcerned. This animal seemed to be walking with a measure of stealth, as if trying to mask its approach.

Crunch. Crunch. Crunch.

The animal was still quite high on the slope but descending. Could it be a bobcat? When Alexa was a child, she'd seen a few bobcats during the summer nights. And their gait had been fluid but silent. She braced for a blood-curdling bobcat scream, but instead, more halting footsteps.

Crunch. Crunch. Then, an ominous waiting silence.

Alexa's throat tightened. This thing was stalking her. Not like an animal. Like a man.

Alexa sank lower, trying to conceal the white gleam of her body. Edging toward the side of the hot tub, she extended her arm to search for the flashlight. She couldn't find it.

Still sensing the watching presence on the hill, Alexa knew she had to make a run for the house. Now. She took a deep breath and sat up, preparing to slip over the side. Just as she moved, the forest exploded with noise. She caught a brief flash of light and heard a loud crack. . Something with an acrid smell ripped into the hot tub cover with a smack, just missing her head. Panicked, she ducked back down into the water.

A gun. He was shooting at her.

With the need for stealth gone, her attacker barreled down the slope dislodging an avalanche of dry leaves. Alexa bolted from the hot tub, bare feet sliding over the wet deck. She regained her balance and dashed toward the walkway.

"Asshole," Alexa hissed when the beam of a powerful flashlight lit up her naked body. Without breaking stride, she fled.

Rounding the corner of the cabin, another rifle crack split the air. Crack. Crack. A chunk of wood sliced her back. Alexa bit back a scream at the sharp pain but didn't break stride until she reached the front door. Inside, a frenzied Scout barked and slammed his body against the door.

She sprinted through the door past the dog, threw the deadbolt, and switched off the light. As she ran to check the back door lock, she murmured soothing sounds to Scout. She needed him to quiet down so she could hear. Keeping low and away from the big front windows, Alexa moved to the living room, maneuvering past Scout's nudges of concern. She rose to hit the living room light switch, and then dropped again to the floor.

Outside, it was quiet. The gunfire had ceased. There was no movement around the house or on the deck. Alexa tugged her clothes from the corner chair, pulling the sweatshirt over her head. After a pause to listen, she shimmied her panties on. Feeling less exposed, she belly crawled across the living room floor to seize the phone. Crawling back to the front corner, she dialed 911 with shaky hands.

"Help. I'm under attack by someone with a high-powered rifle. This is Alexa Williams." She shook as she whispered her address to the man.

"Are you alone?"

"Yes. With my dog."

"Stay on the line, ma'am. I'm going to dispatch a patrol car to your location. Are you hurt?"

"Yes, but it's not life-threatening." Alexa set the phone on the floor. Her panic had given way to a cold, familiar calm. She recalled another life-threatening situation, one that had been far, far worse than this. Repeating a mantra had kept Alexa from losing it that night. She began a silent chant: Panic means death; panic means death.

She looked toward the stairs. Should she make a run for the shotgun in her bedroom closet? Too risky. She decided to stay put and drew Scout next to her. She gripped the phone with one hand and stroked the mastiff with the other, trying to soothe him. As she quieted Scout, Alexa's racing heart slowed almost to normal. She scrunched farther into the corner. This section of the house was part of the original log structure, built of ten-inch logs stacked close with chinking in between. They might stop a bullet.

"Ma'am," the dispatcher's voice came back on the line. His voice seemed to boom through the quiet room. Alexa jammed the receiver against her ear to muffle the sound. He continued, "Troopers are on the way. It shouldn't be more than a few minutes. Has there been any more shooting?"

"No, it's quiet."

"I'll stay on the line until the police arrive."

"Thank you. Can you just hang on? I need to stay quiet and listen. He might try to break into the house."

"Absolutely. Just let me know if you need to talk. The police will be there soon."

Arms around Scout, Alexa burrowed into her corner, phone by her side. On edge in the darkness, she remained alert, waiting for the smallest sound. She feared her attacker would try to scale the back of the house and climb in through a bedroom window. The windows there were only about five feet from the ground. She strained to hear movement outside, but the protective log wall muffled any sound. Her back, wet with blood, throbbed more each moment.

Although it seemed like an eternity, Alexa estimated less than ten minutes passed until she heard sirens in the distance. The sirens drew closer when the police turned into her lane. Alexa jumped at the alarm bell when the police vehicle triggered the early warning system. Scout sprang to his feet barking. She picked up the phone. "Thanks, sir, for staying on the line. They're here." She looked across the room at the mastiff with worry. "Can you tell the cops not to shoot my dog? He won't hurt anyone."

"No problem. I'll relay that message. You'll be safe now. I'll sign off." The dispatcher broke the connection.

When the vehicle stopped out front, the siren died. Alexa stood and plucked her sweatpants from the corner chair. She pulled them on before she walked into the dining area. "Shh, Scout." Seconds later, someone crossed the deck and knocked on the front door.

"Ms. Williams. State Police. I'm Trooper Davis. Are you OK? Please open the door," a woman's voice called out.

"Alexa, this is Trooper Cannon," said a second, familiar voice.

"I'm OK. My dog is very large but harmless. Right now, he's just as scared as I am. Please don't harm him." Alexa unlocked the door. "Sit," she told Scout then opened the door to the two uniformed troopers. "I'm so glad you're here." Trembling, she collapsed into a nearby chair.

CHAPTER FOURTEEN

"Ms. Williams, whoever shot at you has disappeared. The forensic science unit will be here soon to look at the scene and recover any bullets they can find." Trooper Davis removed her full-brimmed hat and unbuttoned her uniform coat. "The FSU might have to wait until daylight to follow the trail down the mountain and discover the shooter's exit route. Cannon and I didn't see any vehicles on the lane when we arrived. The gunman must have parked farther up the mountain and hiked in."

"That sounds right. I have a driveway alarm system. I would have heard a car come down the lane. He might have left when I ran inside the house. I didn't hear anything more outside after I came indoors. But Scout was barking. I was calling 911. So he could have hung around for a while." Alexa couldn't move from the dining room chair.

"You say 'he.' Did you catch a glimpse of your assailant?" Davis pulled out a chair and took a seat across from Alexa.

"No. I guess it could have been a woman, But judging from the sound of the footsteps in the leaves—especially at the end when he charged down the hill—it seemed like a fairly big man."

Cannon walked through the door and stood at the end of the table. "Are you feeling better?"

"A little. This cut on my back is throbbing. It feels sticky too, like it's still bleeding." Alex turned her body to show the trooper the wet spot below the right shoulder of her sweatshirt.

Davis exclaimed, "You're hurt? Were you shot?"

"I think a splinter or something caught me, not a bullet." Alexa lowered her voice. "I wasn't wearing clothes, so it nicked me pretty bad."

Cannon spoke into his portable. "What's the ETA for the paramedics? Victim has possible GS wound or contusions."

Davis said, "While we're waiting for EMS, can you walk us through everything that happened?"

Alexa described how her relaxing soak in the hot tub had turned into a nightmare. "Like I said, I didn't see the shooter. I believe it was just one person, although I can't be completely sure. The gun sounded like a high-powered rifle of some sort. The first shot just missed my head." She winced at the memory.

Cannon looked at the door. "The ambulance is almost here. Alexa, do you have any idea who would want to harm you?"

Alexa tried to concentrate. "I can think of three possibilities. It could be someone who's holding a grudge about my role in breaking up that sex trafficking ring last summer. But most of the key players are dead or in jail, so that seems unlikely. I've arranged Protection from Abuse orders for a few clients. One of the recent ones, Lois Martin. Her husband is an Iraq veteran with a short fuse who liked to slap her around. She finally came to me when he threatened her with a gun. He's pretty pissed that I got her a PFA."

Cannon wrote that one into his notebook. "You said three."

"I'm betting this one is the most likely. You knew I saw Senator Martinelli die. You drove John to Harrisburg so he could bring me home in my car?"

"Yeah. They're calling that case murder now," he informed Trooper Davis.

"I only saw the guy crash into the floor. I have no idea who pushed him. But, somehow, it's leaked that there were witnesses. I'd been hoping the names of those witnesses were still secret." She sighed. "But tonight might mean my name is out there. And the killer might think I can identify him."

"I knew you were there when the senator bit the dust. I didn't know word was on the street about a witness."

Alexa gasped. "Keisha. I'm not the only witness. Keisha Washington could be in danger too."

"Do you know her address?" Davis asked. "We'll send the locals out to pay her a visit."

"Harrisburg, or maybe the suburbs." Alexa leaned over to fish through her purse, sitting on the table. She drew out her phone and located Keisha's number. "Here's her cell number. I don't get cell service here, but there's a landline in the living room."

Davis jotted down the number and hurried toward the door, "I'll be back. I'm going to call this in."

Two paramedics raced through the door.

Cannon said, "I'll leave while they check you out. I called John. He was already on the road home from State College. He'll be here soon."

The EMTs had just finished their examination of Alexa's wound when John came bounding through the door. "Are you OK? Cannon said someone took a shot a you." John managed to weave his way between the two EMTs and gather Alexa in his arms.

Alexa winced when his arm brushed her wound but gritted her teeth and nestled into the comfort of his embrace.

The scrawny EMT who looked barely old enough to drive answered John's question before Alexa could respond. "She's suffered some minor blood loss. That cut below her shoulder should have stitches."

The taller EMT spoke to Alexa. "You can still change your mind, and we'll take you to the hospital."

When Alexa shook her head, he looked at her and then John. "I recommend you drive into the Urgent Care center and get them to stitch it up. Otherwise, you'll continue to bleed and end up with an ugly scar."

"I'll make sure she gets there very soon." John stepped in before Alexa could answer.

The EMT looked uneasy as he said, "OK, if you are refusing transport to the hospital, let me ask again. Are you experiencing any other pain? Dizziness? Are you experiencing chills or lethargy?"

"I'm fine except for the cut. Thank you. I'll head into Urgent Care as soon as I can." Alexa trailed the two men to the door, Scout on her heels. Then she turned back to John. "I'm glad you're here. Weren't you were going to stay with your parents until tomorrow?"

John guided Alexa onto the living room sofa and wrapped a throw around her shoulders. "That's why I wanted you to call me back. My schedule changed. I now have a big meeting tomorrow. A last minute thing. So I decided to hit the road tonight instead of early tomorrow morning."

Alexa sighed. "I got your message. I was going to call after I came in from the hot tub. Then all hell broke loose." She looked at the mastiff lying with his head on her feet. "I never fed Scout either." She slid forward and shrugged off the throw, but John stopped her with a gentle hand on her shoulder.

"I've got this. Come on, Scout, time for dinner."

When John and the dog disappeared into the kitchen, Alexa sat back against the big sofa and closed her eyes. Who would want to shoot her? Could this really have something to do with Senator Martinelli's death? Thoughts bounced through her brain like ping pong balls in a lottery machine. Her eyes opened wide when a question popped to the surface. How did the shooter know she would go to the hot tub? It seemed he'd taken a position up on the hill with quick access to the back deck and the hot tub. Had he been watching her before tonight? How else would he know her habits? Alexa cringed and pulled the furry throw closer. Being watched without her knowledge, maybe for some time. That was almost creepier than being shot at.

Scout trotted around the corner first. Then John. "Hey. Are you OK here alone for a few more minutes? I'm going to check on the status of things outside—and take Scout for a little walk."

"I'm fine," Alexa lied. "I want to go upstairs and dress. Plus I want to check the bedroom walls to see if all that shooting messed anything up. Can you make sure they've warned Keisha Washington?" She pushed off the couch and trudged up the stairs.

In her bedroom, Alexa put on clean clothes, washed her face, and combed her hair. Grabbing a pair of short boots, Alexa perched on the side of the bed to zip them. Instead, she let the boots slip through her fingers and crash onto the floor. The evening's danger finally hit home. A few inches lower, and that first bullet would have killed her.

Weeping, she sank back on the bed and pulled the top quilt over her body.

Some time later, Alexa opened her eyes. Her tears had dried, and she'd drifted off to sleep. Her shoulder hurt like hell. Sitting, she swung her feet off the bed and pulled on the boots with a grimace. She rose and walked along the bedroom wall. Toward the front corner, Alexa found a hole in the drywall and a smattering of dust on the rug below. She turned and noticed a pool of water on a small table, still dripping onto the bedraggled iris on the floor. The bullet had pierced the wall, shattered the vase of flowers, and lodged in the front windowsill.

Alexa tried not to disturb anything. The police would want to see this. But, she had to check the Quan Yin beside the vase. She examined the alabaster statue on the table with a sigh of relief. It was fine. Melissa had given her this Goddess of Mercy and Compassion as a thank you for helping to expose the men who'd murdered her mentor, Cecily Townes. The Bodhisattva was a smaller replica of one Melissa had inherited from Cecily's estate.

As she sat the cherished memento back on the table, a spurt of white-hot anger burned away any remaining fear. This trigger-happy asshole had violated her personal space. The hot tub was her place for respite and contemplation. This guy had fouled it with his nighttime incursion. And, this room, which she'd dubbed her tree house bedroom, was another place of sanctuary. Alexa slipped on a fleece jacket, ignoring the twinge of pain, and strode toward the stairs with resolve. She vowed to help the police get to the bottom of this. And this monster who had tried to kill her? She'd see him pay.

CHAPTER FIFTEEN

THE SOFT CHIME OF temple bells awoke Alexa. For a moment, she thought the tinkling came from one of the many wind chimes she'd hung outside the cabin. But the chimes kept growing louder. "The alarm," Alexa groaned and rolled over, fumbling for the cell phone on her nightstand. Hitting the off button, she remembered she'd chosen a new alarm tone when she'd upgraded the phone software.

She sank back and scrunched up the pillows. Glancing around, she groaned again, remembering why she'd slept in the spare bedroom. When she'd reported the damage, the police asked that her bedroom stay empty until the FSU team returned this morning. So, she and John had dragged Scout's dog bed into this bedroom and collapsed for the night. John and Scout were already up. Alexa focused on the time. Past eight o'clock. She had to get up too. When she scooched across the bed, the stitches on her upper back protested in a flash of pain. Dr. Bradley at the Urgent Care center had told her she might have discomfort. She had even given Alexa a few pain pills to be used as needed. Alexa slid the rest of the way with great care. Shuffling into the bathroom, her entire body ached. That headlong rush out of the hot tub had tweaked a groin muscle and bruised her arms. One little toe throbbed.

A shower helped, but Alexa still limped as she made her way downstairs to join John and Scout.

"Good morning." John looked up from his coffee. "How do you feel?"

Scout ran to Alexa, tail wagging. "Hey, boy." She answered John with a wan smile. "I'm a little worse for the wear. But no permanent damage."

John rose. "What do you want for breakfast? I can cook you eggs."

"I'll just have tea and granola. I can get it."

But, John beat her to the kitchen. "Sit down. I've got this." As he made a cup of Constant Comment and poured cereal into a bowl, John spoke over his shoulder. "I'd like to stay home with you today, but I've got this meeting. I have to be out of here by nine."

Alexa sat at the table. "I planned to go to work, but I didn't expect to be so sore."

"A team will be coming to go over the hill in daylight and examine the bedroom. Why don't you stay home? That way you can answer their questions, keep Scout out of the way." He put a cup of tea and the bowl of cereal in front of Alexa, and then kissed the top of her head. "And you can get some rest. That cut has to hurt like hell."

"A little." Alexa brought up the calendar on her iPhone. "My schedule's pretty light today. A lot of people take a long weekend at Easter. I can stay home—at least all morning. I'll call Graham. He should know what happened here yesterday anyway." Alexa swallowed one of the pain capsules, took a sip of lukewarm tea, and shuffled toward the phone.

Alexa spent most of the morning dozing on the couch, Scout on the floor at her side. The police technicians woke her mid-morning when they knocked to enter the house. Alexa watched as a man and a woman lugged a valise upstairs. She couldn't hear the two working in her bedroom at the far end of the hall.

I'm so glad I made my bed yesterday morning, Alexa thought, then burrowed back into the couch to sleep some more. She never heard the technicians leave the house.

A second round of knocking awoke Alexa in early afternoon. Brushing her fingers through tangled hair, she made her way to the front door. Scout followed her, his fur standing on end. "Ms. Williams, it's Trooper Cannon and Trooper Davis."

"It's all right, boy. It's OK." Alexa soothed the mastiff before she opened the door.

"Our folks are done with their work, so we're wrapping up. We wanted to touch base."

"Come in. I've been sleeping. Can you give me a minute to run upstairs and comb this hair?" Alexa didn't wait for an answer, heading upstairs to the bathroom. Back in the dining room, she joined the troopers, noticing she felt much better. "Would you like a drink? Water, soft drink?"

Davis spoke first. "Water would be good."

Cannon smiled. "You wouldn't happen to have any birch beer, would you?"

"Oh, no. Has John turned you into a birch beer fanatic too?" Alexa laughed on her way to the refrigerator. She came back with two bottles of water and one of white birch beer. "Ever since I found out John loves this stuff, I keep a case on hand at all times."

"Our team has recovered several bullets from the hot tub area, the outer wall of the cabin, and your bedroom. We also found shell casings on the hill that slopes into the hot tub deck." Davis spoke in clipped tones.

"You're goddamn lucky to be alive, Alexa." Cannon shot her an intense look. "He used a semi-automatic rifle, possibly with a night scope."

"I must have moved just as he took the first shot. I was looking for the flashlight."

"A lucky coincidence."

Alexa shivered to think she'd been saved by a quirk of fate. "Did you find anything that points to who this guy was?"

"Knowing the type of weapon gives us someplace to start. FSU might give us more about the make. Beyond that, not much. He was good." Davis looked at a notepad. "The leaves are so thick on that hill we couldn't get a print. The pattern of disturbance suggests he stopped short of the deck, perhaps when you ran inside."

"As best as we can tell, he relied on the element of surprise. When he missed and you ran inside, he must have cut his losses and left." Since Cannon knew Alexa, he seemed to have no qualms about sharing theories despite a harsh look from Davis. "It looks like he retraced his path when he left here. There are recent tire tracks in the lane of a cabin farther up Route 233. Looks like he could have parked there and hiked in. There's a trail that comes that way, right?"

"Yes. A trail comes in over Hunter's Ridge and intersects another unnamed trail that runs parallel to the cabin. That smaller trail goes out to the main road. The other direction heads toward Weaver's Pond." Alexa waved her hand in the direction of the pond.

"It appears he followed the established paths until he got right behind your cabin. Then he left the trail." Davis drew a little diagram on a page of her notebook.

"That's when I picked up the sound of his footsteps in the leaves. If he'd shot from the upper trail, I would have never known he was there." Alexa shuddered.

"There's one more thing." Cannon scowled. "It looks like last night wasn't his first visit to the site. There's some evidence he had been there before—candy wrappers, trampled leaves, and some abrasion on a dead tree. Looks like he sat up there and worked out how to take the shot. Maybe even studied your patterns in using the hot tub."

Davis circled a spot on the upper trail to illustrate Cannon's point.

Alexa quailed to have last night's fears confirmed. Getting shot at was terrifying. But the idea that some man had been watching her for days or even weeks—that made her skin crawl. She rubbed her forehead in agitation. "This cabin is my safe place. An extremist violated it before, but I refused to give into fear. I put in an alarm system and the warning bell on the lane. It's taken awhile, but I felt safe here again. Now you're telling me that safety is an illusion. Any monster can come waltzing down the mountain or creeping through the pines, and I'm vulnerable."

Davis patted Alexa's arm in comfort, but her words belied the gesture. "Ms. Williams, no one is ever completely safe. I'd say that your remote location here, the alarm systems, the big dog, all make you much safer than most. But, it appears you have attracted the attention of one or more people who want to harm you. It's our job to figure out who they are."

"She's right." Cannon stood. "Trouble seems to follow you, Alexa."

Davis cut Cannon off with a piercing look. But his words only confirmed Alexa's own suspicions. She had encountered way too many dead people in her short life. And she'd been in harm's way too often for comfort.

The troopers kept Alexa another forty-five minutes, walking through the entire incident again. They also asked detailed questions about Senator Martinelli's death and the other potential suspects that Alexa had suggested.

When they left, Alexa threw on a jacket and walked outside with Scout. While he frolicked around the open space in front of the cabin, she inspected last night's damage. The bullets had hit the bedroom section of the cabin. A long-ago addition, it was covered in live-edge, beveled cedar rather than the thick log and chinking of the original cabin. Police had cut out a small section of the wall above the hot tub. Several more boards were grooved and splintered. The hot tub was unscathed, but the hole in the cover made Alexa shiver as she thought, That could have been my head. Shaking off a new surge of fear, Alexa circled back to the front steps and walked to the storage area under the hot tub. She found a piece of scrap lumber to tack over the gaping hole in the wall, hoping her stitches wouldn't pop as she worked. Worried about how she'd find a piece of siding to match the vintage cedar, Alexa walked back into the house to notify her homeowner's insurance.

First thing the next morning, Alexa sat on Graham's office couch, getting the third degree from her concerned brother. He had wanted to come to the cabin yesterday, but she'd insisted he stay at work. Now he was demanding a complete rundown of the hot tub incident. "Are you sure you're OK, Lexie? Do you need to go to your own doctor to get checked out?"

"I'm fine. Doctor Bradley at the clinic put in dissolving stitches, so I don't even need to get them removed. I slept much of the day yesterday, thanks to the knockout pills she gave me. But no more pills. I'm feeling much better."

Graham, seated on the adjourning chair, took Alexa's hand. "I'm worried. You barely escaped serious injury—or worse. And the state police don't seem to have a clue who shot at you. Say your theory is right—that it has something to do with this senator's death—I can't see how that puts us any closer to finding the shooter. From all accounts, the cops have no idea who killed the politician. Maybe you should drop everything and fly to Italy. Hang out with Mom and Dad until this is settled."

"I can't, Graham. I'm going to Umbria at the end of May as planned. But, now, I've got three or four cases that are urgent. Both Vanessa and Ted are competent, but I can't dump these clients on either one of them at this stage. Plus I've got this commission report to wrap up. And I still haven't finalized arranging counsel for Jeannie Demeter. I'm hoping to finish that next week."

"When you dig your heels in like this, I know you won't budge. But be careful, Alexa." Graham's exasperation ended on a pleading note.

"I will. Maybe John will stay with me for a few days." Alexa grinned. "My own state police protection detail."

"He spends all his time at the cabin anyway," Graham teased. "Too bad he wasn't there Sunday."

"Mhmm." Alexa didn't voice her concern that the shooter could have picked Easter because John wasn't around. "So we're good?"

Graham shook his head. "Nothing about this is good, Lexie. You should call Mom and Dad. Let them know what happened."

"I didn't want to worry them." Alexa walked toward the door.

"They would want to know what's going on. Call them."

Back at her desk, Alexa looked at the time. Nine o'clock in the morning here. Three o'clock in the afternoon in Umbria. She squared her shoulders and dialed her parents' villa number. The phone rang twenty times with no answer. She considered trying one of their cell phones but decided not to disturb them if they weren't at home.

Next, Alexa called Keisha. The state police had assured her they'd alerted the young woman, but Alexa wanted to speak to her colleague directly. When the assistant put her call through, Keisha exclaimed, "Alexa, I heard someone shot at you on Easter. Are you OK?"

"I'm fine, but that's why I'm calling. There's no way to know for sure this is connected to Senator Martinelli's murder. But it could be, and that means you could be a target too."

Keisha's tone was dismissive. "I'm not worried. That's what I told the police when they came by the house. Of course, I've heard the rumors about witnesses to the senator's death. But the police have kept our names secret. Plus, you know as well as I do, girl. We didn't see anything."

"What about the argument?"

"That ended well before the senator dropped out of the sky. I doubt that the two things were even connected. I'm still betting on suicide. Word is Mrs. Martinelli knew about the good senator's affair. Probably not his first." Keisha's tone hardened. "I see what goes down here. The power attracts political groupies like bees to honey. But this one was different because Martinelli let it become public. Everyone knew about him and Madison Greer. And she's a representative—a woman of substance. Not your typical groupie. It's rumored his wife's family is part of the Philly mob. I wouldn't be surprised if he decided that taking a flying leap was a better choice than waiting for that old bitch, Mama Martinelli, to mete out his punishment."

Taken aback by Keisha's diatribe, Alexa searched for a response. "You could be right. The police are treating this as a murder, though. Maybe Madison Greer's husband. Maybe someone else. They think it's possible the person who attacked me is connected with Martinelli's death."

"Don't you have a lot of other enemies with that sex trafficking business and your law practice? You must have a lot of scumbag clients who hate you for not keeping them out of jail."

Surprised, Alexa answered. "I don't practice criminal law. But you're right. This could have nothing to do with Martinelli. In case it is, be careful."

"Thanks for the heads up. Hey, we got your comments on the commission report. Lauren's making the changes and getting it out to the group, probably today. I'll see you next week. Gotta run, they're calling the Senate to the floor."

Putting the receiver down, Alexa sat for a moment staring at the phone. She knew Keisha had overcome difficult odds to put herself through a good college and work her way up to an important position in the Senate committee structure. She had always thought the woman used tough talk as a tool to inflate her image and to hide her softer side. Perhaps Alexa had misjudged her. Maybe the tough-talking woman she'd just spoken to was the real Keisha after all.

Alexa hadn't built up the courage to use the hot tub yet, but by Saturday, she'd recovered enough to look forward to some fun. Earlier in the month, she'd invited a small group of friends for dinner. Now, she welcomed the distraction.

Melissa and Jim arrived early to help as promised. The redhead swooped through the door, holding something in the crook of her arm. Distracted by a burning smell, Alexa called over her shoulder, "Hi. I just have to check this." With a sigh of relief, she determined the lasagna was fine. The burning smell was just spillover on the oven floor. Turning, Alexa wondered why Scout remained glued to Melissa's side.

"Meet Ansel." With a flourish, Melissa held out a small, white puppy.

Jim walked through the door and scratched Scout's ears. "Are you going to be a good dog with Ansel?"

Laughing, Alexa joined the group. "He's adorable. Look at that smooshed face. Is he a French bulldog?" She petted the little dog.

"Yep. A rescue dog. He's almost a year old and a real sweetheart. I just couldn't bear to leave him at home."

Jim rolled his eyes. "I predict Ansel will be going everywhere with her. Do you think Isabella allows dogs at yoga?"

Melissa laughed. "I don't see why not. Ansel can probably do a perfect Downward Facing Dog. Let's see how the big guy gets along with this little Frenchie." Melissa moved into the living room and placed the dog on the floor. Scout sniffed at Ansel and jumped back when the smaller dog rose to put his front paws on the mastiff's nose. Using caution, Scout approached Ansel again and licked the Frenchie's face."

The three humans broke into delighted laughter as the two dogs ran around the room. Scout was gentle with the puppy, which pattered ten steps for every one of the mastiff's strides.

Jim stayed in the living room to keep an eye on the dogs while Melissa helped Alexa in the kitchen. "Where's John?"

"His shift ends at six. I expected him by now." As Alexa lifted a stack of plates from the cupboard, the alarm on the lane rang twice. "That's probably him."

Melissa opened the silverware drawer. "Are you OK? I know you were still pretty sore on Tuesday and that's why you skipped yoga."

"I didn't want to tear the stitches. I should be back in maybe two weeks. My limp is gone. I just tweaked something that needed a few days to heal."

As they set the dining room table, Melissa gave her friend a long look. "I'm talking about more than your stitches here. What about your state of mind?"

Alexa laid down a plate. "I'm OK. I've been meditating every morning and evening. I'm still scared, but I can't imagine they'll come back here again. I just wish I knew why. Why would someone try to shoot me?"

Just then, John walked through the door, followed by Graham and Kate. Soon, Haley and her husband, Blair, had arrived. Tyrell straggled in alone a few minutes later. The puppy entertained everyone until Alexa served dinner.

When Kate mentioned the shooting, Alexa tried to cut off the conversation. She didn't want this entire group dwelling on the hot tub incident. "I finally connected with Mom and Dad, so I filled them in. But things have been uneventful for the rest of the week. I'm not going to go around looking over my shoulder every minute of the day. Next week, I'm going to be out of town for a couple of days, meeting with a client about a fracking case."

"Fracking." Jim raised his head. The big forest ranger had been putting away the lasagna at an astounding pace. "Where's this?"

"Tioga County, up near Mansfield. Why?"

"There have been some rumors about fracking around here. People are reporting some activity that they think is fracking-related in Michaux over near the Adams/Franklin County line. We're going to look for signs of illegal test activity."

Graham looked puzzled. "I know they're fracking all over Northern and Southwest Pennsylvania, but I've never heard that the Marcellus Shale extends down this far."

"They've been assessing this at the Chamber," Haley spoke up. "From the way I understand it, this area never qualified as first tier shale. But, now with the international climate talks, the industry wants to tap every available source. So they're doing some testing in the tri-county area. The Chamber likes the idea of new jobs but is worried about the impact on infrastructure and air quality."

Blair, an investment banker, added, "I'd like to see a cost analysis on the community benefit of fracking."

Tyrell pushed his plate away. "I'm skeptical about the benefits."

"All I know is fracking has destroyed the beauty of much of Tioga County." Alexa turned to Haley. "The Chamber should take a field trip up north to see the effects of fracking before they decide to sign on as cheerleaders. And look at the heath risks. My friend Jeannie's daughter could die from cancer that they think can be traced to the toxic chemicals used in fracking."

John pushed his plate away. "I can't say much, but we're looking into some illegal activity reported by private landowners." He shot Jim a cop look. "You and I should talk."

"There's a bill in the legislature to open up public lands to fracking. Word is it could pass this session." Alexa recoiled in horror at the vision of a fracking tower in the pristine Michaux State Forest adjoining her property. "It never occurred to me it could affect the public land here in Cumberland County."

Ansel put an end to the glum discussion when he trotted to the front door and whimpered. Melissa jumped up to take the dogs outside, and Alexa cleared the table. "Give me a few minutes to put everything away, and we'll have dessert. In the meantime, there's more wine," Alexa lifted a bottle of red. "And beer in the fridge. One of John's friends brought in a Vienna Lager from Devil's Backbone Brewery down in Virginia."

Kate stayed to help Alexa clean up while the rest of the crew wandered into the living room with their drinks. "Last one." Kate handed Alexa a plate for the dishwasher.

"Thanks for helping."

"That's what sisters-in-law are for." Kate put her arm around Alexa's shoulder. "I know you put on a brave face about your hot tub incident. But, Lexie, you must have been terrified. Promise that you'll be on guard."

"Don't worry. I'll be fine." Alexa stepped to the counter and folded the dish towel into a perfect square, wishing that she could feel as confident as she sounded. Not knowing who shot at her—and why—was a constant strain. She turned back to her sister-in-law with a smile. "I appreciate your concern, Kate. But, tonight, I just want to concentrate on having a good time."

When everyone had left for the evening, Alexa and John stretched out in the living room. "That was fun, but a lot of work."

Alexa laughed and rubbed Scout's ears. "And you've got a new little friend. You were such a good boy with him."

"Excellent lasagna." John patted his taut stomach. "I ate way too much."

"There's a lot left over. You can have some tomorrow night while I'm up north."

"Jim's news about possible fracking activity in Michaux is disturbing. He and I are going to check it out together next weekend. I have Saturday off."

"Speaking of fracking, I have to be out of here by eight tomorrow. I'm going to bed. Thanks for staying with Scout while I'm gone." Alexa rose.

A flicker of yearning passed across John's face. "You know how I feel about that. I'm ready to stay here as long as you like."

Alexa leaned over to give John a long kiss. "I know you're always here for me." She stopped on the bottom stair and exhaled a long breath. "I'm not looking forward to the next two days. This whole situation with Jeannie and her daughter. It is so damn sad."

CHAPTER SIXTEEN

March 30, 1979

This behavior projection is known as the China syndrome.
                              —*Nuclear Physicist Ralph E. Lapp*

Will froze, clutching the scrawled note from Ruth in his hand. He and Randi had to leave town before TMI melted down—but now she'd gone into labor and left for the hospital. His heart beat against his chest in painful thumps. For months he had looked forward to the joy of their child's birth. But now, Will felt only despair. If Brad was right, this hydrogen bubble at TMI could blow up any minute. Will didn't understand exactly what happened in a meltdown—other than what he'd seen in that movie, The China Syndrome. *His mind ran through the awful possibilities. What if the explosion killed Randi and the baby? What if they survived but were poisoned by radiation? Why hadn't he listened to Randi's mother and left two days ago? Why hadn't the government evacuated everyone in the area?*

Grabbing a pack of saltines and a soda from the refrigerator, Will rushed from the house. He stopped short at the car and came back up the sidewalk to lock the door. As he turned the key, he snorted with hysterical laughter. Why bother to lock the house when he and Randi may never make it back alive? Squaring his shoulders, Will dashed to the Thing and sped toward Harrisburg Hospital, only a few blocks away from the office he'd just fled.

Will had spiraled into full-blown panic mode by the time he reached the hospital. Driving well above the speed limit in his frantic trip into the city, he'd encountered little traffic in his direction. But the roads were packed with cars streaming out of town. Tumbling into the hospital lobby, he ran into a roadblock at the empty reception desk. He needed someone to tell him where he could find maternity.

He flew down the first floor hall and grabbed a passing nurse. "Ma'am, my wife's in labor. Where do I go?" Following her directions, he took an elevator to the right floor, tapping his foot at its glacial pace. The moment it came to a halt, Will threw his body through the opening doors.

When he skidded to a stop in front of the nurses' desk, an older woman in a white uniform looked up. "You must be Randi's husband?"

"Yes. How is she? Has the baby come yet?"

"Randi's in the delivery room right now. She was doing just fine when they wheeled her in there. These things take time. Why don't you find a seat in the waiting room? Unless you want to go into the delivery room? We do permit that now."

"No." Will shook his head. "Randi doesn't want me there. She said she didn't want me to see her like that."

The nurse smiled again. "We're a little short staffed. A lot of our employees have left the area with their families. But I'm here for the duration along with some other RNs. One of us will come and find you when it's time." She pointed toward an open doorway. "Your neighbor is still in there; the woman who brought Randi in earlier."

Deflated, Will just stood at the desk after the nurse hurried away. He'd rushed to the hospital, anxious to see his new child. Instead, he had to wait for the baby to arrive. Did that mean they still had time to flee Harrisburg? Will contemplated storming the delivery room and dragging Randi away before the baby came. "Don't be ridiculous," he muttered. "The baby could be here any minute."

With a feeling of incipient doom, Will wandered through the door into a waiting area. Ruth sat along the wall, alone in the sterile room. "Thank you for driving Randi into the hospital." Will seized the older woman's hands in his own.

"Child, that's no never mind to me. That was the arrangement all along. We knew you might be working when Randi went into labor. That girl called me late this morning and said we needed to get on the road. So I hustled over to your house right away. Like I said in the note, I tried to call but couldn't get through. Them contractions were coming pretty fast, so I bundled her into my car and drove lickety-split to the ER. They wheeled her up here right away."

"The nurse said she's in delivery right now."

"Lord willing, that child will meet his mama and papa real soon. You never know how long a first baby will take though."

"Ruth, I feel bad that you've been waiting here this long. With this TMI situation, you might want to head home now—or better yet, get out of town. Can you go stay with your son? Isn't he up in Reading now?"

The old woman looked up at Will and shook her head. The tight braids in her gray hair never moved. "Don't you worry about me. I heard they're evacuating pregnant women and children. And I see how you must be concerned that the baby's coming in the middle of all of this commotion. But the Lord works in mysterious ways, son."

Will lowered his voice and sat down next to her. "It might be worse than they're telling us. You know I work at DER. My friend heard from the NRC in Washington that the plant might be in real trouble."

Ruth patted Will's elbow. Then she leaned over and pulled up the support stockings she'd rolled down to her ankles. "I don't put much stock in rumors and whisper down the lane. But, now you're here, I think I will drive home. That fog this morning was something. It could start to roll off the river again in late afternoon. I hate driving when you can't see the other cars. My night vision's not what it used to be. So I'll say good-bye."

"Think about leaving the area. Call your son and talk to him. See what he says."

"I just might do that, Will. Thanks for your concern. But I'm in God's hands. And you've got a wife and a new baby to worry about. Call me when you get a chance and let me know if it's a girl or a boy. I know Randi's hankering for a girl. But the way she carried so low, it's gonna be a boy for certain."

Will chuckled. "That would make me happy. I've been rooting for a boy. Where's your car parked?" he asked as Ruth picked up her heavy purse and looped it over her elbow. "I can walk you down."

"Absolutely not. I'm perfectly fine on my own." She gave his arm a gentle nudge. "You need to be here to see that precious child the minute he's born."

Alone in the waiting room, Will watched the big, round clock on the wall. Each lurch of the minute hand felt like another dab of mortar sealing the door of his family's tomb. Will tried to concentrate on the good things, the anticipation of seeing his child for the first time. The baby they'd longed for would be here today. But, the clouds of anxiety and fear that had gathered with Brad's warning wouldn't disperse.

Walking to the window, Will looked down on the Susquehanna River across the street. The dark river flowed a little faster and higher than usual with the spring thaw. A slight mist rose from the swirling water. If he opened a window and tossed a stick into the water, it would float over the Dock Street Dam and straight to TMI. Will looked downstream in the direction of the cooling towers, one of which teetered on the brink of disaster. He couldn't see the nuclear facility from here, but this hospital was so close. Just about ten miles away. Well within the radius of contamination if radiation escaped the reactor. Well within the range of certain death if that hydrogen bubble blew.

With envy, Will watched a hawk soar over the dark river, flying upstream away from the towers. Even the birds were fleeing certain destruction.

A tension headache gnawed the back of his neck, just minutes away from roaring into a full-blown migraine. Will leaned his forehead against the cool windowpane in an effort to calm down.

"Mr. Armstrong?"

Will turned at the nurse's voice, the same woman who had spoken to him earlier.

"Congratulations. Randi asked me to bring you back to her room."

Will followed the nurse down a short hallway. "Is she OK? How's the baby?" His voice cracked on the questions.

"Mother and baby are doing fine." She opened the door to a room and smiled. "As you can see for yourself."

"Hello, Dad. This little guy would like to meet you." Randi beamed at Will as she held their newborn in the crook of her arm.

He kissed the baby on the forehead, then his wife on the mouth. "A boy?"

Randi nodded. "A boy. Walden Armstrong, meet your Daddy."

"Really? You're going along with the Walden?"

"As long as we can use my father's name for his middle name, Walden Anthony Armstrong."

An ecstatic Will replied, "Of course, honey. How are you? Was it terrible?"

"Yep. But it's over. And now we have this perfect little angel." Randi looked up from the bed. "He fell asleep already. Do you want to hold him?"

"Is it OK?"

"Of course it's OK. You better get used to it. We'll all be home in a few days. Although they made me sign a paper that said I could be sent home early due to staffing shortages or something.

Something to do with TMI. I hope they don't kick us out early. I'm so tired." Her voice faltered. "I need to just rest for a few days. "

Will didn't want to worry Randi, so he held his silence on the potential danger looming from TMI. His beautiful wife looked so fragile and worn. Heart sinking, he quashed any thought of bundling her and the baby in the car to leave town. Instead, Will cradled the newborn in his arms, supporting the head as he'd been taught in childbirth class. He marveled at the child's tiny size and gently lifted a hand to look at each miniature finger. "Walden, you are perfect." He gave Randi a long, loving look. "And your mother is too." The baby opened his eyes and stared at Will. "Do you want to go back to your mama? Here she is." Full of joy and dread, Will placed his son back in Randi's arms.

Later, the nurses moved Walden to the nursery down the hall so Randi could sleep. Will had called both Randi's parents and his own with the news of Walden's birth. He also reached Ruth, still at home. The friendly nurse, who seemed to be working an endless shift, told Will he could sleep in one of the many empty rooms in the delivery wing and arranged a tray of food for him. Exhausted, Will carried the hospital food to a waiting room farther down the hall and turned on the television, keeping the volume low.

The news did little to calm Will's fears. The local broadcast focused on the thousands of people who were evacuating the Harrisburg area. As Will watched the crowds escaping this coming disaster, he kicked himself again for not listening to Randi; for not fleeing earlier. She could have delivered the baby in a safe hospital up north where her parents lived. The local station showed a news clip of a man from the NRC, Harold Denton, who had flown into TMI from Washington to take charge of the crisis. The balding man told reporters that the White House was concerned the public wasn't getting full reports with hard data. Denton and his team were going to do their own inspection of TMI.

The national news devoted almost half of the show to the crisis. Will's body went cold at Walter Cronkite's opening statement. In a serious voice, the country's most famous newscaster said, "The world has never known a day quite like this. It faces the considerable uncertainties and dangers of the worst nuclear accident of the atomic age." He went on to warn, "It could get much worse. It is not an atomic explosion that is feared, the experts say that is impossible, but the specter was raised that perhaps the next most serious kind of nuclear catastrophe—a massive release of radioactivity."

What about the hydrogen bubble, Will wondered. Wouldn't that be an atomic explosion? Panicking yet again, he lost track of what Cronkite was saying until, "While it is not likely, the potential is there for the ultimate risk of a meltdown."

Will picked at the lump of red Jell-O on his tray while he watched the rest of the report. He shuddered when a doctor of environmental medicine talked about people already being exposed to radiation downwind from the plant. The doctor predicted an increase in cancer in the next twenty or thirty years.

He means right now, before the place melts down. Will closed his eyes and sighed. We'll all be lit up like Christmas trees.

Almost numb with fear and worry, Will pushed the Jell-O aside and shuffled down the hall to the nursery. The drab metal walls of the empty corridor closed around him like a tomb. Will thought they'd evacuated the hospital and left him and his family behind. He rushed down the hall in a panic.

"Is everything all right, sir?"

The nurse sitting outside the nursery snapped Will out of his terror. "I'm fine. I just came to see my son."

The young woman smiled. "Armstrong, right?"

"Right." Will's voice must have given away his puzzlement. He hadn't seen this nurse before, but she knew his name.

"We don't have that many patients this week. I've seen you around."

The nurse giggled as Will looked through the nursery window toward the cradle marked Armstrong. Although there were other occupied cradles, he hadn't seen other parents.

"I'll give you some privacy." The woman walked a few yards away to the nurses' station.

When he looked at Walden, lying swaddled in blue, Will's heart swelled to the breaking point with love. Then, remembering the danger right down the river, he choked on a bitter surge of fear. This boy had only lived for a few hours, and already, Will had failed him. By his inaction and trust in the powers that be, Will had put Randi and his child in unspeakable danger.

If his family survived the next few days, Will vowed never to trust the nuclear industry or the government again.

CHAPTER SEVENTEEN

THIS TIME, ALEXA enjoyed the drive to Tioga County. Departing late enough to miss the morning traffic meant she could take in the subtle signs of spring along the route. Buds kissed the tips of the trees. Fields glowed soft green with early growth. About an hour and a half north, spring's progress became more muted. She passed Williamsport, where the browns and grays of winter still ruled the landscape.

Nearing Granfeld, she followed the same route to Jeannie's house. When she reached the drilling site near the road, Alexa slowed. The frenzy of activity reminded her of swarming insects. Today, the tall drilling rig no longer hugged the edge of the roadway. In its place stood a huge crane. Metal piping dangled from the steel frame, a spinning proboscis piercing the earth below. The crane looked like a giant yellow mosquito, probing for blood beneath the earth's delicate skin. Alexa wondered what infection the mosquito's bite would leave behind. Tractor-trailer trucks, their beds stacked high with pipes, circled the crane like hulking cockroaches. Two crimson tank trucks lurched across the scarred land, their containers full and heavy like sated ticks. At the far end of the gravel-covered flat stood a pool of water. Instead of sparkling in the morning sunlight, the dull, lifeless pond seemed to seize the bright rays and drag them into its murky depths. Battling the feeling that insects were crawling over her skin, Alexa slammed her foot down on the gas and sped off.

When Alexa approached Jeannie's home, she smiled to see the branches of the weeping willows trailing wisps of pale green. The Demeter who'd planted the two magnificent trees must have chosen them as early harbingers of spring. Stepping from the Land Rover, Alexa stopped to watch a truck on the pad below, pumping the contents of a huge green metal container into its tank. Its mechanical whir followed Alexa as she walked onto the wide porch.

Jeannie answered the door and hugged Alexa. "Thanks so much for finding these lawyers and setting up the meetings. We couldn't have done it on our own." Alexa followed her friend into the warm kitchen, bright in the morning sun. Jeannie had taken care with her outfit for the afternoon's meetings. She wore a wide-skirted blue dress dotted with flowers, navy cardigan, and matching pumps.

"I wanted to meet with you in advance of the afternoon meetings so we could walk through all your questions and concerns. That way we'll be prepared for the discussion." Alexa dropped her notebook on the table. "Is Tom here?"

"No." Jeannie kept her voice bright but couldn't hide her exasperation. "I thought we'd have lunch here and then meet Tom in Wellsboro at one o'clock. He's showing a couple of houses this morning. With spring on the way, the real estate market is picking up. He didn't want to miss out on any potential clients. I took Tessa over to my mom's early this morning. She'll keep her until after the meetings."

"Fine. I guess you and Tom have talked through the details." Alexa kept her tone neutral to stifle her disdain for Jeannie's deadbeat husband. "His presence at the meetings is the important part."

"How about we eat while we work through your questions?" Jeannie took two bowls out of the cupboard. "I made vegetable beef soup and homemade bread. Is that OK with you?"

"Sounds delicious." Over lunch, Alexa asked, "How has Tessa been doing?"

Jeannie shook her head. "Not good. She's fading right before our eyes. Although she doesn't seem to be in much pain, she sleeps most of the time. Her appetite is spotty. Some of it's the illness; some is reaction to the treatment." Her eyes brimmed with tears. "But, despite everything, she's still got the sweetest disposition. The specialists at CHOP think she may respond successfully to the treatment. But she has to survive it first."

"I'm sorry, Jeannie. I can't imagine how tough this is on Tessa, not to mention you and Tom."

"It is what it is. We could use the money from this lawsuit to make sure we can pay for anything the insurance doesn't cover."

Alexa took a sip of iced tea. "I saw a tanker truck down below, pumping out one of those huge green structures. What's with that?"

Jeannie sighed. "Those are the saltwater tanks. When the gas is pumped out of the ground, it's warmed in that little structure to the left. The gas goes into the pipeline. But the water byproduct that's separated out by the warming gets stored in those tanks. The groundwater comes from so far down in the earth that it has high salt content. But there are other minerals and such in it." She paused. "I didn't hear the truck down there today. They're hard to miss in the summer, when we have the windows open. The pumps make a whirring sound, like giant mosquitoes—but, like mosquitoes, they usually come at night."

"I'm still trying to learn all the components of this fracking process. But it's complicated."

"I wish I'd learned more about it before we signed this lease." Jeannie shook her head in disgust. "Instead of finding out the hard way." She reached for a tablet. "So, Tom and I put together these questions like you asked."

The two sessions went well, considering. Tom arrived fifteen minutes late for the meeting with Friends of Pine Creek. Alexa apologized to the lead lawyer, Pedro Alvarez, as a surly Tom took a seat. "We're sorry that Mr. Demeter was detained."

"No problem. We'll just walk through the briefing on our class action suit again." Alvarez was very professional.

Alexa wondered how Tom could blow off even a few minutes of this meeting that could be so critical to his daughter's recovery, but she avoided his gaze. The session got back on track soon enough.

After the initial exchange of information, Jeannie said, "It sounds like your class action suit is focusing mainly on drinking water issues and other environmental impacts of fracking. The roads. Traffic. Wildlife. Air quality." She looked at her husband. "Tom and I have certainly experienced some of those things."

He jumped in. "Fucking-A. Our drinking water's shot to hell. It's high in manganese and iron. We have to get it tested all the time. Use filters so we can shower and do laundry. We only drink bottled water."

Jeannie interrupted, tears brimming in her eyes. "And when the pond with the fracking wastewater leaked, it probably ruined the land around it for decades. But our most pressing concern is our daughter's medical problem. When she and our poor dog got into that contaminated runoff, it killed the dog. Now this cancer is killing her. That's what we need immediate money for. The cancer treatment and expenses."

Alexa leaned forward. "Mr. Alvarez, Jeannie has a good point. Your class action suit seems to encompass some of the claims my clients could bring against Monongas. But not all. Do any of the other plaintiffs in the class have acute medical issues as serious as those of Tessa Demeter?"

Alvarez gave his two colleagues a questioning look before he responded. The woman on his left shook her head, a bleak expression on her face. "No. I believe your case is different from most of our plaintiffs in that your child's illness is immediate and life-threatening."

The bushy-haired man on his right, the local farmer who ran the Friends of Pine Creek, spoke in a confidential tone. "I know of two or three other families up here who have had tragic problems like yours. Maybe not the exact same thing. But things went so bad that someone got really sick or their land became uninhabitable. All those settlements are under—what do you call it?" He looked at Alvarez.

"Seal."

"Right, under seal. That's the deal they had to make with the gas company. But, all those families brought private lawsuits."

Alvarez nodded with a sober expression. "I believe your water and environmental issues fit our class definition. We'd be happy to have you sign on as plaintiffs with us. But you're probably better off pursuing your own legal action—and maybe wrapping all the other issues in with your daughter's medical claim."

"We are speaking to someone from Langley and Sloane in about an hour," Alexa offered while Jeannie dabbed at her eyes and Tom glowered.

"That's exactly who I planned to recommend. Although it's all supposed to be on the hush-hush, word travels. They've gotten good settlements for at least two families with problems on the scale of what you folks are dealing with."

The three representatives of the Friends of Pine Creek politely ushered them from the office. The woman, eyes moist, gave Jeannie a hug before they left. "I'll pray for your daughter."

The farmer spat, "They don't call it Mammon-gas for nothin'. I'm so sorry for what them bastards done to your little girl."

Jeannie raised an eyebrow in Alexa's direction at his surprising Biblical reference. Although the allusion to greed seemed to go over Tom's head, he nodded at the farmer's expression of sympathy.

The attorney Alvarez wished Jeannie and Tom good luck. To Alexa, he said, "Call if you decide to opt into our suit."

Out on the sidewalk, Alexa suggested coffee before the next meeting. Seated in the booth of a fading diner, she dipped her teabag into a cup of hot water and studied her clients. Jeannie looked sad, but Tom wore his usual cloak of anger. Alexa asked, "What do you think?"

"They made it pretty clear they didn't want the Demeters in their lawsuit, mucking it up with our daughter's problems." Tom slammed his coffee mug into the table.

"What? Tom, you always see the worst in a situation. They were giving their best advice about getting quicker results that deal with our main issue. Tessa's illness." Jeannie sighed and turned to Alexa. "Is that how you saw it?"

"I agree with Jeannie, Tom. It's not that they don't want you in the class action suit. They believe that an individual civil action will get you the best results. I'm going to withhold judgment until after the next meeting. But I'm inclined to agree."

The session with Don Langley convinced Alexa that representation from Langley and Sloane would be the best option for Jeannie and her family. He couldn't disclose any specifics of the earlier cases against Monongas, but Langley shared enough information to demonstrate his firm's success in similar lawsuits. Alexa sighed in relief when Jeannie and Tom agreed to have Langley and Sloane represent them. Even Tom managed a smile as he signed the papers.

When they left, Jeannie embraced Alexa with tears in her eyes. "I knew we should call you. We can't be sure yet just how this will turn out. But getting us hooked up with Langley and Sloane—now, at least, we have good lawyers and some hope for a good result."

Tom surprised Alexa when he shook her hand with a tearful smile. "Thanks for helping our little girl." He looked at this wife. "I'll go get the car and pick you up."

"Are you sure you won't come back to the house for dinner?" Jeannie asked after Tom loped down the street.

"No. I have an early morning with Representative Jordan for that tour of fracking operations. I have a hotel here in Wellsboro. You have to pick up Tessa at your mom's and get her home. The last thing you need is to worry about a dinner guest."

Tom's SUV pulled up at the curb. "OK. I'll let you off the hook. This time." Jeannie's laugh warmed the chilly afternoon. "Try the China Palace. I know you're crazy for Chinese food, and their fried rice is scrumptious."

Alexa watched Jeannie wave through the tinted window of Tom's vehicle as he pulled away. She exhaled a long sigh of salvation. No way she could have survived a whole evening with Tom. This afternoon had been enough.

Alexa glanced at her phone. Three thirty. Enough time to celebrate the day's success with a short hike.

Standing on the viewing platform at Leonard Harrison State Park, Alexa took in the vista of Pine Creek Gorge below. The dark evergreens stood out against the lighter greens and reds of the budding deciduous trees. Another few weeks and Pennsylvania's Grand Canyon would be even more gorgeous. Looking down the steep incline into the canyon, Alexa nixed the idea of tackling the difficult Turkey Trot trail. It was too late in the day to descend the whole way to the bottom of the gorge. Then she saw the trail sign: "Closed for the Season." Two earlier signs had indicated the campground and gift shop also were closed. Although a few cars were parked in the gravel lot, the area seemed deserted.

Wow. I've got this whole place to myself. Alexa couldn't believe her luck. She craved solitude after the day's emotional meetings. Smiling, she headed toward the one trail that appeared to be open.

At the Overlook Trail sign, Alexa noted several highlighted points of interest. She set out at a leisurely pace; the trail was only a half-mile. The first highlight, a moss-covered incinerator from Civilian Conservation Corps days, wasn't very exciting. Alexa slowed for a quick glance but kept walking until she reached the canyon rim. In the distance, gravel spluttered as a car entered the parking lot. Alexa hoped the passengers would be content with the view from the platform.

Following the rim of the canyon, Alexa stopped a few times to admire the stunning vista. Then, she came to a small wooden platform, marked Otter View, which cantilevered over the steep slope. Alexa loved the wooded, panoramic scene. She could imagine how great the view would be in summer and fall. For a few minutes, Alexa sat on the wooden bench built into the platform, luxuriating in the warmth of the late afternoon sun. With a rising breeze, the creak of exposed winter branches and the whistle of wind gusting through the canyon filled the air with a wild, joyful noise.

With reluctance, Alexa rose from the bench. Although she only had a short distance left on the loop, she didn't want to get caught out here after sundown. She went to the rail to take one last look at the plunging gorge below when she heard a rustle behind her. Two men dressed in brown Carhartt work boots and baseball hats with an MG monogram, stepped onto the narrow platform.

Despite the similar outfits, these guys couldn't pass as twins. The bearded, burly man looked much younger than his lean, middle-aged companion.

"Nice day for a walk." The younger man spoke with a smile while the other man moved toward the railing beside Alexa.

"Sure is." Feeling trapped, she took a step away from the older man who'd sidled next to her at the railing. He was looking at her, not the view. On alert, Alexa reached into her jacket pocket for her car keys, holding them with the pointed ends outward. The smiling younger man stepped forward, his hand reaching toward her. At that instant, Alexa leapt onto the bench and raced past him onto the trail. She sped back toward the main overlook, retracing her steps.

Behind her, one of the men yelled, "Come back, girly. We didn't mean to scare you."

The other remarked, "Jumpy little bitch, ain't she?"

Alexa didn't look over her shoulder until she reached the old incinerator. Stopping on the far side of the structure, she listened to hear if the men had followed. At the faint scuff of footsteps in the distance, she bolted. When she neared the parking area, Alexa approached with caution. The Land Rover stood next to the only other car, a beat-up pickup truck. She scurried to the Rover and pulled out the minute the vehicle's engine turned over. As she left the area, Alexa glanced in the rearview mirror. In the growing twilight, the two men were nowhere to be seen.

On the short drive to Wellsboro, Alexa wondered if she had overreacted. Maybe the men were harmless. Alexa had feared the young guy was going to grab her. Maybe he was just a friendly guy who wanted to shake her hand.

Her heart rate had returned to normal, but Alexa was still second-guessing her actions when she reached town. In the gathering darkness, gaslights flickered along streets lined with charming Victorian homes. Alexa had no problem finding the Chinese place Jeannie had mentioned. Carrying a bag of egg drop soup and General Tso's chicken with fried rice, she rushed into her room at the rustic lodge. Throwing the deadbolt across the frame, Alexa peered out the front window. No beat-up pickup trucks. Then she laughed and exclaimed, "Those guys probably think they ran into a madwoman out at Otter View."

After demolishing the Chinese food, Alexa climbed into bed and turned on the television. She found a movie she'd watched many times before, *Blood Diamond*. The African setting made her think of Reese, off in Kenya doing lion research. Her mind wandered to last summer's visit with her old boyfriend in

Samburu. Alexa regretted their decision to call it quits. But, Reese was a bit of an adventurer, like the movie's Danny Archer. He might never get Africa out of his blood and return to the States.

During a commercial, Alexa picked up a tourist newspaper from the nightstand. One of those things-to-do-in-Tioga County rags. She leafed through the pages until she noticed an advertisement from Representative Walt Jordan. Probably a community service thing. Her eyes traveled to the full-page ad on the opposite page, and she froze. A large logo with an intertwined M and G took up most of the page. Below it, the words "Monongas, a Better Fuel for a Better Future." The Chinese food congealed in Alexa's stomach. Maybe her first instincts at Otter View had been correct. The two men had been wearing baseball hats with the Monongas logo. Were they trying to scare her away from helping the Demeters?

CHAPTER EIGHTEEN

WALT JORDAN CRUISED into the parking lot of Alexa's hotel at nine o'clock, driving a dark gray Toyota Highlander SUV. His secretary had told Alexa this excursion would be casual dress. Still, she was glad to see the representative wore jeans too. She clambered into the SUV with her backpack, which contained water, a notebook, some granola bars, and her wallet.

"We've got a nice day for it, " the legislator said.

"A little chilly for April." Alexa pulled her lightweight down coat a little tighter. "Thanks again, Representative Jordan, for giving me this tour. You could have sent me out with one of your local staff."

"Let's get one thing straight right off the bat. If we are going to spend the day together, you have to call me Walt."

"Sure, Walt." Alexa was still wary. Was his regular-guy vibe real or an act? Either way, the man was gorgeous.

The representative extended his hand. Alexa accepted the handshake but began to blush when he cupped the other hand over hers. "I believe you're a valuable ally to have on our side. So, that's why I wanted to be the one to give you this tour. I've heard what you've done with your advocacy against human trafficking. I'd like you to lend some of that pizzazz to the fight against fracking."

Alexa shook her head and withdrew her hand. "My goal is to help my clients, not find a new cause. After yesterday, I believe I might have them squared away with the right attorneys. Thanks for your help. But when I wrap up this volunteer gig on the Human Trafficking Commission, I need to devote more time to my law practice."

Walt drove out of the parking lot, taking a left turn at the end of town. "If you're not going to fight fracking then why are you here?"

As she studied this appealing man's profile, Alexa searched for an answer. "I have to admit that nothing I've learned so far about fracking has been good."

"That's a start."

"And you helped me and my clients. I didn't want to decline your generous offer to educate me further about fracking." Alexa took a nervous gulp of air. Although they looked nothing alike, Walt's easy style reminded Alexa of Reese. And that made her nervous. She was involved with John.

Walt stopped the vehicle near the entrance to a wide dirt lane. Before he opened the door, he gave Alexa a long steady look. "I'm not sure generous is the word I'd use. I'm being upfront about my agenda. I want you." He paused. "On our side."

Alexa let out the breath she'd been holding. As she slid out her side of the SUV, she muttered, "And I bet you get almost everything you want."

Midway down the lane where they stood, a NO TRESSPASSING sign glared bright yellow in the sun. But the sign looked like a neon speck against the steel tower beyond it. The drilling structure stood in the middle of a huge raft of mobile homes, construction equipment, storage tanks, metal pipes, and more. Alexa's skin crawled, just like yesterday when she'd driven past that site along the road to Jeannie's house. This place too was a mound of activity. Motorized equipment and trucks scurried around the elevated drilling site like the carrion beetles she'd seen swarming an elephant carcass in Africa.

"I'm going to show you the various stages of the process. And then we're going to visit some of my constituents who have leased their land for fracking." Walt pointed toward the tower. "The first stage is to prep the land for all of this. A few weeks ago, that land was a field, just like that one over there." He pointed to a rolling field to the left of the site. "The company comes in, builds up the slope of the land to create a flat pad of earth, covers it in a layer of permeable material, then tops it with several inches of gravel."

Alexa scanned the adjoining acres of rolling, spring-green fields and brought her gaze back to the jarring jumble of metal structures perched on the dull slash of gravel. "Damn. Right in the midst of this beautiful farmland. How big is the area of the—you called it a pad?"

"Around five acres."

"Then what? This drilling? The fracking?"

"We're not at fracking yet. The drilling, which comes first, is a multi-step process. They need to drill through the layer of earth that contains the water supply and protect that with cement-encased steel tubing. Then, they use the same drilling rig to go deeper and drill down to the level where they'll be doing fracking." A big tanker truck came rumbling down the dirt lane. "These trucks are bringing out salt water."

"Jeannie mentioned salt water."

"Yeah. There's a layer of salt water down in the earth that needs to be pumped out before fracking can begin. They case it with cement and steel to protect the groundwater supply and to keep it from seeping into the fracking operation. But, even in the ongoing extraction, the salt water must be separated from the natural gas before the gas is piped out."

"Where are the ponds? The Demeters' daughter got into water from a pond with toxic chemicals in it." Alexa looked toward the pad, searching for a pool of water.

"Theirs must have been one of the early wells. In the first places drilled here in the county, Monongas placed a freshwater pond on site for the drilling process. They also created holding ponds for the salt water and the water that's used in the actual fracking process. They were mostly earthen ponds lined with rubber. Sometimes they leaked, like with the Demeters. DEP cited the company for all sorts of violations. So, now, they use a system of specialized trucks. Some do high pressure pumping of the necessary water, sand, and other chemicals for the different stages of the fracking process. Others haul away the liquid byproduct."

"That seems like a tacit acknowledgment of negligence."

"I'm sure the attorneys will raise that point in their arguments."

As they wound through the rural roads, Walt showed Alexa a complex process. At one site, they saw a wireline inserting steel tubing into the drilled well bore. She recognized this as the same activity she'd seen along the road the day before, the one she'd likened to a giant mosquito boring into the ground. At the next site, the buzzing of a motor made conversation difficult as the drilling rig bored through the shale.

"They dig down a mile and then out another mile at a ninety-degree angle?" Alexa shouted above the din. She pressed her foot down, thinking she felt vibration beneath her feet.

Walt noticed her foot and smiled. "You're probably imagining it." He leaned over and spoke into her ear. His lips were so close they touched her hair. "But, after the well is drilled and piped, they set off explosive charges in the horizontal section to perforate the pipes. People say their houses shake when they set off the charges from the perf gun." Walt explained that the actual fracking process then injected cracks in the shale with water and sand compound to open them up. "Then, the cracks become conduits for the gas to flow into the pipes and up to the surface pumping station."

They stopped at two completed sites, which looked a lot like the one at the Demeter farm. The flat pad that had been constructed for drilling remained. Now it housed a row of pipes and pumps in the center.

"Most sites have six to eight wells." Walt pointed at the eight pumps then moved his outstretched finger toward several metal structures at the edge of the pad. "The gas gets warmed over there in that shed. That separates out the salt water, which is then stored in one of these containers. He gestured at several large metal containers like the ones at Jeannie's farm. The actual gas goes into underground pipes that take it out of the area."

On a nearby hill, a swath of bare ground slashed through the forest like a gruesome scar. "Is that a gas line?"

"It's likely. They run beneath the surface all over the county."

"You want to stop for some coffee? This little place has a nice bakery." When Alexa nodded, Walt pulled the SUV into the parking lot next to the old diner. All the employees and customers seemed to know their representative. Walt called most of them by name as they found a booth.

"Tea, please. And a blueberry muffin," Alexa told the aging waitress with hair wound in gray plaits around her head. "All of these tunnels under the ground, even under some peoples' houses. It reminds me of this movie my brother, Graham, and I used to watch on TV when we were kids. These aliens lived in a tunnel outside a kid's house. It terrified me."

Walt burst into laughter. "*Invaders from Mars*. The one where they put these crystal things into his parents' heads and they changed, acting all weird, like human robots."

"Exactly. It's like Monongas put crystals into everyone's heads up here and got them to sign these awful leases."

"I have to admit I never pictured it quite like that. An alien invasion of Tioga County." Walt raised an eyebrow. "Can I use that in my speeches about fracking?"

"Wait a minute." Alexa twisted her face into a mock frown. "Let me see the back of your neck first."

When the waitress arrived with their drinks, Walt had his head angled to show Alexa he was crystal-free. Turning back, he almost knocked a coffee cup out of the woman's hand. After the server left, he joked, "You're a bad influence."

"Me?"

Walt replied in a husky voice as he gazed into her eyes. "I sort of like it."

Alexa stammered, afraid she was reading more into Walt's tone than he intended. "On a more serious note, I had no idea the fracking process was so complicated. I did some research when I agreed to help the Demeters. But, seeing it like this, it's amazing."

His gray eyes clouded. "That's not exactly the impression I'd hoped for."

"I'm talking about the technology, and the fact someone designed such a complex process. That doesn't mean I'm endorsing fracking. It's hideous. I can't imagine what it would do to your life to have all of that drilling and trucks and noise near your house. And what it does to the land is awful. How long does the process take before it becomes operational?"

"Depends. Usually a few months."

"Jeannie told me they ran night and day."

"Time is money for the companies. They want to get in and out. Start the gas flowing."

"And even when it becomes operational, they have a five-acre plot of pipes and sheds and containers on their property. I saw one of those water trucks coming in to empty a container at Jeannie's. I guess they put that in when they closed down the holding pond."

"Most of the pads are on slopes. It's so hilly up here. DER requires that the company put in a containment pond for water that spills off the pad. So, they still use ponds, but not for storage of the fracking water."

Alexa remembered the brackish pond she'd passed on her way to Jeannie's house. "It must cost the gas company a fortune to drill all these wells."

"I've heard it costs more than a million to come in and set one of these up. But the cost-benefit ratio must be immense. When the gas is flowing and the market is booming, it's like liquid money."

After the waitress brought their order, the conversation veered away from fracking. "Do I have it right that you used to practice law in New York City?" Walt asked.

"After college and law school at Columbia, I joined one of those giant firms in the city. When they put me on the partner track, I realized I just couldn't do it anymore. Too many hours. Too much infighting. No trees. So I fled the city and joined my family's practice with my dad and brother. I'm much happier now, living in a little cabin in the woods. Practicing general civil law."

"Sounds idyllic." He set his coffee cup on the table.

Alexa laughed and tore her gaze from the lean hands wrapped around the mug. "I wouldn't go that far. What's your story? What fueled your meteoric rise to become one of the most admired legislators in Harrisburg?"

"Like you said, I wouldn't go that far. How about I just give you the basics?" Walt continued without waiting for Alexa's response. "I spent most of my life here in Tioga County. Joined the Marines after high school. There wasn't much money for college, and I wanted to get far away from here. I could have gone to Mansfield or another state school, but I opted for seeing the world. Turns out I saw a lot of the worst places in the world as a Marine—but, hey, it wasn't Tioga County."

"Were you in combat?"

"I spent time in Somalia. When my tour ended, I decided I didn't want to spend my whole life in the military, so I went to college. I'd saved a good bit of money, took out some loans, and went to Penn State. By that time, I didn't care if I went to a state-related school or not. I just wanted a degree. Then I got into Dickinson Law. Came back home and joined the district attorney's office for a brief stint. Got political ambitions. Thought I could be the change in the world. I've been in the House for almost eight years now."

"What about the environmental thing? When did you get involved in that?"

"My first term in the House and the fracking boom hit around the same time. At first, most people looked at the gas leases as gifts from heaven. But, little by little, things happened, attitudes changed. I took up the cause, just like a modern-day Don Quixote." He punctuated his words with a sardonic grin.

"I don't think you're tilting at windmills, Walt. You're just trying to hold an industry accountable for the damage they've caused. Look at little Tessa Demeter."

Alexa felt a little flutter when Walt looked into her eyes and said, "Your support means a lot to me."

Following Walt out to the SUV, Alexa sighed. She had a boyfriend. Spending even a minute longer with this charismatic legislator spelled trouble with a capital T. But she couldn't leave. He'd arranged meetings with his constituents, and it would be rude to bail now.

Back on the road, Walt turned into a winding gravel lane that snaked through acres of fields. Most had been plowed under, ready for spring planting. They stopped beside a weathered farmhouse that hadn't seen a coat of paint for years. Across the drive, an old barn leaned into the hillside, its door hanging wide open. Two black and white dogs barked, wagging their tails as they approached Walt and Alexa.

The man of the house opened the door and welcomed them inside. "Howdy, Mr. Jordan. Miss. Come in and meet the missus."

They followed him through the entry room into a warm but faded kitchen. The wife rose from her chair and asked, "Can I get you something to drink? We have soda pop, or I can make coffee."

Walt smiled. "Mrs. Lowry. A Dr. Pepper would taste good, thanks."

Alexa followed his lead and asked for a Coke. Mrs. Lowry wore her iron gray hair in a pageboy with bangs, a style that reminded Alexa of photos of Mamie Eisenhower. In her late sixties at least, she wore a powder pink sweatshirt with a picture of puppies on the front. Mr. Lowry looked ill, his skin drawn tight and pale over the bones of his face.

"Thanks for letting me bring Ms. Williams to visit. I'm trying to give her an introduction to the impact fracking has had on all of us in Tioga County."

"Well, we could spend an entire day telling you about Monongas, but I'll try to keep it short." Mr. Lowry motioned for them all to sit at the kitchen table, then launched into a nervous monologue. "We signed on early, back in 2006. I had some health problems, and it was hard to pass up the money. They hired Dennis Roth's boy, Junior, to go around and pitch the leases. The boy did a good job; made it seem like we were earning money for doing nothing. Said they might not even decide to drill in our lifetime. We own fifty-five acres, so that offer of five hundred dollars an acre gave us more cash in hand than I'd ever seen at one time. We paid off most of the mortgage and put a little away for medical bills and such."

"We wish we'd known then what we know now," Mrs. Lowry said in a gloomy voice.

"They set up the drilling operation within months of signing the lease. What a trial."

"Your drilling site is up above the barn, right?" Walt interjected.

"I'll show you when you leave out of here," the husband said. "Lord, I never saw such a commotion as when those people came on our land to drill. Night and day. Our four dairy cows turned restless and didn't give good milk. Mother and I couldn't get a good night's sleep."

Alexa studied the couple as they described their experience. In many ways, their account echoed Jeannie's fracking story. But these two looked like their losses to fracking had sucked out their very vitality.

"We could live with the drilling because we knew it would end. We could deal with the loss of five good acres of farmland. Hell—oh, excuse me, miss. Heck, we could even live knowing we had them pipes down below the house and the fields, snaking out in every direction. But, when the water turned, that was the last straw."

The Lowrys went on to tell a tale of a contaminated well, relying on bottled water, and struggles with the gas company to get them to install the right filters to make the well water usable. "We had to sell the cows. Couldn't risk them drinking contaminated water. We use it to bathe and for laundry but stick to the bottled water for drinking and cooking."

"Lately," Mrs. Lowry said. "We've had to fight the company tooth and nail for every new filter. They don't pay for the bottled water anymore. That man from the company says the problem has been fixed. Fixed my ass."

Walt rose from the table, bringing the discussion to an end. "Thanks so much for taking the time to meet with us. Any questions, Alexa?"

"What can you do about the water situation?" She looked at the aging couple.

"We joined onto that Pine Creek lawsuit," the husband replied. "I don't usually have no truck with Mexicans. A lot of them have been part of the pipeline crews. Speaking Spanish everywhere you go. But that Alvarez, the lawyer. He seems like the right sort. We're hoping he gets the gas company to accept responsibility. And gets us some money for our water situation."

As they left the farmhouse, Walt pointed out the fracking pad on the hill above the barn behind a narrow band of trees. Alexa had missed it earlier. "I bet that's noisy in the summer with the windows open, especially when they come in to drain the tanks."

Walt took Alexa to two more homes, and they listened to two more stories similar to the Lowrys' tale. One woman's field had washed out, ruining a viable crop of feed corn, because the company had messed up when it constructed the containment pond.

Another family had leased their gas rights but refused to allow drill sites on their property in an attempt to avoid damage from fracking. Alexa had been surprised to learn that this type of lease permitted the drilling bores to extend into the family's land. Even though they had no pad and pumping station on their property, their water became contaminated with manganese and methane after their closest neighbor's land was fracked.

As they drove away from the last visit, Alexa turned to Walt. "This has been a depressing day."

"I'm going to show you the other side of fracking. But we could spend a week visiting folks who've been harmed or disappointed by Monongas. And we still wouldn't cover them all."

Alexa slumped into the seat, overwhelmed. She shook her head in disgust. Fracking was less like a Martian invasion and more like a termite infestation. The termites had bored into Tioga County, undermining the foundation. Any day now, they might swarm to a new location, leaving behind a scarred landscape and collapsed lives that would take years, if ever, to restore.

CHAPTER NINETEEN

OVER A LATE LUNCH, Walt expressed his frustration. "I'm sure you picked up on the pattern. It's the same old story. The gas company addresses the concern right after an incident that affects the family's water or land. They pay for water or filters or restoration. But they don't fix the root cause. So the problems continue, but the company becomes less and less responsive. They don't return calls. They stop sending money or supplies. To make it worse, these days, the company is scaling back their pumping levels because of the lower market price for natural gas. That means the landowners' royalty checks are shrinking.

"How much do they get in royalties?"

"It varies. But one guy just told me that he received ten thousand dollar checks each month right after they drilled the first wells. The initial gas pressure was high. They really pump it out at first. About a half a year into it, things took a turn for the worse. Each month his royalty dropped. Last month, he got less than two hundred bucks. And this guy has a decent amount of acreage."

Alexa toyed with her salad. "All these people are dealing with major problems with no apparent solution—unless this class action suit gets some results. When do their leases expire? Maybe if the fracking stops the groundwater will be restored?"

Walt shook his head. "There are a few rare exceptions, but nearly all of these leases last in perpetuity. Apart from the class action suit, the best hope for these landowners is that Monongas shuts down the wells on their property. Some of them aren't pumping right now, but I don't know of any that have actually been disassembled."

"That sort of puts a crimp in your resale value, I imagine."

"People do sell. But you're right. It can be more difficult." Walt dipped a french fry in ketchup. "But I want to give you the whole picture. In other cases, having a gas lease on the land makes it more valuable. If there are no water or other problems, buyers like the idea of a royalty check coming in each month. And there are many of my constituents, especially the ones with a lot of acreage, who've gotten rich from fracking leases. We're going to visit one of those folks after lunch. And the local economy has benefitted from fracking."

"Jobs?"

"The companies bring a lot of people in from out of state to do the drilling, but local folks have been hired by the trucking companies and other support systems. The drillers need places to live, buy goods and services, and so forth. The companies have improved some of the roads to make them passable for the big trucks. It's a real mixed bag. A lot of people have seen real economic benefit."

"It sounds like Monongas wields a lot of power around here." Alexa leaned toward Walt and lowered her voice. "Do your anti-fracking activities in Harrisburg piss them off?"

He grinned. "Absolutely. They funded a candidate to run against me last year. Tioga County had never seen such fancy television ads. Lucky for me, the people didn't like Monongas trying to interfere in local politics. You know the House runs every two years, so I've got another campaign coming up real soon. Who knows how I'll fare?"

Yesterday afternoon at the canyon flashed into her mind. "Has the company ever threatened you?"

Walt's expression darkened. "You mean a physical threat or something like that? I'd like to see them try." After a moment's pause, he gave her a searching look. "Why do you ask?"

Alexa described what happened at the overlook with the two men wearing Monongas hats. "I might have overreacted. But I picked up a vibe that made me very uneasy."

"Some of these site bosses have been known to run roughshod over landowners, but why would someone from Monongas threaten you?"

"Because of Jeannie's lawsuit? Because I'm spending the day learning from the Master of Anti-fracking? I don't know—just a feeling I had." Alexa shredded the paper from her straw as she talked.

"Do you want to report it to the police? We could swing by there on the way to our next stop."

"No. They didn't assault me. They barely touched me. And I'm heading out of town tonight." Alexa decided again she had overreacted to the two men. Still jumpy from being attacked in her hot tub, she was seeing menace everywhere. Walt's voice drew her out of her thoughts.

"Tonight? Stay the night and come over for dinner." Walt's expression was shuttered. "I'd like you to meet my wife and kids."

At the mention of a wife and family, Alexa went still, surprised at the intensity of her disappointment. Married? Of course he was married—a fortyish politician. But why hadn't the subject come up? Why hadn't she asked? Overcome with guilt at the schoolgirl crush she'd developed on this man, Alexa stole a quick look at his left hand. It was bare. At least she hadn't missed a ring. She felt foolish, deflated, and relieved—all at the same time.

Alexa struggled to keep her tone neutral as she replied, "What a lovely offer, but I have to get back tonight. I have a full schedule tomorrow. This next visit is the last on the tour, right?"

"Right. Just let me text Sandy to let her know you won't be coming over for dinner."

Alexa couldn't decide if Walt looked disappointed or relieved as he texted his wife. Gazing out the window, Alexa sighed in silent self-recrimination. A married man. With kids. And you're involved with John. What ever were you thinking?

"So this is the fair and balanced part of the tour," Walt said as he turned into another driveway. "Marjorie Bannon is very pleased with fracking. I wanted you to hear her point of view."

Marjorie welcomed them into her living room, gushing over Walt. "All the ladies in the church auxiliary always say we've got the most handsome representative in Pennsylvania." She looked Alexa up and down. "Aren't you a pretty little thing."

"We don't want to take up much of your time," Walt said. "But I hope you'll share your thoughts about Monongas with Ms. Williams. I'm helping her learn more about fracking here in the county."

"Of course. I told your girl in the office I'd be happy to help." She leaned toward Alexa and confided. "When my Ronald passed, he left me with this huge old farm and very little cash. I couldn't carry on with the farm. My only option looked like selling the place and moving into an apartment in Wellsboro. Or find one of those retirement communities with all the other blue-haired ladies." She fluffed her lavender-rinsed hair with a bejeweled hand. "But I love this old house. It's where Ronald and I spent fifty years of wedded bliss. And where my two kids were born."

She picked up a family picture from the end table and handed it to Alexa. "Ronald, Ronald Jr., and Shirley."

"Lovely family."

Marjorie continued. "Then Monongas came along with the answer to my prayers. My land sat right in the middle of five other plots of land they'd leased. They needed my hundred and fifty acres to complete their plans. So I leased the whole lot to them for twenty-five hundred an acre. They drilled out on the far corner of the property, beyond the woods. I don't even know they're there."

"So you've had no negative effects from the fracking operations?" Alexa asked.

"Negative effects?" Marjorie scoffed. "My dear, between the initial lease and the little bit I get each month from royalties, I have enough money to live on for the rest of my life. I go to Florida in the winters. And, unless I live past one hundred, my kids will get a nice, tidy inheritance. Except for marrying Ronald and having our babies, Monongas is the best thing that ever happened to me." She looked at Walt. "Would you like some coffee or tea?"

"No, Marjorie. Thank you, but Ms. Williams has a long drive ahead of her."

On the drive back, Walt told Alexa, "Marjorie pretty much summed up the pro-fracking point of view. There are a significant number of families who support it. They think the infusion of money into the area outweighs the negative effects. I'd say there are more people against fracking than for. But a lot depends on people's priorities and their experiences."

"So fracking hasn't impacted everyone's water quality? Or had other negative effects?"

"No. And there are studies out there that say fracking doesn't affect water quality."

"But how do they account for what's happened?"

"They say a lot of these elements occur naturally in this part of the country. And that the water would be affected even if fracking didn't exist."

"But you don't buy it?"

"I don't. And a few more recent studies seem to confirm that fracking can affect water quality." Walt pulled up to the curb behind Alexa's Land Rover.

She turned, hand on the door. "I really appreciate you spending the entire day with me, showing me fracking," Alexa smiled, "from the ground up. It will help me better advise Jeannie. You've gone above and beyond."

"I enjoyed the day. It helps me to touch base with constituents every once in a while, to remind me why fighting fracking is so important." Walt handed Alexa the cell phone she'd left on the seat.

For a moment, their hands touched as Alexa took the phone. Frozen, they looked at each other in silence. Sinking into his gray eyes, Alexa had no doubt she and this man both felt the connection. The sizzle had been there from the moment she'd walked into his office at the Capitol. Then, Alexa collected her wits and pulled the cell phone from Walt's hand, scrambling out of the car. She leaned back in. "I forgot to ask. Did you lease your land to Monongas?"

"No. When I inherited land from my mother a few years back, Monongas put on a full court press for the lease. She'd been too sick to deal with them, but they made another run at me. I told them to pound sand."

CHAPTER TWENTY

RUSHING UP THE Capitol steps, Alexa couldn't help but rejoice. This would be the last meeting of the Human Trafficking Commission. The commission's work had been important. She'd seen some of the lives laid to waste by trafficking and wanted it to end. One way was to make sure the Commonwealth's laws reflected the latest tools to prosecute traffickers and aid their victims. But she just wasn't cut out for politics and wrangling large groups of intense people.

When she reached Senator Gabler's offices, Lauren greeted Alexa. "As usual, Keisha's tied up. I have all the copies of the reports and a brief agenda. Why don't we go into the senator's office? He's on the floor of the Senate."

Seated on the senator's couch, Alexa leafed through the final report and then ran an eye over the agenda. "Looks fine to me."

"Good. It's been exciting working on this project." Lauren summoned a diffident smile.

"I want to thank you for the great job you did on this report. Of course, the committee set the direction. And Keisha and I were involved in the final product. But I know you did the bulk of the writing." Alexa paused. "Your internship ends pretty soon, right?"

"In two weeks. I have to do a written summary of my experience to get full credit. I'm moving out of my apartment the last day of April and will finish my summary at home." Lauren's expression became serious. "I want to tell you, Alexa, that I really admire you. I've learned a lot from you."

"Thank you, Lauren. If you need a letter of recommendation for grad school or a job, just let me know."

The intern leaned in from her chair next to Alexa. "I need your advice on something. That man, the one in the kitchen that day."

Alexa nodded.

Lauren's voice quavered. "There's something going on. Not just the kitchen thing. Something bigger and maybe illegal. Keisha's up—" The girl broke off when the door opened. "Oh, hi, Keisha."

"Did I hear my name?" Keisha asked as she strode into the room.

"Yeah, I was just telling Alexa that you like the final report."

Alexa played along. She knew Keisha had advised Lauren not to rock the boat by reporting the earlier kitchen incident. Perhaps Lauren didn't trust her boss with this new issue. "I agree. Despite the commission ending early, this report captures the key points we wanted to make. Another few months of meetings would have made little difference."

"I, for one, am just glad to get this off my plate." Keisha's tone bordered on disdain. "Senator Gabler has me spending all my time on energy issues these days."

Lauren seemed to have recovered her usual good spirits. "News flash. Did you hear? Keisha has been named executive director of the Energy and Environmental Committee."

"Congratulations." Alexa kept her tone positive. But she couldn't help but remember Keisha plotting this exact scenario the night that Senator Martinelli died at their feet.

Keisha looked at her watch. "We better book. It's ten till. Oh, I forgot. Alexa, Senator Gabler has to brief leadership on an energy matter. He won't make the commission meeting. He asked me to convey his thanks for chairing the group."

The commission meeting went better than Alexa expected. The members voted unanimously to endorse the final report. It seemed like everyone was just going through the motions; the session lasted less than an hour.

When the meeting ended, Alexa looked for Lauren. She wanted to hear what the intern had been about to confide in Senator Gabler's office. But a procession of commission members came forward to thank her for chairing the group. By the time the room had emptied, Lauren and Keisha had both disappeared.

Alexa took the elevator back up to the senator's office. "Is Lauren here?" she asked the receptionist.

She buzzed Lauren on the phone. "No one's answering. Maybe she went to lunch."

"Can you ask her to call me?" Alexa placed her card on the desk.

"Sure, Ms. Williams."

Leaving the office, Alexa decided to grab a sandwich in the cafeteria before she drove back to Carlisle. On the escalator down to the East Wing of the Capitol, Alexa caught sight of Keisha standing just outside the cafeteria, deep in conversation with two men. Alexa recognized them both. They were the guys from that lobbying firm—what was the name? Toland. The fortyish, no-neck guy, Nason Kurtz; and his boss, Walker Toland. She was surprised to see Keisha talking to them. When she'd pointed them out to Alexa at Senator Martinelli's memorial service, the staffer had sounded impressed by their power in Harrisburg but had spoken with a mocking undertone. Alexa had gotten the impression she didn't really know them except by reputation. And that she didn't much respect either one.

Yet, here she was, a few weeks later, thick as thieves with the powerful lobbyists. Then it hit Alexa. Of course. The lobbyists represented energy interests, and Keisha now served as executive director of the committee that controlled Senate energy policy.

She studied the no-neck lobbyist, Nason Kurtz. The arrogant ass who'd reamed out Lauren in the kitchen that day. What a big man, throwing his weight around with a college junior. Alexa curled her lip in disgust.

As she stepped onto the marble floor, Keisha looked straight at Alexa, then glanced away. The three split up. Keisha darted into the cafeteria. The two men sauntered into an adjacent corridor. By the time Alexa emerged into the cafeteria courtyard with her sandwich, Keisha was long gone.

While she finished her lunch, Alexa ran through her emails and made a few notes for a client meeting later that afternoon. But, her mind kept straying to the unfinished conversation with Lauren. Perhaps the intern had decided to report this asshole for that day he went off on her in the kitchen. Or maybe he'd acted the same way with another young staffer? But, Alexa sensed that, during today's earlier conversation, Lauren was speaking about something different. And the word she'd used, "illegal," had an ominous ring. Even more baffling was the way Lauren broke off and changed the subject when Keisha entered the room.

CHAPTER TWENTY-ONE

"OM MANI PADME HUM."

Bundled up against the morning chill, Alexa sat cross-legged in a spot of sunshine on the front deck. She hadn't slept well, besieged by jumbled thoughts of Senator Martinelli's death, the sound of that bullet hitting the hot tub cover behind her head, and Walt Jordan's deep voice talking about fracking. After a few hours of fitful sleep, she'd awakened to bright sunshine, Reese's name on her lips, and a fading dream of their last time together on safari in Samburu.

So, this morning, Alexa searched for inner peace through meditation and chanting. She regretted that she'd let her meditation practice slip in recent months.

Scout, snuggled against her knee, jumped to his feet and looked down the lane, tail wagging. Alexa broke off the mantra when the vehicle arrived a few seconds later. She rose and greeted John as he emerged from his car.

"Good morning, sugarcakes. Great day to be out in the woods, even if it's on a hunt for illegal testing." John kissed Alexa's cheek and patted Scout's head. "I brought some stuff for sandwiches in case we wanted to pack a lunch."

Alexa grabbed the cushion she'd been using and followed John into the cabin. "Where are we going to search?"

"Jim and I want to start up on Big Flat and search from there on the dirt roads. We put together a plan the other evening at that fly-tying workshop."

"Melissa and Jim should be here soon. Let me run upstairs and change."

When Alexa came back downstairs, Scout was chasing the French bulldog puppy, Ansel, around the living room. John,

Melissa, and Jim were in the kitchen making sandwiches. "That looks like enough food for a week."

"I was a Girl Scout. Be prepared." Melissa laughed. "What if we get stranded out there in the wilds?"

Jim raised an eyebrow. "You mean the vast, untamed wilderness where I work every day?"

"Exactly." His girlfriend shook her head in emphasis, auburn hair bouncing.

Ten minutes later the group, including dogs, climbed into Jim's big SUV and hit the road. Alexa felt her spirits climb as they drove the mountain roads. "Look at the daffodils." She pointed to a bank of yellow flowers gleaming in the late morning sun.

"I arranged to meet a guy up on Big Flat to hear about suspicious activity he reported. He does trail rides once or twice a week, usually from Big Flat. Said he passed a big utility truck on some roads that are closed to traffic," Jim announced. "He agreed to meet us at the end of his ride today."

Melissa asked, "Did this horse guy talk to the people in the trucks?"

"I don't think so. He said he decided to give them a wide berth. That they 'looked up to no good.' John and I want to question him and get more details."

"Most of the reports of unusual traffic come from the Adams County side of the forest, right?" John asked.

"Yes. That makes it a little more difficult to deal with. There are still a number of private holdings that jut into state land. The border's not straight like in Cumberland County. So we need to be careful we're investigating within Michaux State Forest and not trespassing on private land." Jim slowed as three deer crossed the road ahead.

"Where were the explosions?" Melissa asked.

Alexa hadn't fully tuned into the conversation until Melissa's question caught her attention. "Explosions?"

"Didn't I tell you about that, sugarcakes?" John's excitement showed. "A couple of Appalachian Trail through-hikers reported they felt the ground shake. They told the park people when they reached Pine Grove Furnace. One of Jim's ranger buddies interviewed them while they were downing the ritual gallon of ice cream at the General Store."

"Where were they when they felt the explosions? Could it have been construction?" Alexa leaned forward toward Jim and John in the front seats.

"That's doubtful. They were a little hazy on the details, but it was somewhere between the Birch Run Shelter and Dead Woman

Hollow Road. There wouldn't be much construction up there," Jim replied.

"Why are explosions significant?" Alexa knew she was slipping into courtroom mode.

"I can't explain the whole thing, but the fracking companies place devices that measure seismic activity at various locations. Then they set off an explosion. The seismic activity from the explosion lets them find the best place to frack." Jim laughed. "Norman Tanner, one of the rangers, has a degree in geology. He explained the details last night, but only part of it stuck. Main thing—we look for marks of explosions or these measuring devices. That gives us evidence of testing."

"After what I saw up in Tioga County earlier this week, just the thought of fracking here in Michaux makes me sick. I took some photos with my phone. I'll show them to you over lunch." Alexa sat back against the cushions as everyone became silent. Sensing her distress, Scout edged forward and hung his head over the back of Alexa's seat.

A few hours later, Jim pulled into an old logging road. After lurching along for a mile or so, Jim stopped the truck. "Look at that old deer trail. Doesn't it look like there's been some foot traffic there?"

Everyone climbed out of the SUV and watched Jim stride around the area, looking at branches and tracks on the ground.

Melissa grinned. "So, what's the story, Natty Bumpo? Has a war party been through here?"

Alexa laughed. "I loved *Last of the Mohicans*. The movie more than the book. I hope Magua's not out here somewhere. That guy was one sick dude."

"This is serious business," John admonished. "But, we don't expect to actually find any of these fracking people today. If we did, we wouldn't have brought you two and the dogs along. We're just searching for signs they've been here."

Jim, who had ignored the entire conversation, returned to the group. "It looks like there has been some foot traffic down that animal trail. It's worth a hike to check it out."

Melissa declared, "I'm not sure Ansel is up to a real hike yet. I'm just going to hang out here. Take some photos of that stream over there."

John looked at Alexa who said, "Scout and I will stay with Melissa."

"Don't forget, she's still recovering from a serious wound, with stitches in her shoulder," Melissa teased.

"I barely notice it. The stitches have dissolved," Alexa whispered.

The two men headed up the trail. When the path crested the top of the ridge, they disappeared from sight. Alexa and Melissa made their way down a gentle slope to the burbling mountain stream. Scout found a sandy spot and waded into the cold water for a drink. More cautious, the puppy stopped at the edge to lap up some water. Melissa snapped photos of the dogs and then wandered upstream to take some more serious photos. "I'm working on landscapes and nature shots now as a counterpoint to the people photos I've been doing for so long," she told Alexa. "It's refreshing, really. There's a lot less misery in landscapes."

"Wait until you see my fracking shots. There's a whole lot of misery in those. It's made me think about adding solar panels to the roof of the cabin."

"Do you get enough light?"

"I'll have the professionals give me an opinion. But I'd really like to wean my energy consumption away from fossil fuels if I can. The fracking tour was an eye-opener."

"You said some bigwig took you on the tour?" Melissa asked as she scanned through the photos she'd taken.

"A representative from Tioga County, Walt Jordan. He's a great guy, not at all the image of a typical politician. He's leading the fight against fracking in state parks. I believe he'll ultimately work to ban all new fracking, like they've done in New York State. I really admire him."

Melissa looked up from her camera. "You admire him?" She emphasized the word admire. "Alexa, what's going on here? That sounded just like senior year when you told Haley and me how you loved Paulo's Spanish accent. What aren't you telling me about this Walt Jordan?"

Alexa winced. "That he's married with two kids."

"WTF, Alexa. You're involved with a married man?"

"I thought you gave up swearing."

"I have. You didn't hear me say fuck, did you? I'm transitioning. Nice try, but you're not going to get me off track, counselor." Melissa sat on a big rock. "What's with you and this married politician?"

"Nothing, really."

Melissa tilted her head and waited for Alexa to continue.

"Well, if he wasn't married, there could be. He's gorgeous, charismatic, and I truly think he's one of the good ones. But I'd never have anything to do with a married man, Melissa."

"Then what's going on?"

"It's John. Or, more accurately, me and John."

"The man's a sweetheart, and he's crazy about you." Melissa's words were matter of fact.

"All that's true. Trust me, I want to be crazy about him. And I just can't. He just too frigging nice. With John, what you see is what you get."

"That's not so bad. John's one of the truly nice guys, not to mention stalwart, brave, steadfast."

"I care for him a lot, but I'm never going to give him my heart. And, I suspect, down deep, he knows. The more I push him away, the harder he pressures me to commit. He wants me to visit his family. He wants to move in." Alexa squeezed onto the rock next to Melissa. "I just can't do it." Her voice dropped. "I've been dreaming of Reese."

The two women sat in silence for a moment watching the dogs. Scout had tired and now stretched out on the forest floor. The French bulldog tugged at the mastiff's ear, trying to get him to play.

"Reese is in Africa, Lexie, and he might never come back. The two of you agreed to end the relationship when you visited him in Kenya. Are you sure this dream of Reese, a man you'll probably never have, isn't what's keeping you from John? And trying to blow up the relationship by running after a married man? None of it makes any sense. Damn, girl. You may need therapy if you can't get your act together."

"Let me say it one more time, Ann Landers. I am not running after a married man. But I can't deny I'm attracted to him. Just knowing I could so easily be drawn to another man—that confirmed what I already knew, deep down. I like John. He's good. He's kind. He's cute and great company. He's always there for me."

"Damn, Alexa. You sound like you're describing your dog, not your boyfriend.

"I know. He's everything I should want. That's why I feel like such a shit for breaking it off."

Melissa walked over to Ansel and picked him up. "Leave Scout alone for a few minutes, shrimp." She came back to Alexa. "So you're really serious. It's over?"

"I've been coming to this decision for a while. But my mind's made up. I need to do it before I say something I'll regret. I want to part on good terms. But every time he calls me sugarcakes, I want to scream." Alexa shook her head.

"When are you going tell him?"

"I don't know. Soon. I'm sort of waiting for the right time."

"Is that fair to John? Waiting, I mean."

"Probably not. I'm just a coward." Alexa rose, her expression strained.

"Suck it up and tell him. Don't wait," Melissa advised.

"I am such a disaster when it comes to men. When I want them, they don't want me or they're taken. If they're really into me, that turns me off. And the rest turn out to be psychopaths and deviants."

Still holding her Frenchie, Melissa comforted Alexa with a one-armed hug and murmured in her ear, "You are a disaster. But I love you anyway."

Giggling, the two old friends broke apart. Scout rose and trotted over to check out the joke.

"I'm thirsty. Let's go back to the car for a drink," Alexa suggested. Melissa put Ansel down on the ground to scamper behind them on their hike up the hill.

Soon after, Jim and John came walking back down the trail. As they approached, Melissa muttered, "Talk about awkward. Now that I know, every time I look at John, I'll wonder when you're going to dump him."

Alexa's reply had a sharp edge. "For God's sake, Melissa. It's a secret, so don't say a thing. Don't tell Jim. For sure, it won't be this afternoon. And he'll still be a friend."

"I'm not so sure about that, sugarcakes," Melissa murmured.

"Did you find anything?" Alexa turned her back on Melissa and yelled to the two men.

When they reached the SUV, the guys buzzed with excitement. John waved his hand toward the hill. "We're pretty sure this is one of the sites. There's some equipment attached to bags, maybe sand bags. We took some pictures on our phones." He passed his cell phone to Alexa and Melissa. "And we got the GPS coordinates."

Jim scrolled through his phone, looking at his photos. "We have to do the research to see if these things are seismic monitors. And to verify this is state forest land. Then we can set up surveillance to get whoever comes back to claim it."

"What about setting up one of those remote cameras they use to track wild animal activities? I saw this TV show about tigers in Nepal where they used them," Melissa suggested.

Jim reached into the cooler for a soft drink. "Not a bad idea. John, a drink?"

"Water, please."

Alexa asked. "Did you see any markings to indicate the company?"

"Just the manufacturer name for the monitor. That might help us track down the owner of the equipment. But we need to make sure we're on solid ground before we proceed." John threw his backpack into the SUV.

"That guy with the horses really helped us narrow the search area," Jim said.

John laughed. "He did. But I would have driven around these dirt roads all day and never have spotted that animal trail. You really are the last of the Mohicans, man."

The group piled back into the SUV and headed toward Route 233.

"What do you think is going on? One of these natural gas companies is trying to get a jump on the competition, right?" Melissa asked.

Alexa leaned forward. "Right. Someone's hedging their bets that this legislation will pass and let them drill on state land. If they have everything mapped out in advance, that gives them an advantage in leasing the gas rights."

As they approached Alexa's cabin, John and Jim discussed their next steps. John said, "Let me talk to the corporal, and you talk to your people. I'd like to come back out here with a team. Maybe next week. And nail these bastards."

CHAPTER TWENTY-TWO

March 31 -April 2, 1979

I Survived Three Mile Island . . . I Think.
    —*T-shirts sold after the Three Mile Island incident*

Randi spent her weekend in the maternity ward in a cocoon of bliss, cuddling little Walden and learning how to feed, bathe, and change him. Will had spent the entire time on tenterhooks, devouring every announcement about the situation at Three Mile Island.

The crisis with the hydrogen bubble had continued throughout the day on Saturday. At a morning press conference, a Met-Ed spokesman assured reporters that they'd reduced the bubble and it was no longer dangerous. Only minutes later, the NRC guy, Harold Denton said the danger was still significant. When Will drove home to shower and change, he turned on the radio to hear a frightening announcement from the NRC Chairman in Washington. He told all residents within a twenty-mile radius of TMI to be prepared to evacuate.

Will packed some clothes in a bag. Although he wasn't really sure what a baby as tiny as Walden would need, he rummaged through Randi's shower gifts and packed some baby clothes and diapers. On his way back to the hospital he gassed up the car so they could hit the road directly from the hospital when the NRC gave the order to evacuate.

Between visits with Randi and the baby, Will hung out with the two floor nurses, listening to the radio for updates. Night had fallen when the public radio station broke a news bulletin from the

Associated Press. The bubble had reached a danger point and could soon explode.

"We should all get out of here," Will cried to the nurses.

The older nurse, still on duty, put a hand on his arm. "Calm down, son. Let's wait to see if there's something more from the governor or the NRC. You don't want to put your wife and day-old baby in a car and subject them to a long ride if you don't need to. They're in no shape for it."

Blanching, the younger nurse looked at her watch. "It's time for young Walden to be fed." Before she left for the nursery, she addressed Will, her voice quavering. "I know this is serious. The hospital is now closed to everything but emergency admissions. I don't want to blow up or get radiation poisoning any more than you do, Mr. Armstrong. But I agree with Nurse Murphy. None of us, especially your wife and child, want to be caught up in a mob of people and traffic running for their lives—unless there's no choice."

"You're right. I'll come with you while Randi feeds the baby." Will bit his lip. He'd been so selfish to only think of his and Randi's situation. He gave Nurse Murphy an apologetic look. "You'll let us know if there's any news?"

Less than an hour later, Nurse Murphy came to the door of Randi's room and asked Will to step out. She whispered, "That last news report was wrong. Although the situation still isn't good at TMI, the bubble isn't going to explode. That man, Denton, says things are not critical. And President Carter is going to visit TMI tomorrow." She gave Will a tremulous smile. "It can't be dangerous if the president is coming, right?"

"I guess. He's a nuclear engineer, so he'll be able to tell if they're lying."

When Will climbed into the narrow hospital bed he'd used the night before, he clung to that shred of optimism. Nurse Murphy was right. No one would let the president of the United States visit a nuclear power plant on the brink of a meltdown. Maybe they really did have the hydrogen bubble under control.

Will headed to Randi's room as soon as he rolled out of bed on Monday morning. He smiled to see his wife breastfeeding little Walden. "Have you seen the doctor yet? Are they going to let you go home today?"

"Not yet, but the nurse says he should be around to sign the discharge order around eleven. Is my mom there yet? She promised to be there when we got home from the hospital and for the first week." Randi bubbled over with excitement.

"I'm going to run home and take a shower. I haven't heard from your mom today, but I doubt she'll be there. She can't come down here with the risk of an evacuation hanging over our heads."

At Randi's look of surprise, Will realized how successful they'd been in protecting his wife from the TMI drama. She had no idea how close they'd come to danger. "Evacuation? Isn't that whole mess over by now?"

"It looks like it's getting there, but they haven't given the all clear yet. Maybe we should just drive straight up north to your parents' and stay there for the first week. That way you'd have your mom."

Randi's sunny mood had vanished and her lip trembled. "Absolutely not. I want Walden to come to our home so we can be a family, right from the beginning. I'm so sick of this Three Mile Island garbage. You said from day one nothing bad would happen. And it hasn't. Why are you getting so weird about it now?"

Will tried not to sound defensive or hurt. "It's just been a rough few days. You might understand after you learn a little more about what's been happening. We've tried to shield you from the worst of it so you could recover from the delivery and enjoy the baby."

"Are you full, little guy?" Randi ignored Will as she whispered to the baby.

"I'll be back. And I'll check in with your mother while I'm gone. We can manage for a few days without her."

At home, Will changed and straightened the house. He pushed the bassinet into the bedroom where he and Randi slept. Although Walden had made his appearance before Will had assembled the crib, it would be weeks before the baby was big enough to graduate from the bassinet. Back in the kitchen, he washed the dishes Randi had left on Friday and listened to the radio for an update on TMI.

After the end of a song, the DJ said, "There's good news from TMI. Just a few minutes ago, Harold Denton from the NRC informed the press that the temperature inside the reactor is going down. And there has been a decrease in the size of the bubble. Mr. Denton called the decrease in the bubble 'dramatic' and said, 'There is reason for optimism.'"

Will threw the dishrag in the sink and sank into a kitchen chair. He tried to smile but instead broke down in tears. Cradling his head in his hands, Will released all the past days' tension and fear as he wept. Raising his head, he wiped his face with a sleeve. For the first time in a long several days, he dared to hope.

CHAPTER TWENTY-THREE

ALEXA RUSHED TO an adoption hearing first thing on Monday morning, so she didn't get a chance to look at the news until lunchtime. Over a salad at her desk, Alexa leafed through Carlisle's newspaper, the *Sentinel,* then pulled up online news on her computer. Looking for references to the trafficking commission report, she came across a small article headlined *Intern Found Dead.* With a sinking feeling, Alexa read the article about a young woman, interning in the legislature, who had been found floating at the Dock Street Dam on the Susquehanna River. The college student had been a resident of Shipoke, the tiny neighborhood located on the river in downtown Harrisburg. The death was being viewed as accidental. Name was being withheld pending notification of family.

Hoping she was wrong, Alexa worried that this dead woman could be Lauren. She interned at the legislature. She lived in Shipoke. After their interrupted conversation last Thursday, Alexa had tried to get in touch with Lauren. She had left a phone message and sent a follow-up email, but Lauren had not responded. It seemed pretty clear Lauren had second thoughts about asking for advice. So Alexa had shrugged it off, not wanting to make a big deal out of nothing.

Melinda walked into the office with some documents. Alexa looked up. "Did you hear anything on the news about this young woman found dead in the river at Harrisburg?"

"Just that. The story didn't have many details. Said that they were testing her blood alcohol levels, so it sounded like they thought she was drunk and fell in. Sad thing, a girl so young."

"I'm worried it could be Lauren Hildebrand, the intern who helped me on the commission."

Melinda gasped. "I talked to her a couple of times on the phone. She seemed like a sweet little thing. Did you call to make sure?"

Alexa felt like a fool. "Of course. Why don't I call?" Alexa looked up the number in her contact list and dialed. "May I speak to Lauren?"

On the other end of the phone, a woman choked back a sob, and Alexa knew. The girl in the news was Lauren.

"May I ask who's calling?"

"This is Alexa Williams. I've been working with Lauren and Keisha Washington on the trafficking commission."

"Can you hold please?"

After a few minutes, Keisha's voice came on the line. "Alexa, I have some terrible news."

"I saw something in the paper and thought it could be Lauren. Awful to say, but I hoped it was someone else."

"No. Lauren drowned on Saturday night or early Sunday morning. A jogger saw her body in the river yesterday around dawn. The police contacted me right away. I guess her roommate gave them my name and number. What a goddamn tragedy."

"How could she have drowned?" Alexa shook her head.

"She was out partying at the Second Street bars. Her parents were coming to pick Lauren up Sunday afternoon, so she and some of the other interns were out for a farewell bash. Her roommate told the police she went back home around one o'clock, but Lauren stayed at the bar. Several other people said Lauren took a taxi back to Shipoke around two o'clock, and she was pretty hammered. God only knows why she would wander down to the river at that time of night." Keisha's voice cracked.

"So her family arrived to take her home. Instead, found out she was dead." Alexa's eyes filled with tears. Melinda, who had been listening to Alexa's side of the conversation, sank into a chair.

"Can you imagine having to deal with your daughter drowning? Look, I planned to call you. I know you and Lauren had developed a good relationship. She looked up to you, Alexa." Keisha sighed. "But I've had a lot to deal with here. The police. Lauren's family. Not to mention the staff. People here liked Lauren and are having trouble coping with such a senseless death."

"I understand, Keisha. I'll let you go. Will there be a memorial service?"

"No. The Hildebrands are real firm about that. They blame all of us in Harrisburg for their daughter's death. They think working here corrupted her. They say she would have never even touched alcohol before she came here to sin city. They're taking their daughter home to bury her and won't sanction any memorial service here."

"Parents often have an idealized picture of their kids. Lauren had been away to college for three years and probably shared a G-rated version of life on campus with her mom and dad. She told me she liked to party, and that was one of the things she missed about being away from campus for her internship. But her parents need to get through this however they can. If they need to blame life in the city, that might help channel their grief."

"I guess." Keisha's voice sounded defensive. "But, I don't like getting the rap for something I had nothing to do with."

Alexa sensed Keisha was struggling with all of this. "I'm so sorry. I can't believe Lauren's gone. I'll let you get back to things. Take care." She ended the call.

Melinda dabbed at her eyes. "My heart goes out to Lauren's parents. They say there is nothing worse than losing a child. I could hear most of what that Keisha woman said, and it just doesn't add up. I only spoke to her on the phone, but Lauren was such a smart, well-mannered young girl. She just didn't seem like someone who would get drunk and fall in the river."

"No, she didn't," Alexa agreed as she recalled her last conversation with the intern. She kept thinking about Lauren's interrupted plea for guidance about something illegal. She decided to call the Harrisburg police and let them know about that last conversation with Lauren. Had the intern stumbled across something that could have gotten her killed?

That evening, Alexa asked John if he could make inquiries about Lauren's death. She'd spoken to the Harrisburg City detective in charge of the case about the intern's run-in with a lobbyist and the interrupted conversation last week. "Detective Campbell promised to look into it, but I got the impression he's convinced Lauren's death was an accident. That the kid drowned because she was drunk. He thinks she fell in the water. Either passed out or tripped and wound up in the river."

"He could be right, sugarcakes. I know your Spidey-senses are working overtime because of that senator's murder. And this lobbyist guy pissed you off because of the way he treated that poor girl. But that doesn't necessarily add up to murder." John put the salt and pepper shakers back on the counter.

"I know. I have to admit that the two incidents I shared with the detective—they sound pretty lame, even to me, as a motive for killing a college kid. And I didn't really know her outside the office environment. Maybe she was a hard drinker. Or maybe she just cut loose this one time and didn't know how to handle it."

"Unless the coroner comes up with something during the autopsy. Or some witness turns up to say they saw her being pushed into the river." John shook his head.

"Yeah. I'll be surprised if they find anything. I just hate believing a young girl with such potential would die such a senseless death." John drew back at Alexa's anguished tone.

Then he hugged her. "You really liked this kid, didn't you? I'm sorry."

Alexa spoke a muffled reply into John's shoulder. "She reminded me of myself at that age." She stepped out of his embrace. "Except for the drinking and drowning. I was never that careless, even at twenty-one."

John got a beer out of the fridge. "Like I said, I'll ask around, just in case there's an angle they're not releasing to the public. That reminds me. I talked to some guys from the governor's detail the other day at that inter-agency training session. Thought they might know something about the Martinelli investigation. There are no new leads. Nobody saw him fall except you and Keisha Washington. Capitol police are stationed at the doors of the Senate Chamber on the mezzanine and the fourth floor when it's in session. But the Senate broke for caucus. Then the senators and staff went back to their offices and waited to be called to the floor. When that happens, the police lock the Senate Chamber and step away from the doors. They're notified before the senators come back into session."

"I wonder why Martinelli was up there, talking to those other men? Why wouldn't they meet in his office?"

"Maybe they didn't want to be seen. It sounds like the entire Senate had returned to their offices."

"Could be. There are elevators and staircases all over the Capitol that those men could have taken to avoid being seen. Especially since the House had left hours earlier."

"Or maybe they just ran into each other. Although that seems unlikely."

"I agree. It sounds like they haven't identified those men yet. I don't know if they have cameras at every entrance and exit of the Capitol. But those men could have come in almost any time during the day. At one of several entrances. They could be staffers or lobbyists or constituents or even other senators. It would be like looking for a needle in a haystack. And it's not certain that those testy guys were the ones who killed him. There was a long silence before he fell. They could have gotten on the elevator and someone else could have thrown Martinelli over the railing. Are they still looking at Madison Greer's husband?"

"Word is he's off the hook. Witnesses put him in Pittsburgh at the time. Plus he knew about his wife's affair. Apparently, he and the representative had some sort of," John made quotation marks with his fingers, "'open' arrangement. She wanted to stay married because it helped her reelection. He wanted to stay married because of her family's auto parts fortune."

Alexa shook her head. "Wow. I wonder if they'll ever solve the case."

John smiled. "This is a prominent state senator we're talking about. I imagine CID is highly motivated to solve the case. They are probably piecing together evidence as we speak."

"I wish I could be as confident as you are. I haven't felt truly safe since that night in the hot tub—another case that hasn't been solved. But I feel in my bones it's connected to the Martinelli murder. I'm seeing bogeymen around every corner. I told you how I freaked out about two guys at the Grand Canyon. Now I'm turning Lauren's senseless death into another murder."

"Of course you're going to be on edge. But I wouldn't want it any other way. The hot tub incident could have just been some sort of warning. But you could still be a target. Just be careful."

"I hate feeling helpless."

John grinned. "Tell me about it." Then his expression sobered again. "I'm here to protect you. Just don't fight me."

"I know you're looking out for me. And I'm grateful, John." She steered the conversation away from their relationship. "Do you want a cup of tea?"

"I'm fine with this beer." John wandered into the living room, Scout on his heels.

When Alexa joined them with her cup of tea, her heart turned over. John sat on the couch, Scout's head resting on his knee. Overcome with guilt, she pondered her plan to dump John. He had been there for her through a lot of bad times, and she really cared for him. But he loved her. He wanted to spend the rest of his life with her. There was no way to let him down gently. Alexa made a vow that she would talk to him this weekend. She just couldn't do it tonight. She dreaded breaking his heart. And Scout would miss John so much. But she felt like she was using him. And it wasn't fair to string him along.

CHAPTER TWENTY-FOUR

LATE TUESDAY AFTERNOON, Melinda buzzed Alexa. "There are two state policemen out here who would like to talk to you. Trooper Davis and Trooper Cannon."

Surprised, Alexa said, "Send them on in." She got up from her desk to greet the troopers and ushered them to the sitting area in the corner.

From the doorway, Melinda asked, "Would either of you like something to drink? Coffee, a soft drink?"

Both troopers shook their heads in refusal, so Alexa asked, "What brings you here today?"

Davis spoke. "We made an arrest related to the shooting at your cabin."

"What?" Alexa leaned forward.

"We charged this defendant with criminal mischief and aggravated assault." Cannon ran a hand over his shaved head. "Over the winter, there were a couple of cabins up at Pine Grove Furnace that had their windows shot out. Then, in early spring, a farmer reported that he'd been shot at while out in his fields on a tractor. We were thinking a turkey hunter's bullet gone astray."

"Until the second farmer called in a similar report," Davis added.

"Where were the farmers shot?"

"In the valley. Not that far from your cabin," Cannon responded. "But neither farmer was hit. We recovered bullets from all of these incidents and determined they were all from the same gun. We did some legwork at the shooting ranges and rod and gun clubs. Without going into all the details, the path led us to this squirrelly punk named Spanky Fulton."

"Is that his given name?" Alexa searched her memory for someone named Spanky.

Davis remained professional. "Frederick Fulton is his given name, but everyone knows him as Spanky. He lives about ten miles from you, up one of those mountain roads. Although he's twenty-one, he still lives with Mama and Daddy. Works at one of the warehouses in Carlisle."

"We think he looks good for the attempt on you, too," Cannon said. "He hasn't admitted anything yet. But we found the gun he used on the cabins and farmers. He hid it from his parents in an outbuilding." Cannon sneered.

"It's a miracle we found it. The Fulton estate has several sheds, filled with firewood, rusted junk, and used car parts. They say they're antique dealers, but in my opinion, the parents are just hoarders." Davis wrinkled her nose as if she were reliving the search.

"I don't recognize either name, Spanky or Frederick Fulton. But you didn't find the rifle he used to shoot at me?" Alexa clasped her hands together.

"Not yet. His lame-ass friends and some of his coworkers said that Spanky spends a lot of time going to gun shows. You know about the gun show loophole people use to avoid registration, right? It's more than possible he could have picked up a semi-automatic rifle there or through a private sale." Cannon sounded confident in his theory.

Davis continued. "His activities show a definite pattern of escalation. He began with shooting at unoccupied cabins. Then he moved up to target practice on those farmers.

"Finally, he combines his love for cabins in the woods with shooting at people and sets his sights on you. We don't know if he staked out the cabins and the farmers before the shootings—like he did with you. But it wouldn't be surprising. Although the farmer incidents were in daylight, we believe the cabins were shot up at night."

Alexa got a sick feeling in her stomach at the thought of this Spanky sitting on the hill and watching her in the hot tub. "Why would he target me? How could he even find me?"

"We're not sure. But he's local. He could know about the cabin. He could have seen you turn back the lane and decided to check it out." Cannon shook his head. "We've already charged him on all the incidents except yours. Davis and I are going to continue to investigate and try to track down the second rifle. We want to charge him with attempted murder in your shooting."

Davis used a reassuring tone. "We arrested him last night. He won't make bail."

"I doubt his parents will even try to make his bail. They say they've washed their hands of him," Cannon interjected.

"Spanky should be in Cumberland County Prison until his trial is scheduled." Davis smiled. "We have to tie up these loose ends, but you can rest easy."

Alexa breathed a sigh of relief. "So you don't think the shooting had anything to do with Senator Martinelli's death?"

Davis said, "We can't rule that out entirely until our investigation finds the hard evidence to link Spanky Fulton to the attack on you. But we haven't been able to discover anything that ties your incident to the senator's death."

"Yeah. We know CID hasn't nailed the person who sent Martinelli for his final ride, but you didn't witness the murder. Just the point of impact. It never made much sense to us that someone would try to kill you over that. But we followed all the leads, and they've come up dry. No way to pinpoint who owned the gun. No DNA on the candy wrappers. The tire track is from a truck, probably a pickup. We're not even sure that the track is related to your shooter. Spanky drives a Honda low-rider. Still, we think it's Spanky Fulton. You fit his pattern."

"I'm glad you caught him. Who knows what he would have done next."

Davis showed the hint of a smile. "We're not sure if he intended to miss you and the farmers—or if Spanky is just a bad shot. But we're lucky he didn't injure anyone, or worse."

"Me too," Alexa declared. She was a little put off by Davis' levity. After all, the trooper was not the one whose head the bullet had just missed. But John used weird cop humor all the time. Maybe Davis felt freer in Alexa's presence since she dated John and knew Cannon.

Cannon shot out of the chair and onto his feet. Davis sank deeper into the couch for a moment, then sighed and joined him.

"Thanks for coming to tell me about this. I've been so jumpy since that night. I'll feel much safer with Spanky behind bars."

Alexa had trouble letting go during Savasana at the end of Tuesday's yoga session. Relief at Spanky Fulton's arrest, sadness about Lauren Hildebrand's senseless death, and anxiety about the coming breakup with John made it impossible for her to clear her mind. She was relived when Isabella rang the chimes to end the yoga session.

"Is it warm enough to sit on the patio?" Tyrell asked as they approached the Om Café.

"Let's go for it," Melissa cried. "Is that OK with you, little mama?"

Haley protested, "I'm pregnant, not sick. And I have a sweater if the baby and I get cold."

"I'll let Ariel know we're out here. The usual for everyone?" Alexa opened the door and caught the proprietor's eye. "Two chai tea lattes, a cappuccino, and herbal tea for Haley." With the order delivered, she walked back out to join her friends at the table.

Haley rubbed her back and groaned. "I'm trying to do yoga as long as I can. But I'm not sure God intended for pregnant women to do Downward Facing Dog in their final months."

"The baby's due in about two months, right?" Tyrell sounded out of his depth with this maternity talk.

"You should have switched to maternity yoga," Melissa grumbled.

"Maybe but then I would have missed our weekly get-togethers." Haley laughed. "Who knows if I'll ever see you again after the baby comes."

Tyrell looked puzzled, so Alexa explained. "They say having a baby changes your entire life. Every waking moment is taken up with the little one. Sleeping moments, too."

"I'll only take a few weeks off from yoga," Haley insisted. "I told Blair he has to stay home with the baby on Tuesday nights."

After Ariel appeared with a tray of drinks, Alexa shared the state police news. "They arrested this guy, Spanky Fulton. Although they don't have a gun to match the bullets in the hot tub and the house, the troopers seem to think he's the one. They have him cold on several similar shootings."

Melissa held her hand in the air, choking down laughter. "Wait. You're saying the guy who shot at you while you were naked in the hot tub is named Spanky? That's a porn name if I ever heard one."

"No, it's not. Didn't you watch Spanky and *Our Gang* when you were a kid?" Haley became indignant.

"You're right. *The Little Rascals*. I loved that dog with the circle around his eye. What was his name?"

"Spot?" Haley asked.

"No, Petey," Alexa answered.

Melissa took a sip of chai. "I always wondered if that circle around his eye was real."

The other three looked at her in disbelief before Tyrell spoke in a dry tone. "I'm pretty sure they painted it on. But, aren't we getting a little off track here? Alexa, it's wonderful they caught this Spanky character. I bet it takes a big weight off your mind to know he's in jail."

"It does. I've been looking over my shoulder ever since that night."

Haley cringed. "I bet you haven't been in the hot tub again. I wouldn't."

"Just once. In daylight. I had Scout with me." Alexa looked at the time on her phone. "I better get home. Scout's been in the house all day."

Although the days were getting longer, twilight had fallen by the time Alexa arrived home. When she unlocked the door, Scout ran out toward the pines. Alexa squared her shoulders and decided to take the plunge. She would celebrate Spanky Fulton's arrest by using the hot tub, even though it was getting dark. Having Scout outside made it easier. An extra two hundred thirty pounds of security. She slipped out of her yoga clothes, grabbed a towel, and walked across the deck to the hot tub.

Sinking into the steaming water with a sigh of contentment, Alexa's thoughts turned to John. He was working a late shift tonight, so she didn't expect to see him. In some ways, that was a relief. She was still searching for the best way to break it off with the trooper. Not an easy thing to do. They'd started dating last October. After the initial thrill of the new relationship had worn off, Alexa had struggled to keep up the enthusiasm. She owed him so much. He'd saved her life when Quinn Hutton had kidnapped her. He'd been there to help her recover from the trauma. But Alexa knew she couldn't build a lasting relationship on gratitude. From the moment John began pressing for something more permanent, Alexa resisted. She knew moving in together was just the prelude to a marriage proposal. And she would never say yes to John Taylor, no matter how much she liked and owed the guy. So she had to break it off. Soon.

Scout came padding up on the deck. He placed his front paws on the hot tub steps, his ears dangling in the water. Alexa scratched his ears. "Hey, buddy. Should we go inside and feed you?"

The dog turned and headed toward the front door. Alexa leaned back and drank in the soothing chorus of peepers down at Weaver's Pond. Soon they would be gone, replaced by the deep croak of bullfrogs and the hum of crickets in the night. Smiling, she got out of the hot tub and wrapped herself in a towel. How wonderful to feel safe again in this place she loved so much.

CHAPTER TWENTY-FIVE

THE PHONE RANG AS Alexa carried her breakfast out onto the deck. Slamming her cup of tea and bowl of granola on the table, she ran into the house to answer the call. "Hello."

"Hi, sugarcakes. I wanted to catch you before you left for work." Alexa carried the receiver back out on the deck.

"I'm just sitting down to breakfast. I don't have any appointments until nine so I'm going in a little late. Are you off today?"

"Yeah. Jim and I are planning another trip up to that area we found this weekend. I'm convinced that someone is surveying the land for fracking. I spoke to the corporal, and he's interested in taking a team up there. Same with the DER people. But Jim and I decided to get some photos of that equipment so we can run them by an expert first. I've got nothing better to do. It's a nice day to be outside."

"I'm envious. I have a full slate of meetings, plus lunch with Darby Kaplan from the Wildness Cooperative. She's coming to Carlisle so I'm pretty sure she wants something from me. First, Walt Jordan. Now, Darby. Trying to get me involved in the anti-fracking campaign."

"It's a good cause. You said so yourself after seeing things up north."

"I know." Alexa sighed. "But I just finished with the Human Trafficking Commission. As much as I'm into good causes, I'd like to have some time to just chill this summer."

"That sounds good, too. Why don't you wait and see what this Darby has in mind?"

"You're right. Melinda would say I'm getting the cart before the horse." Alexa laughed.

"I'll come back to the cabin after Jim and I finish up and just hang out with Scout this afternoon. I want to finish tying a fly or two for the opening day of trout season. Then we could cook something on the grill?"

"That sounds like a plan. Scout will be happy to have some company. I've got some steaks in the freezer. I'll set them out to thaw."

"See you later," John said.

"Bye." Alexa pushed the off button and took a sip of tea. She turned to Scout with resolve in her eyes. "I'm going to bite the bullet and tell him tonight, buddy. It's time."

Alexa met Darby at Legal Grounds. She hadn't visited the coffee shop in a while. When she had volunteered regularly at the Cumberland Family Planning Clinic down the street, Alexa had been a regular here. New owners had kept the coffee shop vibe but added a decent lunch menu.

Darby already sat at a table in the coffee shop when Alexa arrived. "You found it with no problems?"

"Nope, my GPS brought me right to the front door. Parking right out front is a bonus. I'm used to trying to find parking in Harrisburg, and then paying an arm and a leg for it."

The two women ordered their meals from a server Alexa didn't recognize. "Thanks for arranging that meeting with Walt Jordan. I should have called earlier to tell you how much I appreciated it. He connected me with a class action suit against Monongas on mostly environmental issues. My clients talked about becoming part of the class but then decided to go with individual counsel. A firm that's had pretty good success in bringing action against Monongas in cases where there are medical issues."

"Yes. I've heard about the Friends of Pine Creek group. I couldn't remember the name that day we had lunch. But I figured Walt Jordan would point you in the right direction."

"The representative has been very helpful. While I was in Tioga County getting my clients settled with counsel, Mr. Jordan gave me an introduction to fracking. He spent the better part of a day with me, taking me to drilling sites in different stages of development. He also arranged some meetings with families who had been affected—both positively and negatively—by fracking." Alexa winced. "More on the negative side."

An enigmatic smile crossed Darby's face. "I heard about the show and tell. Walt thinks you've become a convert to the anti-fracking cause."

"After seeing what happened to my clients' daughter and then hearing from the Friends of Pine Creek and those other families—it's a pretty compelling argument for the dangers of fracking. Of course, the argument for fracking has some powerful points too. Energy independence. They say it's less polluting than coal. Less impact on global warming."

"But you're not convinced that those things offset the dangers, are you?" Darby speared a fork into the salad the server had placed in front of her.

"I still don't know enough," Alexa demurred.

"Take it from me, they don't. Plus there are renewable alternatives available right now. Wind. Solar. Other cutting edge stuff. But the fossil fuel industry has too big a grip on the decision makers. As a result, the alternatives aren't being funded and nurtured the way they could be."

Alexa nodded. "From the way they're pushing this fracking bill in the legislature, you could be right."

"Which is one of the reasons I'm here. Walt thinks you'd make a good public spokesperson against the bill."

"Me?" Alexa nearly choked on a bite of chicken salad. "I'm hardly an expert. My connection to fracking is very tangential—through my clients. I expected you to hit me up for a big donation to the cause. But act as a spokesperson? Why me?"

"You've been in the public eye on the Human Trafficking Commission. And before that, for breaking open that trafficking ring. Didn't Rachel Maddow interview you about being targeted by anti-abortion zealots? Like it or not, you're a public figure."

"But I'd feel like some gadfly that flits from one cause to the next. Like a pundit on cable TV who has an opinion on everything but knows very little. I wouldn't feel comfortable—no matter how good the cause." Alexa shook her head.

"Think about it for a week or so," Darby advised. She then steered the conversation to amusing stories about working with legislators on environmental issues.

As the women finished their lunch, Alexa asked, "Do you know anything about an industry effort to expand fracking into South Central Pennsylvania? A friend told me they're talking about it at the local Chamber of Commerce. And some other folks in law enforcement believe there's illegal surveying going on in the Michaux State Forest. That at least one company is looking for drilling sites on public land."

Darby frowned. "I've heard some rumors about a new technology, similar to fracking, that would extract natural gas from non-shale areas. Of course, the industry drilled in limestone and sandstone long before they developed hydraulic fracturing. But the goal of this new hybrid technology would open up a lot of previously untouched areas to fracking. I always thought it was an urban myth. This would be a real nightmare if it's true."

"I heard the recent Climate Treaty has affected the industry timelines. That this new thing is real, and they plan to drill everything they can now and stockpile natural gas. They're worried the government will shut down fracking altogether."

"Damn. I'm going to look into this. I wonder if that's what is driving this Senate bill. It's always seemed that the effort to pass this bill far outweighed its potential benefit. But maybe they want to open up a lot more state land than we imagined, using this new technique."

"Maybe you could clue Walt Jordan in as well. I've just learned about this, so haven't spoken to him about it." Alexa felt her face flush when she mentioned Walt's name."

With a knowing look, Darby said, "And you'd rather I filled him in so you can avoid talking to him? Sounds to me like you've fallen under the Jordan spell."

"I'm not sure what you're talking about."

"I've seen it before. Walt is a handsome, charismatic guy. He charms everyone who comes into his orbit—with very few exceptions. A lot of it has to do with his commitment to the cause. All that passion about the environment is so appealing. Like father like son, I guess. You know his dad was a real hero of the environmental movement back in the seventies and eighties?"

"No, I don't know much about Walt, really," Alexa admitted. "Are you saying he's a player?" She wondered if Darby was reacting to personal experience with Walt.

"Just the opposite. The guy's a real family man. Always talking about the wife and kiddies. I'm just saying he has a certain effect on people; women and men alike. My partner, Sabrina, thinks the man walks on water. All the environment groups in the state practically worship the man for his advocacy. You get that same starry-eyed look when you talk about him. That's all I'm saying."

"Oh. I guess I misunderstood. He does seem a bit larger than life." Alexa didn't know whether to be embarrassed her crush on Walt Jordan was so common or disappointed to learn he probably gave everyone the same "special" treatment she'd received. She struggled to change the subject. "Is your partner an environmentalist too?"

Darby signaled to the server for the check. "Only in her spare time. Sabrina is a Pediatric Hospitalist at Hershey Medical Center. What about you? Are you married? Have kids?"

"Neither. I've been in a relationship for a while. With a state cop. But I don't see marriage or kids in the picture—not at this point, anyway."

When Alexa arrived home, she was surprised to find Scout alone at the cabin. There were no signs that John had been there. She checked the steaks in the fridge to make sure they had thawed. Then she ran upstairs to change, figuring John and Jim had decided to stop for a beer somewhere. She hoped he hadn't been called into to work; she'd finally mustered the courage to discuss her feelings about their relationship. She was afraid she'd chicken out again if the conversation got delayed.

Back downstairs, Alexa checked for phone messages on both the landline and her cell. John hadn't called, so she decided to hike to Weaver's Pond. She left a brief note to John on the kitchen counter. "Scout and I went for walk. Will return by six." Locking the door behind her, Alexa and Scout set off through the woods.

She loved this time of year. The leaves on the trees were still fresh with their new growth. Yesterday's steady rain had turned the ground beneath her feet soft and spongy. About halfway to the pond, Alexa spied an early-blooming clutch of Lady's Slippers, the pink blooms balancing on slender, curved stems. She left the native orchids in place, nestled in the hollow of a fallen tree. Scout wandered back and forth ahead of her, snooting the ground and following the scent of small animals that had crossed the path.

Late afternoon shadow blanketed most of the small pond by the time Alexa and Scout arrived. As she gazed at the water, the last rays of sun touched two blooming Redbud trees with their light. Beneath the trees, a patch of water lilies, their buds closed tight, shone blood red in the trees' reflection. Alexa shivered at the eerie trick of light.

"Scout, let's head back home. John might be there." Alexa walked at a steady pace on the return trip, driven by a sense of anxiety she couldn't define. When they reached the edge of the forest, Alexa looked up at the sound of a car coming down the lane.

"What did I tell you? Here's John." Scout was already looking down the lane. But his tail didn't wag its usual greeting. Instead, he stayed by Alexa's side as they continued toward the cabin. When she recognized the Department of Environmental Resources SUV, Alexa thought that John's car had broken down or something, and Jim was giving him a lift. But Jim got out of the car alone. And then Melissa's car drove down the lane.

"Hey, Jim. What's up?" Alexa asked when she reached the SUV. His grave expression was alarming. "Is something wrong?"

"I have some really bad news. Maybe we should go up and sit down," Jim said.

"No, tell me." Panicked, Alexa felt a growing chill. Behind her, Melissa's car came to a stop and the door opened. Melissa rushed to Jim's side. She looked as if she'd been crying. An icy cold settled into Alexa's core as she waited for Jim's reply.

"It's John." He choked out the words. "When we went to that survey site today, we had a run in with the surveyors." Jim grasped her arm. "I'm sorry, Alexa. John's dead."

CHAPTER TWENTY-SIX

April 13, 1979/May 6, 1979

The people put nuclear power on trial. No more Harrisburgs.
    —*Poster for the March on Washington, May 6, 1979*

"*There it is,*" *Will pointed through the Thing's windshield to the four concrete towers sitting on an island in the middle of the Susquehanna River. "The world-famous Three Mile Island. They say everything is safe now.*"

"*Those towers are pretty scary looking. It's almost like having an atom bomb sitting out there. Thank God it didn't melt down.*" *Will's father gripped his son's shoulder with emotion. "Your mother and I were terrified, but you've got a good head on your shoulders. We knew you'd leave if it got too bad.*"

"*Do you want to get out of the car? Get some fresh air?*"

"*Nah. I wanted to see the famous Three Mile Island. But I'm not taking a chance on getting radiated. Let's go somewhere for a beer.*"

"*Fine with me. I hate this place.*" *Will started the car and pulled back out onto the road.*

Sitting in a booth at the neighborhood tavern, Will told his father, "Just one beer, then we better get back to Mom and Randi."

Dad grinned. "It's hard to believe my only son has made me a grandfather. We can leave whenever you want. Let me tell you, though. Your mother has spent this entire time fussing over little Walden and talking baby stuff with Randi. They haven't even noticed we're gone." *He grew serious. "Besides, you look like you could use a break. Has that baby been keeping you from getting enough sleep? Randi doesn't work. Let her get up in the night.*"

Will put his half-empty mug on the table. "That's not it. Randi has been getting up with Walden since she's breastfeeding. But I still can't sleep. I feel so guilty, Dad. I failed them during TMI. With Randi pregnant, we should have evacuated the first day. Instead, I believed the power company and state officials when they said there was nothing to worry about. We didn't know the baby would come early. Still, I should have insisted we leave, just in case. Randi wanted to get out of town, but I pooh-poohed her concern."

"You did the best you could in confusing circumstances. From what I've heard, the powers that be didn't really know what was going on either. Carter sending in that man, Denton, from the NRC—he helped get a handle on things. But, by that time, the baby was already on the way."

"Before we got married, you said I needed to be prepared to protect Randi and my family. I feel like the first time I was tested, I didn't come through." Will rubbed a hand across his forehead.

"I'm glad you took my words to heart." His father gave a soft laugh. "But you did the best you could—and sometimes that's all a man can do."

Will took another sip of Rolling Rock. "I've been thinking about what I can do to make things right. One of the guys I work with, Andy, has been telling me about the anti-nuke movement. Even before TMI, there were a lot of people out there trying to stop nuclear power plants from being built—because of the danger. What happened here only demonstrates that they're right."

Finishing his beer, Dad reached for his wallet. "I'd say these anti-nuke people have a point. I know I'm glad nobody's talking about building one of those reactors near home."

"There aren't enough people in Potter County to make a nuclear power plant profitable. You know, when I took my first class in college, I'd never seen that many people in one place." Will laughed as he followed his father out the door.

"He smiled at me," Will exclaimed and beamed at the baby in his arms.

"Why, yes he did. Did little Walden smile at his daddums? Isn't he such a precious boy? Yes he is." Randi, seated next to Will on the couch, leaned over and babbled at the baby.

"Smiling at one month. That's very advanced, right?" Although Will had read the baby book, most of it remained a blur.

"Of course it is." Randi reached for the baby and rocked him in her arms.

"You're OK with me going to that rally next Saturday with Andy, right?"

"Absolutely. I would go with you if I didn't have to stay with baby cakes. You need to stand up and stop another TMI." Randi leaned into her husband. "With me being in the hospital and all, I didn't really have to deal with all the scary things that were going on. Like that bubble thing. I know that it was a tough situation for you, babe. So go with Andy. We'll be fine. Maybe I'll call and see if Denise wants to visit that day. She hasn't seen Walden yet."

On the first Sunday in May, just over a month after Three Mile Island, Will and Andy joined a busload of protestors from Harrisburg on their way to the anti-nuke March on Washington, DC. When they stepped off the bus, the size of the crowd shocked Will. "Look at all these people."

"It's a righteous cause." Andy grabbed the sign he'd brought from the storage compartment under the bus. Its big block letters cried DON'T FORGET TMI.

Their group walked toward the White House for the rally. Many of the people in the crowd were young, dressed in jeans and sneakers. A lot of the guys sported long hair and beards. Groups were carrying cardboard signs and banners made out of makeshift bedsheets with messages scrawled in paint. When they reached the White House, they joined an even larger crowd. As they approached, the protestors chanted in unison, "Hell no, we won't glow." Caught up in the excitement, Will joined in the chant.

When the crowd switched to "Two-Four-Six-Eight, We Don't Want to Radiate," Andy cackled. "Oh, yeah. Hear that Jimmy Carter, Mister everything's-fine-at-TMI."

Will burst into whoops of laughter before he took up the next chant, "No Nukes. No Nukes. No Nukes." For the first time in over a month, he was having fun. And it was for a cause that could make a difference.

The crowd soon marched toward the Capitol Building, where a big stage had been erected. The program lasted for several hours. A lot of people spoke against nuclear power, many mentioning the recent crisis at Three Mile Island. Will didn't recognize most of the speakers, but he agreed with what they were saying. He'd seen the light. Nuclear power was dangerous, and the government should stop any new power plants from opening their doors. After California Governor Jerry Brown finished his remarks, Will leaned over to Andy. "I can't believe I was such a dumb ass to believe Met-Ed and all their lies about how safe nuclear power is."

"Hey, man, chill. You weren't the only one. But look at this crowd." Andy waved his arm in a semi-circle. "There must be more *than a hundred thousand people here. Especially after that fuck-up at TMI, the word is getting out. The people have spoken, man."*

"I'm not sure it's going to be that easy. These companies have a boatload of money tied up in building nuclear plants. They're not going to give up without a fight." Will abandoned the conversation when Joni Mitchell came out on stage to play her song, "Woodstock." He let the words wash over him, feeling content as the spring sun warmed his back.

On the bus ride home, most of the passengers slept, tired out by the long day. A faint smell of stale marijuana hung in the air, trapped in the confined space. In the back of the bus, a radio played Smokey Robinson's "Cruisin'." Will stared at the passing scenery in the fading light and made a new vow: he would do everything he could to protect innocent people from the dangers of nuclear power. He hadn't been able to protect Randi and Walden from TMI, but maybe he could balance the scale by preventing other nuclear meltdowns.

CHAPTER TWENTY-SEVEN

"JOHN'S DEAD?" ALEXA had trouble comprehending Jim's statement.

Melissa caught Alexa just as her knees buckled. "Let's go sit down. Jim can tell you what happened."

For a moment, Alexa still couldn't process what Jim had just told her. "John's dead? I just spoke to him this morning."

Tears gathered in Jim's eyes. "I can't believe it either, and I saw it happen."

Seeing the stalwart forest ranger break down made his words real. "How?" Alexa cried. "What happened? An accident?"

"Why don't we go inside, and I can tell you everything," Jim said as he and Melissa shuffled Alexa up the stairs and onto the deck. At the front door, Alexa reached into her pocket and handed the forest ranger the key. Scout rushed to get a drink of water while the three humans went into the living room.

Alexa felt numb as she crumpled into the big couch. "You were just going out there to take photos."

"We were. John and I drove out to that place we found last weekend. As we walked down the path, we noticed broken-off trees and tire tracks. It looked like a vehicle had been there since Saturday. When we got to the top of the ridge, we heard engine noise and realized someone was working the site below. We tried to phone it in; neither of us had cell reception. We debated about going back and calling for backup. But John worried we would lose them if we left. It looked like they were finishing up for the day.

"So we decided to confront them. From what we could tell there were just two guys, working out of a big utility truck. They had set up more of those gauge things that measure seismic activity. We drew our guns and walked down the hill, John on the left and me on the right. I don't think they saw us coming at first. They were packing shovels in the truck and getting ready to leave.

The driver opened the door and climbed into the truck. That's when he noticed John.

"John yelled, 'Stop. State Police.' But the driver screamed at the other guy to get in the truck. I ran toward the vehicle, but the driver gunned the motor and headed straight at John. He was less than six feet away by that time. John tried to jump out of the way. I got off some shots, but I hit the rear of the truck. It was moving so fast.

"John stumbled and the truck accelerated." Jim shuddered. "That bastard plowed right over him. And he just kept going. I got off another couple of shots, but the truck bounced like crazy going up the hill. I was more concerned about John." He looked down at his hands and then back up at Alexa. "He was dead when I got there. My God, it was terrible." Melissa hugged Jim as he broke into sobs. "I'm so sorry, Alexa."

"It's not your fault, Jim," Alexa said as she wrapped a throw around her shoulders. She couldn't get warm.

The group sat in stunned silence. Alexa felt numb with shock. When the lane buzzer rang, Melissa jumped at the sound. "This could be Graham. I called him when I heard what happened."

Alexa rose when Graham walked through the door. He rushed across the room and folded his sister into his arms. "What a hell of a thing to happen. I can't believe John is gone. How are you holding up?"

"I don't know," she mumbled into his shoulder. And then, like a dam bursting, Alexa wept. Melissa began to cry too. When Alexa let go of Graham, she stumbled back to the couch, saying, "I can't believe it."

Melissa wiped her eyes and said, "I'm going to make some tea. Or do you want something stronger?"

Jim and Graham opted for a beer. Melissa made a pot of tea for the two women. Then she retrieved a plastic container of homemade chicken noodle soup from the car and heated it on the stove.

"I don't think I can eat." Alexa waved away the soup but managed to down a few bites.

Jim recounted the circumstances of John's death to Graham. Then he went on to describe what had happened next. "It was one of the hardest things I've ever had to do, but I had to leave John's body there and get help. I ran back up the hill and drove out to the main road. I feared those bastards had disabled the SUV, but I guess they were only interested in getting as far away as possible. I called it in on the radio as soon as I could get reception. Then I went back to wait with John." Jim's voice was desolate.

Graham asked, "Did the utility vehicle have company markings?"

"No. It was plain white. No markings. I got the first three numbers of the license, but I'm not sure what state. Not Pennsylvania. Mud covered most of the plate."

"That type of truck can't be that common," Graham suggested. "And it might be damaged. Maybe the cops can trace it. Or that equipment they installed in the ground."

Alexa let the conversation wash over her. She felt like she was caught in a bad dream. That none of this was real. At one point she gathered enough energy to ask, "What about John's parents? Should I call them? Do they know?"

Jim sighed. "One of the state cops took responsibility for notifying them as next of kin. The big guy with a shaved head. Cannon, right? I told them I would break the news to you."

"I can't imagine what this will do to his family. John was their pride and joy. First Taylor to go to college. He's their only son. He has a sister who lives up near the parents' farm in the State College area."

Melissa cleaned up the half-eaten bowls of chicken noodle soup and fed Scout. "I can stay here with you tonight," she told Alexa.

"No. Jim needs you." Alexa turned to Melissa's boyfriend. "I can't imagine how you're still functioning after all of this. You lost a good friend today, right in front of your eyes. Even though you couldn't save John, you tried. Duty and honor were important to him, and you did your best to meet that obligation. He would have been proud of you."

"I just wish I could have nailed that driver before he hit John. We underestimated the situation. It all happened so damn fast."

"You two go home. Leave one of the cars here and collect it tomorrow." Graham took charge. "Kate and I already decided I'm spending the night here. We don't want Alexa to be alone tonight."

When Jim and Melissa left, Graham fussed over his little sister, offering more food, a blanket, a box of Kleenex.

"No, just sit with me. Thanks for staying." Alexa gave her brother a wan smile.

"Kate wanted to be here, but we couldn't get a sitter on such short notice."

"I wouldn't want the kids near all of this grief anyway. It's best she stayed home."

"The state police will pull out all of the stops to find these animals who ran John down. They don't rest when it's one of their own."

Alexa dabbed at her eyes. "John's still gone. Finding his killer won't bring him back. Don't get me wrong. I want these assholes caught and nailed to the wall for what they did. John is—was—such a good man."

"I didn't know him all that well, but I admired him." Graham smiled. "The best testament to John is that you loved him. That says a lot to me."

"But I didn't really." Alexa whispered, wringing her hands.

"What?"

Alexa burst into tears again. "I feel like such a fraud, Graham. If John had made it back here tonight, I was going to break up with him."

Graham looked startled. "Seriously? Kate and I expected to hear about an engagement any day now. But you were going to end things?" His eyes narrowed. "Did he do something to hurt you?"

"Nothing like that. As far I as could tell, John loved me heart and soul. But I didn't love him. Not enough. And I couldn't keep up the charade any longer. I had worked up my courage to end things. Tonight."

"Wow." Graham sat still as if assessing this surprise. "Well, I guess it's good he didn't know. He died thinking you loved him."

"I guess." Alexa sank back into the cushions, wracked with guilt. Died. Dead. She felt like she'd killed John with her cold, screwed-up heart. And now she'd never get a chance to make it right.

CHAPTER TWENTY-EIGHT

THE NEXT WEEK PASSED in a blur. After a long weekend alone with her agonizing thoughts, Alexa decided to return to work. Her irrational guilt over John's death could only be held at bay by keeping busy.

Although spring continued to unfold around her, Alexa was oblivious. Seeing fly fishermen standing thick in the Yellow Breeches Creek made Alexa burst into tears. John should have been among them, using one of the colorful flies he'd spent hours tying. But she barely registered the other signs of the season. The Phoebe building a nest in its annual spot by the laundry room brought her no pleasure. She ignored the patch of bright violet and yellow crocuses by the front steps. Even her mother's arrival from Italy did little to stir Alexa from her funk. Four gloomy days of steady rain mirrored her dull mood.

The following Saturday brought John's funeral. Susan Williams drove Alexa north to State College for the service. Jim and Melissa took Tyrell and one of John's fishing buddies in their car.

"Mom, I don't know what to say to his parents. Mrs. Taylor was so broken up when I spoke to her on the phone, it didn't really matter what I said. But how can I face them today?"

"Lexie, you've got to get out of your own way on this. I know you're grief stricken. You may not have wanted to spend the rest of your life with John, but I know you cared about him. You are not responsible for his death," Susan counseled.

"But I was about to bail on the relationship."

"You know that, and a few of your friends know that. But John's parents still think of you as their son's beloved girlfriend. I know you are kind enough to put aside your own feelings and play that part for the day. Let his parents go on believing their son had a woman who cherished him on the day he died."

"I did cherish him," Alexa whispered. "I just didn't want . . ."

"I know, Lexie. Your grief for John is real. That's enough for today. Starting tomorrow, you can come to terms with the awful fact that this man was killed before you could let him know how you truly felt. I hope you can come to accept that not knowing might have been better for John."

Alexa managed to get through the funeral without totally losing it. Both his parents and friends treated Alexa as John's girlfriend. The minister and several of the people who spoke at the service, among them the state police commissioner and John's former partner, Corporal Branche, included her name among those close to John and most affected by his loss. However, Alexa was glad state police protocol dictated John's mother receive the flag draped over his coffin. As a trooper killed in the line of duty, John's funeral was a military-style event. Nearly a thousand uniformed troopers and policemen from Pennsylvania and other states attended to show their support for a fallen comrade.

Alexa held it together throughout the poignant funeral but broke down at the sight of the riderless horse, empty boots turned backward in the stirrups. She continued to sob in grief and guilt while bagpipers played "Amazing Grace."

After the graveside service and twenty-one gun salute, John's parents invited everyone to a brunch at a huge community social hall. Feeling like a fraud, Alexa stayed for three hours, accepting condolences and hearing people share their memories of John. At the end of the event, Alexa hugged Mr. and Mrs. Taylor and stumbled to the car, exhausted.

"Do you want me to drive, Mom?"

"No. It's nice to drive the Range Rover again. That little Mercedes we have in Italy is like driving a roller skate compared to this baby. Why don't you take a nap? You handled yourself well, Lexie. I know it wasn't easy."

"No, but it was the right thing to do. For John. I will miss him. The service was wonderful. He deserved all the pomp and circumstance. But he didn't deserve to die." Tears ran down Alexa's cheeks as she mourned the man who had given her his heart.

On Monday morning, Susan flew back to Italy, and Alexa tried to pick up the pieces of her life. She plunged back into work, bringing paperwork home each night to read until she tumbled into bed, exhausted. Scout wandered around the house, trying to get her attention. When she looked at the dog's sad face, she imagined he missed John.

On Saturday, Jim and Melissa came by to check on Alexa as she lounged on the deck, trying to read a book. Scout welcomed little Ansel, letting the frisky puppy chase him around the yard.

Jim brought news of the investigation into John's death. "They took two guys into custody in Oklahoma last night. Cannon called to tell me about it. I said I'd fill you in."

"Who are they?" Alexa forced an interest, wondering why it mattered. Arresting these men wouldn't bring John back.

"Their last names are Hudspeth and Poole. They work for a surveying company based in Texas. The Oklahoma Highway Patrol flagged the truck based on the three digits on the license plate and the fact that it was a white utility vehicle. The damage to the truck had been repaired. And it had magnetic signs on the side with the name of the company ERM. Stands for . . ." Jim looked at Melissa when he couldn't remember.

"Earth Resources Mapping."

Rousing from her lethargy, Alexa asked, "Are they the ones that want to drill in Michaux? What kind of company hires guys who kill cops?"

Jim shook his head. "This is where it gets complicated. Who knows if they're lying or not. But ERM told the police they don't know anything about why these two employees were in Michaux. The surveyors apparently work shale fields all over the country. They were up in Northern Pennsylvania for three weeks doing seismic studies. According the company, they assumed the men had returned home to Oklahoma at the end of their assignment, almost two weeks ago. The men were due a ten-day break between assignments. When the highway patrol caught them, Hudspeth and Poole were heading toward their next project in North Dakota."

"Cannon said these two could have been moonlighting, using the ERM equipment," Melissa added.

Jim sneered. "At this point, Hudspeth and Poole aren't talking. So, if they were doing something off the books, we don't know who they were working for. The assignment in Northern Pennsylvania was for Radiant Energy."

"A solar company?" Alexa asked in disbelief.

"You would think, right? Radiant is another natural gas company. Radiant officials say they know nothing about Hudspeth and Poole's activities after they left Warren County."

"If these two were just hired hands, why would they kill John?" Alexa's tone expressed her confusion.

"These guys are pretty rough. They've put in years in the oilfields and natural gas operations. Both of them have records for assault, robbery, and a laundry list of other offenses. Neither one is a geologist. They do the grunt work to set up testing. Someone with skills, higher on the food chain, does the analysis." Jim paced back and forth.

Melissa interjected. "They must have known what they were doing in Michaux was illegal. They panicked."

"I'm sure the cops will continue to press these two for answers." Jim sat down. "Cannon said they plan to start extradition proceedings to get them back to Pennsylvania. The driver will be charged with homicide of a law enforcement officer. I'm not sure about the other guy, but no way he'll walk."

"Good," Alexa replied. "I hope they roll over on the people who hired them. Those anonymous people might not have driven the vehicle, but they're responsible for the illegal activity that created the entire situation."

"Trust me. From listening to Cannon, I don't think the state police are going to rest until they track down everyone involved."

When Melissa and Jim left, Alexa tried to get back into her book. But her thoughts kept drifting from the page. When she had to re-read a paragraph three times to figure out how the character had gotten from the Bronx to Scotland, Alexa threw the book down in disgust. She loved to read, but today she just couldn't concentrate.

Leaving Scout napping outside, Alexa walked into the kitchen for a soda. "I can't believe it," she muttered, shuffling bottles aside in the refrigerator, looking for a soda. "I really wanted a Coke." Finding a bottle behind a half-gallon of milk, Alexa pulled out a soft drink. Closing the door behind her, Alexa saw she'd grabbed a birch beer, not a Coca-Cola. Birch beer, John's favorite. Clutching the cold bottle against her chest, Alexa burst into tears and staggered back against the fridge. She slid down the face of the refrigerator until she collapsed on the floor, sobbing. Alexa remembered the day she and John had begun their romance. It had been his childlike enthusiasm about birch beer that had charmed her into taking a chance on him. Her tears dried, and she smiled as she relived that first, birch beer-infused kiss.

Alexa raised the bottle of birch beer in a toast and whispered to the empty kitchen, "I'll miss you, John. That old line about the good dying young sure applies to you. I just wish I could have loved you more." She took a sip of the beverage and let out a long, tremulous sigh. When she unfolded her body from the kitchen floor, she felt just a little lighter—like she had begun to make peace with what had happened.

On Sunday, Alexa got up early and drove to the Kings Gap Environmental Center to hike the Kings Gap Hollow Trail. She and Scout walked alone for hours, but she found it difficult to escape memories of John.

Only at the end of the hike, when Alexa and the mastiff neared the parking area, did they meet other hikers. Two tall young men, dressed in black sweatshirts, rounded a blind curve on the trail ahead. Alexa's heart pounded as she pulled Scout's leash tighter. She remembered the last time she'd been alone and encountered two men in the forest at the Grand Canyon. She'd convinced herself that those Monongas employees had no sinister intent—that she'd overreacted. But, here she was, tensing again at the sight of two men. When they picked up their pace, she prepared to flee. At least this time she had her mastiff for protection.

The black-clad men were less than five feet away when a group of teenagers in high spirits flooded the trail behind them.

"Tim. Jared. Wait for us," the kids called.

One of the men in black yelled, "Look at this huge dog."

His companion asked, "Can we pet him, ma'am? Or is he mean?"

When Alexa saw the two up close, she realized they were just teenagers. Their black sweatshirts were emblazoned with the words, The Rock, superimposed over a cross. At first Alexa thought the words referred to a local rock and roll radio station. Then it hit her that this was a church group and the rock and cross were religious references.

"Sure, you can pet him. Just be gentle." Alexa kicked herself for overreacting yet again—this time to two fifteen-year-olds. She had to stop jumping every time she came across men on the trail. Spanky Fulton was in jail. It was ridiculous to think everyone else was in on some elaborate plot to harm her.

Before the other kids reached Alexa and Scout, two adults bringing up the rear yelled, "Keep moving, group. Let the lady and her dog walk through."

When Alexa passed the adults, the woman in khaki pants smiled. "I apologize for all the noise. It's hard to contain fifteen teenagers."

"They'll be a lot quieter by the time they reach the summit," Alexa replied. "It's a great day for a hike."

"God's creation in all its glory," said the man, who wore a minister's collar beneath his black windbreaker. He edged toward the side of the path away from Scout. "God bless you both." Safely past, he turned back to observe, "I've never seen a dog that big."

The encounter with the church group left Alexa in a contemplative mood as she drove back to the cabin. It would be so nice to believe God had a plan for all of his or her creation. But Alexa had seen too much wanton death. She couldn't imagine a deity who would design a plan in which some goon would run over a good man like John Taylor. Or a kid like Lauren would drown in the Susquehanna. Or a respected state senator would be tossed from a balcony like a sack of grain.

As if sensing her distress, Scout draped his head over her shoulder.

Alexa had just arrived back at the cabin when Tyrell's car came driving down the lane. She unlocked the cabin door and turned to wait for her friend.

Tyrell unfolded his long lean frame from the car and glided up the stairs. Since they had become friends, Alexa no longer became awestruck by the man's beauty. However, she still regarded the effect of his spiraled dreadlocks and look-at-me confidence as something to behold.

He kissed Alexa on the cheek. "I wanted to check in. See how you're doing."

She dodged the question. "Every time I see you in that Ford Flex, I think I've dropped into an alternate universe. You should be driving a sports car, not a station wagon."

"Excuse me. It's an SUV. Plus it's got three rows of seats so I can ferry around kids from my youth group. It also comes in handy for trucking people and supplies to RESIST events. They didn't tell me advocacy work would involve hauling so much stuff around. Remember, just a few months ago I relied on a county child welfare car for business and rode a bicycle the rest of the time. This baby is a step up."

"You're right. And, the," she paused for emphasis, "SUV has a certain square but ugly beauty." Alexa smiled. "Have you had lunch? Scout and I have been for a long hike. I was about to heat up some chili."

"Sounds good. I came here straight from Sunday services."

"That explains the fancy clothes. You don't want to get chili on that white shirt. Do you want to change into a t-shirt? John's got a few here. He wouldn't mind if you . . ." Alexa trailed off, aghast.

Tyrell put an arm around her shoulder. "Hey, it's natural to have lapses like that. When my Gran passed, it took me months. I'd be at work and think, 'I've got to tell Gran about this or that.' John's been gone less than a month."

"You're right." Alexa walked into the house.

Tyrell followed her through the door. "I will accept your offer of a t-shirt, though."

"I'll bring them all. You can take them with you for RESIST. Just let me get this chili on the stove, then I'll run upstairs for the shirts."

They had lunch out on the deck, Tyrell in a navy blue tee that hung loose on his lean frame. "You haven't been to yoga in two weeks." He stated it as a fact, not an accusation.

"John's death has knocked me for a loop. I've been concentrating on work and not much else. Today, I knew I had to get out and do something. But I'm exhausted after our hike." Alexa took a bite of chili, even though she had little appetite.

"It's hard to lose someone close. And you're dealing with the added burden of a rocky relationship with the guy."

Alexa looked up in surprise.

"It was no secret," Tyrell replied. "It was clear there was trouble in paradise—at least for those of us who know you well. I could see you jump out of your skin every time he called you sugarcakes. You've never really struck me as a sugarcakes type of woman."

"You're right. I was getting ready to break up with John. Then he goes and gets himself killed. If he had lived, we'd have parted ways by now. Instead, everyone is treating me like his ersatz widow. I feel like a fraud. I didn't want to be his girlfriend, but I am mourning his death."

"You need to get off the guilt train. It's not your fault some maniac killed John. The dude picked a dangerous line of work and knew the risks. Hell, he worked homicide."

"I know that."

"Well, I'm not about to lay a rap on you about how everything happens for a reason. Half the shit that happens is totally without reason." Tyrell leaned forward. "But the man died loving you. And when he died, you didn't love him. That's a fact. It's not going to change. You can't let it rule your life."

"Is this how you counseled families and kids in foster care when you were with Children and Youth?" Alexa laughed. "What do you call this technique? Tough love?"

"I call it telling it like it is. Life happens. Deal with it and move on." Tyrell waved a hand to emphasize his point.

"OK. So what's new with you?" Alexa pushed her chili away, surprised she'd eaten almost an entire bowl.

"I'm off to India this summer on a trip to visit the RESIST centers in the north. I really enjoy seeing the progress we're making with retraining these women for new occupations. They just bloom when they're rescued from sex trafficking. India is such an over-the-top country, but I love it. Sensory overload for sure."

"This new job suits you. Moving from being a sometime supporter and volunteer to full-time advocate is a big transition."

"It's good to make a difference." Tyrell smiled. "I hear you've taken up a new cause."

Alexa gave him a puzzled look. "New cause?"

"Fracking. I know Jim and John were looking into some illegal fracking activity when John died. But Melissa tells me you've taken a broader interest in the issue. Something involving an old friend?"

"One of my college roommates has a child who's fighting a rare form of brain cancer. The family believes it's related to a fracking operation on their farm."

"Whoa. What a nightmare. Then I guess you're going to that rally next Saturday?"

"Rally?"

"A bunch of environmental groups are demonstrating against this legislation that's going to open up fracking on state lands. I figured you'd be there to fight back against the bastards that killed John."

Alexa straightened in her seat. "Maybe I will go. I'll call Darby Kaplan at the Wildness Cooperative and find out the details. If it's not stopped, they could be drilling right out there." Alexa pointed to the ridge behind her cabin.

"You go, girl. Find something important to focus all that emotion on. Find out that your problems 'don't amount to a hill of beans in this crazy world.'"

"*Casablanca*? You're channeling Humphrey Bogart now?"

"I am, Elsa." Tyrell laughed.

By the time he left, Alexa had decided that Tyrell had offered good advice. She needed to do something tangible to honor John—and advocating against fracking could be it.

CHAPTER TWENTY-NINE

September 16, 1979

Nuclear power is not healthy for children and other living things. —*Popular anti-nuke poster*

"Not another trip out of town? My God, Will. You're never home. You spend most evenings and weekends doing whatever it is you do with that bunch of crackpots and weirdos, Three Mile Island Alert." Randi's tone was bitter.

"We take samples for radiation. We're monitoring people's health. Even though the state and the feds are saying no one was harmed by TMI, we know radiation was released into the air. There can be short-term and long-term consequences. And someone needs to stay on top of that. The NRC doesn't care. It's just going full steam ahead, authorizing new plants. I hear they might even approve TMI to operate Unit 1—despite the millions of dollars they're spending to clean up Unit 2." Will gripped the back of the chair as his tone became more vehement.

Fussing in his baby seat, Walden waved his arms and whimpered. Will calmed down and handed his son the stuffed bear he'd dropped on the table. "When's Walden's next doctor's appointment? I want to make sure they check him for any radiation effects."

"His appointment is in a few weeks, a six month check-up. Probably while you're gone." Randi paused. "You know, I get the TMI Alert stuff you're doing. I know you want to help after everything we went through with TMI. But I don't get the trips out of town. That protest on Long Island at the power plant."

"Shoreham."

"Yeah, Shoreham. You could have been arrested. Or hurt when they doused you with Mace and hosed the crowd with water. You're the breadwinner for our family. You have responsibilities. What would Walden and I do with you in jail?" Randi put her hands on her hips and stuck out her lower lip. "I'm afraid you're going to lose your job. What does the DER think about you running around the country protesting nuclear power? Don't they run nuclear power in Pennsylvania?"

"Not really." Will took a Coke from the fridge. He knew his anti-nuke activities kept him away from Randi and the baby. But she refused to understand how important this was. "They regulate and monitor some of the operations of the nuclear industry."

"Now you're telling me you have to go to a concert in New York City while I stay home with the baby. How exactly is that a protest? It sounds like you just want to go to the city with your pal Andy for a boys' weekend." Randi curled her lip in contempt.

"The concert is going to be out of sight. Jackson Browne. Bruce Springsteen. Graham Nash. You name it. A whole group of musicians have banded together against nuclear energy in a group called MUSE, Musicians United for Safe Energy." Will took a sip of soda. He refused to let Randi put him on the defensive. He was doing this to keep his family safe. After TMI, she should understand. "But, we only got tickets for the concert because we're going to be there for the protest the next day, on September 23. Thousands of people are gathering to make their voices heard. Numbers like that are the only way The Man will listen. Andy and I will book early to get the train back on Sunday night. We'll only be gone two days."

Randi shook her head. "Do you hear yourself, talking about The Man? I hardly recognize you anymore. The long hair. The beard. The ripped jeans." She broke into tears and lifted Walden into her arms. "What happened to the good, clean-cut man I married?"

"Three Mile Island," Will whispered to his wife's back as she fled the room.

CHAPTER THIRTY

"WHEN TEDDY ROOSEVELT and Gifford Pinchot launched the conservation movement back in the early 1900s, they recognized the importance of preserving land for the good of all. Our public lands are held in trust for all citizens and for the other living creatures that share the planet with us. These lands are essential to our well-being. They provide green spaces where we can hike or swim or simply commune with nature.

"That trust has already been broken here in Pennsylvania when past administrations allowed the oil and gas industry to use public lands for corporate purposes. The past can't be undone. But, now, we have a chance to halt further expansion of the fossil fuel industry into the Commonwealth's most pristine spaces. We must stop the legislature from destroying our state parks and other state lands with further drilling.

"My father was a big fan of Henry David Thoreau, who wrote 'In wildness is the preservation of the world.' Thank you for coming out today to send a message to our senators and representatives. Don't destroy our wild spaces with fracking. Instead, tell them to vote No on Senate Bill 5100 to preserve our world."

Caught up in Walt Jordan's speech, Alexa felt a shiver run down her spine as he roared his closing lines. Rapt, the crowd of nearly twenty thousand people had been silent. Now they broke into frenzied cheering. A chant of "Frack No; Five One O O" broke out, building until the wave of sound bounced off the Capitol Building and amplified the volume.

Alexa stood near the makeshift stage in front of the Capitol's main entrance. When she'd called Darby to ask about the rally, the activist had given her a pass to sit with the rally organizers. So far, Alexa had done little actual sitting, leaping to her feet in support of the various speakers. As Walt left the stage, she turned around to check out the rally. Below, the huge crowd covered the expansive steps and spread out into Third Street and State Street. When she turned back to the stage, Alexa jumped to see Walt Jordan standing in front of her.

"Didn't mean to startle you. Great weather. A day like this has really helped with turnout." Walt grinned.

"Wonderful speech. You've got a real gift."

"Only because my cause is pure."

"I'm glad. I hate to think what would happen if you were up to no good. You had these people eating out of your hand."

"It's nice to see you here." Walt put his hand on Alexa's arm. "I heard about Trooper Taylor. I'm sorry for your loss. From all accounts, he was a good man. And his death exposed another seamy side of the fracking industry. Someone was up there in Michaux State Forest, trying to score an advantage. It's like they have inside knowledge that SB 5100 is going to pass. I wish I knew who was behind the illegal exploration and your trooper's death. Goddamn fracking companies."

Alexa asked, "Do you know who they have on the inside? I guess these companies have a God-awful amount of money to play with. But spending money to explore a long shot. That doesn't add up."

"I agree. But I've been working overtime on this—and I believe there is genuine controversy about the bill in the House. At this point, we have a shot at defeating it."

"What about the Senate?"

Walt frowned. "I'm not sure. There are five or six senators who've spoken out against the bill. But if the leaders turn up the pressure, none of them are known for falling on their swords."

"Senator Gabler's the chair of the committee now. Can't he just keep it from coming up for a vote?" Alexa asked.

Darby had approached in time to hear the last part of the conversation. She lifted her eyebrows in a skeptical expression. "You're assuming Gabler's on our side. Right now, he's officially neutral—but I'm not so sure we can count on him."

By one o'clock the speeches had ended, and the rally had shifted into a feel-good entertainment phase. A local band, called the Green Covenant, had played several environment-focused bluegrass numbers. Alexa enjoyed the next performance, an aging rock band from New York that sounded a lot like Crosby, Stills, Nash, and Young. The lead singer, a skinny guy with wild gray dreadlocks, announced that the band, Levi Bloom and the

Flatbush Boulevard, had been at Woodstock. The band's name sounded familiar. Alexa made a mental note to ask her mother about them.

One of the rally organizers reminded people to call or write their legislators about Senate Bill 5100. Then, a third set of performers moved into the crowd, carrying drums. As the drum circle formed and broke into a wild, pounding rhythm, Alexa decided to leave. She waved a good-bye to Darby and headed back to her car.

People on the steps below were moving away from the center to accommodate the drum circle while others were moving forward to join it. To avoid the chaos, Alexa walked toward the Capitol and cut right, heading toward the parking garage. As she passed the south entrance to the Capitol, she saw Keisha hurrying up the stairs.

"Keisha. Were you at the rally?" Alexa called.

Keisha stopped and turned. "Part of the new job. Since I'm now executive director of the committee that's considering Senate Bill 5100, I decided to hear the opposition."

"I expected one or two of the main sponsors to show up and present their position." Alexa walked to the foot of the steps.

Keisha stayed at the entrance and reached for the door. "Not likely. They all left town on Wednesday night when the session ended. I don't see any of the sponsors being very interested in what a group of environmental activists has to say on the subject anyway. Most of them see this as an economic issue, pure and simple. Plus, we're going to hold a hearing on the bill. That's the time for public input."

"Interesting."

Keisha's tone took on a hostile edge. "What are you doing here anyway? Isn't sex trafficking your little cause?"

"I've begun to take an interest in fracking. Some friends have been touched by it, so I've decided to become more involved." Alexa kept her voice noncommittal.

"Hmmm. Well, all I can say is the issue's a lot more complex than these tree huggers understand. It's interesting to watch Walt Jordan try to position himself as the Great White Hope against fracking. I wonder whose pocket he's in. The solar and wind interests? The coal lobby? You've seen enough to know that, in politics, special interests are usually pulling the strings. He's no different." Keisha opened the door and stepped inside the Capitol before Alexa could respond.

Wending her way back home on back roads, Alexa enjoyed the early May weather. She had put the top down on the Mini convertible and smiled at feel of the soft breeze washing over her bare arms. A short distance from home, she pulled into the gravel parking lot of Keck's store to pick up milk. She had just turned off the engine when her cell phone rang.

"Alexa? This is Jeannie."

"Is everything OK?"

"Yes. Tessa is responding to this new treatment. She seems to be a little stronger. Plus, we've had several conversations with the new lawyers. They plan to file some sort of papers with the court next week. From past experience, they believe Monongas may approach them about a settlement almost right away."

"I imagine Monongas will take a few weeks to look into the complaint. But if a settlement is what you're aiming for, that would be good."

"Tom wants to take them to court and thinks we'll walk away with millions of dollars. I'd rather settle—if it's a decent sum—so we have money right now for Tessa's medical bills."

"Langley and Sloane should be able to advise you on the best course, Jeannie."

"Yeah, I'm getting ahead of things. But that's not why I called. I've been asked to testify at a public hearing in Harrisburg next week. The Senate energy committee is holding a public session on that new fracking bill."

"I just heard about the hearing earlier today."

"Representative Jordan asked me to testify and tell Tessa's story. The lawyers say it could help our case to make her story public. So I wanted to let you know I'll be in the area next week. The hearing is on Thursday, so I'll stay in Harrisburg on Wednesday night. Maybe we could have dinner? My parents are going to keep Tessa."

"Why don't you stay at my place? I'll cook dinner. I need to look at my schedule, but I can probably arrange things so I can come to the hearing."

"I'm not imposing?"

"No way. I have plenty of room, and it's beautiful at the cabin this time of year."

"Then I accept. And it would be wonderful to have your moral support when I testify. I've never done anything like this before. I'm already nervous."

Later that evening, Alexa and Scout sat on the deck, listening to the peepers and the wind in the pines. Despite the calming atmosphere, Alexa kept thinking about her troubling conversation with Keisha. She'd been taken aback by Keisha's recent attitude.

The woman's remarks about Walt Jordan had been surprising, but Alexa knew Keisha saw most things with a jaundiced eye. It was more troubling that she'd lashed out at Alexa. Not that she and Keisha were best friends, but they'd developed a good relationship working on the trafficking committee. They'd gotten along well, and they'd bonded that terrible night when Senator Martinelli died at their feet. But Keisha's manner toward Alexa had changed. In today's encounter, she'd been downright rude.

Maybe Alexa had overestimated the working friendship. Maybe Keisha had played the role of colleague when needed for business—but dropped the pretense now that the commission had ended. Somehow, that explanation didn't ring quite true, even for someone as calculating about her career as Keisha.

Scratching Scout's ears, Alexa tried to pinpoint when Keisha's attitude had changed. "When I got shot," she exclaimed, her words floating away in the wind. Alexa had been baffled by the way Keisha had rebuffed her warning after the hot tub incident. Alexa had feared the shooting was connected to Senator Martinelli's death—and that Keisha could be next on the list. But Keisha had been dismissive and even a little angry at the idea of police watching over her. The young woman had been abrupt with Alexa ever since, even when they'd discussed Lauren's drowning. She wondered whether Keisha was pissed about the fracking bill—or whether it was something more. It felt like the staffer was making a deliberate effort to create distance between them.

Watching the shadows of the pines creep closer and closer to the cabin, an unexpected thought brought Alexa bolt upright in her chair. All along, Keisha had acted antsy at any mention of the police, from the moment Detective Marshall first questioned them. What if Keisha had recognized the voices of the men arguing that night? What if she knew who killed the senator?

CHAPTER THIRTY-ONE

"YOU WORKED WONDERS in rescheduling all of those appointments. And no one complained too much?" Alexa looked at her assistant across the desk.

"Do unto others is what I always say. If you ask nicely, people don't mind changing an appointment. They know someday they might be the ones asking." Melinda bustled toward the door, then turned. "You have that brief due on Monday, though."

"I'm going to ask Vanessa to do the last bit of research, and I can finish it on Friday—or even over the weekend if necessary."

When Melinda closed the door behind her, Alexa turned back to checking emails. In addition to the slew of work-related messages, Alexa read two personal notes. Trooper Cannon's email notified Alexa that Spanky Fulton's trial had been scheduled for early June. At this point, he would be tried for all his offenses except shooting at Alexa. They were still developing that case. Alexa shook her head in disgust. Developing sounded like a euphemism for didn't have a case yet. At least the guy was still in jail.

Darby had sent a message with a link to a news article about the rally. The reporter called it a "powerful message to the fracking industry from a coalition of environmental groups and conservation enthusiasts." Her email also mentioned she was forwarding information about the Senate hearing on Senate Bill 5100.

Alexa scanned her inbox for the second email from Darby but couldn't find it. So she opened up her Spam folder, and there it was, right at the top. Finding this errant email prompted Alexa to review the entire Spam folder. Although their dedicated server emptied Spam older than sixty days, Alexa tried to cruise through the folder at least once a week. It was astounding how many client emails got sidetracked in Spam amidst the ads for Viagra, pleas from Nigerian princes with moneymaking schemes, and sketchy online dating come-ons. The firm had asked their tech company to fine-tune the filters to keep the good emails out of Spam, but they hadn't managed to fix the problem.

In the busy weeks since the commission had wound down, Alexa had neglected her periodic Spam checks, so it took her awhile to page through the entire folder. She found a few items from the bar association along with another email from Darby containing information on fracking lawsuits. She marked them all as "Innocent" and moved them to her inbox. Continuing on, Alexa's heart sank when she found an email from LaurenH.

Biting her lip, Alexa opened the email from Lauren Hildebrand's personal email account. She had sent it on April eighth, the day after the final commission meeting. The day before she drowned.

Sorry I didn't get a chance to talk to you after the Commission meeting. Keisha dragged me off. I suspect she overheard some of our conversation in Senator Gabler's office and didn't want me to tell you the rest. Although I don't think she's in on it, I believe she knows. But, Keisha never wants to do anything that would jeopardize her career. And, I get it. Nobody would ever hire her if she dropped a dime on a powerful Senator and an even more powerful lobbying firm.

Like I tried to tell you, I think that something illegal is going on around this fracking legislation. But, I could be wrong. I know that you could help me figure things out. If I'm right, you could tell me what to do with this information.

Please don't call me at the Senate office. Today is my last day. You can reach me tomorrow and next week on my cell phone.

Alexa sat back and wiped a tear from her eye after she read Lauren's phone number. The intern had tried to reach her, but Alexa had failed the girl—all because of a faulty Spam filter. She printed out the email and raced down the hall to Graham's office, a welter of thoughts crowding her brain. "Is he alone?" she asked her brother's assistant.

At the woman's nod, Alexa sailed into his office. "Graham, I need urgent advice." She handed him the email.

"Hey, Lexie. What's this? The Loomis case?"

Alexa shook her head. "This isn't law firm business. Do you remember that young intern I told you about? The one who helped me on the trafficking commission?"

Graham looked a bit befuddled as he tried to switch gears. "The one who drowned?"

"Yes. Spam just spit out a message from her, from beyond the grave."

Graham read the memo then looked up in surprise. "Do you know what type of illegal activity she's talking about?"

Alexa moaned. "I don't. We had this conversation the day before she wrote this email. We were interrupted just as she was about to tell me what was illegal. I tried to reach out to her that afternoon, and again the next day, but she never returned my messages. Or so I thought, until today."

"We need to get that Spam issue fixed. I'll talk to them again."

"We do. Please focus, Graham. The bigger issue is what should I do with this email?" Alexa remembered her earlier suspicion. "Maybe Lauren didn't drown. Maybe someone killed her to shut her up. Right after her death, I talked to the Harrisburg police about the possibility of foul play, but they were treating her death as a drunken accident. I'm assuming the autopsy revealed nothing to dispute that conclusion. But this email provides motive."

Graham used his most pedantic tone. "You're correct. We need to share this with the police. But I would hardly call this email a smoking gun. We've got a college kid alleging illegal activity with zero details about the activity, the participants, or the proof. She talks about a powerful senator. There are fifty state senators, right?"

"Presumably this one has some role with the fracking legislation," Alexa countered.

"A sponsor, a co-sponsor, someone on the committee that approves the bill, or a fiscal committee that has to vet the bill, or someone in leadership."

"You're right. The fracking connection doesn't narrow things very much. And there must be more than a hundred lobbying firms in Harrisburg. I don't have a clue how many of those might represent hydraulic fracturing companies. They'd be the ones to benefit from this legislation, right?"

Graham leaned forward. "What legislation?"

"Senate Bill 5100, the big bill about fracking on state lands. I went to the rally against it this weekend."

"I can't imagine this is the only fracking-related bill under consideration."

"You're probably right. I know of at least one more that keeps surfacing, related to taxes on fracking." Graham's methodical questions had calmed Alexa. "There is another person who might know about this—Keisha Washington."

"Might is the right word. Your intern assumes Keisha knows what's going on, but she doesn't say it with certainty." Graham again played devil's advocate.

Alexa hesitated to voice her suspicion that Keisha could be shielding Senator Martinelli's murderer with her silence about the men in the balcony. If she could cover up a murder . . . "I know Keisha pretty well, and Lauren was right about the emphasis the woman places on her career. I can't say, though, whether she'd turn a blind eye to bribery and corruption."

"And when the police question this Keisha, she'll say she has no idea what Lauren is talking about. Plus, you're making another leap."

"I know. I know. Lauren doesn't say anything about bribery and corruption. I'm making that assumption since a senator and lobbyist are involved. Classic rookie attorney mistake." Alexa smiled.

"Hey, sis. I understand. This is an emotional thing for you. This young girl's death. A mention of fracking. You're still hurting from John's death, which had a clear link to fracking."

"And I feel like I failed this kid. Goddamn spam." Alexa collapsed into the chair by Graham's desk.

"I get it." Graham's voice was sympathetic.

"I'm not sure you do. This girl asks for my help, in person and in writing. And then she dies before I can provide that help; before anything's resolved. A week or so later, John asks me for commitment. He wants to move in together. Then he dies before I can answer, before anything's resolved. I feel like I'm trapped in a quagmire and the only people who can help me climb out are ghosts. When I reach for one of their hands, I touch nothing but air. So I'll never get out." Alexa heaved a deep sigh.

"Have you considered talking to anyone about all of this?" Graham used a careful tone.

"I am. I'm talking to you. And I've spoken to Melissa and Tyrell. I was getting past my guilt over John. But now this kid's email reaches me from beyond the grave. And it's happening all over again."

"I meant a psychologist or something."

Alexa managed a flicker of a smile. "I know. But I'm OK. This email just threw me for a loop. So, counselor, what is your legal advice on this?"

"It's pretty straightforward. You share this email with the police. I know you'll want to suggest again that her death may not have been accidental. That's it. You don't represent this dead girl or her estate. I don't see any benefit to the parents by raising a suspicion that she could have been killed. If the police find anything, they will adjust the status of the investigation and follow through with her family. I know you'd like to do something more, Lexie. But, you cannot confront Keisha. That would potentially interfere with a police investigation. As an officer of the court, that simply is not an option."

"Thanks. You just confirmed my read on the whole thing. But it helped to talk it through. I'll contact the police this morning." Still distraught, Alexa pushed out of the chair and left the office.

CHAPTER THIRTY-TWO

ALEXA RETURNED TO yoga class on Tuesday. She needed to get back into a routine, and yoga had helped her get through other stressful times in her life. She joined Melissa and Tyrell at the Om Café as usual.

"Where's Haley?" Tyrell asked.

"She called me this afternoon. Said she was just too exhausted to make it," Melissa answered.

"She should be stockpiling extra sleep. She'll need it after the baby comes," Alexa joked.

"I'm glad to see you here tonight." Tyrell had a smug look on his face.

"OK, I'll admit it. Your talk helped." She looked at Melissa. "Tyrell came out to the cabin last Sunday and did his whole social worker number on me. He's pretty good at it." Alexa grinned.

"On Mother's Day? Why weren't you with your mom?" Melissa frowned at Tyrell.

"I spent the whole day this past Sunday with my mama. I visited Alexa last Sunday. It took a whole 'nother week for her to make it to yoga."

"I did go to the rally against fracking on Saturday. Though it still feels like one step forward, two steps back. I got more bad news this week." Alexa filled them in on the email from Lauren. "I called the police detective who investigated her death. He said he'd look into this new information. But I didn't sense a whole lot of enthusiasm to open a closed case."

"If someone killed the kid, they should be jailed for life," Melissa declared. "But the outcome is still the same. A young girl got so drunk and stupid that she fell in the Susquehanna and drowned. Or some bastard killed her because he wanted to keep the girl quiet. Either way, we've got a dead twenty-year-old."

"Damn, girl. When did you become so harsh?" Tyrell shook his head.

"I just mean you can't always save the world. Sometimes, bad things happen. When I went on that trip to India and Thailand with Cecily, we saw and heard all sorts of terrible stories from those victims of sex trafficking. Even the ones who had escaped their traffickers didn't always end up with a rosy life. Cecily taught me that I couldn't expect to lift every burden. Regardless, the intention to help is important. And, when you're lucky, you see results."

"You're right." Alexa appreciated her friends' attempts to rein her in. "But there's more."

"About the intern?" Tyrell took a sip of cappuccino.

"No, about Spanky."

"My God," Melissa groaned. "I can't believe we're going to have another conversation about old Spanky."

"Young Spanky. They said he's only twenty-one." Alexa leaned forward. "I knew Spanky had a hearing coming up in a few weeks. Today, I got an unexpected call from Trooper Cannon. Evidently, Spanky's public defender convinced him to take a plea. He admitted to shooting up all those cabins at Pine Grove Furnace. He admitted to shooting at the two farmers. So he'll be in jail for the next year or so."

"Great," Melissa exclaimed.

"Problem is—Spanky still swears he had nothing to do with my hot tub incident. And Cannon and his partner, Davis, have concluded he might be telling the truth. They expected to turn up evidence confirming he shot at me, too. But they can't find the gun. They viewed his alibi for that night as half-assed, then an independent source confirmed he was at a tractor-pull at the Farm Show. At the very same time someone nearly killed me."

"So who shot at you? Nothing else has happened since he went to jail, right? No strangers around the cabin? Or people stalking you on the street?" Tyrell asked.

"No." Alexa brushed aside the memory of the two men at the Grand Canyon. She'd overreacted there, just like with the kids on the trail at Kings Gap.

"None of this makes any sense. Did the cops look at your client list? You do a lot of Protection from Abuse orders. Maybe some asshole husband or boyfriend wanted to pay you back for a PFA?"

At a loss, Alexa shrugged.

Melissa pushed her empty teacup to the center of the table. "Hate to bail on the moral support, but I need to get home. Jim has a late shift tonight, so I've got Ansel duty."

Alexa pushed back her chair. "I'm going home too."

"Stay out of the hot tub tonight." Tyrell warned as he rose. "I'd feel better if the cops could figure out who took those potshots at you."

Late Wednesday afternoon, Alexa rushed back to the office from a court hearing. She had hoped to leave the office an hour ago to begin preparing dinner. Jeannie was arriving around six.

As she raced past Melinda's desk, she noticed the expression on her assistant's face. "Is something wrong?"

Melinda stood. "Go ahead and put your briefcase down." She followed Alexa into the office. "Your friend Jeannie called. She wants you to call her back right away."

"Is she running late?" Alexa smiled. "That's good news."

"No. She's not coming at all. Some sort of emergency with her daughter." Melinda's solemn expression signaled the emergency was not good.

"Oh, no. Can you dial her for me while I put these papers away?" Alexa pulled the legal documents from her briefcase with a heavy heart.

A few minutes later, Jeannie was on the line. "I'm in Philadelphia at the children's hospital. Our local hospital airlifted Tessa here around noon. I went to wake her from her morning nap, but she didn't respond. At first I thought she was dead. My baby was so pale. But, she was still breathing. So I called the ambulance. The ER got her stabilized and talked to her specialists in Philly. They think it's a reaction to her medication. So they sent Tessa and me here on a helicopter. Tom's driving down. I couldn't reach him at first because he was out showing some homes in a remote part of the county. No cell service."

"I am so sorry. How is Tessa now?" Alexa asked.

"They gave her medication, and she's got some color in her cheeks. But she's still not awake. My God, Alexa. She could die." Jeannie broke down in tears.

"I hope Tom gets there soon. You shouldn't be alone. Did the doctors tell you she could die?"

"No. They're hopeful they can flush this experimental drug from her system—and then she'll be OK." Jeannie's hopeful tone turned bitter. "OK meaning still terminally ill with a rare form of cancer."

"Hang in there." Alexa's words sounded hollow and inadequate to her own ears. Her heart ached for her friend.

Jeannie's voice held an undertone of anger. "I am really upset I won't be there tomorrow to tell Tessa's story to those politicians.

We need to keep this from happening to other little kids, to other families. After some initial apprehension, I looked forward to testifying at this hearing."

"It's more important you be with your daughter."

"I wouldn't think of leaving. But could you give my testimony for me?"

Jeannie's request caught Alexa by surprise. "Do you have your testimony written out? I'm sure they would allow me to present for you, given the circumstances."

"I'll email you a copy of my testimony. This is so important to me, Alexa. I want Tessa to be heard. I am praying she recovers, but she might not. So, that makes testifying even more important."

"You send me the testimony, and I'll go over it tonight." Alexa hesitated, and then plunged ahead. "One way to hammer home the message would be to show the senators a picture of Tessa. Do you have one you could send me?"

"My phone is filled with photos of Tessa. I'll send you one from before the contamination. And a more recent one." Jeannie stopped and Alexa could hear her talking to someone in the background.

"I've got to go, Alexa. Tom's here. I'll send you the testimony and the photos shortly. God bless you for helping out." Jeannie cut the connection.

Alexa sat back in her chair, absorbing the news. Of course she knew Tessa's illness was critical, but she'd never come to grips with the reality that the child could die.

Melinda came into the office. "How bad is it? Poor angel."

"Bad. I'm going to do Jeannie's testimony tomorrow. She'll be sending it through in a little while. I'll revise the testimony with my name. I'll need thirty copies. She's sending me some photos too."

"Whatever you need. I can't imagine what that poor woman is going through."

Twenty minutes later, Jeannie sent the testimony and two photos. The first photo showed a sunny child running with a small, fluffy brown and white dog. This had to be Patches, the dog that had died from the fracking water. Alexa winced at the second photo. Jeannie must have taken the picture just minutes before. It showed Tessa in her hospital bed, connected to machines, a breathing tube, and multiple wires and IVs. Her small pale body, clothed in a colorful printed gown, seemed lost against the big hospital bed and welter of equipment.

Alexa picked up the phone. "Melissa, are you still at the gallery?"

"Yeah. I have that new exhibit opening soon. I'm trying to sort through this artist's work and figure out the best way to present it."

"Could you do me a favor?"

When Alexa hung up the phone, she forwarded the two photos to Melissa. On the way home, she stopped at the gallery and picked up the prints. Melissa had blown up the pictures and placed them on two-foot by three-foot poster board.

"This one is just heartbreaking." Melissa pointed to the shot of Tessa in the hospital bed.

"It is heartbreaking. That's exactly what I want to show these senators. What a vote for fracking can mean in human terms. In desperately ill eight-year-old girl terms."

CHAPTER THIRTY-THREE

CARRYING THE BIG photo posters, Alexa hurried down the corridor that linked the Capitol to the North Office Building. In the office building, she got turned around looking for the hearing room. Wandering, she came across a main door, in front of which sat two Capitol policemen. Following their directions, she finally reached the correct room, tucked away a far corner. Walt Jordan stood out front, looking at his phone, a slim leather envelope under his arm. "Where's Mrs. Demeter?" he asked as Alexa approached.

"Bad news. Her daughter, Tessa, took a turn for the worse yesterday. They were flown to the hospital in Philadelphia. Tessa is a little better this morning—but Jeannie asked me to deliver her testimony." Alexa paused. "Do you think that will be OK? I didn't notify anyone."

"I hope the child continues to improve. I can't see any problem with you filling in for her mother. Substitutes speak all the time in these hearings. Just get up when they call Mrs. Demeter's name and explain."

"Are you staying for the hearing?"

"Yes. We're not in session, so I have all afternoon to hear what people are saying about this bill. It's always interesting to hear what the senators on the committee might ask. They're about ready to start." Walt turned off his phone and dropped it into his envelope briefcase.

The size of the crowd startled Alexa. She and Walt were lucky to find seats near the back. The senators sat facing the packed audience, arrayed behind an elevated desk that spanned the width of the room. Some spilled into tables at floor level. The setup reminded Alexa of one of those PBS shows where the British judges sat on high and harangued some poor, wrongly-accused peasant who stood in the docket. The only thing missing were the white wigs. She assumed the table centered in the front of the room was their version of the docket, the place she and the other presenters would sit.

Only moments later, Senator Gabler pounded a giant gavel and announced the hearing was now in session. As executive director of the committee, Keisha sat beside the senator. Alexa also recognized the scrawny man sitting on the far left, Senator Patterson, the worried man from the kitchen incident with Lauren.

When the crowd quieted, Gabler said, "Before we begin the public testimony, I would like to stress the importance the committee puts on this bill. We understand some citizens oppose the prospect of expanding hydraulic fracturing and maximizing the use of other natural resources in our public parks and state-owned property. We also recognize that the Commonwealth's financial situation continues to require innovative solutions to maintain critical programs, including a number of programs, like Medicaid, that we are obligated to fund under federal law. We've seen the positive impact hydraulic fracturing has had on the economic health of our communities. I, for one, look forward to hearing from the stakeholders, today, before the committee takes any action on Senate Bill 5100."

The room erupted into bedlam, with people cheering and booing. In response, Senator Gabler pounded his gavel and threatened to clear the room if the crowd would not come to order. "Senator Kozlowski, the minority chair, would also like to say a few introductory words."

As the second senator launched into an impassioned speech opposing the bill, Alexa noticed that, beside her, Walt had grown very still. "What's wrong?" she whispered.

"Gabler has something up his sleeve, and I don't like it. Did you hear him? Maximizing the use of other resources? They're going to make this into a larger bill and get every company with interests in mining, timber, water, and God knows what else to support it. It's like shooting the moon with our natural resources."

Alexa hadn't read all of that into the senator's words, but as a legislator, Walt was fluent in politician-speak. With a rising sense of disquiet, she assumed he was right. For a moment, Alexa remembered Keisha's supposition that special interests had Walt in their pocket. If true, he'd just ruled out mining and timber.

As the first person walked to the front to begin his testimony, Alexa took a long, hard look at her father's old law school friend. She had mixed feelings about Senator Gabler. As a child, she'd enjoyed the attention he gave her and Graham. But as she'd moved into her teen years, his hearty manner and tendency to wax on began to feel a little phony. But her dad had good memories of the guy from their school days, and their families got together on a regular basis, even today. During the months they'd worked together on the trafficking commission, Alexa had come to view Silas as a typical politician. While the senator liked the PR he got from taking on a popular cause, he'd delegated everything to Keisha, Lauren, and Alexa. So she'd mainly seen him at the meetings, where the format constrained contact.

Still, Alexa had always believed Gabler was one of the good guys. Without really thinking much about it, she'd bought the line that he moved into this new role as chair of the energy committee because he had seniority and he was a team player. Now Alexa wasn't so sure. He sounded like he really supported this bill. That realization put a whole new twist on things. She felt like the ground had shifted beneath her. Was this hearing rigged?

The natural gas industry dominated the early round of testimony. A series of executives testified in support of the bill, touting the benefits to the economy and energy independence. Alexa wondered why Monongas was not among the companies who spoke.

"What'd I tell you?" Walt muttered as an executive from a coal mining company offered an argument for broadening the scope of the bill to include leasing new mining rights on state lands.

The crowd grew restless as various other industry representatives made similar pleas for their particular interests. At three o'clock Senator Gabler called a break. "I know we are running behind, but we will stay until all the people scheduled have testified. It's important that our questions are answered, even though it might extend the hearing beyond five."

In the ladies' room, Alexa ran into Darby, who was spitting nails. "I can't believe it. They are either setting this bill up as a Christmas tree for all of these special interests, or they're painting such a terrifying picture of all the dire possibilities that people will be happy if they just open up the parks to fracking. I don't know who's playing whom. But I don't like this one bit."

When Alexa took her seat again, Walt and the minority chair were huddled in the front corner of the room. It looked like a heated conversation. When he sat down next to her, he muttered, "Kozlowski says Gabler and the Republicans are running an end game to ram this bill through. This whole hearing's a farce."

Darby led off the opposition testimony with a scathing criticism of the proposed legislation. Alexa noticed with regret that most of the press had left at the break. Jeannie had been scheduled to testify at three fifteen, but the hearing had drifted so far off track, Alexa didn't expect to be called for at least another hour. The packed room grew stifling as the afternoon wore on.

"I have to make some calls," Walt whispered. "I'll be back in before you testify." Alexa turned her attention to the speakers, most of whom opposed the bill. They represented conservation and environmental groups, hikers, hunters, alternative energy providers, physicians, and scientists. Walt came back into the room just as the plainspoken farmer who headed the Friends of Pine Creek began to speak.

Knowing her time slot approached, Alexa made another quick trip to the bathroom to wipe the sweat from her face. That arrogant lobbyist who'd yelled at Lauren stood in the empty hall outside the hearing room. Nason Kurtz. Of course he'd be there. His firm represented some of the energy companies.

"Excuse me." At the entrance of the vestibule, Alexa had to slide past the man to access the ladies' room down the hall. No one in the entire hall, and he had to stand at the one place the passage narrowed to accommodate equipment for the disabled. What a jerk. She rolled her eyes. Although she tried not to stereotype, he looked like one of those no-neck jocks with more muscle than brains. And blocking her like that was something a fifteen-year-old bully would do. Apparently, his nasty behavior with young Lauren was part of a pattern.

When Alexa emerged from the bathroom, the jerk was still there. He watched her approach with an insolent, knowing look on his face—almost like a sexual leer. This time, he took a deliberate step backward and waved his arm with a flourish to let Alexa pass. "I wouldn't want to keep you, Miss Williams," he said in a nasal, mocking voice. Alexa continued into the room without responding, but he'd succeeded in unsettling her. How did this disgusting man know her name?

Still upset, she sat down only to hear Senator Gabler say, "Jeannie Demeter."

As Alexa grabbed the two photos, Walt grasped her arm and said, "Knock 'em dead."

She made her way to the front table. Before sitting, she explained, "Senator Gabler, Mrs. Demeter couldn't make it today because of a family emergency. She asked me to read her testimony."

"Why, of course, Alexa. Go right ahead." The senator was cordial, but Keisha had a stormy expression on her face. As Alexa sat, Keisha gave someone in the back of the room a long look, but Alexa couldn't turn to see who it was.

Instead, she addressed the panel. "Senator Gabler, Senator Kozlowski, members of the committee, thank you for the opportunity to testify today on behalf of Jeannie Demeter, her husband, Tom, and their daughter, Tessa. My name is Alexa Williams. Jeannie and I have been close friends since college."

Jeannie had written the testimony as an account of what had happened with the fracking on the Demeter property. When Alexa read the passage about Tessa getting contaminated by petting the dog that had fallen into a fracking wastewater pool, the audience gasped. She paused and glanced at the panel. Several senators leaned forward, sympathetic looks on their faces. Senator Gabler sat stone-faced. It looked like Keisha was checking her cell phone.

Tamping down a flash of anger, Alexa took a deep breath, then recounted the course of Tessa's diagnosis and illness. She concluded with the words she'd added to the testimony last night.

"The reason Jeannie Demeter could not be here today is because of Tessa. Yesterday morning, Tessa became unresponsive and was flown to Children's Hospital of Philadelphia for emergency treatment. Even if the specialists there are able to save her life this time, they may never be able to cure her cancer. Her parents remain hopeful, as do I. But, the family has paid a terrible price for signing that fracking lease. And their daughter may pay the ultimate price—her life. How can we, as citizens of Pennsylvania, afford to expose other families, other children, to such a terrible risk?

"I believe these two photos say it all." Alexa held up the poster boards to show the photos, first to the senators, and then to the hearing room. "The first is little Tessa Demeter and her dog, Patches, when they were both healthy. Before Monongas drilled on the Demeter farm. The second picture shows Tessa last night, clinging to life in her hospital bed." One of the young staffers sitting behind the senators broke into tears at the second photo.

"The Demeter family and I urge you to vote no on Senate Bill 5100." Alexa finished to a completely silent room. The only sounds were a few muffled sobs behind her in the audience.

"I have no questions for Ms. Williams," Senator Gabler said in a strangled voice. "Any questions?" He looked in both directions at his colleagues who all shook their heads. "Thank you, Alexa. The next witness is . . ."

Alexa felt drained as she collapsed next to Walt. She glanced at her watch. Five thirty? This had been an endless day.

"Very powerful," Walt said. Several people behind Alexa patted her on the back and made complimentary remarks.

"The sad thing," she replied to the representative. "No matter what they do on this bill, it's not going to help Tessa."

"But it could help other children. You look beat. Do you want to leave?"

"No, there can't be that many more people to testify, can there?"

"Kozlowski's staff sent me the list." Walt looked at his cell phone. "It looks like maybe ten more people are scheduled."

"Ten? Maybe I will go."

"Hold on. We both want to hear the next one. Monongas."

"Monongas? Isn't this the opposition segment of the testimony?"

Walt looked at his phone again. "From now on, it looks like a mix. Hell, even AARP is testifying. Wonder what they'll have to say about this."

When Alexa tuned back into the hearing, a skinny guy from a hiking association was finishing his remarks. As the hiker rose, the big chandeliers flickered overhead. Thunder rumbled through the thick walls of the hearing room. Alexa imagined she tasted ozone in the air.

Senator Gabler called out, "Monongas."

A silver-haired man who had been leaning against the wall sauntered toward the front table. Alexa recognized him right away. Walker Toland, boss of the overgrown bully in the hallway, and—if Keisha was correct—the most powerful lobbyist in Harrisburg. She shook her head, thinking, Why am I not surprised that the Toland firm represents Monongas? I saw him with Keisha in the Capitol that day, schmoozing.

Toland thanked the committee and offered a perfunctory apology for the Monongas executives' absence. "They would be here to support the bill in person, but Monongas has its annual board meeting today." When the uber-lobbyist lifted his testimony from the table, the arms of his impeccable charcoal suit slipped to reveal French cuffs. Today's look was diamond cufflinks so big Alexa could identify the stone from the back of the room. Something about the way this guy carried himself pissed Alexa off. He probably held those pages of testimony in the air because he was too vain to wear reading glasses.

Toland continued. "Let me start with the bottom line. Monongas has a long history of partnership with the citizens of Pennsylvania and a track record of stewardship of the land. We employ local citizens in all aspects of our Pennsylvania-based operations. We have improved the roads in many counties to compensate for truck traffic. We are committed to restoring private lands where we've drilled and to ensuring pipeline safety. All told, we have pumped billions of dollars into Pennsylvania's economy.

"Monongas strongly supports the expansion of natural gas exploration and drilling into state parks and public lands. It would be a natural extension of our current work in the state, benefitting both the Commonwealth's taxpayers and the economy—while taking advantage of the state's abundant energy reserves."

As the man droned on, Alexa tried to figure out why his voice sounded so familiar. She was certain she'd never met him in person. But his drawl had a familiar ring to it. She regretted staying for the testimony. He was simply repeating all the same things the earlier industry spokesmen had said. Except Toland's delivery style implied he was too important for such menial work. The fact that he hadn't sent one of his other lobbyist minions, like that hulk Kurtz, to testify must mean Monongas was a pretty important client.

When Toland finished, one of the Democratic senators asked, "Would Monongas be willing to pay an enhanced drilling impact fee or a special tax on gas pumped from state land?"

Toland leaned back in his chair and drawled, "Obviously, I cannot speak for Monongas without a specific proposal on the table. But he who dances must pay the piper. Monongas understands that principle."

Alexa froze at Toland's words. A cold tendril of alarm snaked down her spine. That's why she recognized the voice. Toland had been on the balcony the night Senator Martinelli had died. He and his musclebound sidekick may have been the ones who threw Martinelli over the railing.

She looked up at Keisha, still sitting with the committee. Keisha watched Alexa with a steady gaze as if waiting to see if she'd made the connection. When Keisha's face tightened, Alexa blanched at the realization that the woman had known all along.

Alexa glanced around the room. Only a handful of people remained in the hearing room. "I've got to get out of here. I need the police," she spoke into Walt's ear. Before he could respond, Alexa jumped to her feet and bolted down the aisle, leaving the photos on the floor.

CHAPTER THIRTY-FOUR

March 6 and March 29, 1983

There's reasonable assurance that TMI-1 can and should be safely operated.
—*Nuclear Regulatory Commission; May 29, 1985.*
(TMI Unit One came back on-line in October 1985)

Will gathered his long hair into a ponytail and took his backpack downstairs. "Good morning, Mom. Are you making waffles?"

"We've got real maple syrup and bacon. You always loved waffles on Sunday when you were little." Bettina Armstrong bustled around the kitchen in her apron. "Coffee's on the stove."

Taking a clean cup from the dish rack, Will filled it with coffee and placed it on the table. Then he hugged his mom. "You're the only woman in Pennsylvania who still wears an apron to cook."

"I doubt that, honey."

Dad walked into the house and stamped his feet on the doormat. "It's not even two inches deep out there. This is going to be the last snow of the season."

"Onion snow. That's what my grandmother called it," Mom called out.

"I see you're taking off again." Dad pointed to the bulging backpack in the corner.

Will nodded. "I'm headed out west. This new company, Mononuclear, is constructing a new plant. They're putting it in the desert, right on the only flowing river that intersects forty thousand acres of pristine land. Bastards are even calling it the Oasis

Nuclear Generating Facility. It's like they're thumbing their noses at the critical nature of the habitat they're about to ruin."

"Language, son." Dad joined Will at the table.

"I've heard worse, Herbert." Mom spoke in a mild tone as she laid a towering plate of waffles in the middle of the table next to the platter of bacon.

The conversation lagged as all three turned to the food in front of them. Bettina ate a few bites and then put down her fork. "Are you driving the whole way out there? I'm not sure that vehicle, that Thing of yours, can make it a thousand miles."

Will grinned. "I agree. That's why PANF is paying for my bus ticket."

"Don't they pay all your expenses?" Dad asked. "I mean you do work for this People Against a Nuclear Future organization and draw a salary. Right?"

"I do. But they operate on a shoestring budget. All the money comes from donations and a few grants."

"Honey. We worry about you. Ever since you and Randi broke up, you've been gallivanting all over the country. California; New Hampshire; Washington, DC. I can't keep track of everywhere you've been. And you've been arrested too many times."

"But we're making a difference, Mom. We're keeping new nuclear power plants from coming on line. And we're making our voices heard on nuclear weapons too. Over a million people showed up to the protest in Central Park in June. You can't believe the impact that the will of the people can have on Congress and the White House."

"Son, we know how committed you are to this no nukes movement. But it cost you a wife and son, a good job, and a stable life. We can't help but worry about you."

Will smiled. "It's worth it if I can protect Randi, Walden, you guys, and the world from a nuclear nightmare. TMI came this close." He circled finger and thumb together with a tiny space in between. "It could happen again if we can't shut down all the nukes. That includes keeping TMI Unit One off-line forever."

"Maybe you and Randi will never get back together. I know the divorce is final. But if you settled down, you could see Walden a lot more than you do now." His mother's voice sounded hopeful.

"Not going to happen, Mom. Randi and I are in two different places now. When I stopped there last week, she told me she's engaged to some guy. They're talking about getting married next spring. I'll still see Walden whenever I want."

"We had him here for a weekend last month. He's a fine boy," Dad said.

"Don't you think he's tall for his age? I can't believe he'll be four this month." Will's pride in the child shone in his voice.

"I bet he tops six feet. Maybe more."

"Walden looks just like his father." Bettina wiped a tear from her eye with the corner of her apron.

Will looked at his parents with love. He'd chosen a path they didn't understand, but they always had his back. "It's been great seeing you. But I've got a bus to catch. I'm driving out to Pittsburgh to take a Greyhound. There's a PANF supporter there who's going to hold onto my car until I get back. I might be out west for a few weeks. It's a developing situation, as they say." He pushed back from the table and walked around to kiss his mother on the forehead. "No, don't get up. Finish your breakfast." Will shook his dad's hand and headed out the door.

"I'll be in touch." He turned back with an impish grin and raised a clenched fist in the air. "Power to the people."

The desert sun beat down on Will's back as they hiked cross-country across the hard-baked land. "Damn. This is pretty intense heat. Is it always like this?"

Tanner Lynch cinched the straps tight on his backpack before he offered a laconic response. "Only during the day. That's why we left before dawn." He wiped his sun-baked face with a red bandana.

"Maybe we should have hiked in at night."

"Watch out for rattlers." The burly man pointed at an s-pattern in the sand. "Sidewinders."

Will jumped and threw a suspicious look at the expanse of sand in front of his feet. The two men had left Will's rental car at a scenic view pullout a few miles back. They were hiking across the desert to the Oasis construction site.

"You're sure Dorothy Two-Eagles is going to have the bus of protestors pull into the entrance by eight o'clock, right?"

"Yep."

"How long until we reach the main gate?" Will pulled a pocket watch out of his jeans pocket and flipped it open.

"Not more than an hour. Plenty of time. I'm told the workers never arrive before eight. They're on the clock. Won't get paid if they show up any earlier."

A shadow flitted over the desert ahead. Will looked up to see a dark bird circling high against the sun. An eagle? Or maybe a hawk? Back on the East Coast, Will would have been able to identify the raptor, but the desert felt like foreign territory. His inability to name the bird brought back the nagging feeling he'd *had all morning. That something wasn't right. He knew he was driving Tanner crazy, going over all the details. Maybe he just didn't feel comfortable relying so heavily on people he'd just met.*

He softened his tone. "Too bad we couldn't get that TV station in Desert Forks."

"It's a pretty long haul for them to come way out here." Tanner adjusted course, veering left. "But Dorothy said the town newspaper and one of the TV stations will show up by eight too."

"Righteous. Thanks for hiking in here with me. I might have made it, but with the way this desert goes on and on, I could have missed the construction site. Your local knowledge helps." Will could see a fence in the distance. "You're certain nobody will be on site at this hour?"

"Nothing's certain, man. But a buddy who works for the construction company told me they just lock the gate when they leave at night. No guards." Tanner slowed his footsteps.

Will pulled a pair of binoculars and a canteen from his backpack. He scanned the fence line for movement. Taking a long drink of water, he said, "Looks like we're OK."

The two men easily found the main gate. On either side, an eight-foot chain-link fence stretched long in both directions. Three strings of barbed wire crowned the top. Will turned his back to the gate and gazed down the long dusty entrance road. No sign of traffic. Inside the perimeter, he could see nothing but a line of parked construction vehicles and earthmoving equipment, their yellow paint dulled to a dusty tan by clinging sand.

Will turned his back on Tanner to empty his bladder. The temperature was cooler here near the river gorge. Still, his thin stream of urine dried in the sand before he'd buttoned up his jeans. Pulling his baseball cap lower on his forehead, Will exhaled a long breath. "Let's do this."

Tanner and Will dug thick chains out of their backpacks, along with padlocks. At the point where the two halves of the wide gate met, they threaded their chains through both sides. Then they sat on the ground, a few feet apart, and looped the heavy chains in complete circles around their midsections.

"Ready?" Will padlocked the ends of his chain to the links that ringed the gate. Tanner did the same.

"Here." Tanner held his hand out for Will's key. "I'll throw them out there." He pointed on the far side of the road. When Tanner hurled the keys, Will saw a glint as they hit the desert floor.

The two men sat in silence for a while. As Will breathed the dry air and watched the sun rise higher over the desert, he warmed to the desolate beauty of the place. But it was a far cry from the forests of Pennsylvania he'd roamed as a child and young man. He missed the cool green stillness of the woods.

Will turned to Tanner and smiled. "Nobody mentioned the rattlesnakes when we came up with this plan."

"No worries. They'll feel the vibrations when we move around and stay clear."

Kicking the ground with his boot heel, Will joked. "Like this?"

"That should do it." Tanner answered with a tense expression.

Either Tanner didn't get the joke, or he didn't have much of a sense of humor. Will had only met the guy a few days ago after he'd arrived in town to organize the protest. When they'd come up with the idea of chaining someone to the gate, Tanner had volunteered without hesitation. But, now, the guy looked really nervous. "Having second thoughts about this?" Will asked.

"There's no going back now. We can't unchain ourselves until Dorothy Two-Eagles arrives with the duplicate keys." Tanner ran a sleeve across his sweaty forehead.

"We've got a good plan. It should work. If Mononuclear gets enough bad press, it could slow them down. Force them or the state to hold public hearings before they proceed. By then, that environmental lawsuit will be filed. That's the game; just keep hassling the energy companies until they decide it's going to take too much time and too much money to complete the process. So they cut their losses and walk away. We can't rely on the NRC. It has to be a grassroots effort."

Tanner shook his head. "That all sounds good. But Mononuclear has hired a really rough bunch of goons to intimidate people who oppose Oasis. I heard they threatened two of the county commissioners who were going to disapprove the plant permits. There have been some other incidents too." Tanner's voice quivered.

Will patted his arm. "We're going to have the press here for our protest. They won't do anything weird if the TV cameras are running. He looked at his watch. We've got about an hour before they arrive. I think I'll take a quick nap.

Will had no sooner closed his eyes than he heard the rumble of a vehicle engine. He jerked his eyes open at the unexpected intrusion. Although he knew that noise carried long distances over the desert, this vehicle sounded like it was coming this way. "Do you hear that?"

Tanner didn't reply, but his expression tightened again. He looked like he was about to throw up.

A dart of fear stabbed Will between the shoulder blades. He could see the source of the sound now: a roaring cloud of red dust sweeping across the desert. As it got closer, Will saw a dark jeep with a roll bar at the center of the cloud, barreling toward them, dust billowing from the wheels. "What's going on? This is too early for any workers, right?"

Tanner's face had paled, and he avoided Will's eyes. As a cold, hollow dread surged through his body, Will knew.

"I'm sorry, Will. I had no choice. They threatened my kid. Said they'd kill him if I didn't help them deal with you." Tears streamed down Tanner's face as he dug a key from his pocket, and, hands shaking, opened his padlock. Slipping out of the chains, Tanner took off, stumbling across the desert at a forty-five degree angle to the road.

Maybe they just want to rough me up. Teach me a lesson, Will hoped as he sat there, helpless, chained to the fence. He flinched as a shadow flickered across his outstretched legs. The shriek of the soaring raptor pierced the air. His heart flailed against the cage of his chest, as if trying to break free and join the high-flying bird.

When two hulking men in dark clothes stomped out of the jeep, a hard knot of despair clenched deep in the pit of Will's stomach. He'd been living on borrowed time ever since Three Mile Island. And he feared the clock was about to stop today. A bleak smile flickered across his lips. What a godforsaken place to die.

"Randi, Walden, I did my best. I love you." Will whispered, picturing a green forest glade in his mind. The men halted at his feet, shoulder to shoulder, their faces grim. One man, tall and rangy, dangled a baseball bat from his hand.

Feeding his courage on a flare of anger, Will looked up. His voice never wavered. "I have a right to lawful protest against the Oasis Nuclear Power Station that is being constructed at this site. I'm exercising that right."

The beefy, shorter man spoke with a flat, western accent in a bored voice. "Mononuclear ain't putting up with any of you no-nuke pukes. The desert's a big place, and you won't be the first eastern pretty boy to be left for the buzzards."

"I have a right to protest. The press will be here soon to film our demonstration . . ."

The beefy man ignored Will and nodded to his silent companion. The tall man raised a baseball bat high over his head. He rocked on his heels for a long moment, bat extended aloft. His silhouette looked like a black tower against the bright sun. Then, with a cruel smile, he brought the bat down with an abrupt slash.

Tensing in despair, Will heard a whistle of air, high-pitched like the raptor's cry. "Walden," he thought as his skull shattered with a burst of excruciating pain and a last wild lurch of his heart.

CHAPTER THIRTY-FIVE

WALKER TOLAND'S DRAWL ringing in her ears, Alexa ran from the hearing room, looking for the Capitol police. She slowed at the sight of Nason Kurtz and another beefy man lounging in the far corner of the hall. They were studying Kurtz's phone. Looking up in unison, they moved toward her.

"Alexa," Walt called as he emerged from the hearing room. "What's going on?"

Alexa grabbed his arm and pulled him down the hall. Walt let her manhandle him for a while then stopped. He turned and grabbed both of her arms and demanded, "Look, it's clear something's wrong here. But you need to tell me what."

Alexa glanced down the hall. Kurtz and his friend had backed off, but they were watching her. She kept her voice low. "I just figured it out. The guy who testified, Walker Toland. He was there the night Senator Martinelli died. I have to tell the cops." She nodded in the direction of the main door, where she'd spoken to the Capitol police earlier.

Walt looked confused. "How would you know who was there that night?"

"Keisha Washington and I were in the rotunda when the senator fell."

"So you saw Toland push him over?"

"No, we just heard voices, men arguing not long before it happened."

"And you think Toland was one of those men?"

"Yes. I have to get to the police. Now." Alexa shrugged out of his grip and marched toward the door, a determined look on her face.

"I'll go with you."

"Thanks." Alexa looked over her shoulder at the sound of footsteps hitting marble. Nason Kurtz and his buddy were running down the empty hall toward them. "Walt, Toland's stooge must know I figured it out."

"Let's get to the cops. They can deal with them." Walt picked up the pace. Alexa tried to match his long stride, happy she'd worn flats.

The two dashed into the entrance area only to find it empty. The doors were closed with a velvet rope blocking any exit.

"Let's head for the Capitol. If there are any police in this building, they're out on patrol." Without waiting for an answer, Walt doubled back a few yards and dodged into a corridor.

Alexa looped her purse across her body. Then, she ran after Walt, fumbling with her cell phone. She wanted to dial 911 but had turned the phone off in the hearing room. Every time she slid her thumb to open the emergency screen, she had to look up to avoid tripping. By the time she glanced back down, the security screen had popped up again. Finally, she held the phone in front of her as she ran and tried hitting the emergency button. Nothing happened. Damn. No bars.

"Forget the phone. We'll find police in the Capitol," Walt directed as they fled down the empty hallway. Alexa jammed the phone in her jacket pocket. She could hear the two men chasing them, but they hadn't yet rounded the corner.

Alexa and Walt turned into yet another hallway. Kurtz and his buddy's footsteps echoed behind them, gaining ground. Walt pointed ahead, "That's the door to the Capitol. When we get on the other side, I'll slow them down. You run for the cops. There should be a guy on the back door."

"OK," Alexa gasped. She shrieked as a chunk of plaster hit her hand. A loud crack reverberated through the corridor.

"Weave," Walt yelled. "They've got guns."

Alexa and Walt veered apart. They zigzagged for the last few yards, dodging chunks of falling ceiling. Terrified, Alexa sprinted faster. The racket was unbearable. Plaster dust and the smoke of gunfire filled the air. Covering her ears and coughing, Alexa burst through the doors into the Capitol's East Wing. Taking gulps of clean air, Alexa bent over to catch her breath. She looked up to see Walt flick a switch above the door that had closed behind them.

"Automatic lock. It will only slow them down a minute or two." He motioned to his left as he stepped forward. "There's another entrance down there."

Alexa could feel her heart hammering as she looked at her phone. Still no bars. "You know your way around this maze. Let's stick together. I might get lost on my own."

"Let's keep moving." Walt took off.

"I expected to see police running down here toward the gunshots. Or someone from that hearing." Alexa tried to keep up with Walt, trailing him down another long hallway. They passed a corridor to the right, but he kept going straight.

He slowed to let her catch up. This hall, like all the others, stood empty. "I hoped someone would be watching a security camera, but I guess not. I guess the sound of gunfire didn't carry the whole way back to the hearing room."

"Where is everyone?" Alexa puffed in disbelief.

"The legislature's out of session. That means most of the senators and representatives are in their districts. On non-session days, nearly all the employees hit the road at five or earlier. The Capitol Complex is a ghost town in the evenings."

"Tell me about it." Alexa took several deep breaths to calm her fear.

Behind them, their pursuers were banging on the locked door. Wham. Wham. Wham. Moments later, they crashed through the far doors with a loud bang.

"Run," Walt shouted above the clamor.

Alexa broke into a sprint, not slowing until she reached the cafeteria area. Finally. Help was near.

"This way." Walt veered toward a vacant desk marked Information. He stopped short. "Damn. There's usually a Capitol policeman here."

"No. This is crazy." Distressed, Alexa ran to the back entrance, hoping to find help. She tried each of the doors. All locked.

"We can't get out that way." She came back to Walt's side. Before them, the silent expanse of marble in the East Wing Atrium was empty. The gift shop, welcome center, and cafeteria were shuttered for the evening. The only sounds were the muted burble of a fountain and the chug, chug, chug of the huge escalator that led to the main Capitol building. To the rotunda where Senator Martinelli had died at Alexa's feet.

"Where's the Capitol police office?" Alexa looked at Walt. She shot a nervous glance down the hall they'd just exited. No sign of their pursuers.

"At the end of that corridor. He pointed beyond the cafeteria to a hallway that ran the same direction that they'd just come from."

"Couldn't we have gone straight there?" Alexa snapped. She been relying on Walt's knowledge of the Capitol, but now she was having doubts.

"Yeah, down that hallway we passed. But I don't know if it's staffed at night. I figured this was the best bet. Let's head over there now." He sounded reluctant.

"Why not go up to the rotunda? Someone's sure to be at the main entrance."

"OK. If not, we can duck in somewhere and call for help. How are you doing?" His tone was solicitous as he touched her arm.

"Fine. Let's go." She tried to keep the impatience from her voice. For all this guy knew, she could be some shrinking violet teetering on the edge of total collapse. But she could hold her own. They needed to get help now. Comparing their favorite ways to cope with the stress of being shot at by maniacs could wait for later.

Walt stepped toward the escalator just as Kurtz and the other muscleman emerged from the corridor. The men peered into the visitor's center then turned left into a hall that curved north. Apparently, the thugs hadn't seen them.

Still, Alexa and Walt couldn't take the escalator to the main Capitol. Nor could they cross the open atrium to the Capitol police office. Either route, they'd be sitting ducks if the men came back.

Signaling with a jerk of his head to the left, Walt ducked behind the pillar and slipped off his shoes. A few steps behind, heart pounding, Alexa followed his lead. Then they moved down a hall that curved to the south, a mirror opposite to the corridor Kurtz had decided to investigate. Alexa followed Walt through a maze of halls. Right. Left. Right. Disoriented by the unfamiliar labyrinth, Alexa felt increasingly dependent on the legislator.

An alarming thought hit from left field. What if Walt was in on it? He'd been so quick to offer help. What if he was leading her through this cavernous building right into a trap? Kurtz and the Hulk could just be the sheepdogs helping Walt herd her into a snare. But if she ditched Walt and set out on her own, she might take a wrong turn and run smack into Kurtz.

Alexa remained wary as Walt led her up a set of steps and through a door. The architecture made an abrupt change from modern to an older style; they'd arrived in the main Capitol at last. Grounded by knowing just that little bit about their location calmed Alexa, and she pushed aside her suspicions. Walt was one of the good guys. He was risking his life to help her.

The representative stepped around yet another corner and pulled Alexa to his side. They stood and listened. Complete silence.

"I think we lost them," Alexa whispered. She looked down at her phone, but still no bars. "Do you have reception?" she asked Walt.

"I left my phone back in the hearing room. It's in my briefcase." His expression was sheepish. "Let's keep moving. If we walk down this corridor and take the central stairs, that will bring us into the main rotunda."

"The central stairs? The ones that come up beneath the grand staircase?" Alexa asked. She flashed to an image of Senator Martinelli's body crashing into the angel statue.

"Yeah. We come to the top of the stairs, walk through the rotunda, and the guards are right there at the main entrance." Walt took off down the hall. Alexa followed, glad to resume walking; her bare feet had grown cold, standing still on the marble floor.

Alexa and Walt climbed the stairs with caution. Several times Walt made a hand motion for Alexa to stop. She could see his time as a Marine had kicked right in when faced with this dangerous situation. When they reached the top of the stairs, they faced the top of the East Wing escalators. Although their path from the atrium had seemed erratic, Alexa realized they'd traveled in a long U. But their journey would be over soon. They could turn everything over to the police.

As they stepped onto the floor of the rotunda, loud voices laughed near the front doors. Alexa grabbed Walt's wrist. Still hidden behind the big pillar, he froze.

"You gotta be kidding. That hearing's still going on over in North? Why don't the senators just wrap it up and send everyone home?" a male voice asked.

"Yeah, this place cleared out at least an hour ago. Feels like a tomb at this hour," a woman interjected.

"It's the will of the people, man," another man responded. Alexa thought she recognized Kurtz's arrogant tone.

"Hey, I'm just doing what I was told."

Alexa didn't recognize this new voice, but she feared it was Kurtz's companion. "The senator needs these papers to finish things up, and he sent Kurtz over to pick them up. They could be in his desk on the floor. Could be in his office. I'm going to escort him around to see if we can find what the chairman needs. I wanted to give you a heads up."

"Appreciate it, sir," the first speaker answered.

Alexa eased out onto the main floor next to Walt. They were still shielded by the pillar. A reflection in the huge display case on the facing wall caught her eye. She blanched at the scene, mirrored in the glass. Kurtz stood at the Capitol police desk, speaking to two cops. The fourth person, the one speaking, was Kurtz's buddy as she had suspected. Even worse, his words seemed to indicate he was a Capitol cop.

"Bad guys," she mouthed silently to Walt. From the grim look on his face, he'd already figured it out.

"Let's get out of here," he whispered. Instead of going back downstairs, Walt dashed forward a few steps into the short hall and disappeared around a corner.

"He might have left them in Representative Jordan's office over on the House side too." Reacting to Kurtz's nasal voice, Alexa pushed aside her fear of being seen. She took a deep breath and scurried across the open space to join Walt.

"There's a back stairway here. Let's climb to a higher floor and watch what they're doing. Then we can call for help." Walt jogged up a narrow staircase, not pausing until he'd gone three floors.

When they reached the top, Alexa longed for a rest. She was in good shape, but the adrenalin spike from that long run from the North Office Building—and getting shot at—had left her drained. She leaned over and massaged her feet. They throbbed from walking barefoot over what seemed like miles of marble.

"That man with Kurtz, he must be a Capitol cop. Do you know him?" Alexa looked at Walt.

"No, but from the conversation, he seems to be higher up on the food chain than the two at the door. And it sounds like he has a master key to get into any room in the Capitol. Everything operates on a swipe card system."

"Well they know who you are. Your office is on the list of places Kurtz plans to visit."

Walt moved out of the stairwell and slid to the edge of the balcony. Alexa followed him to the railing. They stood on the highest floor that opened into the rotunda. As she gazed down into the space below, Alexa trembled. Senator Martinelli's last view had been from up here—before he'd been thrown over one of these railings to his death.

She shook off the dismal reflection. Walt was pointing at Kurtz and the cop below. They were opening the door to the Senate chamber. When the two men stepped inside, Alexa said, "They won't be in there long. They're just going through the motions for those guards."

Walt whispered, "I'll keep an eye on them. Call for help." He dashed across the hallway and stood behind the middle pillar, watching the entrance below.

Alexa pulled her cell phone from her pocket. Three bars. She pressed the emergency button to reach 911.

"What is your emergency?" a man asked after a few rings.

"I need help. Someone has been shooting at me and a friend." Alexa replied, her voice breaking at the thought of getting help.

"What is your name?"

"Alexa Williams."

"And your friend?"

"Representative Walt Jordan."

"And where are you located?"

"In the Capitol building in Harrisburg."

"You say someone is shooting at you? In the State Capitol?" The dispatcher squawked.

Walt came running back toward Alexa, pointing to the corner behind him. "They're coming up the elevator. They must have taken a side exit from the Senate chamber."

When she lowered the phone from her ear, Alexa could hear the elevator bell ring and the doors open in the far corner.

"Miss, are you still there?" the man at the 911 center asked.

Alexa put the phone back to her ear just as Walt grabbed her elbow and whispered, "This way." The phone sailed from Alexa's hand and soared into the rotunda. As they fled the balcony, Alexa winced at the crash of the phone, shattering on the marble floor far below.

"Shit," Alexa exclaimed. Nothing was going right. She rounded the corner heading back toward the stairs. But Walt dashed straight through the stairwell and took a ninety-degree turn out onto the balcony above the House chambers. Alexa slowed to claw at the doors into the visitor's gallery on her left, but they were locked. Freaking out, she followed Walt toward the front corner of the building. Alexa stumbled at the sound of gunfire.

"Over here." Walt raced to cover behind a corner wall. Despite her panic, Alexa fretted about the priceless paintings and mosaics on the other side of their hiding place. Then, Walt's hand went to his upper right arm, and he groaned.

"What's wrong?" Alexa whispered. "Were you hit?"

Walt gritted his teeth. "Fine. Just grazed me."

"These assholes just don't give up. I'm scared." Alexa tried to mirror Walt's penchant for understatement. But the terror she was feeling went well beyond scared.

"Me too." Walt grinned. He hugged her with his left arm. "But we've almost got them where we want them."

Alexa knew what he was doing but couldn't suppress a hysterical giggle at Walt's lame joke. Battlefield humor.

"Capitol police. Halt. Hold your fire." The woman cop's shout came from somewhere down below. Footsteps charged up the main staircase just as more shots rang out. A woman screamed, then a man yelled, "Carson? Roxanne?" There was no answer.

Alexa feared the worst for the woman cop but didn't have time to dwell on her fate. The sharp slap slap of leather on marble had resumed, rushing in their direction. It sounded like only one man still chased them.

"Let's get to another floor." Walt broke cover and ran for the staircase in the corner. Passing an elevator, Alexa pushed the button, hoping to confuse their pursuer. She pounded down a twisting and narrow stairway behind Walt, terrified she'd trip and fall. She ran faster, even more terrified at the thought of Kurtz shooting her in the back.

Alexa sighed in relief when Walt dashed out of the second floor exit. She caught a glimpse of white hair on the stairway above before she followed. Kurtz was gaining ground.

Gasping for breath, Walt pulled her close. "I hoped we could make it to the main floor, but I don't think it's safe. They split up. They won't want any witnesses. Kurtz's buddy has probably gone to take out the second guard. Let's deal with this asshole."

Alexa stepped back, glancing around in dread. Here on the mezzanine, they were exposed to the upper floors. She jumped as shots rang out below, hoping the other cop hadn't been hit.

Walt ignored the commotion, intent on Kurtz and the stairs. He grabbed a metal fire extinguisher from the floor and stood to the side of the stairwell exit. "Over here, behind me." When Alexa joined Walt, he said, "Be ready to run back upstairs. We'll take the staircase in that corner." He motioned toward the far side of the mezzanine.

Moments later, footsteps approached, coming down the stairs. The barrel of a brutish-looking handgun poked through the doorway. Then, gripping the gun in both hands, Nason Kurtz emerged, looking to the right. He glanced to his left just as Walt brought the fire extinguisher down on his head. The gun in his hand discharged, bullet striking the marble baseboard and ricocheting past Alexa into the corridor. Kurtz fell to the floor, stunned. The pistol clattered from his hand. Grimacing, Walt dropped the extinguisher to the floor and snatched up the gun. A voice called from below, "Kurtz? Check in."

Walt dashed across the mezzanine to the stairwell on the opposite side of the building. Alexa stepped over the rolling fire extinguisher to follow. As she hurried by Kurtz, lying on the floor, the big man grabbed her right ankle. Alexa wobbled, then came to a complete stop. Her skin crawled at this monster's touch.

"Not so fast, bitch," Kurtz muttered thickly. Although his white hair was turning red from the head wound, Kurtz's grip on Alexa's ankle was tight.

"Kurtz? Where are you?" The second man was ascending the main staircase.

Alexa tried to wrest her ankle out of Kurtz's steel grip.

"Kurtz, damn it. Where are you?" The voice sounded very near.

In a panic, Alexa slipped her purse strap over her head and swung the bag as hard as she could at Kurtz. Thwack. When she connected with the man's injured head, he moaned and collapsed, releasing his grip on her ankle. Alexa sprinted across the mezzanine, fearful that the deadly cop was taking aim behind her. Ducking into the other stairwell, she bounded up the circling stairs.

Walt was waiting at the top of the first flight. "Where were you?"

"Kurtz grabbed me, but I knocked him out. His cop friend was on the main staircase. He's probably reached Kurtz by now."

Walt said, "Wait here."

As he disappeared around the corner to the left, Alexa noticed the red fire alarm pull. She reached out and yanked the lever. Immediately, a loud claxon rang through the Capitol. The sound was deafening. Then she followed Walt out onto a small, secluded balcony that overlooked the mezzanine. He held a finger to his lips and nodded toward the expanse of white marble below. The cop was leaning over Kurtz, who appeared to be out cold. When the cop glanced around, they both stepped back from the railing.

Alexa spoke into Walt's ear, although she doubted the dirty cop could hear anything over the din. "I pulled the fire alarm. They're going to have trouble explaining two dead capitol policemen to the first responders."

"No kidding." He grinned and gestured to acknowledge the clamor. "Good move. But those cops on the desk acted like he was a boss. Who knows how he'll spin things. We need to get to a phone."

"They were going to check your office," Alexa warned.

"I have another idea." Walt pointed to the glass door at the back of the mezzanine below them. The gold lettering said "Lieutenant Governor's Office." From this vantage point, Alexa could see the handle of a mop lying on the floor in front of the door. The mop was wedged into the door frame, preventing the door from closing.

CHAPTER THIRTY-SIX

WALT DREW ALEXA back into the shadows as Kurtz's cop buddy rose. "We need to get him out of there. But it's a dangerous move. He'll be desperate to shut us up before the fire company reaches the Capitol. We don't have much time."

"OK. What's the plan?" For an instant, Alexa wondered why Walt didn't just shoot the cop with Kurtz's gun. But she knew Walt was the type of guy who would only shoot in self-defense. And even that wasn't pretty. She still hadn't fully recovered from being forced to shoot Reverend Browne.

"I'm going to activate the elevator and bring it up to this floor. First, I want you to run down the stairs. There's a cubbyhole beneath the staircase at the bottom. Hide there. I'll be down in a minute."

"But he'll run up those stairs when he hears the elevator bell," Alexa protested.

"Exactly." Walt smiled but he clutched his arm in pain. "Go."

Alexa gritted her teeth and padded down the stairwell. Running up that last flight, she'd completely missed the hiding space nestled behind the foot of the stairs. She snugged her body into the small space, grimacing at the thought of spiders in the dusty nook. A moment later, the elevator whooshed as it ascended, and Walt rushed down the stairway, silent in his stocking feet. He folded his large body into the space behind her. Alexa could feel the pistol in his hand digging into her shoulder. Even over the fire alarm clamor, Alexa could hear the elevator bell chime when it reached its floor.

Seconds later, the dirty cop rushed into the stairwell and flew up the stairs. Alexa held her breath as his footsteps passed over her head, but he never paused. Clearly, he hadn't seen them.

Walt and Alexa stayed hidden while the cop checked out the empty elevator. Alexa closed her eyes, hoping Walt's ploy had worked. They waited until they heard his footsteps thud up the next flight of stairs. Alexa smiled. He'd fallen for the ruse. The cop thought they'd headed toward a higher floor.

"Let's go." Walt urged. He slid out from beneath the stairs and extended a hand. With a glance toward Kurtz, still lying motionless on the far side of the mezzanine, they slipped through the door to the lieutenant governor's office suite. A table lamp in the corner bathed the room in a soft light. The alarm clanged in here too. An annoying light flashed above the door.

Alexa headed for a telephone, skirting a vacuum cleaner sitting in the middle of the room. Is there some code to get out of here?"

"Dial nine and then the number." Walt placed the mop in the corner and locked the door. Avoiding the bucket full of Pine Sol-scented water, he closed the blinds on the glass windows facing the mezzanine. He peered into an office to the right, closed the door, and then disappeared into another door to the left.

Meanwhile, Alexa dialed 911. This time, she didn't wait for the operator to go through her questions. She raised her voice above the clamor from the alarm. "This is Alexa Williams. I spoke to someone there a little while ago but couldn't finish the conversation. I'm barricaded in an office in the Capitol. Two men with guns have been chasing Walt Jordan and me. One of them might be a Capitol policeman. I think they killed the two Capitol police guards at the main entrance of the Capitol. We pulled the fire alarm to get help." Alexa paused to take a breath.

"What is your name again?"

Alexa shouted. "Alexa Williams. This is an emergency. They're trying to kill us. Can you connect me with Detective Marshall of Dauphin County CID? He'll know what this is about."

"Ma'am. We have already notified the Capitol police and the state police assigned to protect the governor. I suggest you stay put. Do you want to tell me where you are so I can relay that information to the Capitol police?"

"No. Let me speak to Detective Marshall."

"Wait and I'll see if I can connect him."

Alexa looked up from the phone. Walt stood in the side doorway with a kitchen towel wrapped around his arm. Before she could ask about it, Detective Marshall came on the line. "Ms. Williams, they tell me someone has been shooting at you and . . ." He paused with a question in his voice.

"Representative Walt Jordan. It's about Senator Martinelli's death. At a hearing today, I recognized the man's voice. From that night. I tried to report it to the police, but these two men chased us. Then they started shooting. They killed two Capitol cops."

"Do you know the name of the man from that night with Senator Martinelli?"

"Yes. Walker Toland. Some high-powered lobbyist. His employee, Kurtz, tried to kill Walt and me tonight. I think the other guy is a Capitol policeman. We need help."

"What does Representative Jordan have to do with all of this?"

"Nothing, really. He was in the wrong place at the wrong time and got caught up in it. I wouldn't have survived without him." Alexa's eyes brimmed with tears. "We're barricaded in the lieutenant governor's suite, but they could find us in here. They want to shut me up."

"Stay put. I'll get in touch with the head of the Capitol police. I'm on my way."

Walt popped back into the center room. After Alexa relayed the conversation to him, he said, "There's a bathroom in there. In the back." He pointed to the inner office he'd just left.

"Good idea." Alexa used the facilities and took an extra moment to splash cool water on her face. Now they'd stopped running, her bare feet throbbed. She sighed and returned to Walt, standing in the inner office. Lamplight from outside the Capitol filtered through a row of huge windows on the front wall. Alexa saw that Walt had closed the door to the center room. With no windows or doors leading to the Capitol mezzanine, this cozy inner office gave the illusion of being safe.

Walt held out a bottle of water. "We're standing in the Ladies' Lounge. In the old days, this is where ladies waited when they came to visit dignitaries. He pointed to the decorative mural on the ceiling of a woman with two cherubs. "Venus, here, was deemed the appropriate decoration for those delicate flowers like you."

"It's actually quite lovely." Alexa gazed up at the ceiling, bathed in a dim glow. She felt like she'd fallen down the rabbit hole. A few minutes ago, she and Walt had been running for their lives. Now here they were, discussing historical architecture.

Walt continued in a conversational tone. "I hear Jackie Kennedy tried to snag the fireplace mantel for the White House, but the State refused. So she had to make do with a replica."

"Maybe I can get the full tour later, Walt. Do you think we're safe here?" Alexa worried that Nason Kurtz might have regained consciousness and seen them slip into this suite.

"I locked the main entrance in the center room and used that here," Walt pointed toward the chair propped beneath the doorknob. "But I still think we'd be safer outside."

"Outside?"

He plucked a throw off the nearest desk chair. Opening a french door in the wall of windows fronting the room, he steered Alexa through it. She stepped through the door, astonished to find they stood on the broad balcony that spanned the main entrance to the Capitol. Below, on the right, three fire trucks formed a line in the parking area, turning the wet streets red with their flashing lights. But the big roof above them had kept the balcony dry. Alexa was tempted to walk to the front of the balcony and peer down at the Capitol steps but didn't want to reveal their presence until Detective Marshall arrived. "Wow. You knew this was here?"

"Yeah. I got the tour after a meeting with the lieutenant governor a few years back. We're better out here than inside. We're not in the line of fire if Nason Kurtz or his lackey try to shoot through that glass entry door out front. The only access to the balcony is through one of the offices in this suite. And, if worse comes to worse, we could jump."

Alexa walked to the side and looked down with a skeptical tilt of her head. "Not so sure about that last one."

"Let's try to stay out of sight." Walt beckoned Alexa to the blanket he'd spread right beneath the door. He had closed the door behind them, leaving just a small opening so they could listen for activity in the office—although the clamor of the fire trucks and the fire alarm made it difficult to hear much of anything.

Alexa sank down onto blanket and leaned her back against the wall. She felt the rough wall scrape against her Armani jacket and sighed. But what did it matter? Her suit was already ruined. "I should have never dressed to impress that committee," Alexa muttered under her breath.

"What?" Walt said.

"Nothing. Lucky for us that entrance door was propped open. Weird though."

"You saw the bucket and the sweeper? I bet someone was cleaning the office and stepped away."

"Or ran away when they heard gunshots," Alexa speculated. Then she returned to an earlier remark he'd made. "You recognized Nason Kurtz?"

"Of course. He and his boss lobby for Monongas. As minority chair of the House Energy Committee, they're always beating a path to my door. I'm not their favorite legislator since I rarely vote the way they want. But they never tried to kill me until I started hanging out with you." Walt summoned a tired smile.

"I'm so sorry I dragged you into this. I suspect they murdered Senator Martinelli. Actually, this past hour, with Nason Kurtz hell bent on killing me; that sort of erases any lingering doubts. When you got involved, they had to kill you too."

"Think of me as the bonus round," Walt quipped.

Alexa tried to muffle her laughter. "We just ran about ten miles, dodged gunfire, and our fate is still up in the air. How can you laugh?"

"Gallows humor. They teach that early in the Marines. Hey, can you help me with this?" Walt pointed to the towel wrapped around his arm. "I thought I'd been nicked by a chunk of marble or something. But it was bleeding pretty good on that last run down the hall. I might have taken a bullet. Just a flesh wound."

Alexa gasped. "Take off your coat." She unwrapped the towel so Walt could slip his arm out of his suit jacket. His light blue shirt was soaked red above his elbow. In the waning light, Alexa could see a tear in the shirt. "I'm not going to mess with that. It's not bleeding too badly. I'll just tie this right over the wound." After she adjusted the makeshift bandage, Alexa plucked the blanket from the floor and placed it over Walt. "I don't want you going into shock."

Walt grimaced and said, "I'm more worried about what my wife's going to say. She got this shirt from some fancy tailor on a trip to New York City."

"I'm sure your wife will look at the bigger picture," Alexa reassured him.

Walt held Alexa's eyes with a steady gaze. "I'm afraid she might do just that."

Alexa looked away. She felt more comfortable with this man than anyone since Reese. Earlier, she'd had a few passing qualms about Walt, but she'd been letting fear cloud her judgment. After that, Alexa had trusted him to guide her to safety. She'd never forget how he'd risked his life for her without hesitation. But she was not about to fall for a married man. She might be vulnerable from John's death, but not that vulnerable. In any case, she didn't think Walt Jordan was the kind of guy who'd cheat on his wife.

"Well, emotions can run high in life and death situations." Alexa took a deep breath. "You know I can't thank you enough. I'd be dead now without you."

"Anything for a fellow environmental warrior," Walt closed his eyes in pain. "And, when you're a Marine, the training just kicks in." He rummaged through his jacket and withdrew the gun he'd taken from Kurtz. "I checked. There are only two bullets left, but if I pass out, don't hesitate to use it on Kurtz or his bent cop friend." He shivered. "I'm a little worried that the cop could be spinning some story that paints us as the bad guys. But, drop the gun if the police come. We don't want any confrontation with them."

"That's why I wanted Detective Marshall here. He's from outside the State structure." Alexa gave Walt a worried look. He seemed to be fading. Although she was certain the bullet wound wasn't life threatening, blood loss and shock were real concerns. She folded her body against Walt for warmth. She chattered on, picking up on his earlier comment in an attempt to keep Walt awake. "I don't think of myself as an environmental warrior. I might think fracking sucks, but all I've been doing is helping out a friend."

"It's more than that, Alexa. You've got a bit of the crusader in you. You want to right the wrongs of the world, and fracking's one of them. That's admirable." He paused. "Did I ever tell you about my father?"

"No, I heard he was involved in the environmental movement?"

"He gave his life for the environment. He died when I was quite young, so I barely remember him. My mother hated his activism with a passion. It broke up their marriage. After that, she took me away to her home in Tioga County. She remarried, and her new husband adopted me. They changed my last name to Jordan, like she wanted to wipe out any connection to my father. When I asked about him, she would call him a worthless dreamer. Eventually, I stopped asking."

Walt's voice was weakening, so Alexa leaned close to hear. "That must have been tough."

"Not really. My new dad was a great guy, so I didn't miss out on having a father. But, when I went to college after the Marines, I did a paper on nuclear energy. Imagine my shock when I read that Will Armstrong was one of the legends of the anti-nuclear movement in the seventies and eighties. He was killed at a protest against a nuclear power plant out west.

"When I confronted my mother, she showed me a scrapbook she'd made about his protest activities. And she told me it all began when I was born during the Three Mile Island disaster."

"So this anti-fracking crusade is in your genes?" Alexa smiled.

"I'll tell you one more secret." Walt nodded off and then opened his eyes.

"You were going to tell me a secret," Alexa prodded.

"My real name is Walden. My dad named me for Thoreau's pond. But Mom changed it to Walt." He watched as if waiting for her reaction.

"Walden." Alexa let it roll off her tongue. Her eyes softened. "I like it."

"OK, now that we're sharing secrets, tell me about Carmine Martinelli's death. I heard a lot of speculation about witnesses, but I don't put much stock in the rumor mill." Walt's voice lowered in concern. "You were there?"

"I was meeting with Keisha Washington in the rotunda. A group of men had an argument on one of the upper floors. Then, the senator's body hit the floor at our feet."

"FUBAR."

"You've got that right. I found out later that the senator was one of the men who were arguing. I didn't recognize any of the other voices until this afternoon when Walker Toland testified."

"I miss Carmine. You may not know. He'd changed his position on fracking. One of his grandkids has cystic fibrosis. It can be exac . . . exacerbated by air pollution." Walt's voice faltered. "The studies about increases in methane from fracking turned the old bastard around 100%. No more drilling in parks. Anywhere.

"We talked about his change in position." Walt closed his eyes but kept talking. His voice sounded paper-thin. "Creepy. Day after he died, I got a letter in interoffice mail. From Carmine. He was all philosophical, taking stock, couldn't support fracking on grounds. Moral grounds."

Alexa sat up straight. "It sounds like the one on his computer when he died. At first, the cops viewed it as a suicide note."

"Yeah, cops asked me." Walt fell silent for a few minutes. "Bet Toland knew Carmine changed." He mumbled, "That's why. Killed him."

"The stakes are that high?"

"Absolutely . . ." Walt's voice trailed off.

As Alexa watched, he collapsed against the wall. "Walt? Walt?" She touched his cheek. He'd passed out, but Alexa had bigger things to worry about. Outside the office, someone was banging on the door. Alexa rose and crept to the next bank of windows where she could see the shadows of several men silhouetted against the closed blinds of the lieutenant governor's door. She scurried back to the french door and slipped inside. As she removed the chair wedged against the door of the Ladies' Lounge, the pounding resumed. Then a deep voice boomed, "Alexa. Please open up. This is Detective Marshall from the Dauphin County Investigations Department."

Alexa's knees went weak in relief. She walked through the center office and opened the door. "Representative Jordan needs medical help. He's out on the balcony." She led them out on the balcony through the open door.

Minutes later, when Detective Marshall appeared on the balcony, Alexa had to hold back from throwing herself into his arms. The detective said, "I have a lot of questions for you."

"Fine, fine, but not until we get Walt to the hospital." Alexa went back to sit with the legislator while the lieutenant governor's office suite turned into a beehive of activity. Officers wound yellow tape around the perimeter and searched the inner rooms of the suite.

Marshall said, "The paramedics should be here in a few minutes. There's an ambulance already on site at the Capitol as part of the fire alarm response. We have taken Nason Kurtz and Dale Hoover into custody for assaulting you and Representative Jordan."

"Is Dale Hoover the Capitol policeman?"

"Yes. Although, I suspect his job is now in serious jeopardy." Marshall clenched his jaw.

"I'm not sure who shot the woman cop, but I think he shot the man. Did either of them survive?"

The detective shook his head, his expression somber.

"That's right." Alexa remembered the gun lying on the floor and pointed to it. "That belongs to Kurtz. Walt took it after he clobbered him with a fire extinguisher. It's still loaded."

Marshall summoned a uniformed policeman to process the gun as the paramedics arrived. Walt roused when they were placing him on the gurney. "Alexa, are you OK?"

"I'm fine. They're going to take you to the hospital."

"Can you come along?" Walt reached for Alexa's hand.

She patted his good shoulder. "These people will take good care of you."

Behind her, the detective said, "We need Ms. Williams here to answer our questions."

"Can someone call my wife and tell her what happened? She's expecting me home tonight."

"Phone number?"

"It's in my cell . . ."

"That's back in the hearing room," Alexa reminded him.

"Right." Walt recited a number.

"We need to get Mr. Jordan to the hospital," one of the paramedics interrupted.

"Go," the detective ordered.

"I'll check in with you, Walt," Alexa called as they rolled him away.

"How about we find a quieter place to talk," the detective suggested and moved toward the window.

Several hours later, Alexa left the Capitol and stopped by Harrisburg Hospital. She didn't want to think about how bedraggled she must look. At least the police had retrieved her shoes. After some pleading, the nurses allowed her to look in on Walt. Alexa paused at the door of his private room to determine if he was awake. She wrinkled her nose at the familiar hospital smell, eau de chemicals and floor wax.

"Come on in." Walt sat against the pillows, with the head of his bed elevated. Several IVs ran into a patch on his left hand. Behind him a humming monitor flashed a series of digital numbers across a screen.

"You're on a medical floor, not ICU. That seems like a good sign." Alexa moved to stand by the bed. The room was dim, lit by a single lamp on the nightstand.

"I'm fine. The bullet just grazed me. The doc cleaned it out and put in a few stitches. My biggest problem was the loss of blood. But they say I'll be fine. I could even go home tomorrow." Walt gave a faint smile.

"Has your wife arrived?" Out in the corridor something crashed, and Alexa shot a guilty look toward the door. She felt responsible for Walt getting shot and more. She wasn't up for a distraught wife asking questions about the woman standing by her injured husband's bedside.

"She's on her way. After they stitched me up, I reached Sandy on her cell and calmed her down. They say she can bunk here with me." Walt nodded toward the corner. "Apparently that chair turns into a bed."

"I'll get out of here and let you sleep. I just wanted to check on you." Alexa backed toward the door.

"Not yet," Walt exclaimed in a stronger voice. "You have to tell me what happened. Did they arrest Kurtz and his sidekick?"

Alexa stopped her retreat and walked back to the bed. "Yes. Both of them were still in the Capitol when the firemen and a contingent of Capitol cops arrived in response to the fire alarm. They arrested Nason Kurtz and the other guy, a Capitol cop. His name is Dale Hoover. Both of the cops on duty at the door died. So, Kurtz and Hoover are facing multiple charges just for tonight. Murder. Attempted murder. Probably a lot more when the DA is done. Those guys shot up the Capitol building. Who knows what State treasures they may have destroyed."

"What about Toland?" Walt grimaced as he shifted higher on the pillows.

"Walker Toland will be arrested and charged with the murder of Senator Carmine Martinelli. Detective Marshall plans to question Keisha Washington about her role as an accessory after the fact. I'm not sure why she threw in with them, but Keisha has a driving ambition. Executive director was her dream job. Maybe she just didn't want to jeopardize her shot at the position, then got in too deep." Alexa shook her head with a puzzled expression.

"I also told the detective about Lauren Hildebrand's death. I could be reaching here. But when she interned with Keisha, she had a run in with two men. I overheard part of it. I think one of the men was Nason Kurtz. The other was Senator Patterson."

"Patterson?" Surprise showed in Walt's voice. "I didn't think that pipsqueak had the balls to get in trouble. He's on Energy too. He was there today." He paused. "I guess it's still today." Walt glanced at a clock on the wall.

"Yeah. But, it's almost midnight." Alexa sank into the chair next to the bed. "Lauren told me she'd learned about something illegal related to a fracking bill. She died before she could tell me any of the details. The Harrisburg police called her death accidental, but it could be related to all of this—maybe Lauren learned who was behind Senator Martinelli's death."

"What some people will do for greed. You know they weren't doing this on their own. They were doing this for Monongas. How much do you want to bet that Monongas will walk away from this scot-free?"

"I hope not, but I've grown cynical in my old age."

Walt laughed and then grimaced at the pain. "How old are you? Thirty?"

"Now I'm leaving." Alexa smiled and rose to her feet. "You need to rest. And I need to get home."

Walt sighed. "You know, I was lying here thinking. The last time I stayed in this hospital was when I was born. Just a few miles down the river, Three Mile Island was in danger of a total meltdown. Here we are, almost forty years later, and we're still in thrall to dangerous energy sources. It's a love-hate relationship in many ways. I'm as addicted as the next guy to lights and heat and phones and electric tools. But there's a price to pay for all that energy. TMI is still chugging away out there on the river. Coal and oil have helped propel climate change. And God only knows about the long-term effects of fracking."

"Keep up the good fight, Walt. But you've done enough for one night to battle the fracking industry. If we're lucky, this scandal will erase any chance of Senate Bill 5100 passing." Alexa leaned over to touch Walt's hand with a soft smile. "Thanks for saving my life tonight, Walden."

Closing his hand over hers, he whispered, "I should be thanking you." With a start he released her hand and broke into an infectious grin. "I definitely want you on my side when the Martians invade."

Giggling, Alexa instructed, "Good night. Get some rest." Her hand tingled as she hurried out of the room. She felt physically drained from both the exhausting brush with death in the Capitol and the conflicting emotions she felt for Walt.

CHAPTER THIRTY-SEVEN

As THE PLANE LEFT the runway at Harrisburg International Airport, Alexa looked out the window at the cooling towers of Three Mile Island below and thought of Walt's father, fighting for safe energy. For a moment her excitement at this upcoming trip dimmed. On the energy front, even as things changed, much stayed the same. Turning away from the window, she shrugged off her gloom and looked forward to Italy.

"I am so glad to be here and finally see this Italian villa," Alexa told her parents hours later, amid hugs.

"Well, you'll have to wait until Monday. We couldn't let you bypass Florence on your first trip here. So we're staying here tonight and tomorrow night before we drive to Umbria," Norris announced.

"Are you too tired to do some sightseeing today?" Susan asked with an anxious look. "We've been so worried about you. We want to hear everything that's happened."

"I got some decent sleep on the plane. I'd love to see Florence. Let's talk about the Capitol thing later. As you can see, I'm fine."

"Now we've seen for ourselves that you're unharmed, we can wait to hear the details." He shot a glance at Susan. "How about we drop your bag off at our hotel? We came up to the city last night." Norris took over Alexa's rolling suitcase and headed toward an exit.

Susan chattered away as she and Alexa followed. "We have tickets for the Uffizi tomorrow and then the Galleria Accademia later in the day. We knew you'd want to see Michelangelo's David. Today, we planned on wandering around the city center and visiting the Duomo and the Ponte Vecchio. We love this one restaurant on the Piazza della Signoria. They have outstanding pizza. We thought we'd have lunch there and people-watch."

"If there's time, we'll go through the Boboli Gardens," her dad tossed a comment over his shoulder.

Alexa's head was spinning in a good way. "It all sounds great. Maybe I can change into something cooler in your room? It's a lot warmer here than in Pennsylvania. I got this really cute striped top from Bloomies, very European."

Although the ancient city teemed with tourists, the excitement energized Alexa after her long flight. The clear Mediterranean light seemed to drive away the heartbreak and horror of the last few months at home. John's homicide and the deaths of Senator Martinelli, Lauren, the Capitol cops—Alexa could feel the weight of those tragedies start to fall from her shoulders. She welcomed the breather, even if just for a couple of weeks.

"Beautiful colors." As they waited in line to enter, the Duomo's walls of green, pink, and white marble shimmered in the sun. Inside, the huge sanctuary provided a cool respite from the warm morning. Listening to the audio-tour on headphones, Alexa was thrown off guard when she looked up to take in the massive curved dome of the cathedral. For a moment, she flashed back to the State Capitol dome. But this structure was much more ornate. The inner dome was decorated with rows and rows of circular paintings embellished with gold leaf depicting the Last Judgment. With satisfaction, Alexa pictured the faces of Walter Toland and Nason Kurtz on two of the bodies spilling headlong into the flames of Hell burning in the lower section of the painting. Then she shook off the disconcerting image. She had come here to get away from all the bad memories—and to have a good time.

Outside the Duomo, Norris said, "We can go up to the top of the Duomo if you want."

"Up there?" Alexa asked in disbelief.

"Yeah. There's a separate line, and you have to climb up the stairs; almost five hundred of them. But you see the inside of the dome. And then you come out up there on the tippy top. They call that tiny section at the top of the dome, a lantern."

"I'll pass." Alexa shivered at the memory of Senator Martinelli's body falling through the air. "You sound like you've made the climb."

"I went up the first time we were here," Norris bragged.

"While I stayed on the ground and shopped. In fact, I picked up this lovely scarf at the outdoor market stalls that day." Susan fluffed the lightweight silk confection looped stylishly around her neck. As usual, her mother's most casual outfit made Alexa feel underdressed.

"Where's that place for pizza? I'd much rather eat than climb . . . how high?"

"Not quite four hundred feet," Norris supplied the number.

"Like I said." Alexa rolled her eyes at her mother.

"No problem. There are a couple of other vantage points. Looking out over the red tile rooftops is a wonderful sight." Norris smiled. "But that's for later. Let's go have pizza."

Over lunch, Alexa briefed her parents on everything that had happened since John's death. Around them, the Piazza della Signoria bustled with tourists. The brick, castle-like structure of the Palazzo Vecchio with its tall tower loomed over the huge plaza. The replica statue of David kept watch over the line of outdoor cafes, their tight rows of tables overflowing with diners. These sights had entranced Alexa when they'd been first seated at the cafe. Now she barely noticed as she fought back tears in the face of her parents' concern.

Norris leaned forward. The slanting afternoon sun highlighted the worry lines on his forehead. "You told us a little bit about your escape from this man, Kurtz. But, we had no idea the extent—"

"Honey, this is absolutely appalling," Mom cut in. "He chased you and this legislator all over the Capitol building? Two policemen were killed?" Susan's hand trembled on her wine glass, splashing the house red onto the table.

Alexa watched the wine trickle across the white tablecloth like a rivulet of blood. She closed her eyes, willing away the image of Senator Martinelli's broken head, bleeding onto the rotunda tiles. "What? Yes, two policemen. And the representative, Walt Jordan—he was wounded."

A tall waiter rushed to the table with a cloth to blot the spilled wine. "Mi scusi, Signora." He offered the wine bottle. "Vorresti più vino? More wine?"

"Per favore."

Taking advantage of the break, Alexa studied the fountain across the piazza in silence. When the waiter left, her father leapt right back into the conversation.

"My God, Lexie. How do you get yourself involved in these dangerous situations?" Norris asked.

Alexa put down her slice of pizza to protest. "It's not like I go looking for trouble. It just seems to find me."

"We're just glad you're safe," Susan stepped in to defuse the tension.

"I am safe. And the bad guys, these lobbyists and their buddies, are going to jail for multiple murders. So Senator

Martinelli; my young intern friend, Lauren; and two Capitol cops are going to get the justice they deserve. John's killers are going to be prosecuted. I just wish they'd been able to prove that Monongas had a role in all of this. Maybe someone there will still be arrested. But there are too many layers between the energy company masterminds and the people they pay to do their dirty work. At least this scandal has ruined the chances for any expansion of fracking in Pennsylvania for the near future. Everybody knows the industry was behind this—and there's been a tremendous backlash."

"I heard about that from Silas Gabler. I guess he's had a real rough time of it, just stepping into that new role as head of the energy committee when all hell broke loose."

"More than that. From his remarks at that hearing on the bill, Silas seemed totally invested in getting the bill passed. He sounded like a real cheerleader for opening up public land to fracking and more. So he must be pretty bummed his side lost. Plus, he lost his executive director, Keisha Washington. I heard she's turning state's evidence to avoid a jail term, but she'll never work in State government again."

"Silas didn't mention that. Of course, he might be embarrassed that her actions will reflect badly on him. That he exercised poor judgment when he hired her."

"Whatever. Let's just say I can't feel too bad for your old friend, Silas."

Susan jumped in. "I understand this whole fracking issue and the lawless actions of these people make you see red, Alexa. But, I hope you can find some charity in your heart for Silas. You know he's been a family friend forever."

"I know. But after working with Uncle Silas on that trafficking commission, and now, knowing his position on fracking—a little bit of the shine has worn off." Alexa turned to her father. "Sorry, Dad. I know he's your friend."

Susan and Norris exchanged a quick glance.

"What?" Alexa knew they were holding something back.

"We didn't plan it this way, but Silas and Cynthia are coming over to stay with us on Saturday. We had wanted to spend the time alone with you, dear. Then Silas called. Said he needed a break and the only time he could make it is next week. I guess the Senate's in recess. We'd invited them to visit a number of times, so it was difficult to say no. I hope you can be civil to Silas."

Alexa sighed. It appeared she couldn't get away from reminders of this fracking mess no matter how far she traveled. "No problem. I'm just glad to get a chance to hang out in Umbria with you. I'm a little disillusioned with Uncle Silas, but I'm not going to make a scene or anything like that. And Cynthia is lovely. Does he know I'm here?"

Norris scrunched his face like he was thinking. "I don't recall if I mentioned that during our conversation. Do you think it would make a difference? Have you two had a serious falling out?" Her father's voice rose in consternation.

"No, nothing like that. But I don't think he appreciated me taking an active role against his fracking bill. I was just curious." Alexa took another bite of pizza, savoring the hint of basil. "We need to bring Graham and Kate and the kids here for Friday pizza night. This might be the best pizza I've ever eaten."

Driving through an ancient gate in the old city walls, the Williams family said farewell to Florence. "What an amazing city. The David is everything it's cracked up to be. And seeing Botticelli's Venus. So sweet," Alexa babbled in excitement.

"We just touched the surface. We'll have to come back on your next trip," Susan spoke from the back seat of the car.

Alexa watched La Bella Toscana unwind from her prime spot in front. They drove the back roads of Tuscany through rolling fields of rippling green wheat punctuated by rows of tall, narrow evergreens leading to hilltop farms.

Alexa chortled to her parents. "I can't believe it. Look at the cypress trees. Tuscany looks exactly like the photos." She took a deep breath of the dry air through the open window. "It smells so green and earthy."

Her mother smiled when she replied, "This is classic Tuscany, the Crete Sensei. While you're here, we'll come back north to Tuscany and see a few hill towns. Montepulciano and Montalcino. Of course, we'd like to you see some of Umbria too. Assisi for sure. Maybe Orvieto."

"The Gablers want to visit Siena. Maybe we can do a day trip the week they're here," Norris chimed in.

"Is that where they have the horse races in the palazzo?"

"In the piazza. A palazzo is a palace. The plaza or square is the piazza," Norris corrected with a grin. "Either way, you'll miss the races, and so will we. They're in July, and we'll be back home by then."

As they drove farther south, the fields were thick with crimson poppies. "I expected to see sunflowers." Alexa remarked.

"You're a few weeks early. They bloom from mid-June through sometime in August. We're almost in Umbria."

They passed another hill, carpeted with poppies, glowing vivid red in the early afternoon sun. A gust of wind sent the poppies into an undulating movement. The languid waves of blood red flowers made Alexa think of John, broken and bleeding after the utility truck hit him. Although she hadn't seen John's body, she'd had nightmares about the blood.

Alexa rubbed her forehead. I really need this break.

Aloud, Alexa told her parents. "Let's make sure to take a few days to just hang out."

"Sure. You can read a book by the pool. Or just sit on the loggia and contemplate the view. Whatever you want to do, dear." Susan smiled.

Less than an hour later, Dad turned the little Mercedes into a white gravel lane that cut through acres of vineyards. As they climbed a steep hill, the terrain became wooded and rocky. After traveling across the hill for a few miles, they drove into a mix of open fields and olive orchards.

"We're up there." Norris pointed through the windshield.

"Amazing," Alexa breathed when she glimpsed the tan stone farmhouse perched on the hillside. Vines covered one side of the ancient stones. A broad veranda fronted the house, with an expansive view of vineyards below. When they emerged from the car, Alexa soaked in the blazing clear light and the stunning view below. "I can't wait to see inside."

Her parents led her past an outdoor eating area shaded by a vine-covered pergola. A long swimming pool on the hill above overlooked the villa. The house embodied everyone's idea of a Tuscan house, painted in dreamy shades of ocher with terracotta floors.

"This is your bedroom." Susan left Alexa standing in the middle of a second-floor bedroom with soft blue plaster walls. An iron four-poster bed, its headboard adorned with painted cherubs, dominated the room. An exquisite wooden armoire and gilded desk completed the Italian country house look. Alexa pulled a comfortable chair up to the open window and looked out across the valley. Several buildings with towers that looked like castles dotted the vista below.

She took a deep breath and sighed. "Pure magic."

CHAPTER THIRTY-EIGHT

ALEXA SPENT THE next week falling in love with Tuscany and Umbria. As her parents had promised, they filled the sunny days with trips to several of the ancient towns that crowned the rolling hills of the region. Their polysyllabic names rolled off her tongue like treasures to be savored. Montepulciano, Montalcino, Cortona, Assisi.

"Every vacation should be like this," she said to her parents over a leisurely lunch at an outdoor café. "It's so much fun to just wander through all these narrow streets. I've lost track of how many ancient churches we've visited."

"Or artisan shops." Her mother nodded at the bag of hand-thrown ceramic plates at Alexa's feet.

Norris took a sip of wine. "I'm looking forward to the wine tasting this afternoon. The Brunello di Montalcino is such a powerful red. We'll take some home to go with our steak tonight."

"I'm usually not that keen on reds," Alexa declared as she took a spoonful of zuppa di fagioli, the thick Tuscan bean soup.

"Maybe next week we'll head toward Orvieto. They specialize in a white down there, Orvieto. Is it Classico, Norris?"

"Yes. And don't forget, we want to run up to San Gimignano. They've got a well-known white DOC."

"DOC?" Alexa asked as she dipped a piece of crusty bread in olive oil.

"It's just a term that denotes regional wines of a certain quality. They must meet a set of controls to get the DOC designation."

"When did you become such a wine connoisseur, Dad?"

Susan replied, "When we bought a house in Umbria. Wine is a way of life here. Personally, I'm fine with most of the local wines they serve in the trattorias and cafes. I can't tell the difference between them and the ones with the fancy labels."

"Do we have time to go into the castle before we do the wine tasting?" Alexa asked.

"Of course. Let's make the most of this last day on our own. The Gablers arrive tomorrow," Norris answered.

"Are you going to drive to Florence to pick them up?"

Susan smiled. "No. That's a special service we reserve for daughters only. They're flying into Rome and taking another flight to Perugia. We'll drive over to Perugia to collect them."

"We've arranged to rent a van from one of the locals for the week. It will be too cramped to do day trips in our tiny Mercedes."

"Sounds like good day for me to hang out by the pool with a book." Alexa looked forward to some downtime.

The addition of the Gablers to the Umbrian house party was turning out better than Alexa had expected. With her parents' attention focused on the new arrivals, Alexa had more time to explore the area surrounding Villa Belle Nuvole. Her parents had named the villa "Beautiful Clouds" for the misty clouds that settled in the valley below on most mornings.

During the first week of her stay, Alexa had discovered a path along the ridge that she liked to walk at dawn. The path ended in an outcrop of rocks where she could watch the morning sun rise and burn off the mist below. As the light warmed the valley, first the turrets of the castles peeked from the pale golden mist. Then the larger buildings emerged until, finally, the full panorama of the valley unfolded. It was a morning scene that hadn't yet grown old. Alexa doubted that it ever would.

After a quiet Sunday by the pool, the Gablers had recovered from the flight and were anxious to see the sights. So the whole group piled into the van for a drive to the city of towers, San Gimignano, and Siena. Alexa made an effort to be cordial to Senator Gabler, and he seemed his usual affable self. By the time the group met for a late lunch in Siena's Piazza del Campo, she had relaxed in his presence. It appeared that Silas was as eager to take a break from Harrisburg issues as Alexa.

At Wednesday breakfast, Susan declared the coming evening would be a night to enjoy an al fresco dinner at Villa Belle Nuvole. "We've had wonderful dinners in our travels to Siena, and yesterday, near Orvieto. Tonight we hope to top those. We have a local chef coming in to cook us a dinner of Tuscan and Umbrian specialties. This morning, we're suggesting a short drive down to Lake Trasimeno and a wander through the surrounding villages. We can take a boat or the ferry out to Isola Maggiore if we want."

Cynthia Gabler exclaimed, "Isn't that island known for its lace?"

"Yes. Norris and I had lunch out there once, too. A lovely little restaurant right on the water."

"Sounds like a fine way to spend the day." Silas nodded.

"What are they cooking for dinner?" Alexa asked. It seemed as if she'd done nothing but eat since she arrived in Italy. The food was wonderful.

"I couldn't tell you even if I wanted to. I've left that up to Emilio and Chiara. They like to cook with whatever's fresh, so it will be a surprise to all of us."

"What a spectacular dinner," Alexa announced to the group seated around the table. They sat outside in the soft night air beneath the pergola. Alexa had dressed in her favorite sundress, blush linen, for the occasion. At least twenty candles flickered in the center of the long table. A string of lights woven through the ceiling of the pergola provided additional illumination. Below, in the valley, Alex glimpsed the soft glow of lamplight shining from the window of the castle with the tallest stone tower. She continued, "I loved the truffle pasta thingy."

As he cleared the dishes, Emilio said, "Tagliolini tartufo. I apologize that the tartufi were not fresh. We made this pasta during the harvest with dried tartufi. Come back in the fall, signorina, and taste the tartufo bianco." He kissed the tips of his fingers on his right hand. "Mamma mia, the tartufo bianco, she is the queen of the Italian truffles. There is even a festival at San Giovanni d'Asso."

With the table clean, Emilio refilled the wine glasses, and Chiara bustled in with plates of cheese, Perugian chocolates, and a dense, spicy cake almost like gingerbread. "This is Panforte. In Siena, they bake this at Christmas. We think it's good enough to serve year-round," she said.

"What's on the agenda for tomorrow?" Silas leaned back in his chair, glass of wine in hand. "Not that I have much energy for anything right now."

"Darling, we're on vacation. We don't really have an agenda, do we?" Cynthia finished her wine and looked for the bottle. Emilio stepped from the shadows and filled her glass.

"I just meant—" Silas protested, but Norris cut him off.

"We wanted to offer you a quiet day here at the house or a drive to Assisi." Norris leaned forward. "Alexa, I know you've been to Assisi. You could join us or take a day on your own?"

Cynthia clapped her hands. "Oh, let's go to Assisi. That's the Saint Francis town, isn't it? I read something about a beautiful church."

Alexa exchanged a quick glance with her mom. It appeared that wine with every course was a little more alcohol than Cynthia could handle. Usually quite restrained, she was bouncing in her seat like a teenager.

"I'm fine with another trip. Let's do Assisi," Silas declared. He did a slow scan of the table and the grounds. "I've got to say, Norris, this is the life. You and Susan have yourselves quite a place here. You're keeping the house back in Carlisle, too?"

"We are. Neither of us is ready to spend the entire year away from the kids and grandkids." Norris smiled. "So, when are you going to retire, Silas? You've been in the legislature for what, thirty years? Aren't you ready to walk away and enjoy life?"

"I've been thinking about it, but I might run for one more term." Silas' voice tightened before he assumed a heartier tone. "Seeing this, though . . ."

Cynthia interrupted, "You tell him, Norris. I keep saying it's time for Silas to retire. We even bought that farm in Adams County for our retirement." Cynthia's voice turned maudlin, "Of course, we might have to sell."

Alexa was glad when her mother took control as the hostess. Even in the dim light, she could see Silas turning purple with annoyance at his wife.

"Emilio. I believe we're finished here. We can take our wine up to the loggia and give you and Chiara a chance to clean up. Dinner was just lovely." When Susan stood, Alexa jumped up too.

"Good idea, Mom. There's a full moon tonight."

Norris grabbed the bottle of wine. "Anyone who'd like a bit more of this, just bring your glass."

When Cynthia lifted her glass from the table, Silas took it from her hand, whispering in an icy tone, "I think you've had enough, dear."

As the group dawdled, Alexa headed straight for the stone loggia. She sat alone for a few moments watching the moon. Then her father joined her, still holding the wine bottle and a glass.

"Silas and Cynthia decided to go up to bed. You may have noticed she was a little worse for the wear. Your mother is helping Emilio and Chiara finish up." He took the chair beside Alexa and poured some wine. "Would you like some?"

"No, thanks. I'm calling it a night soon."

"What about Assisi. Do you want to come with us?"

"I might just take your car and explore on my own, but I'll decide tomorrow. " Alexa gave a soft giggle. "Who knows? Cynthia might decide to stay home for the day if she wakes up with a hangover." She leaned closer to her father and lowered her voice. "Any idea what all that farmhouse stuff was about?"

"Not really. It sounds like they have money troubles. That's plausible. A state senator makes a good salary, but not one that would make you rich. I know Silas has dabbled in various business ventures over the years, but maybe they haven't been as successful as he'd hoped."

"Well. None of my business, really." Alexa leaned back in her seat. "It is so beautiful here, Dad. I am glad you and Mom bought this place."

After a few minutes of companionable silence, Alexa's eyes closed. She jerked them open before she fell asleep. "I'm going to bed." She rose, kissed her dad's forehead, and climbed the stairs to her dreamy bedroom.

Her head on the pillow, Alexa drifted toward sleep, contemplating the wonderful evening. Then a thought jerked her awake. Cynthia had said they'd bought a farm in Adams County. John had been killed by that fracking exploration team in the part of Michaux that bordered on Adams County. She remembered how Monongas had leased almost all the land in Tioga County. Wouldn't they plan to do something similar, leasing nearby farms, if their state forest scheme were successful?

Wide awake, Alexa sat up in bed, her mind racing. She remembered Silas' impassioned speech in support of Senate Bill 5100. And the fact that Keisha had worked for him. Had she fallen on her sword for her boss? Was Silas involved with Toland and Monongas?

"Alexa, get a grip," she said aloud. "You're getting as bad as Fox Mulder, seeing conspiracy theories behind every corner." She brushed away her crazy suspicions, lay back, and fell asleep.

CHAPTER THIRTY-NINE

WHEN SHE OPENED her eyes, Alexa indulged in a moment of sheer delight. She gazed at the gauzy white clouds painted on the arched blue ceiling and padded out of bed to look out her window. Dawn was just breaking over a valley wreathed in billowing mist. She slipped into her sweats and sneakers, anxious to make her way to the rocks for sunrise.

Alexa tiptoed down the stairs to the kitchen, where she downed a glass of milk. Then she stepped out the back door onto the dining terrace. Alexa stopped short in surprise.

Silas sat at the table, fully dressed, looking at his smart phone.

"I didn't mean to startle you," he said in a hushed voice.

"No problem. I just didn't expect anyone to be awake."

"I couldn't sleep, so I decided to get out of bed and walk to the rocks you told us about. Is it OK if I tag along?"

Alexa wanted to say it wasn't OK. That she loved the solitude of her morning pilgrimages to the rocks. Watching the sun unfold over the valley was like mediation for her. But, Alexa was her mother's daughter, so her answer was polite. "Of course. The track is a little rough. Are you wearing sneakers?"

"I am." Silas rose and dropped his cell phone into the pocket of his black polyester tracksuit.

As Alexa stepped onto the path, she hesitated. Remembering her wild conspiracy theories of the night before sent a sudden chill down her spine. Then her good mood kicked in, and Alexa shrugged off any reservations about her hiking companion. Those crazy nighttime fantasies seemed silly in the light of dawn.

They walked in silence for most of the way, Alexa in the lead. Halfway to the rocks, Silas stopped. "Do you know if these olive groves are part of your parents' property? That one looks really old." He pointed at one gnarled tree, its trunk twisted beneath silvery leaves.

From the way Silas was panting, Alexa suspected the question was more a pretext for a break than a sincere interest in olive orchards. She played along. "They are. They have an arrangement with a local farmer to harvest and press the olives this fall. Who knows, we all might get bottles of Villa Belle Nuvelo virgin olive oil for Christmas."

"Cynthia uses olive oil in a lot of her cooking. So I wouldn't refuse a gift like that. It would be even more special since we've seen the trees where it comes from." Silas was breathing more evenly, so Alexa turned and stepped back onto the trail.

When they reached the top, the mist had cleared the towers but still hovered in much of the valley. Silas acted impressed. "What a fantastic view. Just beautiful. Look at that fog. I see why you come up here."

His delight sounded a little over the top to Alexa, but, of course, false enthusiasm was part of a politician's stock in trade.

"Yes. I love the mist. A few days it's been misty up here on the rocks when I arrived. Then it just slips down into the valley, revealing first the castle turrets, the tile roofs. And then, poof. Everything becomes clear."

Silas marched to the edge of the rocks and peered down. "Whoa. That's quite a drop off."

From her earlier jaunts, Alexa knew the edge of the rocks formed a cliff with a three hundred foot drop straight to the rocky valley floor. The land directly below was too rough for cultivation, and the vineyards stopped on either side of the rocky scree. "Umbria is more mountainous than Tuscany, that's for sure." She leaned on one of the two boulders that flanked the entrance to the rock ledge.

As they watched, the sky turned a vivid pink. The mist below reflected the same bright color until the entire expanse of earth and sky before them took on a deep rosy glow.

"Wow," Alexa exclaimed. "This is the first time I've seen something like this. It's spectacular, but a little eerie."

"Why don't you let me take your picture in this light? Something to remember from Italy." Silas pulled his cell phone from his pocket. "Go on. Stand out there." He pointed toward the edge of the rocks with a big smile.

Alexa would have rather watched the sunrise, but she decided to be a good sport. "Sure. Then I'll take one of you for Cynthia." She walked forward, stopping at least five feet from the edge.

Silas held the phone's camera up to his face and snapped a photo. "Stay there. Or even move back a little. Let me get a few more," he directed, the smile slipping from his face.

As Alexa stood firm, she felt a clammy breeze at her back. A tendril of mist rode the wind up the mountain and enveloped the rock ledge in a sudden fog. Disoriented by the lack of visibility, Alexa froze in place.

As quick as the mist came, it disappeared on another gust of wind. And with it went Silas' false bonhomie. When Alexa looked up, his face had contorted into a mask of anger. With an abrupt movement, Silas shoved the phone into his pocket and strode forward, "You don't fool me, you little bitch." He pointed a finger at Alexa. "You're a cool customer, but I know you figured it out. I should have never let Cynthia drink so much. Her mouth runs like a duck's ass when she's had a few."

Taken aback, Alexa took a step to the left, but she had little room to maneuver on the rock. For a moment, she couldn't understand why Silas had snapped. But his anger seemed very real. And she was in a precarious position out on this ledge. This felt like the Grand Canyon with those two men. But this situation was much, much worse. With a three hundred foot drop behind her and no way out other than the narrow passage through the big boulders, Alexa would have to talk her way out.

"Excuse me, Silas. I don't think that type of language is called for. I have no idea what you're talking about. Sure, Cynthia got a little tipsy last night, but we're on vacation. Did I do something to offend you?" As she babbled on in a polite tone, Alexa put it all together and began to panic. Silas was right. She had figured it out last night. She should have trusted her nighttime musings. Her father's old friend was up to his neck in the fracking conspiracy.

"Alexa, cut the crap. Did you mention any of this to your father? Or text one of your friends?" When Alexa made no reply Silas kept talking. It was like he couldn't contain himself. "You have no idea how much I hate you. I had a good thing going. Until you blew it all to hell.

"First, you turn up in the rotunda during Carmine's final flight. Who knew you and Keisha would be there? Then, you encourage that little piece of fluff, Lauren, to eavesdrop on private conversations. We couldn't be sure what she told you, so we sent Hoover to take you out at your cabin."

At this point, Alexa realized she couldn't talk her way out of this. Rage had turned Silas' face a mottled purple. His whole body quivered in anger. She tried to circle behind him, but the big man darted to cut her off.

"No, no, no." Silas shook his head. "I'm sick and tired of people screwing up. That idiot Hoover missed the shot. Those Monongas boys let you get away up at the Grand Canyon. Toland, Kurtz, and Keisha got caught. What a clusterfuck. Sometimes you gotta do the job yourself."

Silas feinted toward Alexa. She bobbed to the side, calculating the odds of scrambling up a boulder. But the massive rocks looked too high and too smooth for her to get a foothold.

"At least we got your cop boyfriend. You didn't let any grass grow under your feet though. The statie wasn't cold in his grave before you teamed up with that self-righteous bastard, Walt Jordan. You screwing him too?"

Silas took several steps forward. Terrified, Alexa glanced toward the cliff. She had to keep away from the edge. Pulse racing, she steeled herself for a fight. Silas was a big man, much taller than she. But their walk had proven he wasn't in the best physical shape.

Alexa held her hand out to fend him off. "Uncle Silas, can't we work this out?" She pleaded, hoping to touch a sense of family obligation.

"Honey. I'm not your fucking uncle. Your father and I go way back, but it damn near ruined my vacation when we arrived at the villa and found you here."

Abandoning any pretense of ignorance, she tried to keep him talking. "I can't believe you're involved in this. It was the farm, right? Monongas leased the rights to your farm?" Alexa sidled toward the boulders.

"They were going to pay me thousands an acre. It was going to be part of a huge Michaux drilling field. If their new process worked, they could expand it everywhere.

"I let Cynthia think we were going to actually live there—but there's no way I'd live near a fracking operation. That would be crazy. Too toxic. No, that place was my checkbook to an easy retirement. With that money plus what Monongas paid me to get rid of Carmine and pass their bill, I could've bought a place like your parents' somewhere. Lived like a king. Just like all those guys from law school with silver spoons in their mouths."

As Silas spat out those last words, he rushed toward Alexa. She jerked to the left, but he caught her. The senator wrapped his arms around Alexa and dragged her toward the edge of the cliff. Twisting and turning, she tried to free her hands. She kicked at Silas' shins, hard with her heels.

"Ompf," he grunted, grip loosening at the pain. Alexa tried to slide out of his arms, but Silas tightened his hold. Trembling with effort, Alexa bent her legs and went limp in his arms, feet dangling off the ground. Silas stumbled backward. Frantic, Alexa worried he might take them both over the cliff. Then Silas' legs buckled, and he collapsed under her dead weight just a few feet from the cliff edge. As he crashed, he dropped Alexa, freeing his hands to help break his fall.

Alexa tumbled out of his arms. In a flash, she jumped up and brushed past Silas. But the old man surprised her. With a swish of his arm, he swept her legs out from under her. Alexa tumbled, hitting the ground hard. She couldn't breathe. Opening her eyes, she quailed at the sight of rocks, hundreds of feet below. She'd landed with her head over the edge of the cliff. Terrified, Alexa scrambled back onto firm ground and rolled over, still gasping for air.

Silas leapt on top of her and planted a knee in the center of her chest. Hooking his hands under her armpits, he dragged her back toward the cliff. Too terrified to even scream, Alexa fought for her life. She bucked and writhed as they inched nearer and nearer, ignoring the sharp stones that dug into her back. But the larger man had her overpowered.

"Damn you," Silas cursed. Struggling against Alexa's constant motion, Silas straightened from his crouch to a more upright position. As he rose, Alexa took her last chance. She rammed her knee and shin into Silas' crotch as hard as she could.

His grip loosened. His face turned pale. With a high, thin scream, Silas fell to the side and toppled over the cliff.

Lying on her back, Alexa took deep, shuddering breaths and gazed at the bright blue sky above. Daybreak had arrived. And she was alive. Giving in to a mixture of horror and relief, Alexa wept silent tears. The sound of a dove cooing jarred her into action. Holding her breath, Alexa turned onto her stomach and slid to the edge of the cliff, loosing a thin stream of pebbles into the abyss. Shaking, she spotted Silas Gabler's body crumpled on the rocks far below, his black polyester tracksuit shimmering in the morning sun. There was no way he could have survived the fall.

Gazing down at Silas' body, she felt nothing but contempt for this man she'd known most of her life. He'd shown no remorse for the fracking conspiracy that led to John and Lauren's deaths. He'd admitted to helping throw Carmine Martinelli off the Capitol balcony. He'd sent Dale Hoover to kill her.

"Karma's a bitch." With those bitter words, Alexa pushed away from the precipice.

EPILOGUE

LUCKY FOR ALEXA, Silas' wife had still been abed when she'd fled to her parents' villa, bruised and disheveled from the fight on the cliff.

"My God. Silas tried to kill you?" Susan folded Alexa into her arms. "Are you all right? What happened?"

Alexa kept it together as she told them about the fight on the cliff, keeping her voice low.

"I thought he was my friend." Norris' face was grim. "Now I need to protect you. Listen to me, Lexie. You're going to tell them it was an accident. Nothing about a fight. Nothing about Silas' crimes. Tell them he slipped over the edge while taking a selfie. Every week, you read about another incident where someone dies taking selfies."

At Alexa's look of doubt, Norris became adamant. "You do not want to tangle with the Italian legal system, Lexie. It is nothing like the United States. Remember that college student in the news? I can't say if she was guilty or not, but the legal process was Byzantine.

"Susan, can you stay here in case Cynthia wakes up? Don't tell her anything."

After Alexa had washed her face and brushed off her clothes, Norris followed Alexa to the site of his old friend's body. He found a path that took them below the ledge where the senator lay, blood soaking into the ground beneath his broken form.

"You're right, Lexie. He's gone." Her father's face was like stone as he checked his old friend's pulse. "Where's his phone?"

"Jacket pocket."

Norris slid Silas' phone from his pocket with the hem of his shirt. He thumbed through the recent photos and deleted the ones of Alexa standing on the promontory. Then he took a photo of the sky before he threw the phone against the rocks a few feet from Gabler's body.

Even through her shock, Alexa marveled at her father's unexpected gifts of deception. She knew covering up a crime was anathema to her dad. He lived by the rule of law. And Silas had been his friend for almost half a century. This had to be tearing him up.

Hugging Alexa, Norris apologized, his voice tight with self-recrimination. "I'm so sorry, honey. I asked you to get involved in that bastard's trafficking commission. Then I couldn't refuse when he hinted about coming here to visit. Even in college, Silas had a nasty greedy streak, but I ignored it because of the good times we shared. Are you all right?"

"I've been better." Alexa felt so tired. All she wanted to do was climb into bed and make this all go away.

"When we get back to the house, you need to fall apart just a bit. You don't want to be too calm when we tell Cynthia what happened. Or when you talk to the polizia. Lucky your face isn't bruised." He took a long, angry look at Alexa's battered arms. "Remember to wear long sleeves."

Alexa managed a wan smile as she wiped away another tear. "Piece of cake. It's all I can do to hold it together."

The police investigators accepted Alexa's story about Silas' selfie accident. When Alexa told them about the senator's fatal misstep, the investigators nodded. In animated tones, they shared examples of other selfie accidents involving cliffs, moving vehicles, guns, wild animals, and other strange situations.

"However, most of these accidents are with young people. So impulsivo, the young. And always the telefonino; the Twitter. The Instagram." The lead investigator shook his head. "But an unusual accident for someone of so many years."

"The senator liked his photos." Alexa didn't know what else to say.

"Ah, un senatore. Si, si, signorina. Il politico. Say no more."

Surprisingly, even the distraught Cynthia Gabler accepted Alexa's tearful explanation. Norris arranged for a local lawyer to help Cynthia with the complicated process of dealing with the American embassy, local death registration, a post mortem, the Examining Magistrate, and the insurance company. Following several days of formalities regarding the senator's death, Cynthia flew back home with his body.

Her parents' support helped Alexa through the difficult week. She hated lying to Cynthia and the police. She hated letting Silas get away with murder. Even though he'd already paid with his own death, she felt his crimes should become public. But she heeded her father's warning. She didn't want to become the next Amanda Knox, caught in the wheels of an uncertain Italian justice system. When the Italian authorities ruled Silas Gabler's death an accident, Alexa trembled in relief.

She decided to spend one more week in Umbria, glad her parents gave her the space she needed. So, Alexa spent her days walking through hill towns, wandering into dusty churches, and sipping wine at outdoor cafes. In the late afternoons, she'd hole up in her magical room at the villa and sip more wine. The week before Silas and Cynthia arrived, she and her parents had visited a monastery in Tuscany, the Abbey of Sant'Antimo. She'd been so entranced by its monks' famed Gregorian chants, Alexa had bought their CD. Listening to the soothing rhythm of their voices as she watched the evening shadows steal over the valley below brought Alexa some measure of peace.

"We're coming home in a few weeks. The renovations to the villa are complete, and we need to spend time with you and Graham and the kids," Susan told Alexa on the drive back to Florence.

"You know Kate and the kids are spending most of the summer at their new beach house?"

"We do. They've invited us to stay for a few weeks in July," Norris interjected.

"Then we'll head back here for August and September. I want to see the sunflowers in full bloom."

"Honey, take care of yourself. Silas Gabler and those fracking industry robber barons wreaked death and havoc on too many people. It makes me sick that you and John got in their way. We are heartbroken about John, but your mother and I are so glad that you survived Silas' attack."

"Silas got what he deserved," Susan muttered.

"You're right, Mom. Silas paid with his life, and Keisha and the lobbyists are going to jail. But I'm not sure that balances the scales. John, a young intern, Senator Martinelli—they're all dead. Little Tessa Demeter may not survive to see her next birthday. And how many other people's lives have been ruined by fracking?"

Alexa leaned back in her seat and watched the fields whiz by the car window. Although they'd taken the Autostrada on this return trip, she still caught glimpses of La Bella Toscana from the superhighway. Olive trees, wheat fields, clear blue sky. Despite the ugliness of Silas' death, Alexa had fallen in love with Italy. She spied a field of plants, their spiky stems brimming with furled green buds. She sighed. "I really wanted to see the sunflowers bloom."

"You'll be back, dear." Susan smiled. "Italy's now your second home."

Back in Pennsylvania, Graham, Kate, and Alexa's friends overwhelmed her with their concern. They'd all seen the twenty-four-hour news coverage of the "Senator's Deadly Selfie" and wanted to make sure Alexa was OK. When Melissa brought Scout home the day Alexa arrived, she'd insisted on spending the night. Alexa appreciated her friends' support. But, after a few days, she pushed them all away. She threw herself into work, but spent her spare time alone, with Scout, attempting to process everything that happened.

One weekday evening in June, Alexa had a surprise visitor. Stretched out on a deck chair, she listened to the wind sigh through the pines. When she recognized Walt Jordan, Alexa swung her legs over the side and rose. Scout stood at full alert, tail wagging in anticipation of meeting someone new.

"I hope you like big dogs." Alexa moved to the deck railing and tried to quell her misgivings. She hadn't seen Walt since she left his room at the hospital.

"I'm not sure I've ever met one with a head that big, but I love dogs." Walt walked up the steps and addressed the mastiff directly. "What's your name, boy?"

"Scout. He's harmless."

"I see." As he spoke, Walt rubbed the dog's ears. "I don't want to intrude."

"I'm surprised you drove the whole way out here. But it's nice to see you."

"Right. I worried when I learned you were there in Italy when Senator Gabler died. It happened at your parents' home, right?"

Alexa nodded. "They own a little villa in Umbria now. Really, more of a farmhouse."

"The Capitol is buzzing. How totally weird is it that the last two chairmen of the Energy and Environment Committee died in falls. Of course, Martinelli was murdered. I guess you'd call Gabler's death careless." Walt's tone was chatty, like he was gossiping with a colleague. "But I can tell you. Nobody's lining up to take the chairmanship now, even though it's considered a plum position."

"Sit, please." Alexa gestured to a chair at the outdoor table. "Would you like a Coke or iced tea?"

"Iced tea would be good." Walt removed his suit coat and took a seat. He chuckled as he watched Scout chase a ball around the yard.

When Alexa returned with two glasses of iced tea, she took the chair next to the representative. "Anything new on the fracking bill?"

"Good news. When the truth came out about Senator Martinelli's death, the Senate took a big leap back from that bill. With the Toland gang arrests and Monongas under investigation, leadership got very nervous. I don't think they'll touch fracking with a ten-foot pole for the next several sessions. No one wants their constituents asking questions about how deep the corruption might run."

"That is good news. Something positive blooming out of the ruins. From what I've heard, you played a major role in engineering the backlash against the Senate bill. You've led the charge on every major TV and newspaper outlet, right?" Alexa tried to find the right tone. She and Walt had let their guard down during their flight from Nason Kurtz. But, that had been a unique situation.

Walt sidestepped her praise. "What's the news on the little Demeter girl?"

"With all the negative publicity, Monongas was anxious to settle the case. And they were very generous. Jeannie and Tom will have millions of dollars to pay for Tessa's medical bills and any long-term consequences of her illness. But, on the medical front, I don't know. After that crisis at the time of the hearing, they got her into a new clinical trial. Last time I spoke to Jeannie she said this treatment seems to be working. But they won't know for quite some time. They're hopeful. The whole thing is a damn shame."

Walt nodded. "I can't imagine something like that happening to one of my kids." After a moment of silence, he said, "Look, I hope you don't mind I drove out here uninvited. But we haven't really spoken since that night everything went down in the Capitol. You've had a rough few months. Seeing Carmine die. Dealing with your boyfriend's death. Then Gabler's accident. I truly just wanted to see how you're coping."

"I've been better. But I'll survive." Alexa gave him a crooked smile as she weighed what she was about to do. But she owed it to Walt, and she felt she could trust him. "Is your law license still active?"

Walt looked puzzled. "Of course. I need an occupation to fall back on when they finally kick me out of the House." He grinned.

"I'd like to retain you then." Alexa pulled a worn dollar bill out of her shorts pocket. She'd stuffed it there when she'd made a run to Keck's store for milk.

"I don't really practice, you know. What's this about?"

Alexa handed Walt the dollar. "Humor me."

He accepted the bill and laid it on the table. "All right. I agree to represent you."

"I doubt I'll need your representation beyond today's consultation, but I wanted to ensure confidentiality." Alexa leaned close to Walt even though they were alone amid acres of uninhabited forest. "The Italians ruled Senator Gabler's death an accident, which it was. But what they don't know—the senator toppled over the edge in an attempt to throw me off the cliff."

"What?" Walt sat up in his chair. "Why would he try to harm you?"

"Kill me," Alexa corrected him in a somber tone.

"Bastard." Walt's shout brought Scout running back to the deck.

"It's OK, boy." Alexa turned from the dog back to Walt. "I'm trusting you because it's the answer to the riddle. The end game with Martinelli's murder. It'll never come out in court, because it doesn't help either Toland or Monongas in their case. Especially now Gabler's dead. But killing Martinelli had a dual purpose. Yes, he got cold feet on the fracking bill. But, more important, Gabler wanted that chairmanship. Toland acted as the conduit, bribing Gabler with Monongas money to get the bill passed."

"So Gabler was in on it?"

"Yeah. And he had an even bigger stake in the outcome. He'd been buying up land in Adams County—on the border of Michaux where Monongas had determined there were deposits of gas. They were going to use this new drilling process to tap the gas. They'd promised him thousands of dollars an acre to lease the land. Then they were going to point to their success in Michaux and leapfrog onto other forest land with the new technique."

Walt let out a long whistle. "That explains a lot. Keisha covered for him. I'm surprised."

"They must have been paying her off, somehow."

Walt wrinkled his brow. "But why did he try to kill you? He escaped the indictments. No one was going to know the role he played in the whole conspiracy."

"At dinner, his wife let something slip about this land in Adams County. He knew I would put two and two together eventually. Plus, he was furious you and I blew it all up. It was personal. He'd dreamed about all the money for so long he wanted to make me pay."

"What happened?"

"I don't want to relive the details. We struggled. He got too close to the edge. It could have just as easily been me." Alexa shuddered at the memory. "And I lied about what happened." She let out a deep sigh.

"As your attorney, I'm bound by attorney-client confidentiality. Although it sounds as if the Italian authorities are satisfied with their verdict of accidental death?" Walt's reassuring lawyer-babble reminded Alexa of Graham.

"They are. I don't want to burden you with my secrets. But you deserve to know the whole story." Alexa took a long sip of tea.

"Wow, I can't believe what these fracking monsters have put you through. And, of course, your state trooper friend, John, paid the ultimate price. All to stop a conspiracy based on greed, pure and simple."

"Don't forget, you took a bullet."

Walt raised his arm. "It's all better. Just a twinge every once in a while if I knock this arm against something."

Alexa smiled. "Your dad would have been proud to know you've followed in his footsteps."

"He would've been proud of you too."

The talk of conspiracy and death faded into lighter discussion of Walt's kids. Alexa felt a passing ping of regret. Though she felt a real bond with Walt, she could never get involved with a married man. The two sat, drinking tea and chatting until shadows lengthened over the mountain. An owl hooted in the distance. "What a great place you have here, Alexa," Walt spoke after a few minutes of silence. "It's good for the soul." He touched her hand then rose. "I better get back to Harrisburg. We're in session tomorrow."

Scout followed Walt down the stairs to his car, but Alexa stayed on the deck. "Thanks for coming out here to check on me."

"I'm glad I did. If you need further legal advice, just let me know." Walt hesitated a moment, then climbed into the car.

With a pensive smile Alexa watched the car fade into the twilight.

On Saturday morning, Alexa could barely contain her excitement. Haley had delivered a healthy baby girl last night. Blair had called with the good news and insisted she come to the hospital to meet baby Charlotte. Leaving Scout at home, she jumped into the Mini and hit the button to open the top. It was a glorious day, warm and sunny. Perfect convertible weather. As she drove out the long lane to the macadam road, Alexa took it slow, savoring the sounds of birdsong and the fresh smell of pine wafting on balmy air. At the intersection of the lane and Route

233, Alexa pulled on a baseball cap to corral her hair and popped a CD into the player.

Heading down the mountain, wind rushing through the car, Alexa smiled in sheer delight. Hard to believe the first day of summer was just a few days away. She stole a glance at the envelope sticking out of her purse. Just yesterday, she'd received a letter from Reese. A long letter, not an email. He was coming home from Africa for a while. He said he missed her. Just looking at the envelope made Alexa's wounded heart sing.

When Alexa downshifted into a right turn, the whistle of the wind eased, and Gregorian chants filled the car. She'd become quite of fan of the Abbey Sant'Antimo's Gregorian chants. She giggled. How small the world had become. Here she was in Pennsylvania, driving a German car, thinking about a guy in Africa, and listening to a CD of French monks chanting in Latin from their monastery in Italy.

The slower speed required by the narrow, winding road allowed Alexa to take in the profusion of greens and reds around her. The trees had all unfurled tender new leaves. Beneath them, masses of mountain laurel displayed delicate sprays of blush pink. New growth sprouted in the wheat field to her left.

The monks' voices soared into a chorus of Alleluias just as Alexa caught a flash of red to her left. She lowered the audio and slowed the car to watch the gleaming red fox, prancing a path through the tender shoots of wheat. Alexa brought the Mini to a complete halt so she could watch the beast. She was astounded when he also stopped, no more than twenty feet away. As he stood there in a shaft of sunlight, dust motes dancing around his body, the animal's glossy coat took on an ethereal crimson glow.

For a moment, Alexa and the fox gazed at each other as if caught in a spell. Then, the fox broke the magic moment. Unafraid, he ambled across the road ahead of the car and disappeared into the hedgerow.

Alexa put the car into gear and moved forward, a beatific expression on her face. These several months had been difficult, but the fox and the blooming spring around her reminded Alexa of the resiliency of nature. She was resilient too. It might take more than a season, but Alexa knew she would survive.

AFTERWORD

Dead of Spring is a work of fiction, and its characters are drawn from my imagination. Any resemblance to actual people is purely coincidental. The only exceptions are public figures, such as those who played a role during the Three Mile Island crisis.

Many of my references are based in fact. Hydraulic fracturing is taking place in the Marcellus Shale across Pennsylvania and in other places around the country. It's a well-publicized fact that fracking is controversial. There are many opponents and proponents for the process. To my knowledge, the "new" process that would allow the non-shale areas to be fracked exists only in my imagination.

The Pennsylvania State Legislature and the committees named in the novel also exist. However, the legislators and activities of those committees in this book are entirely fictional. On the other hand, Pennsylvania's State Capitol Building is a National Historic Landmark. Everything described in the building and the Capitol Office Complex does exist. I fear, however, that I have fallen short in describing the beauty of the Capitol building and the national treasures it houses.

The near-disaster at Three Mile Island in 1979 holds a unique place in American history. The Nuclear Regulatory Commission states that the partial-meltdown of TMI's Unit 2 reactor was "the most serious accident in U.S. commercial nuclear power plant operating history." The description of the Three Mile Island event is drawn from my own memories as a State employee who worked in Harrisburg at the time. I also relied on news articles and academic research on the incident.

The quotes that introduce the Three Mile Island chapters are drawn from news broadcasts, press conferences, and memorabilia related to the incident. However, Randi and Will's Three Mile Island story in this book is fiction.

Many of the places in this novel, both in South Central Pennsylvania and in Italy, are real. However, others exist only in the pages of this book. There is no environmental organization called the Wildness Cooperative. However, there are many dedicated environmental organizations—both governmental and non-governmental—that act as advocates for clean energy and the preservation our planet. Organizations such as the Sierra Club, the Natural Resources Defense Council, the FracTracker Alliance, and many others at the local, state, national, and global level work to protect people and the environment from potentially harmful energy expansion.

ACKNOWLEDGMENTS

I WANT TO THANK all the people who helped with *Dead of Spring*. First and foremost, my husband, Mike, who supports my writing in so many ways. For *Dead of Spring*, he gave me feedback on the manuscript, plus he accompanied me in my travels to Northeastern Pennsylvania and Italy. On a daily basis, he copes with all the hours I spend hunched over a computer in the world of Alexa Williams.

I also want to thank the Knowlton/Kuehn clan, who give me feedback on manuscripts, information on guns, and help in untold ways with my writing. This group includes my son, Josh Knowlton, and his new wife, Laura; Dave and Nancy Knowlton; Steve and Pam Knowlton; and Dennis and Coe Kuehn. Denny and Coe also provided me with the spark for the Three Mile Island story. Their daughter, Laurel, was born in a hospital within the TMI danger zone during the 1979 crisis.

Once again, Trooper Jessica Williams of Troop H provided technical assistance on state police and other law enforcement procedure. Lieutenant James Rhoads provided information on the responsibilities of the Capitol police. I have the utmost respect for all the law enforcement agencies that figure in this novel. These women and men perform hard, dangerous jobs, which often go unrecognized.

The Honorable Jessica Brewbaker, judge in the Cumberland County Court of Pleas, gave me valuable input on proper criminal charges under Pennsylvania law.

Jason Wilson, a historian with the Pennsylvania Capitol Preservation Committee, assisted me with the history and treasures of the Pennsylvania State Capitol. Although I'd been in the Capitol hundreds of times, he introduced me to secret nooks and crannies of the building that I'd never seen. Eric Pettis, executive assistant to Lieutenant Governor Michael Stack, was gracious enough to provide me with a tour and history of the lieutenant governor's offices—which helped me place the historic suite front and center at a critical point in the novel.

Bill Phillips and Dave English were invaluable in helping me with the technical aspects of hydraulic fracturing. If I've made any errors about fracking in the book, the mistakes are mine in translating the input from Bill and Dave onto the written page. Bill Phillips was extremely gracious in sharing his own experiences as a landowner who leases to a fracking company—as well as showing me the various aspects of the fracking process. Dave English brought an entirely different perspective from his work as a regulator for the Department of Environmental Programs and, before that, Environmental Resources. I must note, however, than any conclusions and opinions about hydraulic fracturing that are embodied in the story are strictly my own—not those of either Bill or Dave. I also have to thank Bill and Tina Krivenko for connecting me with both of these fracking experts. They also spent a long day with my husband Mike and me on Bill Phillips' guided tour of fracking fields of Northeastern Pennsylvania.

Finally, I would be remiss to not thank Val Muller, a fellow author and teacher, who always gives me valuable feedback on my novels. I also want to thank the crew at Sunbury Press: Publisher Lawrence Knorr, who continues to support my Alexa Williams series; Jennifer Cappello, who is the best editor an author could ask for; Crystal Devine, who is a wizard at the technical aspects of production; and Amber Rendon who is responsible for another eye-catching cover for *Dead of Spring.*

Thanks to all these generous people who have helped make *Dead of Spring* more accurate. If I've misinterpreted your information, the fault is purely mine.

Finally, I want to thank all my readers. Your continuing interest in the Alexa Williams series is heartening and inspires me to keep writing. I would like to ask all my readers to help spread the word about my novels by leaving a brief review of *Dead of Spring* and my other Alexa Williams books on Amazon, Goodreads, Barnes and Noble, IndieBound, or Sunbury Press. Thank you.

ABOUT THE AUTHOR

Sherry Knowlton is the author of the successful Alexa Williams suspense series, *Dead of Autumn, Dead of Summer and Dead of Spring*. Sherry (nee Sherry Rothenberger) was born and raised in Chambersburg, PA where she developed a lifelong passion for books. She was that kid who would sneak a flashlight to bed at night so she could read beneath the covers. All the local librarians knew her by name.

Sherry spent much of her early career in state government, working primarily with social and human services programs, including services for abused children, rape crisis, domestic violence, and family planning. In the 1990s, she served as the Deputy Secretary for Medical Assistance in the Commonwealth of Pennsylvania. The latter part of Sherry's career has focused on the field of Medicaid managed care. Now retired from executive positions in the health insurance industry, Sherry runs her own health care consulting business.

Sherry has a B.A. in English and psychology from Dickinson College in Carlisle, PA.

Sherry and her husband, Mike, began their journey together in the days of peace and music when they traversed the country in a hippie van. Running out of money several months into the trip, Sherry waitressed the night shift at a cowboy hangout in Jackson Hole, Wyoming and Mike washed dishes in a bakery. Undeterred, they embraced the travel experience and continue to explore far-flung places around the globe.

Sherry lives in the mountains of South Central Pennsylvania where her novels are set.